DARK GROWS THE SUN

AND THE HEAVENS BURN, BOOK 2

MATT BISHOP

FENSALIR PUBLISHING, LLC

Dark Grows the Sun, by Matt Bishop

Published by Fensalir Publishing, LLC

PO Box 473 Lemont, IL 60439

https://mattbishopwrites.com

fb.me/mattbishopwrites

Cover by J. Caleb Design

Editor: Lisa Poisso

All errors in this book are Matt Bishop's fault.

Ebook ISBN: 978-0-9986789-1-7

Print ISBN: 978-0-9986789-2-4

QUICK GUIDE TO PRONUNCIATION

All examples are for modern American English.

Ráta = Rawta *or* Máni = Mawni
 the "á" sounds like the "ou" in "bought"

Sól = Sohl
 the "ó" sounds like the "o" in "road"

Fylgja = fulg-yuh
 the "j" sounds like "yuh"

Heimdall = Hame-dall

Emphasis in the non-English words is always on the first syllable.
Examples:
 1) VAF-thrudnir
 2) THRUTH-gelmir
 3) MUS-pellheim

MAIN CHARACTERS & PLACES

PEOPLE

- **Frigg:** Almother, wife of Odin, mother of Baldr and Hodr.
- **Odin:** Alfather, husband of Frigg, father of Baldr, Hodr, Vidar and Thor.
- **Loki:** Blood brother to Odin; husband of Sigyn; father of Hel, and Narfi.

PLACES

- **Gladsheim:** Main city of the Aesir.
- **Ifington:** Large port city, largely inhabited by the Aesir.
- **Jotunheim:** Main city of the Jotunn.

1

ODIN

The night of Baldr's murder

Odin swung a leg over Sleipnir's saddle. His sodden cloak caught and he fell, graceless, into the mud.

Baldr . . .

Groaning, he pushed himself up to all fours, vomited, and dragged a shaking hand across quivering lips. He'd failed. He'd been tricked.

Baldr was dead.

He slammed his fists into the ground. Dank mud splattered into his mouth.

His son was dead.

He settled back onto his haunches and turned his face up to the gray sky. Cold rain trickled down his neck, and he shivered. An ache grew in his eye socket, the one that held the golden orb placed there by . . .

. . . Baldr.

Despite himself, a sob broke free of his chest and escaped into the dark woods. He screamed, eye closed, fists clenched. He screamed till his throat was raw.

Another chill slithered down his back. Angrboda had snared him with a curse. He'd underestimated her, hadn't realized what she was doing. She had delayed him, yes, but it was his own pride and arrogance that had let it happen. Were it not for the roaring of Heimdall's horn, he might still be wandering these woods. Heimdall's horn—a horn that never would have sounded if not for Baldr's murder.

What was Frigg thinking now? One son dead by the other's hand. A husband who'd broken another promise.

Why, Hodr, why?

Angrboda's voice rang in his head: *Your son will fling the far-famed branch.* The dead spoke the truth to him even if they didn't want to. The pact he'd struck with Angrboda had made that certain twice over. Only the mistletoe in which Baldr's spirit was hidden could hurt Baldr. That simple plant would become "far-famed" indeed once word spread of how it had killed the Alfather's heir. But how had Hodr learned the secret about Baldr? And how had a blind man gathered the plant without anyone discovering the damage? Mistletoe was a soft plant. How had Hodr crafted the "branch" into a weapon?

Angrboda had spoken true words—Odin's magic had compelled it—but she still could have woven a lie with them. He'd done the same with his own words often enough. She'd never actually said "Baldr was killed." When he'd begun torturing her, she'd said Hodr had "wielded" the branch. He'd leaped to the conclusion that Hodr had killed Baldr. Maybe he'd misinterpreted her words?

Thunder rumbled as if the sky itself mocked him. How far he had fallen, if he hung his hopes on maybes.

Sleipnir whinnied and shook her head, bridle jingling. He looked up into smart blue eyes that looked too much like her mother's. That thought sent a shiver of disgust down his spine, and he looked away. You couldn't blame a child for their parents; if you did, his own children would carry heavy burdens indeed.

He pushed himself up, muck sucking at his knees and his feet. Sleipnir's bristly muzzle tickled his face as he wrapped an arm around her neck. "Yes, girl, I'm back."

She whickered, blew hot horsey breath into his face, and stomped one of her forefeet. She thought something was wrong.

One hand on her halter, he cast his eye down the ragged path. Sól was hidden behind a pall of gray clouds, so while it looked like early morning or evening, he couldn't be sure. He examined the underbrush lining either side of the ragged path. No sign of anything alive besides trees stretching upward like stork legs and the mist slinking across the forest floor.

Was something coming?

He turned and looked back the way he must've come, judging by the hoofprints in the deep mud. The glinting pate of the hill where he'd summoned Angrboda was close, so close that he hadn't even crossed back over the Gjoll. How long *had* he wandered this dead forest?

Sleipnir whickered and stomped one of her hooves.

He thumped her neck. "I know. The charm hit you, too. The fault is all mine."

And the guilt.

The crackle of breaking branches reached his ears. Sleipnir whinnied and stomped in place. Something *was* coming.

"All right, girl, let's move. Take us home."

He hauled himself up into the saddle. He clucked his tongue and Sleipnir trotted forward, the mud popping and squelching as she pulled her hooves free and placed them again. Her ears flicked back and forth.

A heartbeat later, the distant, sharp sound of splintering wood. Then a dull, angry roar. Oh yes, something was coming.

Sleipnir snorted, blew, and pranced, eager to be moving.

"It's all right, we're leav—"

The golden orb that Baldr had placed in his ruined eye socket flared. Blood seemed to drip across his missing eye's sight and through the searing pain he saw, squatting on a branch to his right, a naked woman. He shook the pain away; the blood-red film over his sight vanished. On the same branch sat a large gray and black bird with yellow-clawed feet, a wrinkled bald head, and a hooked beak. It stared at him, then sunk its head low as it spread its wings and launched itself into the air with a squawk.

Odin dug for his spindle. With a flick of his wrist, he sent the witchthread arrowing toward the gray bird. He began to sing. The thread snared itself in the bird's clawed feet. He sang it up the bird's body, beneath its feathers, and out around the dark wing feathers. The bird beat the air heavily, frantically, trying to gain height and distance.

He spoke a word. The witchthread flared golden all along its length, and the bird began to change. The wide, outstretched gray wings became a woman's legs bent up and backward over her shoulders. Framed between them, the savage beak and bald head became a face contorted with fear and surprise. The bird's crooked claws became hands reaching out to grasp bare tree limbs that were too far away.

The witch hit the muck with a wet thud, her breath blown from her lungs.

Another roar rumbled through the trees, again accompanied by the sharp splintering of wood. Whatever was coming was drawing closer. Would Hel have set the traitorous hound Garm on him? Possibly.

Odin swung a leg over the saddle and slid to the ground, calling Gungnir to him as he stalked toward the stunned witch gasping in the mud. He poked her in the side with Gungnir's tip. Red blood blossomed. She hissed and rolled over onto all fours. She met his eye, her face twisted in a snarl that already looked too much like a great-cat's. She was already trying to shift again.

He leveled Gungnir's sharp promise before her eyes and he watched her indecision bloom. Her body relaxed, and her features slipped back into an unlined brow, tawny skin, and a wide nose.

"Wise choice," he said.

She pushed herself up, her large breasts shaking, and settled back on her knees. Dark mud covered most of her youthful, smooth-skinned nakedness. Her eyes were dark and narrowed; a shaman's tattoos crawled along her left temple.

She spat mud and in a low, strawberry-sweet voice said, "You've broken my spell, Ygg. Now what?"

"And what spell was that, child?"

She smiled, teeth white and straight. She rested her hands on her hips and almost imperceptibly arched her back so her breasts seemed more prominent. If she expected her flesh to distract him, then she was very young indeed.

"The one that held you here. Kept you mazed."

"Come now, that wasn't your spell. We both know that."

Slowly, she came back onto her heels in a squat, legs spread. Was she going to try escaping again? He slid forward a step and poked her in the chest with Gungnir hard enough to draw blood. She fell back on her rear.

"We have much to discuss—"

Another roar cut through the air, this time much closer.

"—and little time to waste, it seems. Who is your mistress? Does the oncoming beast serve her?"

The witch said nothing.

He flicked Gungnir across the rounded swell of her shoulder, opening a shallow cut.

She pushed herself up with her elbows and hissed. "No need for threats, Ygg. You can have me if you ask." She drew her ankles up toward her body so that her knees were high and arched her back, displaying her breasts.

Two hundred winters ago he might have been tempted, but now he found it amusing. Behind him, Sleipnir whinnied. He heard the mud sucking at her hooves as she impatiently shifted. Time pressed. And there could be another, more practiced member of this child's coven nearby.

"Who leads your coven?"

She laughed at him, a sound full of hatred and mockery.

He flicked Gungnir across her other shoulder, opening another slit.

She winced but stayed silent, inching her hands in toward her body.

Loud crashing came from the forest. The beast, Garm or otherwise, was moving fast. Odin's blood roiled at the prospect of a fight, but the golden orb in his eye socket was burning again, and something loomed at the edges of his missing eye's vision.

Maybe he'd looked distracted or maybe she'd picked her moment, but either way she lunged at him, hands curving into leathery black fists coated with coarse black hair. He brought Gungnir up in time to save his face, but her hands closed around the haft, tore it free with unnatural strength, and flung it wide. Gungnir tumbled away and vanished.

Odin pulled hard on his fylgja's strength. Reflected in the witch's eyes shone his own—the living one and the one Baldr had given him—flaring golden.

He punched her in the head.

Had the rest of the witch's body not already begun swelling into some black-haired, heavily muscled beast, he would have broken her neck. Instead, he only knocked her down into the mud. The impact must have dazed her, because her body began to revert to her Jotunn form. He kicked her in the ribs. She cried out, and her arms came up to cradle them.

Odin called Gungnir to him and leveled the spear at her.

Sleipnir whinnied again, sounding much more alarmed than she had before, only two paces away. A heartbeat later, the din of falling trees preceded a tremendous roar from whatever beast was coming.

"I'm out of time, child. Who leads your coven?"

She glared at him, blood dribbling from the corners of her mouth. "Out of time? No, you're too late, Ygg. Far too late. My mistress planned for all of this."

"Who is your mistress?" He stepped back, angling himself so that his one eye could see both her and the forest's verge.

She spat in the mud.

Another tree splintered. Another roar. He could now see some massive shape bulling through the forest of bare trees. In the time it'd take to kill the beast, this witch would flee. If he took her with him back to Gladsheim, she'd do nothing but slow him down.

He plunged Gungnir into her chest and ripped the spear back

out. Blood poured from her mouth and from the wound. Such a waste.. He swung Gungnir and severed her head.

He put a boot in the stirrup and mounted. A massive, misshapen, horned beast plowed through the trees in a straight line toward him roaring its challenge.

Garm hadn't come for him. It was some other monster.

He raised Gungnir and shook the spear at the beast. As Sleipnir pranced in a half circle to face the correct way on the mud-covered path, he shouted, "Go, Sleipnir, take us home."

2

FRIGG

Day 1, dawn

Frigg turned her back on the rising sun. She tugged her cloak more tightly about her shoulders and shivered. Her son was dead. But Sól still rose, twice now since Hodr had killed his older brother. The wind still blew. Life went on.

And Odin still wasn't back.

So she'd walked here, Heimdall's tower. Built upon the pinnacle of rock that overlooked her city, the tower provided chilly calm before what would likely prove another too-long day. The dawn's light reflected off thousands of snow-covered roofs that filled Gladsheim nearly to bursting. To the east, Gladsheim was bounded but not constrained by the River Silfr. To the south, along the banks of that same river, rolled farmlands, pastures, and dozens of villages. To the west lay Arnheim's Forest and beyond that, the high grasslands.

Every morning as dawn set foot upon the world, wardens put their backs into opening each of the three gates into Gladsheim. No doubt Heimdall could see the men and women pushing on the gates and hear their grunts of exertion. She couldn't. But if she squinted and shaded her eyes, she could make out people beginning to move through the western gate. That was the gate she expected Odin to return through. At her direction, Heimdall searched for her husband now, peering northward toward the dark notch in the mountains that marked the path to the Gjoll's shores.

When men were away, they missed all the little things that no one ever valued until they never happened again. Breakfasts with the children. A good-morning kiss. A friendly wave to a neighbor. Sometimes men missed the birth of their child. Maybe a marriage.

This man had missed the murder of his son. By his other son.

Frigg snatched up a log from the pile stacked against the stone wall and flung it onto the brazier. Sparks darted up, eager to escape. Odin had said he'd be back in time. Another promise broken. Not that he wouldn't have a good reason. He always did.

She sighed and rubbed her face.

From behind her, Heimdall said, "He'll be here."

"Too late." As usual.

"Are you sure about that?"

Confused, she spun around. Fair-haired and pale like a wave's crest, Heimdall leaned against the waist-high stone wall that circled the top of his tower and stared southward.

"What do you mean?" she asked.

"Death is no bar to Odin. You've seen that. I saw the wound in Baldr's chest. Odin's healed similar on the battlefield."

"But Baldr is dead."

He frowned and turned his extraordinarily blue eyes on her. They were more piercing than icicles in the dead of winter. "Death is a journey on a long river. There may still be time."

Sól blazed out from behind one of the easternmost crags and blinded her. Was Heimdall right? Less than a week ago, she'd seen Odin bring Baldr back from the brink of death. Maybe he could do more now. It was a small hope to cling to, but a little hope was better than none.

She blinked away the bright spots across her vision, watching the familiar vision-flames kindle in the air above Heimdall's head. In those vision-flames, a gore-streaked blade slid out from between his shoulders. Just as she was about to glimpse his opponent, the angle of her vision staggered sideways to Heimdall's bloody lips, split in a wild grin as he pulled his killer in close.

Heimdall had fought in a hundred battles even before he earned the deadly sword he now bore. Only a few could best him now—Odin, Tyr, Thor. They wouldn't kill Heimdall, much less fight him. So who would? No one she knew of.

Maybe *what* could kill him was the better question. Maybe something had followed Odin back from his long winters spent in the west. Or perhaps the creature that slept beneath Urdr's Well? It had nearly killed Odin. Surely it could do the same to the other jarls.

But more than who or what, she wanted to know *when* Heimdall would die. If her visions of Baldr's death were any guide, then it might happen within months. But were they a guide? Her shaman mentor likened visions of the future to sailing through storm-tossed seas. At the top of a swell, she could glimpse the waters ahead, behind, and all around, but only for that brief moment. Once she dropped back into a trough, she saw no more than anyone else. By the time she again rose atop a swell, the future might be different.

Odin had said something similar recently, hadn't he? She yawned again, her jaw aching, and stretched her back. She couldn't remember.

Thunder rumbled from the cloudless eastern sky.

"Thor will be here shortly," Heimdall said, not taking his eyes from the north.

Long ago, the jarls had agreed to ready their armies when the Gjallarhorn sang. If Heimdall winded the horn a second time immediately after the first, they would march. A third sounding would call Freyr and Freyja back on their fast, magical steeds. Thor had agreed to answer the first call, and yet his father still wasn't here. And Heimdall couldn't find him.

Frigg closed her eyes sighed and leaned against the cold stone wall.

"I'll let you know when I find him," Heimdall said. "Get some sleep."

"I did." But only thanks to a draft Eir had given her. Hermod had drunk it, too, and she still slept. Ah, youth.

Light bloomed in the darkness as she rubbed her eyes. In that light, she saw her son die again. *Why, Hodr? Why did you kill your brother?* There'd been no hint of his intent when he'd showed up last night. Aegir's breath, had it only been last night?

"How is Hodr?" she asked. She'd had him locked in a stout long-house near the Great Hall.

"I think he's just lying there."

"Is he . . ."

"No, I can hear him breathing. He's just not moving anymore. I had them shorten the chains after he tried to end himself."

Oh, her poor son. How had they let it come to this? She blew out a long breath and watched the mist escape eastward on the wind's back. She'd sat on Odin's High Seat often enough, checking that her orders as Almother were being followed while also stealing a few moments to check on her blind, estranged son. Hodr had seemed happy with his life in Ifington. He'd found a woman, work, maybe even some friends. So why hadn't a vision danced above Hodr's head two nights ago? Neither had one flickered above the head of that old, scruffy, half-drunk smith—nor over Yelena's head, either, when she'd attacked Frigg and killed Gulfinn.

A fresh wave of grief washed over her. Sweet Aegir, she'd done nothing yet to honor Gulfinn's sacrifice. Ráta and Gulfinn were like family.

"How is Ráta?"

Heimdall's head swung toward the Einherjar garrison in the upper tier where the baresarks were quartered. "Awake. Readying herself, from the sound of it."

Had she expected something different? Ráta had been a warrior since before the Last War. She knew death. When she saw Ráta later, she'd ask her how she wanted to honor Gulfinn's death.

There. That was something good she could accomplish today.

Unbidden, she again saw Baldr standing, arms spread wide on the tree stump in the center of the Great Hall. He was smiling, having shouted something to his brother. And again, the wicked branch sprouted from his chest. She wanted to turn away, to push the memory away, but this time she forced herself to focus on the faces of the folk behind Baldr—laughing faces, some clapping, some swaying or dancing in place. Most were drunk. She couldn't tell who they were. She hadn't been paying attention to them.

In her memory, she traced the flight of the spear back to Hodr's outstretched hand even though she hadn't really been paying attention to him, either. Vaguely, she remembered the smith standing beside Hodr, one arm pointing toward Baldr while the other was maybe on Hodr's shoulder.

Then her memory jumped to the moment she saw through the veil hiding the spear. The word *mistilteinn*—mistletoe—had been cut in runes into the spear's shaft. She'd traced them with her fingers, and if she'd felt them, Hodr would certainly have been able to. Unlike his brothers, he had no gift for seidr—for magic. But he knew the runes. Would he have wielded a spear named Mistletoe if he'd known that Baldr's spirit had been hidden in mistletoe?

Again, she saw the smith's hand on Hodr's shoulder.

The spear had been veiled. Magic had therefore been used. Even then, she'd suspected that Yelena was involved, so why hadn't she closed the hall? Why hadn't she canceled Baldr's procession through the streets? Because she was a fool. But Yelena could shape-shift, so she could have slipped in regardless.

Frigg hissed in a sharp breath. She *was* a fool. It was all right there in front of her.

Yelena was Lopt.

That's why they hadn't been able to find her; she'd taken the smith's shape. And that's why they couldn't find the smith now. Yelena had sloughed that skin like a snake and moved on. She could be anywhere—or anyone—now. The use of seidr helped everything make more sense. She distinctly remembered Hodr setting aside his spear. Would a man planning murder give up the weapon he intended to use? Only if he knew he'd get it back. So who'd given it back to him? The smith, of course. And the smith was Yelena.

And now came the question that she had to ask Hodr: Were you a willing participant in your brother's murder? Her heart said absolutely not. But could she trust herself? Yelena had charmed Harald and Klakki and Bera's parents. If she could do all that, surely bewitching Hodr was within her powers.

She opened her eyes. Sól had shed a little more light on the city below. "Do you remember the smith who entered the hall as Hodr's guest?"

Heimdall stared fixedly northward.

"Heimdall?"

He cocked his head to one side. "I heard Vithi's horn from Utgard. Vidar speaks. He says, 'I've driven back much of the warband that attacked me and mine. More than half my warband is dead. I'm making the journey back through the mines now. I believe the Jotunn will pursue me through the mines. If you do not hear from me again . . .'" His concentration deepened, as if he was trying to overhear a whispered conversation. "He's repeating all that he's already told me, about the lake and what he found."

She'd failed to save Baldr, allowed the Jotunn to destroy one of Asgard's towns, and now one of Odin's other sons might get killed. And there was probably a witch coven active in Gladsheim, along with a rebel group with a penchant for fire.

Heimdall blew out a plume of breath, grimaced, then opened his eyes. "That's it. That's all Vidar said."

Twenty winters of peaceful rule over Asgard tasted like ash in her mouth. "We're under attack, aren't we?"

"It certainly seems like it, Almother."

And just like that, she was a failure.

Tears sprung to her eyes, and she turned away. And then, of all things, she felt a mad, wild laughter bubbling up. She'd been so sure that she'd done well—that Baldr's plan for peace with the Jotunn, which she'd fully supported, was the right, necessary thing to do. And yet here they were, betrayed by the Jotunn.

"It's not your fault alone," Heimdall said, his deep voice gentler than she'd ever heard. "Odin left. I became a drunk."

"But everyone else remained true."

"Did they? We had forty winters of peace. Thor spent his time in his land, as did all the others. Sure, they came each Midwinter, but . . ."

"Had Odin been here, he would've seen the danger. He saw it immediately when he came back."

"Haven't you ever lost something in your own house? A pin or brush or whatever?"

She wiped the wetness from beneath her eyes.

"And then a friend comes in, you tell her, and she finds it right away in an obvious spot?"

She smiled wanly and shrugged.

"It's like that. Sometimes we don't see what's right in front of us, and it takes someone from the outside to see what we should."

Maybe he was right, but that didn't lessen the guilt. She was the Almother. Alone or not, she was responsible for what was happening. She'd have to fix it.

"But you asked me about a smith?"

She shivered at a bit of wind that sneaked beneath her cloak and nodded. "The one who entered the hall as Hodr's guest. Did you see him?"

Heimdall shook his head. "I heard Hodr mention him, but I didn't see the man. I stood here."

Rán's cold fingers, of course he'd been here. She'd asked him to stay at this post. Who else might remember the smith's face? Hermod might; she'd been there. Nanna had been, too, but grief had left her incoherent. Still. And Fimafeng had seen him, too.

"Could you find him if he was described to you?" Even as she asked, she wondered what good it would do. If she was right, then Yelena wouldn't be stupid enough to retake the smith's shape. But what other options did they have?

He pursed his lips and shrugged. "It would be very difficult, but I'd certainly try."

She smiled and gripped his arm. "Thank you."

Heimdall's head snapped northward. He took two quick steps to the tower's wall. She joined him. Sól was well above the eastern mountains now. The sky had become a bright blue with a fading border of red tinge below.

Heimdall grinned, his gold teeth flashing. "Odin has emerged from the fog blanketing the Gjoll's chill shores, him and Sleipnir. They look a little worse for wear, and they're pushing hard. Foam whitens her flanks. He'll be here tomorrow if they keep—wait, no."

"What?" Though she could guess: Odin had used his magic to speed his pace. Usually he sent his wolves ahead, but he'd left them behind when he rode down to summon Angrboda.

Heimdall shook his head. "He's just done something stupid and dangerous."

"He used his magic."

"Yes, but I can still see him, so he's not going as fast as he could."

"He knows, then."

Heimdall pushed back from the stone and faced her. "Oh yes, I believe he does."

"Well, I hope his little jaunt was worth the price."

And if he didn't kill himself getting back, maybe he'd prove Heimdall right. Maybe there was something he could do for Baldr. But since there was nothing she could do—and since she couldn't postpone it any longer—it was time she spoke with Hodr. Herself.

3

LOKI

Day 1, dawn

Loki strode into a Great Hall empty of anyone except the thralls readying it for the wake of Baldr. Nobody paid him any heed—no different than Midwinter two nights ago, when he'd guided blind Hodr's aim, sending the spear he'd crafted flying true, splitting Baldr's chest wide open. Nobody had given Loki a second glance then or when he'd slipped outside to watch the crowds gather, savoring their grief like a warm stew.

His plan had worked. The thought still gave him a thrill of satisfaction. And that was the main reason he'd waited till this morning to present himself to Frigg. Yesterday, he'd still been afraid that she might perceive his satisfaction. She wouldn't have known why he was satisfied, but it would've struck an odd note. He could spin as fine a lie as anyone, but there were limits. The Aesir always suspected him of something, and this would be a spectacularly bad time to carelessly trigger that sense. Besides, the sooner he presented himself, the more time he'd presumably have to spend pretending to chase down the smith who'd been with Hodr.

For two entire nights, he'd waited. He'd used the time well, reestablishing an old identity of his as a man who was a member of the Sons of Muspell, and then getting word to Yelena that he wanted to meet. As luck would have it, he'd be meeting both the Sons and the witch today. Which meant he needed more time.

So this morning, he'd waited for Frigg to depart for Goldtooth's tower, then made a show of arriving in Gladsheim and walking into the Great Hall. Goldtooth would hear everything, but that was the point.

"You there," he called to a bald, golden-skinned thrall dragging gnawed bones out from beneath one of the many tables on the lowest of the three levels.

On the first level, dozens of tables and benches were arrayed on either side of a long central path that ran between the stout carved pillars that held up the roof. Fire pits were interspersed among those tables. The second tier was about half a sword's length above the ground, with benches built flush against the wall behind a long row of tables. The third tier was another half a sword's length up.

The thrall looked up, clearly considering scurrying away, then bowed. "May I be of service, jarl?"

"Do you know where the Almother is?"

"I do not, jarl, but let me fetch the steward. He'll know."

Loki summoned his power, took the thrall by the shoulder, and set his will upon him as if he were moving a heavy door. "Fimafeng is where, exactly?"

"In the kitchens, I believe, jarl." The thrall's eyes widened under the effect of Loki's will.

"Excellent. I need a private word with Fimafeng. Fetch him for me."

The thrall headed for the opposite end of the hall, where the jarls sat during meals. By now, Loki knew that everything he said was being overheard by Goldtooth. That wasn't necessarily a bad thing; ostensibly, he had nothing to hide. But he did in fact have much to hide, and that meant avoiding being tracked by Goldtooth, with the help of distractions or things to hide behind or crowds to blend into.

He strode half the breadth of the empty hall to the spot where he'd stood two nights earlier to guide Hodr's throw. The thralls had done a good job cleaning away the blood, though the place Baldr had fallen was still apparent.

He turned at footsteps behind him. Fimafeng approached with the golden-skinned thrall, who he sent back to his labors with a wave of his hand. Fimafeng stopped an arm's length away and bowed from the waist, one hand on his heart. "Jarl Loki, welcome back to Gladsheim, even on such a sad occasion. I'm told you seek the Almother."

His voice sounded less hoarse than a few nights ago, when he'd shuffled up and down the road outside the hall shouting about how no weapons were permitted inside. The Almother's unexpected decree had presented an unexpected roadblock, but not insurmountable.

"I do, Fimafeng." Loki gestured at the well-scrubbed planks. "This is where it happened?"

"Indeed, jarl."

"And the rumors are true?"

Fimafeng looked him straight in the eye for the briefest moment before dropping his white-haired head. "Yes, jarl."

By the Gap, what had that look meant? Goldtooth would be listening intently by now, so rather than press this ancient turd on the matter, he blew out a long breath and asked, "My brother couldn't stop him, then?"

"The Alfather was elsewhere, jarl. We hope he'll return soon."

"Elsewhere? Where did he go?"

"To the shores of the Gjoll. That's all I know." Again, the steward gave him the briefest hard-eyed look, as if he suspected that Loki knew more than he was saying. And who didn't aspire to that goal? It certainly made lying easier.

"And he's not back yet? Frigg must be beside herself."

"The Almother's handled this tragedy with her usual grace, jarl, though I don't doubt it's been hard on her. As you'd expect."

"Of course. And where is the Almother now? I would lend what aid I can."

"She's been with Heimdall since the early hours, jarl, and next, I believe she intends to speak with her son."

He meant Hodr.

"And I believe Thor will arrive soon, if he hasn't already. My ears aren't what they were."

That was a little worrisome. His nephew was much like the storms he commanded, slow to build and when he struck, it was best to be elsewhere. Not that he couldn't trick Thor as easily as the rest of them. But he'd traveled with Thor. Truth was, he respected him. Thor was simple, direct, and honest, unlike the rest of his family.

He gave the old man another look. He wasn't sure why Fimafeng had volunteered all this information. Ever since Goldtooth had beaten him in retribution for stealing Freyja's necklace, the other jarls and even their lackeys had treated him with disdain. What none of them understood, though, was that this had been his plan. He'd allowed Goldtooth to best him. This disdain was exactly the result he'd wanted. No one would suspect weak Loki of anything at all.

Unless that's what everyone wanted him to think. Had Frigg and the others seen through his plan and were now treating him as he expected to be treated? Did they suspect him of something? Is that why Fimafeng was giving him these odd looks and telling him that Thor was coming?

No, there was no layered guile in those rheumy eyes. He was over-thinking this; his plan had worked. And even if they suspected him of something, they couldn't link him to the smith. Ever. Loki had been someone else entirely when he'd first met Lopt. There was no link—not unless he made a mistake now.

He laid a hand on Fimafeng's thin shoulder and laid his will upon the old man. "Thank you for all you've said. It sounds like the Almother has a long, busy day ahead of her. I will present myself to her in the evening."

Fimafeng shuddered, gave a weak smile, and ducked his head. "Yes, Jarl Loki. That's very considerate. I'll inform her."

He squeezed Fimafeng's shoulder once more and again exerted his will, this time to briefly cloud the man's mind. Fimafeng closed his eyes.

In that instant, Loki became a fly. It wasn't the first time he'd taken that shape—nor, he suspected, would it be the last. Now he'd find that Alvar thrall, or another thrall who was headed outside, and alight upon them. Goldtooth was either looking and listening very hard for Loki to leave the Great Hall or he was passed out drunk beneath a table somewhere. Loki didn't know which so with this, as with so many things, he'd best careful.

4

FRIGG

Day 1, early morning

Frigg didn't know what to do with her hands other than clasp them together so tightly that her knuckles were white. Hodr didn't have the same problem. He was shackled to one of the columns supporting the longhouse's roof. His hands moved expressively, clenching and releasing as if he were speaking in the Jotunn hand language.

His anguished expression appeared all the more intense for the lack of tears on his cheeks. For an instant she saw him as a boy, brown hair tousled, cheeks wet and deep brown eyes red-rimmed. He'd fallen from a tree and broken his arm. Baldr had improvised a sling, helped Hodr up onto his horse and brought him back.

Frigg blinked tears away when Hodr said, "Mother, I was tricked. It had to be that smith, Lopt. Have you found him yet?"

Then her memory jumped to when Hodr and the remnants of his warband had held the Old Bridge in Ifington against concerted attacks by what seemed like half the Jotunn army until he had been reinforced by Baldr and his warband. In what then proved to be the final, vicious battle of that too-long war, Baldr's impenetrable skin had deflected a snow bear's venomous spittle and sent it splattering across Hodr's face where it burned his eyes from their sockets. Baldr had brought his brother home that night, too, except Baldr had been the one weeping.

If Baldr hadn't reinforced his brother, Hodr probably would have died in that battle. If Baldr hadn't been impervious to harm, the snow bear probably would have killed him. Instead, he had lived and Hodr had been blinded.

She given up her visions of what was to come because she didn't want to live with knowing what was to come—and then relive those events when they inevitably happened no matter what she did.

Yet the visions had come back. And now Odin wanted her to tell him what she saw . . . so they could choose among acceptable dooms.

Her fingers started to hurt, so she released her grip. "Heimdall's searching. None of us remember what he looks like, except Hermod."

All she could remember from a few nights ago were things she wanted to forget. And useless things. The cloth covering Hodr's eyes had been blue. The smith had been drunk, scruffy, and nervous. But his face? Just a grizzled brown beard.

"Good, that's good," he said. "Of course she'd remember his face. She always had a good memory—she remembered me, after all, right?"

The light from the witchlamp she'd carried in was full upon his beaten face. His lips were split. His right cheek was swollen and purple. It glistened wetly with the ointment Eir used for such injuries.

"I only ever had to show her a strike or a block once and she'd remember," he continued. "And now she probably wants to kill me. Probably everyone in the city wants me dead. Or worse. I'd give myself to Rán if it'd bring him back."

"So why did you do it?" Rage growled in her voice, and her nails dug into her elbows. She thought she'd shackled her rage and left it behind. Clearly it had pulled up its stake and slunk in behind her.

Hodr shrank in on himself like a flower closing up for the night. "I didn't." He said it as if he knew that she didn't believe him.

"Everyone in the hall saw you do it, even me." She wished she could unsee it—or at least stop seeing it over and over.

He gave a sharp, quick shake of his head. "I was tricked. I had a rock in my hand—a rock. I could feel it."

In her mind's eye, she again pierced the heat-like shimmer that had masked the spear in his hand, making it look like a smooth stone. She still didn't understand how she'd pierced that shroud. No one else had, not until the spear had sprouted like a branch from Baldr's chest.

"But it wasn't a rock, was it?" he whispered. "Sweet Aegir, it wasn't. It was that spear he gave me. A part of me knew it, but there was this fire in my arm and my mind and I . . ."

She ignored his pain and hated herself for it. She was questioning a murderer, like she'd questioned Harald a week earlier—and dozens before him. "How did you learn of your brother's weakness?"

"What weakness?" he said, shaking his head. "He is—he was—one of the strongest among us."

"Was it that witch?"

"I don't know any witches."

"It was a woman. She called herself Yelena. She's already tormented one family I know of here in Gladsheim."

"I don't know her."

"But you knew the smith. Where did you meet him?"

He hunched further into himself. Were he a turtle, she'd be talking to a shell. Flames kindled on his shoulders, the first hint of a vision shimmering like rising heat. That gave her pause. A vision might actually help in this situation.

Hodr continued. "I came to Gladsheim to get your blessing, Mother. And Father's. I was going to ask for a boon. At the very least, I wanted to set things right between us."

"What boon?" Probably that woman he'd been living with for several winters.

His shoulders twitched in a brief shrug. The vision-flames stretched up above his head, and in them she saw . . .

. . . a lean-faced man with long, uncombed black hair and a black beard wilder than his gray eyes, sprinting across . . .

"Forty-odd winters ago, when I slipped away during the night, I was angry and bitter and lost. I wasn't a warrior any longer, just the blind son of Odin who'd been a hero once." His lips quirked. "So I lost myself in the wilds. I gave Kona slices of the fruit Father sent so she could stay with me, and she's saved my life a dozen times over. You'll keep her alive for me?"

"Yes."

. . . a snow-covered field, past smooth stones set in rings, toward a longhouse . . .

"After a very long time alone, I realized I wanted to see people again. So I closed up my little hut and set off toward Ifington. A night or two in, five bandits attacked me—scum thinking a blind man an easy target. By then my ears and nose had become as keen as the spear I killed them with. They stank so bad that even without Kona, I would've known they were coming. Still, they hurt me. Knife in the belly. I bound it like Baldr had taught me, hauled myself up onto her back, and asked her to bring me to Ifington. The rest is a blur. Rot set in, the healer told me later. Foulness on the blade, or just bad luck."

He snorted and sneaked fingers beneath the cloth to rub at the thick scars where his eyes had been.

. . . he held a long, heavy-bladed seax . . .

"Turned out Kona brought me to Alara's way house. It wasn't hers at the time—her parents were still alive—and they took me in. Helped me. Her father never said, but I think he recognized me. He was old enough to remember firsthand how Hodr Odinsson had stopped the Jotunn attack at the Old Bridge—and then been blinded for his trouble."

"I'd wondered how you met her." He was unburdening himself; that demanded some response from her.

. . . he set a broad, hairy hand on a weathered door and pushed . . .

That door looked familiar. Her view in the vision kept switching between above his right shoulder and looking back at him. She

should be able to see his face, but all she could see were the gray eyes
and the unkempt black hair and beard.

Hodr nodded, taking it as a given she'd known of Alara. "I stayed
on after I recovered. Helped out. I was about to leave when her father
died, then her mother shortly after." He shrugged. "I had nowhere to
go. Kona was happy. And after a while, a long while, I realized I was
too."

. . . the door swung open, a dim hearth before him . . .

She'd often sat on Odin's High Seat to watch her blind, wandering
son. Odin had said to leave him be, that he'd return when he was
ready. And then he himself had left her. Despite that, she'd continued
to resist the urge to go to Hodr. It got harder when Hermod's questions about her blind brother had changed from a child's wonderings
to pointed accusations, but even then she hadn't sought him out.

"For a long time, I was angry at both of you for letting me go—
and then for not coming after me," he said, reading her thoughts in
that uncanny way of children. "Then after maybe twenty winters, I
started hoping that you'd never come find me."

. . . the wild man stepped into a dark room . . .

She suppressed a gasp when she realized that the man in her
vision stood near where she did now. And that he was . . .

. . . looking down at the ragged remnant of a man, cloth around his eyes,
arms chained to the wall behind him. The broad seax glinted in the man's
fist . . .

Her stomach lurched. She bit her tongue and forced herself to
focus on Hodr.

Hodr shifted into a cross-legged sitting position, both before her
and in her vision. The chains rattled as he straightened his back. "I
came back, thinking I'd ask Father to give Yggdrasil's fruit to Alara.
And her brother. And our children, should Aegir bless us. But now I
think I was going to ask him to stop sending me that fruit. Alara
didn't want it. And I wanted to be with her."

. . . Hodr looked up, smiled sadly, knowingly; the black-haired man
darted forward . . .

Tears leaped to her eyes, and her arms uncrossed. She went to

Hodr, arms extended even as the man in her vision did the same. Except the man led with the knife.

"I didn't come here to kill my brother," he said, burying his face in her shoulder as she wrapped her arms around her and hugged him tightly. He held on hard, just as the little boy he'd once been had so often done. "I came here to die."

5

LOKI

Day 1, early morning

Loki strode toward the ringing bang of Smith Gundri's hammer upon anvil. Most of this section of Gladsheim was given over to the louder, smellier trades. The streets were busy with people buying wares, placing or picking orders, or making deliveries. Gladsheim's favored son might be dead, but life went on for everyone else. Particularly for those who plotted against the long-lived rulers of Gladsheim; folk like Smith Gundri.

Gundri knew Loki well.

The person he thinks you are, at least, whispered the clever voice from the back of Loki's mind.

Bent over his forge, his watchful apprentice behind him, Gundri appeared to be in the final stages of rough-shaping a blade. Which was good, because it meant Loki would have less time to wait till Gundri reached a point when he could stop without ruining the work he'd done so far.

The forge's heat was impressive even standing just outside the smithy itself. Loki stepped inside the two main doors, which were thrown wide open to either side. The forge was built into the rounded back wall of mounded earth and stone. Across the wooden walls hung all manner of tools, as well as the finished products of Gundri's labor.

Once Gundri had reviewed the work with his apprentice and the young, heavy-shouldered man had set the rough blade aside, Loki called out, "Hot work this early in the morning, eh?"

A broad smile broke across the smith's face. He wiped big hands on a well-scarred leather apron and extended his arm. "Ah, Bolverk, it's been a while. Back from Alvheim, was it? Or was it somewhere else?"

Loki grasped Gundri's thickly muscled forearm and clapped him on the shoulder. "I'm not sure I said, did I?"

"You traders are all alike—too secretive by half."

"Share my markets? You never know who's listening."

Gundri's smile faded. He quirked a grizzled eyebrow.

"And I'd look quite the fool if other traders took advantage of my simplicity and my family went hungry because of it," Loki added.

Or you let a word slip and Goldtooth caught you.

"What is a man without healthy sons and daughters, eh?" Gundri said. "Are you back for another order, then? I've finished a new batch of axes and spears."

"I'm happy to look at them—your weapons always sell well—but I'm really here for custom work. I need a pair of blades. Skymetal, preferably."

Gundri gestured for his apprentice. The young man had the sparse beard and smooth skin of early manhood, along with the obligatory beefiness of a smith. A bit of silver chain glinted around his neck. "Fetch our friend, won't you, Madr?"

The apprentice nodded, ducked out of the apron protecting his simple brown clothing, and left. Smart enough to keep his mouth shut, at least.

Gundri nodded toward a table built into the deep hollow between the forge and the wall behind it. A cup and a bowl sat atop it. "Have a seat, and we'll go over the details."

———

Sól was bright on the rooftops by the time a graybeard showed up along with a tall, thickset henchman. Both were cloaked and moved with a surreptitious air that screamed *look at me*. The graybeard consulted with Gundri, who gestured with his chin toward Loki and the nook where he sat. It seemed this graybeard was a contact for the Sons of Muspell.

Gundri set his hammer on the anvil and motioned toward the forge. His apprentice brought a dull red ingot, nestled it in among the coals, and started working the bellows. The heat in the forge doubled. Loki blotted the fresh beads of sweat from his forehead.

The graybeard patted the smith's shoulder, then walked over to Loki. He moved smoothly for such a seemingly old man. Was this a disguise, then?

"You've been gone a long time, Bolverk." Rather than offer his arm in greeting, the graybeard rested his thin, long-fingered hands on the knob of his walking stick.

So this was how they'd play it.

It's likely a test, said the patient, clever voice. *See where it goes.*

The apprentice brought the bright-yellow ingot back to the anvil. Gundri's hammering began again. An attempt to prevent Goldtooth from overhearing what was said inside the smithy? It should work; the Jotunn sometimes did the same.

"I'm a trader, friend. From here to Ifington, Alvheim, even Vanaheim."

Clang, ting-ting. The smith's hammer blows rang loudly in the small forge.

"And what's your trade again?" The graybeard put an odd emphasis on the word *trade*.

"You know me," Loki said flatly. "What's your name?"

The graybeard ignored the question and spoke in the Jotunn hand language. "You didn't join the Sons here in Gladsheim, did you, Bolverk?"

"Are you questioning my loyalty?" Loki replied in that same language.

The graybeard leaned back and made a small gesture with one

hand. The man who'd remained outside came in and leaned against the back wall of the smithy. He folded big arms across his big chest and stared down at Loki. Even to a casual observer, it'd be obvious they were trying to intimidate him. It was a wonder these fools hadn't been caught. Actually, it wasn't. Ygg had been gone for most of their lives, and Goldtooth was a drunk.

The old man picked up a nearby poker and thrust it into the forge just deep enough so that the tip would heat up. "Of course not," he said aloud. "We're checking that you're who you say you are."

This was going well.

Clang, ting-ting.

Loki made his voice quaver, and he swallowed hard. The heavy sweat on his forehead and upper lip from the forge's heat would further the appearance of nervousness. "I joined in Ifington. But you probably knew that already."

The old man smiled thinly beneath flat eyes. "Been a long time since you were there. We checked."

That was a lie. How would this oaf check on his story? Regardless, he'd better stick to his own story and not try to improvise. "I told you, I'm often gone—"

"And you trade in what, again?" The old man withdrew the poker. The tip had turned a bright cherry red.

"Timber, worked metals, weapons. That's why I was here." He gestured toward the smith, whose hammer still rose and fell. "He makes 'em. I sell 'em."

Clang, ting-ting.

"It's curious that you show up after more than a season and say you have a job for us."

"Listen, I—"

The graybeard swung the poker from the forge. Loki's gaze focused on the cherry-red tip. He was prepared to suffer cuts and broken bones; he could fix those. But burns? Missing eyes? Short of Yggdrasil's fruit or a healer like the one he'd just murdered, those were unfixable. And maybe not even then.

The poker stopped beside his cheek. The heat was intense. He could smell his hair singeing.

You can kill them all in a heartbeat. They are testing you, said the patient voice.

Even so, Loki readied a familiar shape, the powerful white-furred bear. He could become that bear between the blinking of this suspicious old fool's eyes, but he'd rather not slaughter four people and vanish. He had a job for them.

So he'd first try a good lie.

Clang, ting-ting.

A convincing lie.

He cringed away from the poker, but the henchman's powerful hands caught him and held him.

He dropped the nervous ruse. "I've been very patient with you, graybeard. Stop being foolish. I've work for you."

The poker moved closer. The old man's eyes were hard, disbelieving. His lips set. He was prepared to burn Loki.

In the Jotunn hand language, Loki said, "The Skrymir himself sent me. I'm one of his."

6

FRIGG

Day 1, morning

Frigg climbed down from Heimdall's tower under rumbling skies as Thor circled above the hilltop, one hand raised in greeting. The shod hooves of the pair of goats pulling his cart, Toothgrinder and Toothgnasher, hammered sparks from the air. Frigg raised her hand somberly in reply. Thor wouldn't know why he'd been summoned; he'd flown faster than the news had spread.

The hilltop boomed as the cart landed and again beneath Thor's voice. "Why was the Gjallarhorn sounded? I see no army at the gates or any trace of an enemy within miles."

He vaulted over the cart's side and strode toward her, Mjolnir jouncing on his left hip.

"I have bad news, Thor."

He was before her now, a wall of sweat and leather and goats. He was dressed for battle in iron gauntlets, a heavy brown overtunic, woolen trousers, and a wide leather belt. His red hair was wilder than his full beard. Usually, his broad face was open and creased with laugh lines. Now, his clear blue eyes grew serious and fixed on hers.

"What's happened? Is it Father? Couldn't happen to a n—"

"Baldr is dead." Her mouth went dry. This was the first time she'd uttered those words to someone who didn't already know.

He snorted. "That's not possible. Even Mjolnir never hurt him."

He patted the hammer at his side. It didn't look like much, she had to admit. The handle was a thumb's breadth longer than Thor's fist. Twin-headed with a rounded peak in the middle, its sides were intricately carved with what almost looked an interlocking pattern of drainage ditches. The Svartalvar had crafted this hammer—well, those Alvar who ended up becoming the Svartalvar.

"That's just the beginning," she said.

"Mother?"

Oh, he sounded worried now. Heartbeats earlier, he was all bluff denial, but now?

She forced a lifeless smile. "Hodr killed him. Not on—"

He laughed, a short, sharp noise like a clap of thunder. "Now you're having a go at me."

Heimdall's voice drifted down from above. "She's telling you the truth, Thor."

Thor's expression went from amusement and disbelief to fury as fast as one of his lightning bolts. His hands curled into fists. "Well where is he, then?"

"No, Thor, stop. It wasn't Hodr who did it. And he's in chains, regardless, until we can figure out what exactly happened."

"What? Either Hodr killed him—however he did it—or he didn't."

She took his fists in her hands and drew them toward her. "It's not that simple. Let's go back to my longhouse. We'll sit and eat, and I'll tell you everything that happened."

He shook his head. "I think you should tell me right now."

So she did.

She told him of the shape-changing witch who'd tried to kill her, and how his father had cut his own eye from his head and then left to summon Angrboda's shade for answers. She told him about Hodr arriving on Midwinter's Eve in the company of a smith named Lopt. And how she'd seen through the veil that someone, probably the witch, had cast over the spear and how she'd been too late to stop Hodr from hurling it at Baldr. And how the smith had been beside Hodr the whole time.

"And that's when Heimdall sounded the Gjallarhorn," he said.

"Yes."

He grunted. "And you saw Hodr throw the spear."

In her mind, she saw it flash through the air yet again. She pushed the memory away before she could see it hit Baldr.

"So Hodr did kill him."

Frigg shook her head. "He says he didn't intend to—that he didn't even know he held a spear. I believe him."

Thor considered her for a long, shrewd moment, every bit his father's son. Then he blew out a long breath, pushed his big hands through his unruly red hair and stared up at the sky before meeting her eyes again. "Well, mother, the Hodr I knew never would have done such a thing," he said. "We were—are—much alike. He'd no more strike such a cowardly blow than I would."

She couldn't help the smile that spread across her face nor the tears she felt on her cheeks, chill in the cold air. "Thank you, Thor, I can't tell you how much that means to me."

He hugged her. It felt like being crushed, gently, in a landslide.

When he stepped back, he said, "So you think the smith was the witch."

"Yes," she said. Why people thought Thor dim-witted was beyond her.

He blew out another breath in a long cloud. "That's more father's area than mine. When is he back?"

"He should be here soon—by midday."

A herd of emotions stampeded across Thor's face. There'd been bad blood between father and son since the Last War. The first time she'd seen a crack in it was a couple weeks earlier at Ithavoll. But now it was back.

"Would you like to see him? Baldr, I mean."

"I would, yes," Thor said.

She pointed at his cart. "How much room do you need to land that?"

"Not much more than where I just did."

"I'd hoped you would say that. Let's go."

———

FRIGG AND THOR stepped back out of the larder that had been cut, ages ago, into the cliff beneath Heimdall's tower. The cold radiating off that rock cut right through her.

"I can't believe he's dead." Thor looked back down the gloomy, witchlamp-lit corridor from which they'd emerged. "This whole time, his spirit was in mistletoe? That's what killed him?"

"And it's what made him unkillable," Frigg said. "My people's magic. Very old. I wish I knew how that witch learned the secret."

"Probably used her own magic." He rested one hand on Mjolnir. "I wear the only bit of magic I trust. The rest of it . . ."

Thor wore quite a bit—more than any of the other Aesir. She herself only had the falcon cloak given to her by Freyja. "Speaking of magical things we distrust, I have a favor to ask of you."

He lifted one bushy red eyebrow.

"Remember that Jotunn attack on Háls and how Vidar pursued them?" she asked. "Well, he killed their rear guard at the entrance to an abandoned mine under Háls and then chased a few survivors into the mine and all the way—"

"Good to know Vidar's fighting again rather than tinkering."

"Indeed, but he chased them all the way into northwest Utgard— a very remote section."

"From a mine in Asgard, he got to Utgard?"

She nodded.

His brow clouded. "And here comes the bit about untrustworthy magic."

"Vidar said he went through a doorway of some kind," she said. "It led from the mine to Utgard."

"How is that possible?"

She shrugged. "We need Vidar or your father to explain it. But we think that's how they got to Háls with no one noticing."

Thor's face darkened still further, the squall threatening to loose its fury. Then he blew out a breath, and his mood brightened. "That must relieve your mind."

"How so?"

He tucked his thumbs behind his thick belt. "I'm sure you were kicking yourself for having let the Jotunn sneak into Asgard and slaughter every man, woman and child in Háls. Now you know that you didn't make that particular mistake."

He might as well have punched her in the stomach.

"They could still be sneaking in," she said.

Which was true—but on the scale necessary for sneaking a full Jotunn warband past the Fortress at the Breach, south to Ifington, through that bustling city, south about two nights travel to Glad-sheim, and then out west for at least another two nights' travel? That could only be possible with the complicity of many people: merchants, residents of the areas through which the Jotunn were traveling, wardens, even members of the army and the Einherjar. So far Saglund, who led the Einherjar, had found no evidence that his warriors had helped the Jotunn, nor had Orgrandr of his wardens or Tyr and Ullr of the army. So far.

Yet.

Aloud, she said, "The doorway appears to be the simplest explanation."

The look in Thor's eye was very keen, as though he'd guessed her thoughts. "And your favor, Mother?"

"Vidar saw the Jotunn hauling something from a lake into a cave. My guess is he came across one of those ancient Jotunn cliff strongholds."

"What were they removing?"

"He didn't get close enough to see. Whatever it was, it required sledges pulled by several Jotunn at a time. Beyond that . . ."

Thor frowned. "How will I find this place? Did Heimdall see it?"

"He glimpsed it through heavy clouds. And Vidar described it, both the landscape and its position relative to Aurvandil's Toe."

Thor rolled his eyes. "Well, that's useful."

"I know it's a long trip, even for you, and I wouldn't ask except—"

"Except you fear that all these events are not as unrelated as they appear." He looked up toward where Heimdall stood, and then at the rising sun, now well on her way toward midday. "It's two nights for me to fly directly to Jotunheim, and then longer to find this cliff and lake, assuming I even can."

"I know, you'll be gone—"

His grin came and went like blue sky between storms. "I'm not objecting to going. It's why I carry these weapons. But I'll be gone a week, maybe longer. If something happens here, as you seem to fear..."

"It's a risk," she said. "But I'm sure your father can manage till you return. And we've several Einherjar warbands stationed in the city. If something should happen, well, you'll hear Heimdall call."

7

LOKI

Day 1, morning

Loki didn't allow his stern expression to soften even as the gray-beard swung the hot poker away from his cheek. He was playing the role of a secret Jotunn envoy playing the role of a simple trader, and he'd hooked this man.

"I bear his mark," he said with his hands.

"Prove it," the graybeard said out loud, his eyes still narrow with suspicion. He gestured for the henchman to check.

Clang, ting-ting.

Each of the Skrymir's secret, personal messengers bore a rune painted on their shoulder as an identifying mark—a stupid affectation, in Loki's opinion. The Skrymir changed the rune every so often, but Loki didn't know how knowledge of the current rune was spread. It might have something to do with the shaman, but even after more than a hundred winters of working with the Jotunn, he hadn't quite cracked this particular secret.

Fortunately, the Skrymir had shown him the current rune. It was a simple matter to make it appear where it should. If this ruse didn't work, he'd have to bend their minds to his will. But that option left traces that could, potentially, show his current identity to be more than it seemed.

And we do have more to do today, his inner voice added.

The henchman yanked Loki's cloak to one side and pulled his shirt down, exposing his shoulder. "It's there."

"Of course it's there," Loki said.

The poker swung further away, the dull orange tip smoldering against the forge's lip. The graybeard gestured, and the henchman released him. If that was a fake beard, it was a good one; if it wasn't, then the man was stupid. Good schemes required layers upon layers of separation between who you really were and your assumed identities.

Clang, ting-ting.

"Well, no hard feelings," the graybeard said. "We have to be careful."

"I understand," Loki said, slouching as if in relief as the henchman backed away a pace. "And I told you—"

He stood and spun in one fluid motion, striking the henchman in the side of the head with his left fist. The man dropped like a slaughtered cow. Loki continued the spin and kicked the graybeard in the stomach as he came back around.

Clang, ting-ting.

The graybeard dry-heaved and wheezed as he tried to draw a breath.

Loki grabbed him by the beard and whispered into his ear. "I don't appreciate hot pokers in my face."

He shoved the old man's head down and stepped back. Real beard, just an unusually spry old man. This would be the last time he could use the Bolverk identity.

Clang, ting-ting.

Neither the smith nor his apprentice seemed to have noticed the altercation. The street beyond the forge's doors was empty, and the hammer's pounding was still loud enough to have drowned out his whispers.

The old man got control of his breathing, spat blood into the dirt and ash of the floor, and pushed himself up. Tough bastard. He glared at Loki, wiped his mouth, and said, "We have to check. You know that."

With his hands, Loki said, "I have a job for you. Are you ready to listen?"

The graybeard spat more blood and stood. "You kill him?" he asked, pointing at the unmoving henchman.

"If I did, it wasn't my intent. You'll need all the help you can get."

The graybeard's scowl deepened, but he nodded once and offered his arm. "I'm Afi. We're at his service."

THEY HAD TUCKED themselves deeper into the shadowed nook behind the forge. Using his hands, Afi said, "And all he wants us to do is burn some buildings? We can do more."

"The food stores," Loki emphasized, using his hands to reply. "He knows you can do more. He didn't say, but I've no doubt you and yours will be called upon to do more before long. But this first."

The Skrymir had said nothing of the kind, nor had this plot been devised by either the Skrymir or Vafthrudnir. But they needed Ygg and the Aesir distracted for a full month before they attacked. Murdering Baldr had been a good start, but that distraction would last two weeks at most. Setting the city ablaze would keep the Aesir occupied for much longer, and these Sons of Muspell were the perfect tool for the job.

"All right," Afi said, looking somewhat mollified.

"How soon can you get it done?" Loki asked.

"The lower storehouses are easy enough, but we need a couple of nights to get everyone in place. He wants the upper stores burned, too?"

Loki nodded. "Ideally."

Afi pursed his lips, thinking. "That'll be more difficult—"

"But doable?"

"Yes. Absolutely."

"Best to do all at once."

"Obviously," Afi said, frowning as his hands answered. "Three nights from now."

"You're certain? Our friends need a distraction. The more we coordinate, the bigger the distraction."

"Yes, I'm certain. Only a matter of getting the right means into the right place. After that, it's easy enough to set spark to tinder."

Loki clapped him on the shoulder just as a fellow in arms would. "You won't see me again. I'll tell the Skrymir that he has trusted and valuable friends in Gladsheim."

Afi stood and offered his arm. "What we do, we do for our people."

"For we are the sons of Bergelmir and Thruthgelmir," Loki replied with his hands. He took the old man's arm and gripped it tightly before he left.

By the time he'd reached the crowd of folk milling about for the midday meal, Loki wore the face of a young man he'd seen herding sheep in a village east of Ifington. Afi's last words kept repeating in his head. While Loki's actions were indeed helping the Jotunn and supporting the Skrymir's plan, that wasn't why he was doing any of this. He did what he did for his children. And for his dead wife.

Ygg and the Aesir had a large debt to repay. In blood.

8

FRIGG

Day 1, late morning

Frigg pushed back her feathered cloak and stepped out of the Great Hall. The iron-banded doors stood open behind her. A part of her really wished she could go back inside, have the doors closed, and mourn her son. But no. With the rumbles of Thor's departure to Utgard hardly faded, she now stood in front of a thousand-strong crowd—a mob, if she handled this wrong—to call for calm when there was none in her heart.

"Heimdall, hear me," she said, trying not to move her lips. "Watch this crowd before the Great Hall."

The late morning breeze had grown chilly. The shadows of clouds flowed across the ground. Sól peeked from behind them, but the clouds kept pouring in from the west. The air smelled of snow. And like the night Baldr died, the air above the crowd burned with vision-fire. It looked like grasslands aflame, but without heat or smoke. Frigg looked straight at an older Aesir woman, gray-haired and stout. Solid. She leaned on a staff clutched in worn hands, red-knuckled and coarse from the work of winter piled upon winter. In the vision-fires above her head . . .

. . . *tears coursed down her face like water running over a boulder.*

Buildings burned behind her, black smoke rising, snow-covered ground churning . . .

Was the old woman kneeling? Behind her in the vision it looked like a building was burning.

"Well, Almother, what say you?" shouted a nearby voice.

. . . a spear, black with blood, burst through the matron's chest . . .

More visions of a battle coming. But when? The matron didn't look noticeably older in the vision than she did standing before Frigg now. The crowd's grumblings were growing louder. She'd fallen silent at the same time she'd asked them to be.

"Another few moments of silence are all I require as we ask for Aegir's mercy," she called.

With only a few more protests, quickly hushed, the crowd complied.

Before they could buck the silence, she said, "You've come seeking answers about Baldr's death."

"His murder," shouted a deep voice from the far end of the clearing.

From the broad platform at the front of the Great Hall, she stood a sword's length higher than those packed tight into the clearing—not a great vantage point to see who exactly she was speaking to.

"We'll wake him when Odin returns. All are welcome, both in the hall and where you stand now. We'll have the fires going, so you'll have warmth and plentiful food and drink."

From the left side of the crowd cried a high-pitched voice. "We heard it's your blind son Hodr who killed Baldr!"

A rumble of assent followed. This is what they wanted, then, the custom met. A murder demanded blood. Death for death. She swept her gaze across the crowd and saw . . .

. . . arrows falling around a young man cowering behind a shield, his face wet with tears . . .

. . . a door slammed shut and barred; a woman ushered two young boys and a girl toward . . .

. . . a man with a bloody cloth tied around his head shouting orders to warriors arrayed in a long line before him . . .

She'd seen others dying the night Baldr was killed, but not so many. Not so widespread. She knew what war looked like; she'd seen enough of them. Her stomach churned. Sweat broke out on her forehead. Her palms felt clammy.

War was coming.

She gazed down at the churning crowd, their faces wore every expression between anger and confusion and grief. Some among them blood and death. But it'd be their own, not Hodr's.

Odin thought he could change what was to come. Perhaps he'd be able to. But for now, she had to deal with the problem before her.

Frigg thrust out her hands. "You loved him, too. I know that, just as I know you want answers. We do, too. That's why we seek a smith named Lopt. From Ifington, or thereabouts. Spread the word! If you know of him, tell Fimafeng—"

"That's not who threw the spear!" From another place in the crowd, a hoarse, old-sounding man shouted. "Who cares about some smith? I saw who threw the spear. It was your blind son!"

A shrieky voice cried "Vengeance! Vengeance for Baldr! Hodr must die!"

Frigg shouted to make herself heard. "He's my son! If custom applies, then I have the right of vengeance."

"If it were one of us, we'd be strung up already—" shouted someone from the back.

"Two nights and nothing!" yelled someone else. "Were it my son, he'd be dead by now."

"Stand forth if you question me," she shouted back. "Only cowards hide themselves in a crowd."

Her only answers were more angry calls: "Too long!" and "One set of rules for you and yours, one set for us!" and "What's right is right! Hodr must die!"

And above their heads, her visions burned on—scenes of violent death and battle and armored figures laying waste to a city that looked far too much like Gladsheim.

9

LOKI

Loki grasped the elbow of a bald man in front of him. Startled, the man turned toward him. Quickly, Loki traced the rune he used to cloud men's minds and set his will upon the man.

"Who cares about some smith? You saw who threw the spear, didn't you? It was her blind son. I tell you, friend, were it you or me who'd done it, we'd already be food for the ravens."

The bald man's liver-spotted face went black with rage. Spittle whitened the corners of his lips and he turned away, threw his fist in the air, and bellowed, "Who cares about some smith? I saw who threw the spear. It was your blind son!"

The impossible part was guessing when Goldtooth's gaze would be upon him, even assuming Goldtooth was watching and listening from his high tower. Which he had to assume. Loki was too close to success to get caught now. Even so, he'd promised to distract the Aesir and what better way than with a few fires and unruly mobs.

A shrieky voice on the opposite side of the open area, which was packed shoulder to shoulder with many folk, screamed out, "Vengeance! Vengeance for Baldr! Hodr must die!"

Move now.

Loki slipped past several people, subtly shape-shifting his face, stature, and sex as he went, making himself more and more womanly.

That scream would've woken the dead. Which would be funny—Baldr come back as an afterwalker, staggering out of whatever hole Frigg had stuffed his body into.

More shouts rang out. He paid them half a mind; all his attention was on Frigg. She appeared worried, as well she should. A few more shoves would turn this crowd violent. Unchecked, they might bring that hall down around her ears. That'd be quite the distraction for the Skrymir—the Almother and Baldr both dead and Ygg come back to Gladsheim, whenever that might be, to a city in outright rebellion.

He moved further to his left, lengthening his hair and rounding out his hips. Even if he was noticed now, he'd leave the clearing as someone entirely different. Once he had the tall cliff between himself and Goldtooth's tower, he'd take an animal's shape to get to his meeting with Yelena.

Loki passed through pockets of shouting people with upraised fists. Others muttered and swore. All faced the Great Hall where Frigg stood, arms upraised as if she could calm this mob.

Too easy.

Behind Frigg, the baresark Ráta stepped into the sunlight. Hermod was beside her, looking more like her father than she had the last time he'd seen her, a good ten winters ago now. In the comparative gloom inside the Great Hall, he thought he could see more figures. He made his eyes become an eagle's for a moment and yes, a small group of Einherjar had assembled inside. Perfect.

He settled into the shape of a young woman with loose golden-brown hair and bewitching green eyes. He touched a burly man's arm and smiled prettily up at the piggish face that looked down at him. "Are those warriors behind the Almother? There, inside the hall—I can see the spears!"

"What's that now?" The man's voice rang with a note pleasantly at odds with his rough features. He squinted at the hall. "Well, so there are."

Loki was about to set his will upon him when he reached forward and jostled the arm of a whip-cord lean man in front of him. "Hey, Ogmundr, look. Inside the hall."

Ogmundr grunted, sneered over his shoulder, and with his hands said, "Maybe one of 'em is on our side."

With his hands.

All thought of setting his will upon the rough-featured man flew from Loki's head. Ogmundr had used the Jotunn hand speech. He'd just stepped in a pile of—

"You head on home now, girl," the rough-featured man said, giving Loki a gentle push. "Not safe here."

Loki let himself get pushed back by the man's big hand. He watched as the big man and Ogmundr shoved their way forward through the crowd, grabbing other men by the arms and shoulders as they went. The rough-featured man had understood the hand speech. He and Ogmundr were gathering other men. They were Sons of Muspell. They had to be.

Loki suddenly felt very aware of Heimdall's tower looming high above the Great Hall and the clearing. He began shoving his way through a crowd whose mood, he realized, was finally growing uglier. A few more pushes should send it over the edge and perhaps aid the Sons.

He ducked behind taller, broader folk, shifting his features and height till he was an even younger girl than he had been. He wound up beside the fence along the cliff above the road that wound its way up from the second tier. Off to his right blazed one of the tall bonfires that was used to help warm the gatherings.

"Child, what are you doing here?" asked a matronly woman with very blue eyes and blond hair in a long, loose braid.

A distant shout echoed up from the road below; another came from near the Great Hall. He couldn't see what was happening at the hall. He'd made himself too short. But he could guess. Couldn't be good for him, though, particularly since he'd heard Thor arrive and depart. Maybe Tyr or Ullr had arrived, too—or even worse, Ygg himself.

Time to go. But not before he made a bad situation even worse.

"I can't find my daddy," he said to the blond-haired woman.

"Shame on him for even bringing you here," she said, holding out her hand. "I'm Mjoll. I'll get you out of here."

"Thank you so much. I'm so scared."

"Why's that, love? I heard the Alfather's riding up from the second tier even now. He'll get this mob in order." Mjoll threw an annoyed glance back over her shoulder toward the hall.

Ygg was here? Definitely time to go.

"My daddy says he only protects his own, no matter what they've done," Loki said, squeezing Mjoll's hand tightly and setting his will upon her.

She stared down at him with very wide, very green eyes. "He wouldn't. He's supposed to protect us."

Croaking loudly, a pair of huge ravens fell from the sky. They landed on the nose and tail of the prowling wooden wolf carved into the lintel above the door to the Great Hall.

"Look, he's sent his ravens," Loki shouted. "They eat his enemies. Please, stop him!"

Mjoll's expression grew hard and fierce. Much as the big man had done, she grabbed the arms and shoulders of the women near her and shouted a few words. The women glanced at Loki, nodded, and they pulled him into the center of a group of women who started moving toward the road down to the second tier. The same road Ygg was riding up.

As the crowd moved toward the road, with a touch here and there, Loki set his will upon the surrounding women, emphasizing their fear, the desire to protect him, and their desire to not be here when violence broke out.

When he was close enough to feel the heat of the large, blazing bonfire, he flicked a small black pebble into it.

A deep-voiced roar went up from the men Loki assumed had attacked the Almother's guards.

Then Ygg himself appeared above the old wall that bordered the road.

The green-eyed matron, whose hand still gripped Loki's tightly, pointed and shrieked. "There he is! There's the Alfather! He'll kill our men!"

Loki slipped from the grasp of the green-eyed matron and ran toward the stones of the old wall as if he were seeking shelter. Which proved necessary because a heartbeat later, Ygg set his wolves on the women.

As Loki reached the wall, the pebble he'd flung into the bonfire exploded in a shower of sparks that rapidly expanded into a cloud of black smoke.

Good luck, brother.

10

ODIN

Day 1, late morning

Odin rode through Gladsheim's western gates. Sleipnir's eight hooves struck a unique cadence from the hard-frozen earth. His wolves had run ahead, opening a path, while his ravens flew toward the upper tier. Merchants' wagons and farmers' carts ran aground on the road's narrow banks. Their drivers and passengers stared at him in silence, twisting to keep their eyes on him. Judging by the droves of people flocking to the road, news of his return was rippling through the city.

A cloud's shadow swept across them, dappling the hill he was about to ride up, and then sped out over the eastern wall to rush across the snow-covered plain of Vigrid. There was a sadness hanging thick about the city, thicker even than the stench of night-soil kept at bay by the cold air.

Wing-Father, trouble above, Huginn said.

Trouble ahead, trouble behind. And he was tired. Worn, like the filthy cloak around his shoulders.

Show me.

Through Huginn's eyes, he saw a large crowd packed into the clearing before the Great Hall. Fists upraised, arms pumping, mouths open in shouts, they advanced against the steps up to the hall. Frigg stood strong before them, Ráta and Hermod beside her, Einherjar behind.

Should he go there now? Or ride up there? Heimdall knew he was coming and what was happening with Frigg. No doubt even more Einherjar and wardens were already on their way.

Tell me if weapons are drawn, he told his ravens. *And make your presence known to the crowd and to Frigg.*

Yes, Wing-Father.

He leaned forward and thumped Sleipnir's sweaty neck. "Only a little further. Then you can rest."

Sleipnir shook her head and snorted, then trotted a little faster.

"All right, girl, all right. Get me there so I can rest, then."

Up ahead, his wolves howled. The roadside was as thick with people as a riverbank with reeds. They'd left their work and trades and chores to watch him ride through the city he'd left a week ago, staring at him with mixed expressions—doubt, concern, awe, mistrust. Perhaps they'd heard stories of what the Alfather had done long ago, but many of these folk had been babies when he'd left twenty years to go wandering. To them, he was a mud-stained man in a wide-brimmed gray hat astride an impossible horse.

His missing eye began to itch behind its patch.

He raised an open hand in greeting as he rode. Some of those he passed returned the salute; others doffed their hats. Some bent to whisper into their children's ears, pointing up at him as he rode past. Others muttered sidelong to one another. Nothing he could hear, though.

The gate to the second tier hove into view as the road curved northward. At the outward bend of the road's curve, his gaze fell upon a big, weathered-looking man with fair hair, a long-braided beard, and an ugly mouth. Hate burned in the man's blue eyes.

Odin's missing eye burned in its socket. A bloody haze crept across his sight. Through it, he saw the blond man charging across a battlefield with spear and shield in hand.

Odin blinked; the vision vanished.

Muninn, remember this man's face, he said, pushing the memory to her.

He felt her croak in answer.

You and your brother will look for him later.

Yes, Wing-Father.

He was nearly even with the fair-haired man now. He didn't want to turn his head or, worse, turn in the saddle to keep his eye on him. A brown-bearded man with black eyes and burly shoulders pushed through the crowd to stand beside the fair-haired man. A woman with long black hair pulled back into tight braids leaned against the wall beside the fair-haired man. She had a scar across her nose. None of the three could've seen more than thirty winters.

Remember these, he said, sharing the image of all three together.

Did they hate him personally? Had they allied themselves with the Sons of Muspell? And what did the vision mean? Frigg might see more, not that she'd tell him what she saw. The Norns would know, but they'd stopped answering his questions. He nearly spat in the dirt at the thought of speaking to those farmyard hens again. He would, though. Somehow, they saw what had happened, what was happening, and what would happen. They'd sometimes told him what would happen. Other times, they lied about it or didn't tell him everything—more the fool he was for trusting them. They'd said that Baldr would be protected against all harm, but they hadn't said that protection would cost Hodr his sight. Nor had they said that Baldr would be killed by the very thing used to safeguard him.

He rubbed his brow beneath the eyepatch covering the golden orb that Baldr had placed there after he sacrificed his real eye and cast it into the waters beneath Mimir's head.

The eye was opening. He was glimpsing future events, if his visions worked the same as Frigg's. Even if they didn't, they still provided more knowledge than he would otherwise have, and that was the whole point. The more he knew, the better choices he could make. He could prevent tragedies like those that had befallen Baldr and Hodr.

He was beginning to see.

He couldn't help it; he grinned.

That smile was echoed in the face of a towheaded boy beside the road. The child clapped and bounced up and down in sheer happiness. Odin winked at him just as the red veil dropped across his vision and his missing eye saw . . .

. . . *a bearded man, stout, with a battered shield in one hand, a bloodied axe in the other, and a determined expression on his face. Behind him and other men similarly armed, women carried children, boys and girls held hands and tugged smaller children behind them, and . . .*

Sleipnir whinnied. Odin blinked back to awareness. They were passing through the tall gate to the second tier. Freki and Geri padded a spear's throw ahead of him, keeping the road clear.

Hurry, Wing-Father, Huginn called from his perch above the Great Hall. *Quickly.*

The gate to the third tier wasn't far; the road was clear. He urged Sleipnir into a canter.

———

ODIN CRESTED the hill and passed between the stout gateposts built flush against the wall's heavy stones. On his right, the old wall stretched upward along the steeper slope to the hill's crest, lined with anxious people. Some had begun fleeing back down the road to the second tier.

"There he is! There's the Alfather! He'll kill our men!"

A horde of shrieking, wild-eyed women with fists upraised were charging toward Odin along the waist-high stone wall to his left. Most were gaudily dressed—bright dresses, rings, earrings and arm rings of gold and silver and set with precious stones glittered and flashed in the sunlight.

Another, distant shout came from the steps of the Great Hall. Even from here, he could see the dozens of men throwing themselves against a shield wall formed by Einherjar. The defenders in the second row held their spears reversed, using them like a ship's fending poles to push the attackers back. Barely visible, Frigg stood behind Hermod and Ráta.

How is Frigg? he asked Huginn, who had taken wing above the fray.

Safe. Your pup and she-bear stand before her. But many attack.

The screaming of the women charging him was louder now, a few spears' lengths away. What madness had taken these people?

Stop the women, he told his wolves, *without killing them.*

Freki and Geri's heads came up to the shoulders of most men, and they were easily twice as massive. Geri threw himself at the charging women first, turning sideways at the last moment so that the entire length of his huge body slammed into them. He knocked down the first three rows of women, landed on his feet, and spun to face those who skidded to a halt. Freki crashed into the remaining women, flattening them like long grass in a field.

"Forward, girl," he said to Sleipnir. "Slowly now. Let's try not to crush our own folk."

Most of the folk directly in front of him and Sleipnir had backed away, the older among them with arms outspread to push back those behind them. Confusion and fear reigned. One of the bonfires on his far left exploded in a huge, expanding cloud of black smoke. The surrounding folk screamed and stampeded away from it toward him. He had to move before the panicked crowd swamped him.

To me, he called to Freki and Geri. *We're headed to the Great Hall.*

The wolves leaped smoothly toward him, knocking aside those unfortunates who'd been forced in toward Sleipnir. With Sleipnir as the tip of Odin's wedge and the black wolves on either side, he split the hundreds-strong crowd like soft wood.

The attackers had pushed the Einherjar shield wall back from the bottom of the stairs to the top. They'd begun hauling themselves up onto the platform by the sides. Ráta and Hermod had seen that threat and were even now shouting orders. Slowly, the shield wall began withdrawing to the next bottleneck—the Great Hall's entryway.

Freki looked back over her shoulder, eagerness alive in her golden eyes.

Not unless I order it, he said to his wolves. *We'll try to do this without killing anyone.*

Both wolves woofed aloud in reply and then growled at those in their way.

They were still fifty yards from the Great Hall. The attackers had forced the Einherjar back another few feet. Hermod and Ráta fought the men who swarmed them from the sides. Frigg stood inside the hall. For the moment, she was still safe.

Huginn cried out. *Wing-Father, blades are out!*

On the steps of the Great Hall, axe blades flashed in the fists of the attackers. The Einherjar were still using the blunt end of their spears, but it wouldn't be long before they spilled blood. Odin brought Gungnir to his hand and hauled upon his fylgja's power until the air buzzed around him. He'd seen no weapons among those fleeing, but now any skymetal, iron, or steel would blunt itself against him.

He stood in the stirrups and shouted, "Make way!"

Sleipnir stood a spear's length at the shoulder, had eight massive legs, and was half again as long as any other horse save the Builder's horse who'd sired her. Those folk before her parted easily. Odin and his wolves surged another thirty yards with no resistance until they came upon a shoal of men clad in brown leathers and gray cloaks, bearing axes, knives, and determined expressions.

Take them down, he said his wolves. *Kill only if you have to.*

With a pair of growling barks, Freki and Geri leaped forward and slammed into the men. Jaws snapping, white teeth flashing, they laid into the men.

Sleipnir trotted around them.

The fight on the steps of the hall had grown more dire, and Odin couldn't see Frigg anymore. Hermod and Ráta stood on either side of the hall's doorway, shoring up the line of twelve Einherjar. All of them were still using the flats of their axes and the butts of their spears against some thirty men still attacking the hall.

Odin leaped off Sleipnir and dashed up the stairs. Wielding Gungnir like a staff, he began clubbing the men besieging the hall.

There was a time when he'd have killed them. That time might come again, but he didn't want to shed blood on the steps of the Great Hall. Not today. That would turn more people against him, and that memory—of him killing his own people—would be harder to cleanse than bloodstains from the stairs. Instead, he knocked the attackers down with quick, brutal strikes.

As the pressure on the shield wall eased, the Einherjar advanced toward him. Hermod grinned hugely when she saw him but kept laying about with the flat of her sword. Ráta nodded, power buzzing about her shoulders, as she knocked the attackers senseless with precise strikes using the hammer sides of her war axes.

Frigg emerged from the Great Hall's dark entrance, her expression a mix of anger and concern. Her eyes went frosty when she saw him, but she also seemed relieved.

And then the fight was over. Red-faced, sweating, and breathing hard, the Einherjar put away their weapons and began collecting the ones wielded by the attackers. Odin surveyed over the remaining crowd. Many hundreds of folk had apparently chosen to watch.

From the platform's edge, he shouted, "What was all this about then, eh?"

The closest hundred heads remained locked on him, mostly men but more than a few women mixed in.

"Well?" he shouted again, louder than before.

Some brave man in the far back shouted, "We came to demand justice and fair treatment!"

"For what?" he called back.

"The murder of your son!" yelled another man, as if it was obvious.

With Gungnir, Odin pointed toward the attackers strewn across the steps and the platform. "This is a good way to plead for justice or fairness?"

Another man shouted, "Custom demands—your own custom . . ."

Odin slammed Gungnir against the wooden platform. It boomed like thunder. He left her standing there. "And were I to besiege your house and threaten your wife and child, how would you respond?"

Silence.

Join me, he said to Freki and Geri.

His wolves leaped atop the platform and flanked him, snarling. The closest spectators blanched and edged away. The expressions on the faces of many others grew resolute. That showed promise.

"Go back to your homes," he said. "If I see a mob like this again, I will turn my wolves loose."

One among the resolute was a young woman around Hermod's age. Her brown hair was bound up in a thick braid that rested on one green-cloaked shoulder. Her left hand rested on the hilt of a long-bladed knife. She stared up at him with serious blue eyes. The dispersing crowd flowed around her like she was a river rock.

Odin acknowledged her with a grave nod. She jumped at that, her face coloring. A black-bearded man stepped up beside her and touched her arm. She glanced at him, nodded, then looked back up at Odin. She gave him a respectful nod and turned away.

Odin's chest filled with warmth and he grinned. Oh yes, some among the Aesir remembered who they were. Some had kept their temper.

Stay alert, he said to Freki and Geri. *Watch for more like her.*

He turned his back to the crowd and walked back toward where his daughter, wife, and his baresark stood waiting. Only one of the three looked annoyed.

"Well, Odin, it's about time," Frigg said. "You better be able to do what I hope you can."

"Take me to him, and I'll let you know."

11

LOKI

Day 1, midday

Loki stepped inside the way house, escaping the carts rumbling through Gladsheim's eastern gate. He blinked, letting his eyes adjust from the brightness of midday to the darker interior of the way house. Hopefully, Yelena was already here—he was late, so she should be. This meeting shouldn't take long. He couldn't afford to delay much longer in meeting with Frigg—and Ygg, now that he'd returned from wherever he'd been. Again.

"Pardon, trader," said a short, stout man who glared up at him.

"Apologies." Loki touched his forehead and stepped aside; he'd been blocking the door. He'd taken the shape of an ordinary traveling merchant who'd picked this way house for a meal after completing the last leg of the journey from Ifington. That was his story, should he be asked.

The man grunted and walked outside, tugging his hood up against the chill. The best part of cities and towns' growing ever larger was that people cared ever less about those they didn't know. That made it much easier to move unremarked among them.

Or to rile up a mob.

Loki checked the far corners of the way house first, looking for the agreed-upon signal: two witchlamps on a table, one glowing bright, the second turned low. He didn't see either till he checked— there. A brown-haired, brown-bearded, plain-faced man sat at a table in the far right corner.

The man winked. "Come join me, friend." He lifted his cup with one hand; the other formed the letter Y in the Jotunn hand language.

———

"I see that you're well," Loki said after the lady of the way house had bustled away from the table, leaving behind plates of hot meat, flatbread, and cups of mead.

Yelena shrugged the rounded shoulders of the man's shape she'd taken. "No worse for wear. Not yet, at least."

"Your voice is deeper than I remember," he said, gesturing toward his throat. "Bit of a cold?"

She yawned. "Have you been in the city a while, then?"

"Arrived this morning," he said, hiding the lie behind a casual sip of mead. Too much honey for his taste.

"You've heard the news though, yes?"

"That Jarl Baldr was murdered by his brother? I could hardly not have—every third woman weeps about it. It was an ill deed, and I grieve for the Almother and Alfather."

No doubt old Goldtooth had heard so much of this sentiment over the past few nights that he'd begun ignoring it. Still, other ears might be listening.

Yelena doused the brighter witchlamp's flame. Shadows crept in. She leaned back in her seat so that she could speak in the Jotunn hand language beneath the table's lip. Loki could see her hands, but no one else in the way house could. Presumably. And as long as he kept his own hands in front of his chest, no one could see his replies. Though he hated having his back to the room.

"Why did you want to meet? I thought our arrangement ended when I handed over the mistletoe," she said in the Jotunn language.

"It did, but I have more work for you. If you're interested."

"Well, that depends," she said aloud, spearing a slice of meat on the point of her knife.

"On what?" Like every witch he'd ever met, Yelena was only interested in one thing: increasing her power.

She chewed the meat till it had to be softer than the pap fed to babies, then washed it down with mead. "I'll take more of that same coin you paid me with before."

He snorted. "Silver is the coin for this deal—and plenty of it, too."

With her hands, she said, "Oh, I've had enough silver to last me a lifetime, as have my sisters. We like gold much better."

When he hired Yelena and her coven to get the mistletoe, he'd agreed to pay her with a slice of the golden apple he received from Idunn each Midwinter. The Aesir and Vanir ate them every Midwinter, and as the slight ache in his joints attested, he was overdue for his —though he'd been within stealing distance of a dozen not two weeks ago.

Of course she wanted more of that currency. Few would turn down the chance at a long, healthy, youthful life. When he'd married Sigyn, she'd gotten an apple, as had Angrboda before her. His boys, Vali and Narfi, weren't old enough to receive theirs—not that they ever would. If Loki had his way, there'd be no one left to pluck the apples from Yggdrasil's branches. Perhaps he could persuade Idunn to tell him which branch yielded the fruit.

"I'm not much for riddles, Yelena." He needed a few moments to think. Getting more apples would take too long, even assuming he could. They were better guarded now than when he'd stolen some. Idunn, too, was better guarded.

She leaned forward. "You've stolen them before. You can do so again."

"You overestimate my capabilities," he said, noting the hard glint in her eyes. He should have thought this through a bit more. He'd planned to use Yelena to add still more unrest to the city, but he couldn't afford her services if the only currency she'd accept was an apple.

He put his hands on the table and stood. "I'm sorry to have wasted your time. An agreement's just not possible."

"Don't be like that," she said, amusement heavy in her manly voice. "Besides, if you leave now, you won't hear the message your wife wanted me to convey."

He froze. He knew of only one man who could speak with the dead, both the recently deceased and the long dead. That was Ygg. Was Yelena now claiming the same power?

"Did I catch you off guard?" She patted the table with one broad hand. "Please. Sit."

Contacting this witch had been a mistake.

Angrboda had gone to her barrow a grieving, angry, hate-filled shell of the woman he'd married. With good reason, of course, but he'd thought that the grave had swallowed her rage just as it ate everything else.

He sat. "Out with it."

She switched to the Jotunn hand language. "Your wife has sent us to do what you wouldn't."

A sick feeling rose in his stomach. He crossed his arms and clenched his jaw. He knew what was coming.

They were here to kill Ygg.

12

ODIN

Day 1, early afternoon

Odin wiped tears from his face. It was true. His son was dead. The evidence was right there in front of him, cold and flat on a table that was equally cold and flat. And so faded the small, hopeful part of him that had nursed the hope that Baldr might not actually be dead.

He shivered. It was cold in the hill's belly.

The steady, pale light of the witchlamps lent little heat but did impart the larder with a still, eerie quality that brought back dim memories of the time he and Loki had crept into a dead man's barrow. They'd been standing at the door of the chamber, arms loaded with the treasure the widow had dispatched them for, when a sound came like branches breaking. They turned to see the dead man smiling, arms wide open, a grin on his bloated face. Then the draugr had spoken: "But you didn't even say please."

The dead man's body had been blue-black and swollen, heavier than the immense stone they'd had to lever out of the way to get into the barrow. The ensuing fight had been the second time Loki saved his life.

By contrast, Baldr's body was still. It hadn't yet begun to bloat.

Odin gestured with his chin at the body. "Frigg, how long ago . . ."

How many dead men and women had he seen? How many had he dispatched to the shores of the Gjoll? He couldn't count them all, and yet he couldn't bring himself to say the words about his own son. Coward.

"Two. Nights."

He winced. Those sharply bitten-off words would've hurt less had they been knives.

She was right. This was his fault. He'd left, thinking that Baldr would be fine despite her portentous dreams. He'd left, believing that the charm protecting Baldr would keep him safe.

He'd also left knowing that someone had found the mistletoe and realized its significance. But they'd taken precautions, hadn't they? Frigg had barred wood from the Great Hall. They'd added guards. It wasn't as though they could have canceled the Midwinter festival, nor could they have swapped out the man playing Aegir. They couldn't afford to seem weak, not after the Jotunn burned Háls to the ground and murdered most of those who'd lived there.

But if he'd returned in time, Baldr would still be alive.

He rested one hand on his son's cold head, the soft curls compressing beneath his palm. With his thumb he traced a rune on Baldr's forehead and breathed out, sending his awareness down into the dead flesh, seeking the wound in his son's chest. He explored its edges and examined the damage the spear had wrought. Fixable. It was all fixable. Frigg had made a good choice. The cold in here had mostly kept the rot at bay. There was a good chance he could heal both that rot and the wound.

He reached into his satchel and withdrew his spindle and shears. Then he drew back the blanket covering his son.

"Odin, what are you—"

With the shears, he sliced through the fresh, clean clothes in which Baldr was dressed and exposed the wound, gaping like a mouth, reddish pink with torn flesh around the edges.

"For this to work, I have to repair his body before I put his spirit back into it. Otherwise, it'd be like filling a wineskin with a hole in it."

"I see."

"Good. Now please, let me work."

"Fine."

She didn't stomp her feet or yell at him or slam the outside door. She just . . . left. That immediate sense of her being gone, of his being alone, nearly unmanned him.

Nearly.

He had work to do. And if saving his son cost him his wife, well, he'd pay that price.

So with numb fingers, he unspooled a double arm's length of witchthread and began to sing—roughly, at first, but strengthening as he regained control of a throat too full with sorrow. When his hands and his mind were steady, he pinched the end of thread between thumb and forefinger and began to sew the spear wound shut, using the power to quicken the dead flesh. At times there was resistance, as though he'd hooked a fish. And just as if he'd landed such a fighter, he went easy, making sure to not snap the thread. He repaired the rot as he worked, with particular attention to the dark spots on his son's face. They reminded him of the decayed bark he'd found on Yggdrasil.

He hauled free another length of witchthread and was disturbed to feel how little was left. One of the three spindles he'd harvested from the Gjoll was nearly gone.

He found another spot of blackness on Baldr's right thigh and thought of the worms that had exploded from the ground when he'd gone to save Mimir. Was all this related somehow? Or was he remembering unconnected things?

He stepped back and examined his work. In his witchsight, Baldr's body glowed a greenish gold. All he had left was to tie the weaving so it'd sustain itself for . . . for how long? Investing too much witchthread into the weave would be wasteful; too little, and rot would quickly set in. It shouldn't take long to retrieve Baldr's spirit. They should be back by nightfall. So he stretched another loop of witchthread around Baldr's body to strengthen the weave. He tied the final knot, bent to kiss his son's icy forehead, and drew the blanket back over Baldr's body.

His missing eye flickered. Pain shot through his head. With the resounding crack of his firstborn's hammer striking a Jotunn skull, he was . . .

. . . in a green field. The sweet smell of crushed, broken grass was heavy around him. A huge stone block lay to his right, gold runes cut into the face he could see. The sky was thick with flocks upon flocks of birds all flying in one direction. He stood. More stones littered the field. The birds threw themselves toward a familiar mountain more heavily blanketed with snow than he remembered. Overhead, with a roar of a thousand great-cats, a sword of fire cut the sky, black smoke bleeding from the wound. Quickly it passed out of view beyond the mountain. The sky flared. A huge hand knocked him off his feet.

———

SOMETHING COOL LAY across his forehead. He sat up. Eir stumbled back to avoid getting hit.

Frigg knelt on his other side, emanating angry concern. "Well?"

He'd had a vision, more profound than the one he'd had riding up the hill. Another wet cloth clung to the back of his head. He peeled it off.

"You cracked your head against the floor when you fell," Frigg said.

Quite the vision it had been. A sword of fire in the sky? He'd never seen or heard of anything like that. "I had a vision, Frigg."

"You're kidding." Her tone was drier than his mouth.

"I'm serious."

She rolled her eyes and gestured with her chin toward Eir. "Let her have another look at you. Your head's grown softer."

He stood, head pounding. Both women watched him with concern. He was achingly aware of Baldr's dead body behind them all. Would the visions become predictable? If not, he'd better walk around in full armor to save himself from more cracked skulls.

"I'm fine," he said, turning away from Frigg. "What did you bring with you, Eir?"

Her pale brows knotted in confusion. "Alfather?"

"I assume you brought your full healer's kit? Anything else—a cauldron, perhaps?"

"My kit, yes, but not—"

He held up his hand. "That's fine. We can get the rest. Is your woman around, Frigg?"

"If you mean Gná, then yes, my 'woman' is outside."

"Have her fetch a pot, a pair of witchstoves, and several blankets."

"What are you planning to do?"

"Not just me. You and I need to go for a walk."

Her eyes widened. "What?"

He laid his hands on her shoulders. "You did well to place him here. Because of that, at least in part, I can bring him back. But we need to start now."

13

FRIGG

Day 1, early afternoon

Frigg blew out a long white breath, shivered, and pulled her cloak tight around her. The earth's cold was creeping through the thick, red blanket she sat on. Light from witchlamps pooled in the room's corners.

She sat with her back to the table on which Baldr's body lay. A pot bubbled atop the witchstove before her, throwing a wine-sweet smell into the room. Odin sat cross-legged on the opposite side, his wrists on his knees—the same posture he'd told her to take. His face was dirty from travel, his eye downcast and his expression hard. He pulled his bag around in front of him and started rummaging, removing items as he went—a mortar and pestle, several small bundles of herbs, a short thick-bladed knife in a sheath, small silver shears, a spindle of witchthread.

They hadn't spoken more than maybe two dozen words since he'd gotten back. They hadn't embraced or kissed or even looked at each longer than necessary. She felt even more alone now that when he'd been gone. It felt wrong. But there was also a hot ball of anger boiling in her stomach. He'd left before Midwinter for a good reason. She hadn't liked it, but he'd gone to try to help Baldr. She knew he wouldn't have left if he'd even guessed that he wouldn't make it back in time.

She knew that, didn't she?

Yet she was still angry.

He dumped a hot, sweet-smelling liquid into the mortar, followed it with some herbs, and ground them together. Then he picked up a paintbrush, dipped it into the mixture, and met her eye. "Here we go."

She looked down at the red paste he'd made. After a heartbeat's silence, he started painting interlinked red runes around his left forearm. Their vibrance showed how faded the blue tattoos underneath had grown.

Ráta knocked on the threshold. She held another two witchstoves. "Where do you want them, Sigfather?"

"Close to Frigg, please, Ráta. She'll need their heat when we get back."

Frigg looked from Ráta to her expressionless husband. "How bad is this going to be?"

He turned his missing eye to her and went back to his bag, rummaging till he found a short rod. He stood and began cutting a wide, circular furrow in the dirt floor around them both.

"Odin?"

Dirt piled up on either side of the line as he worked. She gritted her teeth.

Ráta waited till he'd finished the outside line to place and light the two witchstoves. She was in the hallway before he said, "Thank you, Ráta. Make sure we're not disturbed."

"Of course, Sigfather."

Odin sat in front of her. "I'll need to hold your hand as I paint your wrist."

Frigg shoved up her left sleeve. Her skin prickled as he took her hand, holding it so he could move her forearm up, down, and around as he painted the red runes. He painted in silence, his grizzled, unkempt, mud-caked head bent over his work. She shivered with each touch of the cold brush.

An icy gulf the length and breadth of their dead son stretched between them. Another gulf loomed beyond the first—the same size as the soon-to-be-dead body of their second son, if the mob got its way.

They could be talking right now. Should be talking.

"I know you didn't intend to be gone as long as you were, but—"

He flinched and had to fix the line he'd painted with his little finger. "But if I hadn't left, he'd still be alive."

Yes. Exactly. She bit back those words and instead said, "There was some enchantment at work. I didn't see through it till the spear was in the air."

He paused at that. "So Hodr did throw the spear?"

"Yes. One made of mistletoe."

He released her arm and leaned back. His face was streaked with dried mud. "You kept it?"

"Of course. It's in my longhouse."

He gave a sad little smile at that. "Angrboda told me a 'branch' would kill him—right before she landed a curse that I should've seen coming."

She said nothing.

"Because of the curse, I wandered in the forests of the Gjoll long enough for . . ." His eye flicked to Baldr's corpse and then back to the dirt floor between them. He shook his head. "Were it not for Heimdall's horn, I'd still be down there."

So that's what happened. The icy grip of anger around her heart thawed a little. As ever, a good reason for breaking his promise. At which hot anger flared. He was actually wriggling off the hook—no, she was *letting* him, as she'd always done. Not this time.

"You mean if it weren't for Hodr killing Baldr," she said. "This is your fault, Odin."

He recoiled.

She jabbed a finger at him. "You left to get answers—against my advice, if you recall. You said you'd be back before Midwinter. You weren't. But if you'd been here, you could've stopped Hodr and that witch who was with him."

"What?"

"Oh, that's right, you missed that, too. There was a witch named Yelena. She's been in Gladsheim for who knows how long, disguised most recently as a pregnant woman. I exposed her deceit and then she tried to kill me. She would've succeeded, actually, except Gulfinn and Ráta stopped her. Gulfinn *died* saving me, Odin."

He paled at that.

"And then on Midwinter, Hodr showed up with a friend named Lopt. A smith. I was stupid enough not to think twice about it, because Hodr vouched for this friend. Hodr gave up the spear he walked in with, supposedly made by this friend of his. Only later on, when Baldr stood on the stump, Hodr had it back in his hand, but it was charmed to look like a rock..."

Odin looked confused. She was aware, vaguely, that she'd begun rambling, but she pressed on. "... and then as he raised the rock to throw at Baldr, I saw through the charm—saw that it was a spear. I couldn't stop it. But you could have." She jabbed her finger into his chest, emphasizing each word. "You. Could. Have."

He looked absurd leaning back, eye downcast, paintbrush between thumb and forefinger of one hand and paint pot in the other. "Frigg, I—"

"I don't want to hear it. No more excuses. You broke another promise"—she pointed at Baldr—"and he paid the price. So will Hodr. You saw how angry the folk are."

"I understand."

"Do you? You're back less than a month to deal with one problem. One. And then everything else falls apart."

"We'll fix it," he said, meeting her gaze for the first time. His cheeks were flushed beneath the grime, both with chagrin and not a little bit of anger. Maybe no one else dared to speak to him like that, but he'd better get used to it from her. "I know I failed, Frigg. I know our sons paid the price. We will fix it. All of it. Together."

He stood and held out his hand.

She stood without it.

———

FRIGG COMPARED the red runes painted on her arm to those he'd painted around his own. They matched. Odin said the runes would tether them together once they entered the spirit world.

"How far apart can we go?"

"About a spear's length, maybe two," he said while opening a small pouch. Then he looked up and locked her gaze. "A rope will fray and break if stretched too far from its cleat, Frigg."

She suppressed the shiver that ran down her spine. She wouldn't deliberately go off on her own. "I understand. This will be dangerous."

He shook his head. "It's not that. You saw what happened when I got hurt in the spirit realm. Where we're going is the River Gjoll. Do not fall overboard."

"What would happen?"

"Think of it like falling overboard during a bad storm. Maybe you can hold fast to a rope you're thrown, but more likely you lose your grip and get swept away. There's no coming back from that."

He sounded curious, as if maybe there were a way back. Not that she wanted to find out.

"Are you ready?" He held the small pouch above the bubbling pot.

She nodded.

He dumped the pouch's contents into the water, set it aside, and offered his left hand. She took it, savoring the warmth rising from the witchstove and the smell of cinnamon from the pot.

"Breathe," he said quietly. "Relax, as much as you can."

The scent wafting from the pot mellowed into the smell of wet grass in the hot sun after a summer storm. The sun. Her son. Her eyelids felt heavy.

"No, Frigg," Odin said, his voice sharp, like the spear that had split—

He squeezed her hand, grinding the bones of her fingers together. Pain shot through her hand, and her eyes flew open.

"Stay awake. Take deep breaths. Relax. Be a torch in still air. Steady. Calm."

The smell grew richer, like fresh-turned soil, and then thicker, like horse dung in a hot stable. Like the stench of rot escaping from a fallen tree split by an axe.

Split open.

Fallen tree.

Her stomach dropped. She was floating.

"Focus on the frame of the doorway," Odin said, his voice thrumming like a taut sail. The empty doorframe leaped into her vision. She could see the grain's whorls in the wood, the darker knots, the light lapping at the passageway.

"The threshold separates this room from the hall. We cross that line without thinking. Back and forth. From here to there. From there to here."

Her eyelids felt heavy, yet her heart raced. She fought to keep her eyes open.

"Breathe in, breathe out," he said, his voice slower and even deeper. "Stay focused on the doorway. Keep breathing."

He let go of her hand. She kept her eyes on the doorway. She heard him rummaging through his bag, and then his low-voiced song took her by surprise. She nearly pulled her hand away when he tied a wisp of thread around her wrist, but she let him work. Then he pressed the knot into where her life beat and spoke a word. The spot he touched burned as if she'd touched a hot pan. She hissed in a pained breath, but already the sensation was gone. Heartbeats later, the shears snicked, Odin spoke the same word again, and the rope between them wriggled to life.

"Can you hear it yet, Frigg?"

Hear what? Just her breath in her nose and the bubbling water and the popping flame and then the distant creak of rigging.

The smell of seawater. Moisture on her face.

"The doorway is a gangplank. Do you see it?"

She sucked in a breath. She did see it. It was right there. The room she sat in was a dock, and the gangplank was hoisted up.

"Step toward it."

Without the popping of knees or any sense that she'd physically done so, she stood before the gangplank.

Odin squeezed her hand again. "Lower the gangplank and walk across it."

She saw both the gangplank itself and through the doorway into a place where the shadows billowed. Her stomach lurched like the first time she'd been at sea in a storm. She still remembered it. The wind's voice had doubled upon itself until finally, sounding like an old woman who'd lost everyone she'd ever loved, it blew the sail off the mast. It had fluttered away like a crippled bird and vanished. Her father had bellowed at the crew: "Bend to your oars! Keep Rán's chill fingers from our throats. If she wants us, make her fight for us."

But this time it was her husband's voice reverberating. "Go, Frigg, now! Step across!"

So she did.

———

FRIGG SPLUTTERED and wiped her eyes. She was in a skiff big enough for three. The mast was before her on the right. A red-and-white striped sail, bellied out from the wind, hauled the ship through choppy white-tipped seas. The sky was gray with looming storms.

Spray dashed in her face and she shivered, pushing damp hair back from her forehead. Moments earlier, she'd been in an earthen room and now—her stomach lurched, and she retched over the gunwale. She had a sense that something from below was watching her. She jerked back from the side. A shiver ran down her back as she drew a shaking hand across her mouth.

"I'm . . . here?"

"Welcome to the spirit realm," Odin said from behind her. "You're aboard the skiff of my mind, sailing upon the River Gjoll. I, too, was confused and sick the first few times Mimir led me here."

He sat calmly beside the steering board, one hand guiding the skiff through the water. His teeth flashed in a quick, mirthless smile and he leaned forward, peering beneath the full-bellied sail. His good eye was lost in shadow, but his missing eye glimmered like gold in a witchlamp's light.

"Not that you're sick any more than you're wet and cold," he said, pulling the steering board slightly toward him so the skiff came gently to starboard. "Don't forget, anything that happens to you here also happens to your flesh."

She rubbed her eyes, ran her hands through her wet hair, and pulled her falcon cloak closed. The spirit realm. The River Gjoll. Odin had told her he was riding down to the shores of the Gjoll when he went to summon Angrboda, but he'd ridden Sleipnir out through Gladsheim's western gate and then turned northward.

"I . . . I don't understand."

He pointed to leeward, steadying the skiff's course on that tack. "And that's where we're headed."

She followed his gesture and saw the biggest longship she'd ever seen—bigger even than Skidbladnir when it carried a dozen warbands. Hundreds of shields lined the gunwales. Even at this distance—and they were closing fast—the ship's overlapping planks looked like her grandfather's toenails. The prow was a carved sea-dragon with blazing ruby eyes. She couldn't quite see the ship's stern, but she had the sense that a tall, dark figure manned the steering oar. The single mast rose high, and from it billowed and snapped a gray-and-white checkered sail.

"That's the Naglfar," Odin said. "The dead ride her down to the last march they'll ever make. Seems bigger each time I see it. Baldr's spirit should still be aboard. Hold fast, Frigg."

The skiff lurched forward like a colt eager to test his legs on the plains. He brought the ship back to larboard, and the Naglfar vanished behind the skiff's sail.

Hold fast, indeed.

14

LOKI

Day 1, midafternoon

Loki massaged his forehead. Yelena had said that Angrboda had sent "us" to kill Ygg. A full coven—a mere seven witches—against Ygg? Even if they made him spend all his magic, and lived through his doing it, Ygg still had other resources at his disposal. Yelena, her coven, and his own dead wife were all mad.

"And you're telling me because . . ."

"I should think it obvious," Yelena said in the Jotunn hand language. "You will help us."

"I wish you all success, but I have neither the time nor the inclination to pit myself against him."

Which was exactly true and the answer she should've expected.

Yelena's sharp, fast smile could have split a log. "Still a coward, I see. She said that'd be your answer."

Always the same insult, even from beyond the grave. Angrboda had screamed it at him for months—every time she'd set eyes on him. Many of the Aesir and Vanir had thought the same. They still thought it. Which is what he wanted.

He wasn't a coward. He wasn't.

But he was aware of his limits, and going head to head against Ygg was idiotic. Over the last two hundred winters, he'd made sure that his enemies underestimated him—be it as cowardly, weak, or otherwise. Mostly, it had worked. And when it hadn't, with a touch upon the shoulder, he'd carefully clouded the minds of those who were suspicious by their very nature—Ygg, Tyr, and Ullr.

"Is that all, then?" he asked. "If so, I'll take my leave."

The way house's main door opened behind them. The angle of the sunlight left their little corner even darker than it had been. A young woman stepped inside, glanced at him, and smirked. She joined a man sitting at a table on the opposite side of the room.

Quickly, he counted those in way house. Besides himself, there were seven total, including Yelena, the new entrant and the matron of the house. Great, Yelena's whole coven was here.

"Oh, sit down, Loki," Yelena said. "Another afternoon won't change how the Almother and Alfather receive you. With all they've gone through these past few nights, I'm sure they'll welcome you with open arms."

Ygg would. He'd smile as he plunged a knife into Loki's back. Frigg might be capable of the same by now, too. She'd ruled Gladsheim long enough to have acquired the knack of saying one thing and doing another.

"And why should I?" he said aloud, putting his hands flat on the table. He leaned down till he was within a foot of Yelena's face.

She didn't flinch. The threat she uttered came in the hand language. "Because if you don't, I'll tell all your secrets to Ygg before my sisters and I drink his blood."

He switched to the hand language. "You don't mean that literally, do you?"

"What?"

"Drink his blood?"

She shook her bearded head slowly from side to side. "Sad, tired humor from a sad, tired man."

"It's been a long day." He shrugged and glanced around the way house, noting again where each of the other six witches were. Yelena made seven. "What's stopping me from revealing your plans to old Goldtooth right now?"

She snorted. "Common sense? How exactly would you explain knowing me without exposing yourself for the liar you've been all these winters?"

"This is why you won't kill Ygg, Yelena. You're thinking too directly. All I would need to do is speak in a loud, firm voice what you've told me. Then I turn into a fly and . . . I'm gone."

"Fair enough. Yet I can do the same and pay no price at all. You, however—you have a lot to lose. Two sons. A lovely Aesir wife. How is Sigyn these days?"

He could simply kill her, right here—now—but he knew she was seeing right through his bland little smile to the red core of rage she'd stoked. More than that, she was right. He did have more to lose. All he needed was time. When the Jotunn attacked in another month, he could move. But not before then.

He sat down again.

"That's a good boy." She grinned widely and gestured for the lady of the way house to bring another round of mead.

He drained his cup, considered it for a moment, and placed it to one side. "So what help do you want from me?"

"I want you to distract him."

Seriously? "So what, should I do a little dance for him? Sing, maybe?"

She smirked. "I was thinking more along the lines of stealing the apples and giving them to us."

"I knew my former wife liked servants who did as they were told, but I didn't realize she also preferred idiots."

"The apples, Loki. That's what we want."

Four people entered the way house. Now there were ten people inside, excluding himself and Yelena. He waited for the newcomers to find seats before he hitched his chair in, met her eyes, and signed quickly. "They already ate the apples. I watched them do it."

"So there aren't any others? What about the one you get?"

"I haven't yet presented myself to either Frigg or Ygg. They'll give me my apple." Hopefully. "I can't go to Idunn and get it. No one can."

She lifted an eyebrow.

A very long time ago, a Jotunn named Thiazi had forced him to steal the apples and lure Idunn from the safety of Gladsheim. What he kept having to remind everyone was that he'd also saved Idunn and the apples and, in so doing, helped Ygg and the others kill Thiazi.

He sighed. "Even after all this time."

"Then I suppose I'll have to tell Ygg who really killed his son."

Bitch.

"Fine. I can get you half of one now and then a whole one within a month." The first would be his. He could get by on half. Vidar, Ygg, and Frigg had been doing it, after all. In another month, he could take a bushel of apples.

"Don't be ridiculous," she said, sneering even as her fingers danced. "In a month, it won't matter. I want seven."

"Forget it. I have no idea how many Yggdrasil produces, much less where they are kept—or even where Idunn picks them from. Ygg guards that secret most jealously."

"Then three now and four in a couple nights."

He tapped the side of his head. "You. Are. Not. Listening."

Yelena's eyes went dangerously flat.

"You're going to start a fight here?" he said. "You'll be dead before you clear the chair."

Yelena feigned a fearful expression and raised her left hand. All six of the men and women in the way house turned and looked at him.

Was he supposed to act surprised? It was worth a try.

He held up his hands as if beaten, then lowered them so he could speak. "All right, you've got me. I still can't get that many."

Her fingers began to move, but he interrupted her. "How about this. I give you half my apple as soon as I get it. You've done quite well on the sliver I paid you with earlier. Even half an apple split seven ways will restore some youth—maybe even some of the beauty you crones might've possessed."

He let the tension grow. He probably shouldn't poke this particular bear, but it was so much fun. And angry people made bad choices.

He looked from one fake, unsmiling face to another till he came back to hers. "Not good enough? Tell you what, I'll even arrange for a distraction in the city. I have contacts here. I can make something happen." Of course, he'd already arranged for that to happen. "It won't be easy, and it'll cost me, but I'll do that. For you."

Yelena stared at him. Had the sarcasm been too much? Then she gave a slight gesture with her chin, and the six witches turned around. Loki felt the tension drain away.

Yelena pointed a thick, hairy finger at him. "You'd better deliver."

He hid his scoff. Or what? Stupid witch would be dead within a week. "Absolutely. I will." And then he said, not understanding why he was saying it, "You'll fail. I wish you luck, but you and my wife are delusional to think you can kill him."

"He has his weaknesses, just as we all do," she said. "Not three nights ago, your dead wife laid a curse on him that kept him mazed."

"So? He's back."

She shrugged. "I don't deny his power. These are my strongest sisters. We can defeat him."

"There's always a road between 'can' and the actual accomplishment of the deed. The road you walk is very long indeed."

He should know. He'd walked every inch of his.

And the end was in sight.

15

FRIGG

Day 1, midafternoon

The cold wind whipped spray into Frigg's face and her wet hair across her eyes. When she smoothed them away, the receding Naglfar and its indifferent captain had sunk below the river's horizon.

She shifted and looked forward. The wind came from the larboard, so the skiff's single sail was angled slightly away and the boat itself heeled slightly to starboard. Odin had said this was the spirit realm, but everything felt completely real, down to her chattering teeth and trembling hands. Yet Odin sat untouched by the cold or wet. Nor did the wind pluck at his hair or cloak like it did her own.

He must've felt her eyes on him, for he winked and with his chin gestured forward. His right hand rested on the steering board. "We'll find him, Frigg."

Thankfully, he left the second half of that sentence unsaid: *before he rejoins the Ginnungagap.*

Odin's plan had been to rescue Baldr's spirit from where it took passage on the Naglfar. As they had come up alongside the ship, it had appeared no longer than the Great Hall itself. But once aboard, she never reached the bow no matter how many rows of dead men and women she passed.

She'd passed hundreds of spirits—thousands, maybe. Some hauled on their oars; others sat listless. Some wore colorful, well-made clothes; others wore outlandish garments. Only the amount of jewelry and ornamentation seemed to mark those who'd been higher status in life. Yet in death, thrall, karl, and jarl sat side by side on the ship of the dead.

And there'd been no sign of her son.

After a time, Odin had called to her. The ship and its passengers wrung themselves out in a heartbeat. In the next heartbeat, she stood beside Odin, her hand in his, at the Naglfar's stern.

A tall, broad Jotunn man with dark skin, a bald head, and a braided, graying beard had stood before them. He leaned against the starboard gunwale, one hand on the steering oar. He was dressed like any trader plying the seas: a thick wool cloak over a heavy wool tunic and pants, all of it beaded with spray.

Odin called him Hyrm and asked where Baldr's spirit was, for they could not find it aboard. Hyrm had looked down at Odin then pointed downstream.

"My mistress plucked your son's spirit from my ship," he said in a booming voice. "Take your skiff to the shores where I'm headed. Maybe you'll find him there."

Then Hyrm had lifted his black eyes to the horizon as though he didn't care.

She shivered at the memory and drew her feathered cloak tighter about her. Why would he care? Was Hyrm real in the same way she and Odin were? How could a Jotunn man live here? Maybe he was dead. A draugr, perhaps?

More spray dashed across her face. She wiped it away. Then she glanced beneath the sail at the waters ahead. Nothing but foamy wave crests and shadows beneath the waves. She'd first noticed the shadows when they arrived; Odin had said not to worry. But how could animals—or whatever they were—live here?

Or were they also dead?

Odin leaned closer. The silver line of his magic, which tied her to him like an anchor to its ship, glinted. He said again, "We'll find him, Frigg."

Something slammed hard into the skiff's side. She gasped and clawed for the gunwale, keeping herself from tumbling over the opposite gunwale into the cold river. Odin swore and fought the steering oar. The sail spilled its wind. The yardarm banged against the mast.

Frigg looked to windward and saw a pair of long black fins slicing spearheads of white foam as they cut a curving path away from the skiff.

"Odin!" she cried, flinging out an arm and pointing before they slipped back beneath the curling waves.

"I know," he said, pulling the steering oar closer until the skiff steadied and regained speed. The sail snapped and fluttered.

"I thought you said we were in the spirit realm," she shouted over the rising wind.

"We are." He eased up on the oar till the sail's fluttering eased and the skiff settled back into its swift dash downriver.

"So what was that in the water? It looked like a sea-wolf."

He nodded. "So it did. There's life here, others like us. They can enter and leave as they choose. Still others are spirits traveling from life to the Ginnungagap."

The wind gusted and blew some of her hair across her face. She pulled it free and tucked it behind her ear. "Are those things alive?"

"What should concern us more," he said with a quick grin, "is that they attacked us."

She sidled along the gunwale so she at least didn't have to shout. "Meaning what, exactly? You said not to worry."

He held her gaze. "Meaning that I've missed something huge."

The water hissed along beside them; spray flew and was carried away.

"What?"

"It happens."

That response hardly answered her question or addressed her concern. Concern? Dread, more like. She turned sideways to him and forced down the impending sense that despite all this, they would fail to get Baldr's spirit back. And how crazy was this journey? A few weeks ago, she'd imagined herself on a longship with Odin sailing away from all their responsibilities. And now here she was, that dream become a nightmare.

The sail began flapping again. She felt the skiff's direction shift slightly and the sail quieted, unlike her rising sense of failure and panic. Off to her left, she spied the fins rising and then disappearing.

"Who did Hyrm mean, Odin? Who's his mistress?"

When he didn't respond, she faced him. He'd wrapped another turn of the rope around his left arm and was intently watching the sail and what little he could probably see behind it while making slight adjustments to the steering oar.

She grabbed the gunwale as the skiff began thudding against the waves rather than scudding across them. The black fins appeared directly to starboard, maybe a spear's length away.

"Odin, they're back!"

"I know." His lips formed a thin, bloodless line. His eyes jumped from the sail to the waters ahead to her to the fins and back again.

The skiff slammed against the increasingly rough water.

Behind her, the water hissed. Another pair of black fins surfaced. That made at least four sea-wolves, maybe more.

"What are they?" She looked for a harpoon beneath the starboard gunwale, which was opposite her, then behind her. Nothing.

"No friends of ours." He gestured ahead with his chin. "But we're getting close."

One hand on the gunwale behind her, feet braced against the skiff's ribs, she peeked beneath the sail and saw a brown loom of land ahead. The river bucked against the skiff. She bit back a startled scream. The fins cut closer.

"Odin . . ."

"I know. Not much farther."

Another pair of fins surfaced. Something bumped the skiff directly beneath her. Odin caught her eye, and the silver line of magic that linked her to him glimmered with dark runes. As though they were alone in their bed, Odin whispered in her ear. Except it wasn't in her ear; it was inside her mind. The sensation sent a shudder down her back.

When I tell you, take your falcon shape.

"How can I—"

His lips didn't move, but he spoke. *We're spirits here. We can take whatever shape we choose—or none at all. But you should take the falcon form you know.*

Panic bubbled up. How could—

"Frigg, relax," he said aloud. And then again in her mind—she could almost feel his hands resting on her shoulders: *You brought the cloak with you.*

She quashed the reflexive anger at being told to relax and instead made an effort to speak with her mind alone. *But the cloak isn't real.*

She could feel his approval.

It's real here because you brought it, he said. *How do you shift into a falcon back in Gladsheim?*

I think it.

Do that here. I'll be with you the whole time.

This is why he hadn't wanted her joining him when he went to find and ultimately rescue Mimir. Those first learning to swing an axe didn't fight in the shield wall.

But here she was.

He reached for her hand as the starboard pair of black fins cut directly at them. The black-and-white sea-wolves broached the water.

With Odin beside her, Frigg leaped into the wind, wings beating to gain height. They put the skiff behind them, then wheeled about. Frigg looked down. She'd expected broken timbers and floating debris, but instead saw nothing but the slick backs, fins, and axe-like tails of the sea-wolves as they churned the water to froth.

16

ODIN

Day 1, late afternoon

"Well, look how you've grown, Hel," Odin called to the young woman who stood a few spear lengths away on the stony bank of the Gjoll. "Your father must be proud."

Hel said nothing. She wore a simple gray dress, a darker gray cloak with the hood thrown back, and a dark leather belt and boots. Behind her lay a man-sized shape swaddled in gray burial cloth. Wasn't hard to puzzle out who that was or the reason she'd taken him.

Of everything that had gone wrong today, these setbacks in the spirit realm were the worst. They ate into the time Baldr had left before rot consumed his flesh beyond his own ability to heal. He couldn't let that worry show. Obviously, Hel was the mistress Hyrm had referenced. That meant she had somehow gained power over the dead—power he'd thought only he possessed.

And since he was wrong about that, what else had he been wrong about?

He and Frigg walked a few paces closer, pebbles crunching beneath their feet. The Gjoll rushed along behind them. Two huge birds with strange, pointed heads flew in wide, slow circles above them. One of them shrieked; the other jabbered a reply.

"Is that my son lying there?" Frigg asked, her voice full of barely controlled grief.

Hel said nothing. He put a gentle hand on Frigg's arm, trying to calm her.

They stopped a spear's length from Hel. She was of an age with his daughter Hermod. Where Hermod was broad-shouldered and strong, tanned and golden-haired, Hel was slight, black-haired, and pale. And they were close enough now that her condition was apparent.

Frigg ripped her arm free of his hand and advanced on Hel. "Is. That. My. Son!"

Above, the birds shrieked. Behind, the river burbled.

Hel spoke in a deep, throaty voice. "Yes, Hár Frigg, and if I—"

Frigg lunged, hands coming up to throttle Hel. She took two steps and sprawled flat on her face.

Hel hadn't moved; her solemn expression hadn't changed.

If your will was strong enough, you could bend the spirit realm as you chose. Mostly. Some things couldn't be changed: the river that flowed behind them. That was real, no matter which realm you stood in.

He stooped to help Frigg up. She batted him away.

Through the silvery link binding them together, he said, *Go easy, Frigg. There's more going on than either of us expected.*

Frigg glared at him. To Hel she said, "I want my son back."

"And I want to give him to you, Hár Frigg," Hel said, spreading her hands. "That's why we're here."

A blue-black stain marred the left upper half of Hel's face, ran down beside her nose, bled across her lower lip and chin, and flowed like paint down the left side of her neck. The blue-black skin wasn't thick or twisted like a scar; it was just skin. He knew because he'd tried to heal it.

"What are your terms?" Odin asked.

Frigg rounded on him. "Terms, Odin? Terms? She's probably the one who had him killed to begin with."

"I wasn't involved in Baldr's death, Hár Frigg," Hel said. "All I've done is take advantage of it."

"Liar! You sent that witch to kill me, and then she killed Baldr."

"I know nothing about that, Hár Frigg. I told you, I wasn't involved in his death." Hel's deep voice took on a smoother note. "In fact, given how long it took you both to get here, you could say that I've saved him from rejoining the Gap."

Frigg lunged at Hel.

Odin grabbed her by the arms. *Frigg, please—*

How can you take her word for it?

What choice do we have?

Take Baldr from her.

He couldn't tell Frigg that she was making this situation worse. Nor could he tell her to calm down. He blew out a long breath before replying.

I don't know how she's keeping his spirit here, preventing its natural progression from life to death. That concerns me. Besides, that body behind her is probably a figment spun from her mind.

Frigg radiated such angry heat it was a wonder the stones beneath her feet weren't scorched. *Just get him back. Give her what she wants. Let's be done with it.*

And with that, Frigg turned away.

"So, Hel," he said, spreading his hands. "What are your terms?"

———

THE WATERS of the Gjoll hissed across the stones behind them. Hel gave Odin another tight-lipped smile. The blue-black blighted half of her face moved as smoothly as the unmarred half did.

"Beforehand," she said. "You need to free us all before I let him go."

"I've already agreed to free all of you," he said for the third time.

"But you have to see how unreasonable it is to demand that I free you before getting his spirit back."

She shrugged. "Those are my terms."

"You say you don't trust me, but what reason do I have to trust you? I could do as you ask and then be left with nothing. Or you three could attempt to kill me."

Hel crossed her arms.

Time for a new tack and a little careful deception. "You know that bodies rot, yes?"

Her features settled into a bored expression.

He held up his hand. "Baldr's body will rot beyond my ability to heal in a few days."

"Sounds like we're wasting time, then."

Odin, this is going nowhere. Frigg's voice was loud inside his mind. *Kill her and take Baldr's spirit back.*

Killing her would likely undo whatever she's done, and he'd slip through our fingers.

Won't he go back to the Naglfar?

I don't know, Frigg. That's the problem.

Not knowing was the common, infuriating thread marking the weft and weave of his return to Gladsheim. He gritted his teeth.

Besides, Hel was likely prepared for him to try killing her. His reputation was well earned, after all. Hel had also demonstrated considerable skill at manipulating the spirit realm and commanding the creatures of the Gjoll. She'd be ready for him.

He'd gained power over death when he'd won the runes from Yggdrasil's roots. He'd then used that knowledge to take Slídr as his fylgja. Had Hel done something similar with another disir? He knew of six other disir, each associated with a river of power that ran through all the realms. The Jotunn had bound at least two of them through means different from his own. Behind them flowed the Gjoll, the seventh river he knew of. It had never seemed to be a disir—and he'd examined it—but perhaps it was.

Unexpected events. Things he didn't know. They'd be the death of him.

"Can you at least acknowledge that Baldr's body will continue rotting?"

Hel nodded. She wore a light smile, as if she'd followed the current of his thoughts.

He continued. "I've done what I can to stave off the rot's hunger. Even so, I've bought three nights, maybe four, before it starts again, worse for having been delayed. That's not enough time. Consider that aboard Skidbladnir, it's at least three nights' travel from Ifington to where Fenrir is chained, but my ship is with Freyr in Alvheim. Figure five nights along the coast to bring the ship up to Ifington. Jorm is another week's sailing beyond Fenrir."

He shrugged. "So you see, it's impossible for me to free all of you before I can save Baldr."

A suspicious frown creased Hel's face. "Convenient."

"There are rules even I cannot break," he said. Not yet, at least. "So I again propose what I originally offered: You give me Baldr's spirit, I revive him, and then I ride back down to the shores of the Gjoll and free you. Then you and I go to free your brothers. Your father will join us. The two of you can make me keep my word—not that I'll break it."

"That's unacceptable." Her eyes flicked to Baldr's shrouded spirit and back to him. "I don't trust you, Ygg. Or my father."

She made a point of using the name the Jotunn had given him, which meant something like "the terrifying one." She meant it as an insult; he rather liked it.

"Then we truly are wasting time," he said.

Frigg cleared her throat. "What if I stayed here as your hostage, Hel? If Odin does not keep his word, then you can do with me what you will."

"Frigg—"

Hel interrupted him with a snort. "You're probably the only one who can get him to keep his word, Hár Frigg."

What are you doing, Frigg? I could've gotten her to—

You said yourself that Baldr doesn't have much time. I'm trying to get this deal made.

"But I like the idea of a hostage," Hel said, one gloved finger tapping her lips. "It'd have to be someone important to you . . ."

"A jarl, perhaps?" he asked.

"No, you don't care about your 'normal' Aesir jarls. And your kin are far too dangerous." Hel snapped her fingers. "My father said you have a daughter. Hermod, isn't it? She's young still. She'll make an excellent hostage, I think. Once she's here, I'll release Baldr's spirit."

"Absolutely not," Frigg said, her hands bunching into fists.

Through the link connecting them he said, *Frigg, how can we not agree to—*

I'm not losing another child.

You won't.

I remember your saying something similar a few nights before Baldr was killed in front of me.

He looked down at the slick pebbles between his boots. *I deserve that. But I don't see a choice here.*

We send someone else.

He took Frigg in—raven-black hair, tawny skin, arms folded beneath her breasts, eyes flashing. *So we should send someone into a danger that we ourselves aren't willing to brave?*

She looked uncomfortable. They both knew that wasn't what she'd meant.

I can't lose another child. I can't.

You won't. We won't. And I promise you, I'm not going anywhere this time.

Frigg said nothing.

"We agree," Odin said.

Frigg wore a black look, but she remained silent.

"It's two nights for her to get down here. That doesn't leave me much time."

"Better get moving, then," Hel said. The ground where she stood folded in around her like a sail into which someone had thrown a heavy rock. She vanished.

"Come, Frigg."

He tugged on the line connecting them and exhaled. His next

breath took in frozen earth, smoke, and tea. The magic was a fading hum in the air, like insects at night.

When he opened his eyes, the first thing he saw was his son's cold corpse.

Soon, Baldr. Soon.

17

FRIGG

Day 1, night

As a girl, Frigg had once jumped from a high cliff into a deep snowbank. Her friends had all leaped before her. Laughing and hooting, they'd dug themselves free of the tall drift below the cliff. One night later, she'd awoken in her father's tent, bruised and aching from head to toe.

She awoke now feeling much the same as she had then. She rolled to her side and retched.

Except for that.

She hauled in a shuddering breath. The smell of dead ashes and cold dirt were heavy in her nose. Her stomach heaved again. She coughed, gagged, and threw up bile.

The gurgle of pouring water sounded sweeter than the music plucked from Bragi's harp. She caught hints of sweet warmth in the larder's cold air. She dragged a shaking hand across her mouth and spat again.

"The same happened to me the first few times," Odin said, his voice barely audible above the clink of stoneware. "This tea will help when you're ready."

She pushed herself up to her knees. Baldr lay dead on the table behind her. Odin sat before her.

She didn't want to look at either of them.

Instead, she stared down at her hands, the palms black with soot and dirt from the floor. She wiped them on her dress.

"Don't lose hope, Frigg."

She snorted. Hope? She caught up the sleeves of her dress and rubbed the tears away, then ran her dirty fingers through her hair, roughly braiding it and draping it across her left shoulder.

She jumped at a light touch on her shoulder. Odin's grimy fingers were already retreating, palm up, while his other hand proffered a cup of the tea he'd mentioned. Steam wafted toward her, carrying a warm, spicy smell. Her eager stomach gurgled. She nodded her thanks and took the cup in both hands.

The dried mud still streaked his face, small clumps caked in his unkempt beard and hair. With the patch covering one eye, he looked more like a hunter than he ever had. He withdrew across the room and sank down behind the witchstove he'd used to brew the tea. He picked up a small cup, blew gently on it, and took a sip.

The tea was warm, spicy and a little sweet. After a few more sips, her stomach's warnings faded to an irritated grumble.

"Keep drinking, and how you're feeling will pass," he said.

She looked from him to their son's body and back again.

He grimaced and added, "The sick feeling, anyway."

In the silence that grew between them, she noticed a faint buzzing sound, as if bees were hovering over Baldr's body.

Odin cleared his throat. "I bought us more time by strengthening the weave that keeps the rot from his body."

"I don't understand. You told Hel you'd already done that." Right before they agreed to send their daughter as a hostage. After offering herself—forgetting, apparently, that she had another son she could still save.

Her stomach churned, and she took another sip. This time, the descending warmth didn't affect the sickness she felt. Because that was guilt. No amount of tea would drown that.

"I'd assumed that retrieving his spirit would be relatively simple,"

Odin said. "So before we left, I'd only done enough to mend the wound and keep the rot from him till nightfall."

"And how long have we—"

"Night has fallen."

They'd left after midday. That was the entire day gone, somehow. Wasted. And she had so much left to do. She had to check in with Heimdall, prepare for tomorrow's wake for Baldr, check in with the chief warden regarding the prisoners they'd taken after the riot, and deal with a dozen other minor things.

"And how much time before . . ." She glanced at Baldr's covered body.

"Nine nights, including tonight."

She put the tea aside and stood. The room spun. She staggered, and suddenly Odin was there, helping her stand. She leaned into him, enjoying his musky smell and the lean hardness of the muscles in his arms and chest. Everything this past week had been disastrous, one disappointment, one failure after another.

She pushed herself away.

"Frigg, I—"

She blamed him for it all because he'd been absent, but she was every bit as guilty. She should've seen through the charm on the spear sooner. She should've set a better trap for Yelena, one that Gulfinn might've lived through. Worst of all, she should've seen the rot chewing through her city and the lies spun by the Jotunn.

"Baldr's wake is tomorrow—"

"A wake?" Odin sounded surprised. "But he isn't—"

"I didn't know that at the time. I had to do something. It was expected."

"Cancel it."

She snorted. "I need to go. Gná and Fulla will be wondering where I am."

"Ráta's been outside. She sent your women away earlier."

"My *women* have done much to help me, husband."

And what had she done to help anyone? She'd failed Baldr, and now she'd thrown Hermod to a wolf.

"That's not what I—Look, Frigg, I know I've let you down."

"Let *me* down?" She glanced at the door behind him. It would feel so good to walk out.

"They're my children, too. I know what I've done. And not done."

He reached for her. She stepped back. His arms fell slowly till they were by his sides, his hands twitching upward, conveying a sad helplessness she'd never seen before.

"We'll get him back, Frigg, I swear it. And no harm will come to Hermod."

"What about Hodr?" she asked.

"Nor to him, either."

"Even though he threw the spear?"

"If it's as you say—and I believe you," he added quickly, "then I've no reason to seek vengeance against my own flesh and blood."

"The folk want him dead."

"The folk want lots of things."

"He didn't do it, you know," she said. "Not really. He says he was tricked, and I believe him. And yet I feel this need to prove him innocent. I need that, Odin, and I hate it."

She found that she hated confiding in him—and hated that it felt good. The door behind him again beckoned to her.

He spread his hands. "I understand why you do. I don't blame you for needing to know the truth behind what happened. There's more going on here than it appears, from Baldr's murder to the attack on Háls to the rioting folk."

"And I've been blind to all of it," she said, "either willfully or through total ignorance of what's going on in my own city. I'm not sure which is worse."

"It's not your fault, Frigg. I wasn't here. I should have been."

She snorted. "So I need you to see what I should've seen?"

He shook his head. "That's not what I meant."

Who was she really angry at here. Him, for being gone? Certainly. But also herself, for being here. "Maybe you should have. I still missed it. All of it. And now look where we are."

She held up her hands, showing him her palms. "My hands are

dirty—first time in a long time. The opposite was true when I was a girl and a young woman, even when I was your young wife."

Confusion creased his face.

"Your hands—and Thor's, Tyr's, Heimdall's, Ullr's, even Vidar's—are all dirty. You all do things. I can't help but think that's what I need. To do something. Myself. And the only thing I can do right now is prove my son's—our son's—innocence."

She moved toward the door. "So Odin, I'm leaving. Tomorrow, after the wake."

He stood there, ragged and dirty. Hands spread. Looking spent. Shocked.

She walked out.

18

LOKI

Day 2, morning

Loki waited outside the Great Hall. Again. Yesterday morning he'd presented himself only to be turned away by the old fool Fimafeng, who'd said the Almother was unavailable. He'd done the same last night only to be told that both Almother and Alfather had retired. So now, the morning after, with Sól brightening in the east, he stood at the back entrance to the Great Hall in fresh, ankle-deep snow, staring at a stand of fir trees.

Obviously they'd been told he'd tried to speak with them. To be summoned this early, though, was either a good sign or a terrible one.

He warmed his hands over the brazier outside the entrance and ran his gaze over the firs again. No sign of lurking wardens or Einherjar. No footprints in the snow.

The door creaked open. Fimafeng stepped out onto the platform.

"They'll see you now, Jarl Loki, and they both apologize for asking you to give them a few moments. They're in their private room behind the chairs, so if you'll—"

"I completely understand." He jogged up the three stairs to the platform and was inside the Great Hall before Fimafeng could finish his sentence.

The corridor was gloomy, tight, and too reminiscent (as usual) of the ship's hold in which he and Ygg had met a very long time ago.

"—follow me," Fimafeng finished lamely from behind him.

Over his shoulder, Loki said, "I know the way."

He had two main worries. First, he needed a believable excuse for why he was so late getting to Gladsheim after Goldtooth had winded his horn. He'd been visiting Fenrir, perhaps. That was close enough to the truth. He visited all three of his exiled children every year around Midwinter.

His second worry was harder to overcome. Ygg had been busy since his return, even speaking with Loki's dead wife, Angrboda. He could have learned something about Loki's plans. Maybe. Though she'd been long dead before his plan was fully developed.

But this was Ygg. Loki had seen him in action far too many times to underestimate him. He also couldn't worry that Ygg had figured something out. He either had or he hadn't. If he did suspect something, well, he'd dealt with their suspicions for a hundred winters now.

He paused outside the thick, iron-banded door to the room where Ygg and Frigg waited. He dropped his worry that his plans would fail. The first had already worked. Baldr was dead and Hodr framed. The other plans would also work.

So he adopted a somber expression. He had to show sadness for the loss his blood brother and wife had suffered. Easy enough; he'd been grieving for two hundred winters, one son chained, the other asleep, and his daughter exiled. All three still alive, hating him, and his wife dead. Like a carefully blown ember, his grief burst into fiery life. He covered his mouth so his sob wouldn't travel but failed to force back the hot tears that coursed down his cheeks.

Ymir's sagging tits—if he overdid it, he'd sound every wrong note possible. Time to become the weak, cowardly Loki. He'd tricked Ygg before. Time to do it again. He wiped his face on his sleeve.

Reddened eyes would help, maybe even a well-timed, manly hug. But naked tears? Far too dangerous.

He must work the plan. They didn't know what he'd already done.

He put his ear to the door and listened. Either it was too thick or they weren't talking. So he rapped on the door.

"Enter, Loki." It was Ygg. Was that amusement in his voice?

Despite himself, panic thrilled through him. Sweat burst from his forehead and upper lip. He was undone. Ygg knew. Somehow, he knew! But he had to open the door, even if this meeting was a trap. He forced the somber expression back onto his face, hoped it looked natural, and pushed the door open.

Firelight threw shadows on the red curtains separating this room from the rear of the platform where the jarls sat. The stairs up to the platform were to his left. To his right were a pair of wide and tall oak chairs before the hearth. Ygg sat in one chair facing the hearth, his back to his wife.

"Welcome, Loki." Frigg stepped down from the stairs, the thick curtains swaying behind her. She examined him like a mother would an unruly child. She'd always looked at him like that. To be fair, he usually was up to no good—far worse, in this case, than his usual mischief.

Her rich brown hair was neatly braided, and she wore a dark green dress with little ornamentation. A daughter of Draupnir hung on her wrist, identical to the one he himself wore.

Another thrill of panic went through him. He was wearing his, wasn't he? He shook his wrist slightly and felt the answering weight of the heavy gold ring. The daughter of yet another gift he'd laid at his blood brother's feet.

How many gifts? Too many.

Before he could do more than duck his head in reply, Ygg stood and faced him, the witchlamp picking out the gray hair in his black beard and hair. With half his lean face in shadows and despite the smile of welcome on his lips, he looked much the same as ever—grim, humorless, and dangerous.

They looked haggard. Butter scraped too thin across cold flat-bread. More than that, Loki had no sense that he'd interrupted anything intimate at all between them. Could it be that husband and wife were at odds? It was so hard to fathom why that might be. This might be fun . . . if he could avoid tripping himself up.

Fimafeng's old feet caught up to him. "My apologies, Almother, Alfather. Jarl Loki outpaced me."

"He has that tendency, old friend," Ygg said, stepping closer. The light from the witchlamps fell full upon his face.

Loki immediately saw the patch covering Ygg's eye. Before he could stop himself, he asked, "What happened?"

Ygg touched the patch and shrugged. "Long story."

To Fimafeng, Frigg said, "Please see we're not disturbed."

"Yes, Almother," the old thrall said with a bow. The door banged shut.

With his arms wide, Loki walked over to Frigg and embraced her. "I'm so very sorry, Frigg. I came as soon as I heard—would that I'd gotten here sooner."

If she were a bowstring, she would've snapped. Was Ygg's absence at least partly behind this tension?

She broke the embrace. "Thank you, Loki. All that matters is that you're here now."

Was that sarcasm? Not judging by her expression. She was pale and drawn, sparking an unwelcome memory of Angrboda's face looking much the same. Except Angrboda had reeked of contempt when she looked at him; in her eyes, Loki had been a coward.

But he wasn't then, nor was he now. They shouldn't try to stand before the avalanche. They should've known to get out of its way.

"Indeed, my friend," Ygg said, directing a meaningful glance toward Frigg.

Loki took the few steps to Ygg and embraced him, too. "I grieve with you, brother."

"Thank you, Loki," Ygg said, clapping him on the back and then stepping back. "You look well."

"Sigyn keeps me fed," he said with a shrug. "She asked me to convey her deepest sympathies. She's putting the house in order and following along behind—less swiftly than I, unfortunately."

"Thank you," Frigg said.

He listened hard to those words. Were they said too neutrally? Did she know something? Suspect something? He'd tried to keep her off balance, but there was only so much he could do. She was smart, savvy. By now, she had to suspect something wicked was coming. Ygg, too.

Silence slunk into the room. The hairs on the back of his neck started to rise. He shifted slightly so he could see both of them. What did they know? What were they planning?

Neither one seemed willing to speak, either to each other or him.

Which shape would allow him to escape? What form would Ygg not expect? Who would be waiting outside to catch him? He'd seen Thor arrive and depart, so it wasn't him. Tyr and Ullr were at the Breach. Freyr and Freyja weren't here. Goldtooth would've attacked him already; Vidar would've started asking questions. Those were the dangerous ones. Idunn was harmless; Bragi was useless.

But neither Ygg nor Frigg had made any threatening gesture, much less said anything accusatory. That meant he was letting his guilt guide his thoughts. That was dangerous.

Finally, Frigg gave a slight nod, and Ygg cleared his throat. "Our apologies for turning you away last night and summoning you so early this morning. We have news for you that, if not for our own exhaustion, we would have delivered immediately."

Well, that was disturbing. He edged up onto the balls of his feet, ready to move. "Odin, Frigg, I can't imagine what you both must be—"

Ygg cocked his head to one side. "Oh? I think you do, brother."

There were three ways out of this room: through the door he'd entered, through the curtains into the hall, or up and out through the gap between roofs. A huge bear would be best at first; he could knock them both down, then shift again and escape as a fly. Frigg was closer, but Ygg was the threat. Give him anything more than a few heartbeats and—

"You must have felt like we do now when I followed the Norn's advice and banished your children. And when Angrboda passed back into the Gap."

Relief began to trickle in a chill line down his spine. Of course he'd mention the Norns. Nothing like taking full responsibility for your choices, eh, Ygg?

Ygg continued. "It saddens me more than I can say that I caused you such pain."

"You believed you were doing the right thing," he heard himself say. "I did, too, having heard their prophecy." Sometimes the best lies were the old ones that everyone had swallowed the first time around.

Unless they'd figured out those lies.

"Nonsense," Ygg said, advancing a step, his voice low and mean. "The Norns, those clucking hens, tricked me. Tricked *us.*"

Loki glanced from Ygg to Frigg and back again. "Tricked? I'm not sure what you—"

"The Norns also prophesied that Baldr would not—could not—die," Ygg said. "And yet here we are."

"Here we are," Frigg echoed, her voice a whisper. She was staring down at her clasped hands. The knuckles were white.

"But you've always said that what the Norns said was true," Loki said.

"I've heard you tell the cleverest lies without speaking a single untrue word, my friend," Ygg said.

Loki felt his balls retract a little. It'd have to be one of those short-nosed bears. Or maybe a snow bear? The horns might be useful.

He could not be caught now. "I'm not sure I follow—"

Ygg took another step forward and raised one hand, palm out. "I mean no offense. Rán knows I've been known to tell a lie—"

You think? Loki had to glance away.

"—but when I do, it's to protect my folk. My family."

He should keep telling himself that. Maybe one day it'd even be true.

"But put all that to one side for now," Ygg said, glancing at Frigg. Something passed between them, and then Ygg was speaking again.

"I can bring Baldr back to life. Frigg and I were in the spirit realm, but Baldr's spirit wasn't aboard the Naglfar."

He could bring Baldr back to life?

Ygg edged a half step closer, hands out as if he were approaching a spooked horse. "I realize this sounds a little crazy, but what—"

"Just say it, Odin," Frigg said. She crossed to a small table and began pouring wine into stone cups.

Ygg nodded once. "Loki, your daughter's taken Baldr's spirit hostage. She's demanded that I free her and her brothers before she'll release Baldr's spirit to me. Also, she's also demanded I send my daughter Hermod to her as a hostage."

The room began to spin. Hel had done what? And how? How had she taken Baldr's spirit?

Ygg continued. ". . . agreed to release Hel and her brothers, but I need to know that she'll do as she promised."

Blood began pounding in his ears, and he took an involuntary step back. "I, uh, I'm not sure I . . ." Dimly, he saw Frigg and Ygg exchange such a shrewd look that he realized he'd passed some kind of test. But between his pounding heart, the sweat beading on his forehead, and his dry mouth, he found himself incapable of getting past what he'd been told. "Hel . . . She did what now?"

Frigg touched his arm. She held out a cup of wine with a concerned, motherly expression. "Sit, Loki, please. We're sorry to spring this on you. We thought you might have already known and that's why it took you so long to get here, but . . ."

She directed him to a chair and he sat. He sipped the wine. Sweet, but he could taste the barrel it had soaked in.

Hel had taken Baldr's spirit? How? She'd never been able to shift her shape, much less exercise power over the dead. No witch he knew of could do that, other than the man standing before him.

That same man was staring intently at him now.

He sipped the wine again. Not too much; he couldn't afford even the slightest diminution of his wits. "I'm sorry, Y—" He coughed, trying to cover his slip. "Y-you know I visit her every winter, sometimes more often. I'd no idea she could—what did she do, again? Took Baldr's spirit?"

Ygg nodded. "That's what she did. Right from the Naglfar. And then she confronted me, and Frigg, in the spirit realm."

How had she done any of that? And what was the Naglfar?

"Did you know she had that power?" Ygg asked, his tone sharp. His single gray eye was a drill boring into him.

He shook his head. "Absolutely not."

Frigg patted his hand. "This must be a huge shock, and we *are* sorry to spring this on you. It's just that we don't have a lot of time."

"I've set a charm over Baldr's body," Ygg said. "That, along with the chill place he's in, will keep the rot from his body for a short time —another six nights at most."

He couldn't blame Hel for having seized the opportunity, but . . . How had she even seen the opportunity? No, he had to get past the how. It didn't matter, not now. She'd somehow acquired power over the dead, kept it secret, and then used it when she had something to gain.

But oh, daughter, what a target you've painted on your back.

"We'd like you to speak with her. Convince her I will keep my word."

Loki blew out a long breath and spread his hands. "I'm completely taken aback by this. I'd no idea."

But he was proud of her. It wasn't easy to pull one over on Ygg, particularly when magic was involved. She'd done it, though.

"Loki, did you hear—"

"I did. Of course I'll go speak with her."

"Thank you," Frigg said, touching his shoulder. "That means so much to me—to us. Particularly since—"

He raised a hand. He didn't want to hear their empty regret. What he wanted was time to think without Ygg's piercing eye on him.

But when had he ever gotten what he wanted?

19

LOKI

Day 2, morning

Loki glanced from Ygg, to Frigg, to the exit and back again. His armpits were damp and he could smell his own sweat. The only sound in the small room was the fire's occasional pop and hiss.

By agreeing to intercede with Hel, he'd thrown away the little leverage he'd had. He needed to slow things down—he needed time to figure out how Ygg's revelations would affect his plans.

Maybe an outburst? Ygg had said he'd been wrong to trust the Norns, hadn't he? That left him an opening. He could shout, wave his arms—the whole thing. But would that ring false now?

"When can you leave, brother?" Ygg asked, his gray eye glittering. "I'm too blunt by half, but Baldr doesn't have much time."

Well, thank you, brother. That was exactly the excuse he needed. He slid forward in his seat.

Frigg looked shocked. "Odin, show some—"

"Hold a moment," Loki said. "Didn't you say—nearly two hundred winters too late for my wife and children—that the Norns were wrong and you were wrong to trust them? But now you're pushing me to leave as fast as possible because *your* son's life is at stake? What about *my* wife and *my* children!" He shouted the last few words, surging to his feet and clenching his fists.

Carefully, said the clever voice in his head.

Ygg blinked. He looked taken aback.

"Well, old friend?" Loki reflexively shifted his body, becoming taller and stronger. "Will you bring my wife back, too? Or bring back all those winters I lost with my children?"

He jabbed a large finger into Ygg's chest and knocked him back a couple of steps. Ygg's jaw tightened, and his eye took on as wicked a cast as Loki had ever seen. A dim golden glow peeked out from behind the patch covering his missing eye.

He felt a feral smile stretch itself across his lips. This felt so good. Maybe he could take Ygg.

He jabbed Ygg again. His blood brother stumbled back another few steps, then frowned and raised his hands. His back was against the wall of the small room. He hadn't brought Gungnir to his hand, though—another gift Loki had delivered to his blood brother.

Loki jabbed Ygg in the chest again. Harder.

Ygg's pupil turned golden, and the air buzzed. The next jab would be answered.

Let him.

The careful voice in his mind said, *You're a fool. He'll kill you.*

He won't. He needs me.

Does he? He already struck the deal with Hel.

That was a fair point. But he was committed now.

And what's changed? Yesterday you told Yelena she was a fool for doing what you're about to try.

I've grown stronger in the last two hundred winters.

You think he hasn't? What's with the missing eye?

I'll take the other one.

The voice inside his head laughed at him. *And maybe he'll take your chance at revenge from you.*

So I'll try to kill him instead.

Try? You told the Skrymir that if he went after Ygg directly, he'd better make sure his first strike would kill. Now you're not taking your own advice.

That was different. He's not expecting me.

Seriously? You don't think he's prepared for you now?

Frigg had squeezed in between them, her back to Ygg. Loki loomed over both of them. He'd added nearly a foot of height and the muscle to go with it.

She held her hands up, palms out. "Loki, I can't imagine how you're feeling—overwhelmed with grief and anger at all you've lost and all you could've had. Maybe you even feel betrayed . . ."

The calm voice said, *Listen to her. Let her talk you down. Stay angry, but lock it away. Save it. Use it later.*

". . . begging you to save our son when we didn't save your children. I can't imagine that. I can't imagine how I'd feel. Frankly, I'm shocked you even agreed to help us."

Loki stared down into Ygg's now golden eye. Ygg stared right back, lips a tight line, jaw clenched.

Without breaking eye contact, Loki said, "You're right, Frigg, you've no idea how I feel. Your husband ruined my family."

Carefully, the voice said. *Don't betray yourself.*

"I went along with it because he said the Norns were always right," he continued. "Because I trusted him—and because he said he wouldn't kill my children. I convinced myself that exile wasn't that bad. Angrboda and I could still visit them, right? Or leave ourselves."

He snorted. "And now he says he was wrong? Or worse, that he's not even sure what's happening? What am I supposed to tell my daughter? Or my sons? 'Sorry! I made a mistake that left you, Jorm, asleep beneath the sea and you, Fenrir, chained to a rock in the middle of nowhere and you, Hel, with suffering that began when you slipped from your mother's womb. You each got to spend the past two hundred winters utterly alone. And me? My wife blamed me, went mad, and took her own life.' "

Too much, the voice in his mind said. *You've given too much away.*

So what? Let him come for me. He released his grip on his shape, shrinking as he stumbled to the chair he'd flung aside, righted it, and collapsed into it.

Frigg was right behind him. She knelt beside his chair and took his hand in hers. Tears rolled down her face. "I'm so sorry, Loki, so very sorry. We'll make this right. No, what am I saying? That's impossible. But we'll do everything in our power to make amends, won't we, Odin?"

She threw a look over her shoulder at Ygg that was so heavy with meaning that it went beyond Loki's ability to guess. There'd be time to think about it later.

Loki covered her hand with his and squeezed. "I apologize for my outburst, Almother—"

"You've nothing to be sorry about. It's we who are at fault."

"I take full responsibility for what I've done," Ygg said. He hadn't left the corner he'd been backed into. His single eye was still wolven. "I'll make whatever recompense I may that doesn't compromise the safety of the Aesir."

He'd make recompense, all right. He'd pay in blood for Angrboda's death and the exile of the children. They'd been brothers. He had broken that oath.

He looked into Ygg's face. *Just as I broke faith with my family because you would have killed me.*

"Thank you, brother." He stood and extended his arm. "That means a lot. Apologies for my outburst."

If the Norns had really been wrong, then all this had happened because Ygg made a mistake. He willed his arm not to waver.

Ygg crossed the room in two quick strides. The wolven gleam left his eye; the buzzing faded. "Don't give it another thought."

Loki clasped the proffered wrist and allowed himself to be pulled in for a clap on the shoulder.

I'll remind you of that when all you've built is burning down around you.

Because of me.

20

FRIGG

Day 2, late morning

Frigg's vision winked out the moment Loki closed the door behind him. In it, Loki had been gaunt and pale. His normally well-kept black beard had instead been wild and matted, and he'd been wearing wet, tattered clothes. He'd also been bound. His muscles had stood out like a ship's ropes as he strained against restraints that left red-brown stains on his skin and clothes and the rock beneath him. Worst of all were his eyes, which had shifted from one type of animal's to another and then back again. He'd been screaming as he thrashed, his mouth a wide circle flecked with spittle.

She'd no idea what the vision meant, and worse, she knew Odin would ask her about—

"What did you see, Frigg?" His eye bored into her.

"A furious man full of new, unexpected hope," she said, surprising herself at the note of sadness in her own voice. "And you? What did you see?"

"Much the same," he said, frowning. Her sidestep had been obvious enough. "His anger's directed toward me."

"Can you blame him? You admitted to being wrong in following the Norns' prophecy. That decision cost him everything he loved. I'm shocked he's remained loyal."

"Has he, though? His anger was more . . . raw . . . than I've ever seen from him. And then there's that memory I uncovered."

He was referring to the memory he'd dredged up after cutting out his own eye. In it, Loki had promised to destroy everything Odin had built. At the time, they hadn't been sure the memory had been true; the creature who attacked Odin and lived beneath Urdr's Well could have manipulated Odin's memories. In fact, they still weren't sure. But having witnessed this outburst from Loki and the vision that came with it—well, Loki had clearly been bound against his will. Things like that didn't happen. Maybe the memory of Loki's vow was real.

So why not tell Odin what she'd seen? Telling people never mattered. Whatever she saw always happened, anyway.

But that's not why she was avoiding Odin's question. She was dodging him because they needed Loki, for whatever good he might do. She needed him to get Baldr back.

"Let me ask you this," she said instead. "If you hadn't uncovered that memory, regardless of its authenticity, would you be questioning Loki's loyalty now?"

His gray eye narrowed in thought and then flicked away to stare into the crackling hearth. "A part of me has always wondered why he didn't attack me when I sent his children away. We'd fought before, several times, but . . ."

He shrugged.

Odin had always won.

"Was he always like he is now? Smart, clever? Calculated? Whenever I speak with him, I feel like I'm getting the response he thinks will best suit the situation."

"Pretty much."

"And then there's the nasty streak, like what he did to Heimdall."

"What are you getting at?"

"Do you think Loki's capable of killing Baldr and framing Hodr?"

"Of course he's capable, but I doubt he did it."

She stared at him, one eyebrow rising.

He frowned. "I didn't kill his children, Frigg, even though that's what the Norns wanted. I should have. Tyr lost a hand to Fenrir because we were trying not to hurt him."

"But Angrboda—"

He leveled a finger at her. "She took her own life. That's not on me."

"I know that, but you're the reason all that happened."

"So he should come after me, then, not strike at me through my— our—children."

Was he deliberately being thick? "He can't beat you in a fight, Odin. That's the point I'm trying to make. So he's going to come at us sideways."

Odin fell silent, considering her words. "All right, let's assume he's turned against us, then. How did he know about Baldr?" Then: "Haven't we had this conversation before?"

They had. Loki could be anyone or any animal he chose, as could Yelena. Either of them could have followed her on her annual trip to Baldr's tree, regardless of how careful she'd been. And then there was her old, deaf attendant, a woman named Laun. She'd often been close enough to overhear her whispered conversations with Odin, including the one in which they'd discussed Baldr's tree, the mistletoe, and how they'd care for them. They'd only let her get that close because she was deaf. But what if . . .?

Frigg cast her mind back to a distant memory. She saw their . . .

. . . *old longhouse, the packed dirt floor strewn with ash, dimly lit by witchlamps. The acrid smell of burning wood hung in the air. The cooks banged and bustled. The old woman brushed Frigg's bare shoulders with dry fingers as she helped Frigg dress . . . then Laun stumbling, catching Frigg's elbow, fingers and thumb pressing in hard, the thumb burning hot, as she said . . .*

"Frigg?"

She jumped and opened her eyes. Odin was in front of her, brow creased in concern, one hand on her shoulder.

"Are you all right?" His hand tightened a little on her shoulder.

She leaned back, breaking his grip. "I'm fine. Just remembering a long-ago conversation."

He withdrew back to his chair and spread his hands. "It looked like more than remembering. You're clutching your elbow like it hurts."

"Am I?" She looked down; she was. She opened and closed her hand and bent her elbow. "Feels fine."

"Good. So did you *remember* anything?"

"I'm not lying, Odin. I didn't have a vision."

He grunted.

"I remembered that old deaf woman, Laun. You do too, don't you?"

He held her gaze and then looked into the hearth. The firelight betrayed no emotions on his face. After the last time they'd found Laun close enough to overhear one of their private conversations, they'd found her dead in her quarters. Frigg had always suspected Odin of killing her. She'd never had the guts to ask.

Regardless, it seemed unlikely that either Loki or Yelena had taken the shape of an old deaf woman back then. Loki been a staunch new member of the Aesir at the time of Baldr's birth. Why would he skulk about? He hadn't even been married to Angrboda. If Yelena had been present back then, she'd be well over two hundred winters old now. Frigg knew of only one source of such longevity. Could there be sources other than Idunn's apples?

Odin tapped the patch over his missing eye. "I told you I've started seeing glimpses of . . . I guess 'events' would be the best word to use. I don't know when or even if they'll happen." He looked right at her. "A moment ago, I saw you standing on a rocky shore watching a burning ship float away."

Frigg's stomach dropped. Here they were again.

Months ago when her visions had come back, she'd seen Baldr aboard a burning ship. The visions had portended his death, though she hadn't wanted to admit it. Although she'd always said that talking about her visions never changed them, she wasn't above trying to change them herself. She'd sent Baldr with Odin to Háls, thinking he'd be safe there. And he was, just as he was the time he ran onto that burning ship in Gladsheim. The vision had come true, but not in any way she could have expected. In her youth, she used to tell anyone who asked what she saw. The telling made no difference. Those she saw die still died. Like Baldr. And yesterday, she'd seen a wild-haired man coming to kill Hodr. Was she wrong to keep her visions to herself? She'd kept quiet about Baldr, and he'd still died. Maybe she could prevent Hodr's death by sharing her vision?

She leaned back in her chair and examined Odin, from the loose, lean drape of his limbs, to the one gray eye staring back at her, to the wolfish ghost of a smile on his lips. Everything about it said *I know what you're thinking.*

But he was wrong. She'd never told anyone like him what she saw —someone of his age and power and knowledge.

So Frigg told him what she'd seen in the vision-flames above Hodr's head. He listened intently, his smile fading. Then she told him what she'd above Loki's head. His expression grew both worried and thoughtful.

They sat in silence a long while, the silence broken only by the pop and crackle of the burning wood in the hearth.

"Well, Odin," she asked, "is it everything you hoped it'd be?"

"I can honestly say that no, it isn't. I'd hoped that your visions would have more clarity and context than what I'm beginning to glimpse."

"Sorry to disappoint."

He shrugged. "We work with what we're given. Why did you change your mind?"

"Because staying silent has never worked in the past. I don't want Hodr to be killed." She leveled as frank and honest a gaze at him as she ever had. "Something bad is coming. We both know it. We should try everything we can to stop it."

21

ODIN

Day 2, midday

Odin stared down at the ugly-faced blond man—the same man he'd seen on his ride up yesterday morning.

"Well, *Alfather*," the man spat, "we want answers!"

Aesir were packed shoulder to shoulder in the Great Hall. It was so quiet Odin could hear the child coughing back by the main doors. Most had come to grieve Baldr's death, but a few—apparently led by this karl—had challenged *him* on the day of his son's wake.

Odin drew upon his fylgja's strength, without which a knife in the back would be as fatal to him as to any other, and hopped off the platform. The folk nearby pushed back, giving him and the blond man space.

Up close, the blond man was even wider of shoulder and taller than he'd seemed. He had prominent teeth behind full lips framed by a thick, unkempt beard that matched his long hair. His hairy brows lent additional savagery to his furious expression.

"What's your name?" Odin asked.

"Why, so you can use your woman's magic on me?" the man said, his teeth gnashing.

"I don't need your name for that."

The man's hands clenched into white-knuckled fists, but they stayed away from the axe on his belt. "Skarp."

"I'm Odin." He put his arm out into that middle space between them.

Confusion clouded Skarp's ice-blue eyes, but after a heartbeat he took Odin's arm in what was a strong grip for a normal man.

Loudly, Odin said, "You brought a weapon into my hall, Skarp—"

Anger flashed in Skarp's eyes, and his ugly mouth twisted. He tried to let go, but Odin tightened his grip. Surprise joined the anger in Skarp's eyes.

"—which I salute you for. We Aesir should always go armed. But tell me, are you an Aesir, or have you chosen to stand among the Sons of Muspell?"

Skarp spat on the floor. "Those bastards burned my ship and nearly killed my nephew and his daughter. That's why I'm here."

Odin let go of Skarp's arm. "You interrupt my son's wake to claim damages?"

"No! Baldr, and your daughter, saved them—"

"It's true, Odin," Frigg said, "I saw it."

"I didn't doubt him," Odin said, without turning around. To Skarp he said, "Continue."

"So I'm here to demand what's right when brother kills brother—"

"Death for the killer," Odin said. "Yes, I'm well aware of the custom. But what if Hodr was *made* to do it?"

"So you admit it, then," Skarp said.

Odin lifted his chin. The man was outspoken, brash, and totally fearless. *I like him.*

"Who was here two nights ago?" he called out. "Who saw a *blind* man accurately throw a spear?" He looked right at Skarp. "Did you?"

Skarp shook his head.

"Did you?" Odin pointed at a random man in the encircling crowd. And then another. "Or you?"

Both men blanched and shook their heads.

From the platform, Frigg said, "I saw it."

Muttering broke out—many *ayes* and *hear her* and *the Almother says it*. Odin held his hand up for silence.

"I saw it," said a blond-haired woman a few rows back.

"Then step forward," Odin said, gesturing to her, "and tell us."

Looking equal parts bewildered and angry, Skarp made space for the woman. She wore a sea-blue dress with long sleeves and a collar embroidered to resemble white foam. "I saw a man—Jarl Hodr, if the rumors are true—throw the spear at Jarl Baldr."

The crowd rumbled and growled.

"I'm not finished," the woman shouted, raising her hands. When the crowd's noise diminished, she said, "And I saw a man who stood at Jarl Hodr's shoulder and guided his aim."

Another uproar began.

Odin glanced at a tight-lipped, angry-eyed Frigg. Her expression said, *See, I told you.* He'd never disbelieved her; he couldn't free Hodr without proof that he was innocent. And Frigg couldn't, either—not publicly, at least, which is why she was leaving. One reason, at least.

He help up his hands again and called for silence.

When a reasonable semblance of it again descended on the hall, he asked loudly, "And what's your name, mistress?"

"Gudrun," she said, her cheeks flushing.

Odin gestured inclusively toward both her and Skarp. "If neither of you are married, you two should spend some time together. You're both brave and outspoken—a good union that'd make for the strong children we Aesir need." He stepped back up onto the platform and held up his hands again. "If you in the back couldn't hear, we've heard from a woman who saw a spear thrown at my son Baldr. And yes, my other son, our son"—he put his arm around Frigg's waist —"who was blinded by snow bear spittle in the Last War did hurl that spear."

The folk in the hall rumbled like an oncoming storm.

He shouted. "But I tell you, as one who knows, foul magic was involved. A blind man throwing a spear clear across this hall? Who here can explain that?"

He waited a few moments to let that sink in.

"You know that witches are at work in our city. The Almother uncovered one witch's corruption, and then that same witch tried to murder her. And these Sons of Muspell who destroyed this man's ship, among others"—he pointed at Skarp—"also tried to kill the Almother yesterday. The Jotunn destroyed Háls not three weeks ago. Even now, my son Vidar battles Jotunn warbands in remotest Utgard. I tell you truly, my people, we stand on the brink of renewed war!"

Cries of "No!" and "Don't believe it" and "At peace!" bounced off the rafters. But it was the shouts of "Lies!" and "Excuses!" that disturbed him. Those were the troublemakers.

"Peace?" He shouted the word. "We're here waking my murdered son, and you dare shout 'peace' at me? Baldr's murder is part of the Jotunn's plot against us. I don't want war. But I won't stand idly by while my people—you—have their ships burned out from beneath them and are killed or turned against each other by the wiles of some coven. But I hear you. You want peace, do you?"

The hall shook with the shouted replies of "Yes! and "Aye!"

"Would you have Jarl Baldr back if you could?"

More shouts of assent.

"I can do that."

A silence so complete that his ears rang fell across the hall.

He pointed at Skarp and Gudrun. "Do you believe me?"

They gaped at him. Gudrun recovered first. In a shaky voice, she said, "If you say you can, Alfather, then—though this is the first I've ever seen you—then I . . . I believe you."

"She believes me," he shouted, "though I've been gone most of her life. The graybeards among you, do you remember my power? Do you believe me?"

A dozen shouts of "Yes, Sigfather!" reached him.

"Hermod, come forward."

Another silence fell upon the hall. He stepped to one side as his golden-haired daughter approached, eyes wide. He reached into his satchel and withdrew a spindle and silver shears, hooked the spindle on his belt, and unspooled a length of witchthread.

"A witch has trapped Baldr's spirit upon the shore between death and life," he said. "Hermod, before all assembled here, will you deal with this witch?"

"Yes, Father," she said in a voice so full of pride and joy that it nearly brought a tear to his eye.

"Then take this gift of my magic. It will give you the strength to travel night and day till you reach the shores of the Gjoll."

And then he sang, weaving the golden, glowing witchthread through his daughter till she burned with its light. Then he snipped the thread, tied it off, and took her by the shoulders so she'd stand before the hall.

Frigg stepped forward and embraced Hermod. He heard her whisper: "Wait for us in the chamber behind the chairs; we have more to tell."

Aloud, so the hall could hear, Frigg said, "Fetch your father's horse, Hermod, and ride fast northward, winding ever down, on the ways Sleipnir knows well."

When Hermod had gone, Odin again faced the crowd. "Fellow Aesir, return to your food and drink and rejoice. Baldr will live again."

22

ODIN

Day 3, evening

Leaning on Ráta, Odin stepped off the hard-packed road into the ankle-deep snow. The ox-drawn cart trundled past them on the long-house-lined street in Gladsheim's second tier.

The driver touched his woolen cap and said, "Good evening to you, grandfather."

Odin, in the shape of an elderly man, doffed his wide-brimmed hat. Above the cart's noise, he called out, "To you as well. Late to be out delivering firewood."

"Cold winters keep me busy, sure enough," the driver said. He was thickset, red-cheeked and heavily bearded. "I've never loved the smell of burning wood so much as I do now."

The crisp evening air did indeed carry the tangy bite of wood smoke.

"May your prosperity long continue," Odin replied, "but this chill sets in my bones."

"Thank you," the driver said, touching his cap again before turning back around.

Odin and Ráta stepped back onto the frost-rutted road. "Wasn't this section of the city still forested when I left?"

Ráta nodded. "The last trees were felled about five winters ago to make room for these houses."

So much change in only twenty winters. These last few weeks were example enough. Baldr dead; Hodr chained. Hermod riding down to Hel. Unrest in the city. And this was the first he could remember actually being without Frigg in Gladsheim—she had left for Ifington before dawn this morning.

Odin snorted.

"Sigfather?" Ráta asked.

"Just thinking. Despite all my years, I'm still amazed at how quickly things can change."

The snap of leather reins cut through the smoky evening air. The cart lurched to a halt about twenty feet further down the road. A thrall who'd evidently been riding in the cart stood up and began dragging cords of firewood from the front of the cart to the back.

The driver called out, "Helga! Firewood's here."

The thrall jumped down, carried a few cords of wood to the longhouse's door, and stacked them. A woman emerged from the longhouse. She handed over a few coins.

"Same again next week, Eik," she called to the karl.

"I'll be here." Eik clicked his tongue and flicked the reins, and the cart lurched forward on the rutted road. The thrall hopped back into the cart.

Odin and Ráta came up opposite Helga's longhouse. Already on their short walk, Odin and Ráta had passed several dozen houses like hers. It was roughly one hundred feet long and twenty-five wide in the middle. The main doors faced southward. Another six such houses lined both sides of the road between them and the market a few hundred yards distant.

Helga stepped outside again. Odin raised his hand and called, "I hope this evening finds you well, matron."

Helga glanced up, smiled, and gave a friendly wave. "It does indeed. May Máni guide your steps till dawn."

"And yours," Odin said. From inside Helga's longhouse he caught the smell of cooking meat and frying bread, though it was nearly overwhelmed by the smell of wood smoke in the evening air.

When he'd awoken in the early afternoon, Odin had met with Chief Warden Orgrandr and Hersir Saglund, the leader of the Einherjar. Both men said that despite recent events, the folk were generally happy. Crime was minimal. Trade with Vanaheim and Alvheim was good—and growing, despite all expectations, with Jotunheim. And, thanks to an excellent growing season, Gladsheim's storehouses bulged with surplus bounty.

"The chief warden told me how peaceful the city's been despite recent events," he said to Ráta. "I was skeptical, but I'm less so now because of what I see around us."

"The wardens are always busy dealing with minor crimes—thieving, brawling," Ráta said, "but yes, Gladsheim's been peaceful these past twenty winters."

They ambled past more houses, their doors also open wide. Smoke drifted up from the holes cut in roofs. Some folk were out in their yards, bustling with minor chores as Helga had been. Other folk leaned on fences and spoke with one another. Groups of small children ran among the houses playing.

The smell of burning had grown so strong that he could taste it. He glanced over the few nearby longhouses, but he found nothing amiss. The wind gusted. It brought the heavy, acrid stench of a bonfire to him.

"Fire!" came a distant shout.

He exchanged a glance with Ráta. More shouts of "Fire, fire!" joined the first.

Odin released his staff; it vanished. Ráta's form blurred. A lean, white-chested snow cat bounded away from her footprints as Odin beat into the sky on eagle's wings.

———

ODIN FLARED golden wings and landed in front of the hall. The heat tightened the skin on his face. The burning hall before him dominated the eastern end of the market. Its front doors were wide open and ablaze, red tongues of fire licking the underside of the roof. Folk in a bucket line threw one ineffectual bucket of water after another onto the hall. Others shoveled snow onto the hall; still others had clambered onto the nearby roofs to help prevent the fire's spread. More quick thinking. The sight of his people acting so decisively filled him with pride.

But he still needed to act.

Ráta took shape beside him.

"At least six more buildings in the lower tier are burning," he said, bringing Gungnir to his hand. "Find some wardens, Ráta, and start looking for those who did this. Check in with Heimdall. He may have seen or heard something."

"Yes, Sigfather." Ráta dropped into her snow cat shape and sprinted away.

With a groan, the front half of the hall's roof collapsed, exposing the building's bones, pillars and beams wreathed in roaring, triumphant flames.

Odin slammed Gungnir into the frozen earth. He reached into his bag and withdrew his spindle and shears. He slotted the spindle onto Gungnir's cross guard, tugged free a long strand of witchthread, and hung his shears from the small hook on the front of his belt. Then he began to sing.

The fire recoiled backward, seemingly aware of his intent. Those laboring around him, throwing buckets of water, shoveling snow and dirt onto the blaze, slowly stopped.

With his right hand, Odin cast the witchthread outward into the burning hall. It shot through the sagging doors, wove through the flames, and darted among the fallen beams. He called the thread's tip back to his left hand, passed it to his right, and flung it back into the flames. With each cast, he sang more of the flames into the witchthread.

The fire fought him, but little by little, it yielded more of itself to the thread and his song until only the thread itself burned. He cast a third loop and, still singing, caught and held the witchthread in his left hand. It writhed like a fish. He snatched the shears from his belt, snipped the thread, and flung the witchthread, coated in flames, slithering up into the night sky.

The flames that had engulfed the building went with it, lighting the immediate area like midday.

Then night flooded back in. The building smoldered and popped, creaked and groaned. Those dozens who'd crowded in to save the hall stared at him—shock, horror, fear, amazement. Awe. He saw all those expressions in their pure and mixed states.

The Aesir hadn't seen him work in a long time.

23

LOKI

Day 3, evening

Loki flew through a steady drizzle. He had hoped, despite knowing better, that the skies above the land where Hel lived would be clear and blue. But as usual, gray, fleecy clouds dominated. Far ahead, a gray, white-flecked sea stretched northward.

After emerging from that weird realm in which Yggdrasil thrived, he'd slept as an owl tucked beneath the shelter of an evergreen. Now he soared above a stream that plunged down from the snow and ice coating the steep mountains behind him, one of many streams that flowed into mist-laden lake surrounded by tall peaks. At the far end of the lake was a glacier; at the other end, the Gjoll spilled out and flowed down to the sea, gaining strength and volume as the snowcaps fed the river.

It was almost funny how all his planning these past hundred winters and more came down to taking Ygg at his word. Again. Even so, Ygg hadn't been wholly forthright. Most of it was probably true, but sifting out the lies would be difficult. Vafthrudnir could probably help, but he was in Jotunheim. Loki couldn't go there first; Goldtooth would expect to see him outside Hel's home tonight, tomorrow morning at the latest.

An updraft blew Loki to one side. He rode it till its fury was spent, then resumed his course.

Who would ever have thought it possible that Ygg could restore the dead to life? Frigg hadn't even blinked when her husband had said he could restore Baldr's life. Was it something unique to Baldr and the ritual they'd used to protect him? Or was it something else Ygg could do—an extension, maybe, of the magic he used to create freakish Mimir?

Did it matter to his plans—or the Jotunn's—that Baldr might live again?

He tried to focus on that question, but his thoughts flew ahead to what Ygg would do to Hel. Ygg was always jealous of his magic, let alone when someone did something he didn't expect—and then thwarted him as well. He'd never let Hel's challenge pass unanswered.

He'd kill her.

Besides, Ygg had promised only to release Hel, Fenrir, and Jorm. What did that mean, to "release"? Death was a release. He could free them from their prisons but still bar them from returning to Asgard or Utgard. Or he could release them and then kill them.

Your pardon, my old friend, what do you mean by "release"?

Why, just that—to free them, Loki. I'm concerned that you'd ask.

I see. And would you tell me what you mean by "free them"? Would they be free to return to Asgard? To Utgard?

Why, Loki, I think perhaps you don't trust me after all.

Yes, that would've ended well.

Ygg wasn't above playing with words, but he was also desperate. That's what Loki wanted: Ygg in pain, desperate. He'd promised the Skrymir that Ygg would be distracted, and he was—just not in the way Loki had expected.

How did you do it, Hel? And why did you keep your powers secret from me?

For the same reason he'd kept his own plans secret: It was his nature. She was his daughter. If he hadn't been secretive, then maybe she wouldn't have taken Baldr's spirit as the coin with which she hoped to buy freedom for herself and her brothers. She would see it differently, of course. She didn't know the true value of Ygg's word, not really. She did know everything about how she and her brothers had ended up where they were, including how her mother had died. He'd never lied to her about any of it, even when that meant enduring her anger and her hate. He'd borne it because he deserved it. Now he'd have to tell her how he'd chosen the long road to revenge because he'd seen it as the only option.

But they might have other options now, if they worked together.

Loki swept lower, right above a jumbled mixture of stony, broken teeth that marked the River Gjoll's most precipitous drop to the valley far below. Far below lie the smooth patch of stony shore near the falls where he'd often sat beside a crackling fire, waiting for Ygg to finish harvesting witchthread. Angrboda had used this same spot.

Would that he'd heard what Angrboda's shade had said to Ygg. Would that he'd seen her curse cause Ygg to stumble away blind and befuddled, unable to use the knowledge he'd won. Would that he could laugh in an owl's form.

Instead, he dropped through the river's deep-voiced roar toward the snaking gray river below. It was time to include Hel in his plans. Maybe together they could find their way free.

———

LOKI STOPPED short of the split-rail fence he'd built around his daughter's house. It was far larger than she needed, but in this wet land beneath these gray skies, a warm, large house with a high roof and plenty of room to move around in was the least he could provide to the daughter he'd wronged. He'd cut every stone of its foundation. He'd dragged each one from the cliffs. He'd felled every timber for the posts and rafters and dragged them down here for shaping. Every time his strength had flagged, his guilt drove him on. It wasn't a bad place to live, he supposed, though there was much less sun than he'd prefer. Up in the foothills, the soil was rich and game plentiful. The sea was close and easy to fish. One summer, he'd brought her sheep and goats; another, he'd brought her a few chickens.

He put one hand on the cold, damp stone that anchored the fence and called, "Hel, it's your father."

Goldtooth would hear him and tell his master, but that was the point. When the enemy saw you, you made sure you were doing as they expected.

A warm yellow rectangle of light split open the house's long side, followed by a dark shape that stepped in front of it. "Back so soon?"

"Were I the master of my wyrd, I would never have left."

Stone-faced, she asked, "Why have you come?"

Every time he saw Hel, he wanted to apologize for the agony he'd put her through—and her brothers and mother. He'd stopped apologizing long ago, but each time it required an effort of will. But this time, having heard Ygg admit that trusting the Norns had been a mistake? It was all he could do to simply say—he knew who was listening: "I've come at the behest of others."

"What a surprise." She walked back into the house but left the door open.

As much an invitation as he ever got. He glanced up at the sky; the gray clouds had packed in tighter. He pushed open the gate. Damp with rain, Loki walked up the path to Hel's home.

24

ODIN

Day 3, late night

With his boot, Odin rolled the corpse onto its back. It was a man, young, judging by the sparse beard and smooth skin. The corpse wore the remnants of a happy smile on bloody lips.

Odin's hand rasped along Gungnir's smooth grain as he sank to his haunches. "This is one of the bastards who set the fires?"

He and Ráta stood in front of another burned-out hulk of a hall. He'd arrived in time to stop the fires from spreading to the surrounding buildings, but that was it. Easily a hundred folk slumped nearby, exhausted and soot-stained from fighting the fire before he'd arrived and sung the flames to sleep.

"Yes, Sigfather, the only one we've found so far," Ráta said, an angry note in her voice. "He ran when the wardens called out to him. They stopped him, but..."

But they hadn't stopped him from killing himself. One savage tear down his arm, another across his left wrist, and then he'd buried the short blade in his stomach. Bad way to go. Odin reached down and examined the corpse. The young man had big, strong shoulders, a thick chest, and beefy arms. His hands were similarly big, scarred, and calloused. Simple clothes of brown and tan, worn but not ill-made.

A bit of silver glinted in the filth around his neck. Odin dug his fingers in and pulled free an amulet with a stylized tooth pendant. That meant nothing to him other than reminding him of the tooth he'd seen in Angrboda's longhouse. He put the pendant in his satchel.

Boots crunched against the frozen ground. Ráta pivoted toward the sound. It was Chief Warden Orgrandr, middle-aged, stout, and dour. He'd lost his arm at the elbow. Beyond him, a thin line of blue-cloaked wardens held their spears crosswise before them. Hundreds of folk were crowding into the square along the roads; more were slipping between buildings and around the line of wardens. It looked like a gathering of angry people.

With his chin Odin, gestured toward them. "Will that be an issue, Chief Warden?"

The chief warden glanced back at the gathering crowd and shook his bald head. "No, Alfather. Word's spread that you were here. The folk have come to see you."

Odin stood. "Have your wardens fall back here. I want a few spear lengths of room to work, but otherwise the folk may come as close as they choose."

"Yes, Alfather." The chief warden saluted and jogged away.

Ráta gestured toward the corpse. "Sigfather, is letting the folk see you work the best decision?"

"I've been away too long," he said. "They need to understand that there's more to this world than gathering crops, staying warm at night, and raising a family—that they have those things because people like you and I stand watch and fight."

Ráta didn't look convinced.

The first dozens of folk had instinctively formed a half circle around where he and Ráta stood by the corpse. They were regular folk. An older man, filthy from fighting the fires, who carried himself as though he'd been a warrior. A matronly woman holding the hands of two children, neither more than ten winters old and each dirtier than the one beside them. A young Alvar woman, her golden skin streaked with dirt, her clothing singed and scorched, leaning on a young man with his beard barely upon him. Behind them gathered row upon row of more folk. Still others scrambled upon the roofs of nearby buildings.

The air began buzzing as Ráta drew on her fylgja's strength. He did the same. Otherwise, a bowman atop those roofs could kill either of them, and given the events of the past few nights, an attack wasn't an outside possibility. The wardens pushed through the crowd. They formed a blue-cloaked perimeter which Chief Warden Orgrandr bulled through as he approached Odin.

Blood dripped down Odin's sight and he saw the chief warden . . . *stumble, an arrow through his throat. Blood gurgled in his mouth. Another arrow buried into his shoulder and he fell . . .*

Odin shook his head, and the blood-vision cleared. The chief warden wore a curious expression; the crowd was oddly silent. Had he asked Odin a question?

He snapped his fingers. "It's just come to me, chief warden, but I believe your father was an Einherjar during the Last War."

The man reddened and ducked his head. "Yes, Alfather. You were kind enough to attend his funeral."

"Kindness had nothing to do with it, Orgrandr." Odin pitched his voice a little louder. "He fought to keep all we have, all we've built. None of it comes free of toil and sacrifice. I honor that courage whenever I see it."

The chief warden reddened further.

"I remember him well. You carry yourself much as he did. Did he ever tell you why I chose him?"

"No, Alfather. He never spoke much of the war."

"Those who've lived it rarely do," he said. Then, more loudly so the surrounding folk could hear, he said, "Report, Chief Warden."

Orgrandr coughed and cleared his throat. "Alfather, throughout the city, twenty-seven buildings were burned right down to their foundations or near enough they'll have to be rebuilt, anyway. Most of those were outbuildings, but we lost seven storehouses, three halls, and two stables. They got the animals out in time."

Gasps and swearing came from those folk nearby. The news was whispered backward through the crowd. So much for the summer's bounty. The city would have many lean weeks ahead of it, and the folk knew it.

"This was all done at the same time?" Ráta asked.

"Yes, Baresark. Or near enough."

"How many dead?" Odin asked.

"We're still waiting on the final tallies, Alfather, but at least one hundred and twenty-three."

More muttering and curses from the folk. Good. They needed to be outraged. They needed to understand that they had enemies.

He pointed at the corpse. "And this one was among those who set the fires?"

The chief warden nodded. "We believe so, Alfather, but he killed himself before we could question him."

"That's not a problem." Odin gestured toward the folk. "Make sure everyone stays back."

Ráta nodded and faced the crowd. The chief warden also nodded, confusion plain on his face.

Odin leaned on Gungnir and stared down at the dead young man. He spoke one of the rune words he'd seized for himself when he'd hung from Yggdrasil. The air resounded with the crack of a breaking branch.

The corpse twitched.

As the sound of the word faded, the corpse's arms flailed and its heels drummed against the ground.

The mutterings from the crowd died like the wind at sea.

"Rise," he commanded.

The corpse sat up. The crowd gasped. A woman to his right somewhere shrieked, a sound that was shortly muffled as if a hand had been clapped over her mouth.

The corpse clambered to its feet and stood before Odin like a living man would have. Except his chest didn't rise and fall.

"Tell me your name."

"Madr."

"And who am I, Madr?"

"You are the Valfather."

That gave him pause. The dead had never used that name before. The Norns had named him that when he'd gone to speak with them a pair of weeks ago.

He made a sharp upward gesture with his chin. Madr rose to his toes, straining as if trying to relieve pressure around his throat. "Why did you burn this building?"

"I was told to." A spot of decay blossomed on the man's face below his right cheekbone.

"By whom?"

"The leader of my group."

"And who is that?"

"Afi." The decay spread up to the man's temple, down to his jaw and beneath his bloodstained overtunic.

"Describe him."

"Gray hair, gray beard. Brown eyes. Wrinkled."

That described every old man in the city.

"Where did you meet him?"

The decay spread into the man's hair; a hunk fell out and wafted downward. A rich, sickly-sweet stench began to roll off the body.

"In this hall here."

That was gutsy, burning a place you'd been seen in.

"When was that?"

"Midday yesterday, Valfather." The decay slunk from beneath the man's stained, rent clothes and appeared on his hands.

"That's when you were told to burn these buildings?"

Madr's pants flapped in the breeze as a thick, ashy dust spilled from the tops of his boots.

"Yes, Valfather."

"And you belong to the Sons of Muspell?"

"Yes, Valfather. They will bring fire and—"

"Be silent."

The dead man's teeth clacked shut. The vines of decay grew thickened into black snakes that slithered and writhed across his exposed flesh.

"How many in your group?"

"Seven." The vines tightened. Flesh flaked and crumbled away from his hands, exposing white bone.

"Describe them."

Madr shook his head. "I won't. The fire is all, it—"

Odin touched the dead man's shoulder, and the man shrieked in agony. "You will."

"They cloaked themselves, Valfather! I couldn't see their faces."

The red faded from Madr's beard; the hair fell out and drifted away. The folk nearest the tumbling tufts of hair pushed and shoved to get out of the way.

"What did you do in the city? Do you have a family?"

Odin could feel Madr resisting the compulsion so he touched his shoulder again. Madr gave a long, muddled moan. Vines of decay ate his lips. Not long before this traitor's body could no longer speak.

Madr's voice was a syrupy whisper that Odin had to lean in to hear, and even then it was barely audible. "I'm apprenticed to Smith Gundri. I have no family. My father died in the Last War. Bandits murdered my mother when I was a boy. I was alone. But the Sons"—Madr looked right at him, his white eyes turning yellow and shriveling—"we are *everywhere*."

The man's teeth became visible as his lips rotted away. The rest of his long red hair faded and blew away, accompanied by the battlefield's familiar blood stench. More in the crowd scrambled away.

Madr's bones hung loose in the grip of his power. Odin released his hold, and the corpse rattled down into a heap. The skull rolled away. The crowd gave a collective gasp of horror and dread and disgust, yet Odin could remember a time when not a single warrior would have batted an eye at what he'd done.

He looked a question at Ráta.

She nodded. "I heard. I'll find the one he mentioned, Sigfather.

Finding the other Sons might take longer, but once we have one, it'll be easier."

"Agreed. I leave it to you alone."

She held his eye for a long moment and nodded again, proving that she understood the implications of what Madr had said. If the Sons truly were everywhere—likely an exaggeration—then only a few whose loyalties were time-tested could be fully trusted.

"Chief Warden," he said.

"Yes, Alfather?"

"I want the gates sealed and guarded. No one leaves or enters until I say otherwise."

"Yes, Alfather. I'll see to it."

Odin looked around at the folk surrounding him in a much looser half circle than before. Word would spread quickly about what he'd done and said. Fear would build in the city, of him and those who had set the fires. Left alone, that fear would grow until it proved more destructive than the flames had. But it wouldn't come to that. His city wasn't lost yet.

Raising his voice, he pointed at one of the nearby wardens. "Bring me a cart and shovel. I have a mess to clean up."

25

LOKI

Day 4, late morning

Loki swore to himself. She wasn't hearing him. He tried again, his fingers dancing in the Jotunn speech. "Hel, please. You didn't think this through. You took his son's spirit hostage. Once he gets Baldr back, you're dead. And probably your brothers, too."

"He swore an oath. And he's sending me a hostage. He'll do what I want."

"Yes, he will. And then he'll kill you." He sat about a sword's length from his daughter, the hearth on his left. He was rested, full-bellied, warm, and comfortable, unlike when he'd arrived the night before.

A light smile played across her lips, and aloud she said, "He's welcome to try."

"Hel, I don't think you quite under—"

She reached out and touched his knee.

The room lurched around him, his stomach grew queasy, and then he was in a cave. The air smelled of salt water. The sound of crashing waves boomed around him. Hel stood before him, her eyes an intense black with specks of starlight and—

His stomach lurched again.

Now he stood beside a shrouded body flat upon a stone table. A sheathed seax with a golden hilt lay beside the body. Wind shrieked in his ears.

Hel's eyes flared white. His stomach lurched again.

Now he was on his knees, dry-heaving, before the hearth in her longhouse.

"Do you see now?" she said aloud.

Loki dragged a shaking hand across spittle-thick lips. No, he didn't understand at all. What had she done? And how? He coughed, hauled in a ragged breath, and pushed himself up to his chair. Hel handed him a cup of something, and he drained it. Sweet mead.

When he was ready, he spoke with his fingers. "What did you do?"

"I gave you a small taste of what I can do now." Thankfully, she answered with her hands.

"Which is what exactly?"

She smirked. "I can touch your mind. I've gained power over the dead. And I've grown capable in other things, too, thanks to speaking with those who've died."

"So you claim the same power as Ygg?"

She shrugged. "I don't know if it's quite the same, but I proved his equal not three nights earlier."

It was a mistake, but he laughed. Hel's eyes blazed white, she grabbed his arm, and the room vanished.

They stood opposite each other on the surface of a windswept sea. But his footing was solid. And the sea was white. The sky above was black and flecked with stars and smears of colorful clouds.

"This is impressive, Hel, but—"

The river vanished, and a white wyrm loomed behind Hel as tall as Gladsheim's Great Hall. Its head alone was the size of a cart.

He stumbled backward. "Hel—"

She looked up at the wyrm and laid her hand on the monster's taloned foot. She was no bigger than one of its claws.

"This is the Gjoll, Father. She and I have become one."

The what? "I don't understand. Neither what you're telling me nor where I am."

He recognized the wyrm shape, though. Jorm had been born with slitted eyes similar to the ones that transfixed him now. He'd favored the wyrm shape as he grew up, so much that he refused to shift back to his birth form. Green-scaled Jorm now slept beneath a distant sea.

"I've pulled you into the spirit realm, Father." She stroked the Gjoll's claw, and the wyrm lay down beside her. Its eyes were a more brilliant blue than any sky he'd ever seen. "And she is the River Gjoll that stretches from life to death. She is one of the Elivagr and has ten sisters. Ygg knows most of them very well, as do his baresark."

Was that supposed to help? He remembered what it was like to show off. As a child, he'd bragged enough for any dozen children, so he wasn't unsympathetic to what his daughter was doing. He also didn't want to further insult her. Not only would that be counterproductive, but it might get him hurt. Or her. So he took a different tack.

"It's not that I'm unimpressed. But I really don't understand what you're showing me. I've paltry gifts when it comes to seidr, though they've proved useful enough."

Hel raised a hand, and everything went black. Then he was back on his knees dry-heaving beside the hearth. He was vaguely aware of Hel standing, the clicking of stoneware, and the pouring of water. After a time, he dragged himself back into his chair. After another short time, the blackness receded and Hel gave him a warm cup of a sweet-smelling tea. As he sipped, his stomach's lurching eased.

She sat back down opposite him and spoke in the Jotunn language with her hands. "Let's start with what we all know. At the heart of all the realms lies the Ginnungagap. Within that void churns the Hvergelmir, driven by the ever-flowing rivers of ice and fire from Niflheim and Muspellsheim.

"What most do not know is that eleven rivers flow outward from the Hvergelmir. They are called the Elivagr. They are all sisters—disir. And they are alive. Back when Ymir lived, Ygg sought power by sacrificing himself to himself. He saw what I've described to you.

Then he gained great power by enslaving one of the Elivagr. I've done something similar."

Loki wanted to ask her what she meant by *sacrificed* and *something similar*, but he didn't want the answer. Instead he asked, "You enslaved a river?"

Hel gave a quick shake of her head. "Gjoll and I joined willingly. Only the Aesir enslave."

If only he'd known what his choice would do to her . . .

"No, Father, you don't get to do that," Hel said, jabbing a finger at him.

He wiped his eyes. How could he not? His grief dueled with his guilt, a duel he lost no matter which won. This had all happened because he'd chosen to twist Ygg's mind rather than fight him. But if he had it to do over, he would make the same choice. Opposing Ygg directly was stupid.

"I don't even hate you anymore," she said.

Anymore? The word stabbed him.

"Or your cowardice."

She gave the knife a good twist. But he wasn't a coward. Only fools fought Ygg. Many tried. All of them failed.

"I've become what I am now because of it," Hel said.

His family had paid the price for his choices, and now his daughter had attempted what she believed her father would not.

"My brothers and I will be free because Gjoll gave me the ability to catch Baldr's spirit like a river's eddy catches the leaf. Not even Ygg can do that."

As far as she knew.

Hel's eyes were intense. Her lips drew a tight line from the unstained half of her face to the blue-black side. "My plan will work."

All his questionable choices and decisions were in the past. Unchangeable. As for the guilt and self-loathing he lived with—and the fear that his painstakingly laid plan might fail—he had to put it all aside. If he didn't, then he'd truly lose his children this time.

"It might, Hel. But I wish you'd confided in me. Because I fear we're working at cross purposes."

Worse than jeopardizing his plan, she'd drawn Ygg's attention. So even when Loki freed her Ygg would pursue her. He massaged his temples and blew out a long breath. That was a problem for another day. First he must adapt his own plan to free his children. And that meant doing what he rarely ever did.

Loki confided in his daughter.

26

ODIN

Day 4, midday

Odin tugged the oak door open and stepped from the bright winter daylight into the dark longhouse.

Hodr sat slumped in a chair set sideways to both the door and the low-burning hearth. "Who's there?" He sounded disinterested. A long chain led from his hands to one of the posts that held up the roof.

"It's been a long time." Odin tugged the door shut behind him and moved toward his son. In his left hand, he carried a three-legged stool. In his right, he carried a spear.

Hodr turned stiffly toward him, as if his ribs hurt. His face was a mask of bruises shading into yellows and browns. A brown cloth hid his missing eyes; his brown beard had grown grizzled. He wore a simple overtunic, shirt, and breeches, simply cut but clean.

A sad smile ghosted across Hodr's lips. "Hello, Father. Have you come to kill me?"

Odin sat on the stool about two arm lengths from Hodr. "Some would say you deserve death, but that's not why I'm here."

"Ah, well."

He held the spear out to his son. "Take this. It's an arm's length in front of you."

"What is it?"

"The spear you killed Baldr with."

Hodr seemed to shrink into himself, and he raised his hands as though to push the spear away. "I don't want that thing. It's evil."

Odin snorted.

Hodr turned his face away.

"Take it."

Hodr frowned but reached for the weapon. As his right hand closed around the spear's shaft, he shivered and looked up at Odin. "So those runes—"

He doubled over, retched, and flung the spear away. It skittered, danced, and clattered to the floor.

Odin jumped up and backed away. "Rán's tits, Hodr, what—"

Hodr dragged a shaking hand across his mouth. "Your eye, Father. What happened to your eye?"

Ice ran down his back. He snatched up the spear and slammed it down in front of his son. "Take it."

Hodr shook his head. "I don't want to see it again."

"I don't care what you want. Take it."

Hodr resisted, even as Odin shoved the spear into his son's hands and wrapped his own around them, holding them there.

"Tell me what you—"

This time Hodr threw himself forward and vomited into the ash-covered dirt.

What was Hodr seeing that was so terrible?

Odin angled the spear in his hands so that the firelight ran across its length. The leaf-shaped blade seemed to grow out of the oak shaft not unlike, he supposed, how the mistletoe plant itself dug into a tree's branch.

The runes cut into the blade and shaft were familiar—they made the weapon stronger and more accurate. He rapped it with his knuckle. It rang like metal should. He ran his thumb gently along the blade. Sharp. Oily. He sniffed it. It didn't smell like anything, certainly not like weapon oil.

The dead Jotunn shaman he'd taken the charm had told him that the only thing that could wound the body of the one warded by the charm was the vessel in which their spirit was safeguarded. He'd learned the way to undo the charm without killing the one protected. Someone either knew what he did or had guessed well.

And this spear was supposedly crafted by some unknown Aesir smith? Unlikely. He couldn't shake the feeling that the Svartalvar had been involved in this spear's crafting, but they worked in metal, stone, and gems. The Alvar worked in wood and stone almost exclusively, particularly those flakes of black stone that were sharper and more delicate than most metal blades.

So, yet another mystery piled atop all the others.

Hodr knelt on all fours, spitting into the dirt floor. "Don't make me do that again, Father."

"Depends what you tell me about what you saw."

Hodr blew out a shuddering breath and hauled himself back up into his chair. He rested his head in his hands. "A wave of fire rolling fast across plains; warriors marching; gemmed eyes in a man-shaped helm; women raped, their men torn apart; ravens gorging on the eyes of the dead; water running down a tree; chisels hammering wood that bled like flesh; you standing bound and unburning in a fire; a woman with an axe facing Thor; Vidar forging a sword; a goat milked; a boar slaughtered and reborn; a field of the dead with flame-haired women riding black clouds above it.

"All the sights flowed one into the other across a starry field where your eye should be—as if that part of your head had been sheared off by an axe."

No wonder he'd thrown up. "You saw all that? You only held the spear for a moment. How do remember all of it in such detail?"

"There was more I don't remember. It was all moving so fast, like a school of fish swimming in a cresting wave, and it only happened when I faced you. Everything else looked as it did when I first took up the spear."

Odin again ran his thumb across the finely cut runes. "These runes shouldn't do that."

Hodr's laugh sounded like dead leaves. "That's what Lopt said."

Leaves on a seemingly dead fire would sometimes start burning. Maybe Hodr had the gift of foresight, and these runes had somehow kindled it.

"You had no visions when you were with him?"

"None. All I had was a dim sight when I held the spear; I still have that. You're the one who's different."

He knew the eye he'd sacrificed to see more had opened, but he couldn't control it. Not yet. Perhaps the spear's magic somehow let Hodr see into that link that flowed between himself and the pool beneath Mimir?

That didn't make much sense.

"And the smith gave you this spear because his horse knocked you down and cracked your skull?"

"He did. It was one of many I tested. This was the last one I tried. And when it somehow gave my sight back—even the shadow of it . . ." He gave a slight smile and shook his head. "Of course I kept it. I got to see Alara's face."

"Your mother told me you had a woman."

"She's why I'm here. To make peace with you finally, to get your blessing and your decision on whether we could get—"

"Stop. You know we don't speak about that outside of Ithavoll."

Hodr changed what he was about to say into a clearing of his throat.

"When did you figure out how your mother and I protected Baldr from harm?"

"What?" He was clearly confused. "I never—"

"Don't lie to me, son," he said, rapping Mistilteinn against the hearthstones. "Someone figured it out. You had reasons to hate your brother, perhaps reasons enough to kill him."

"What? Father, I—"

He cracked the spear against the stones again. "No, Hodr, don't lie to me. You wanted Nanna, and your brother took her. When you were blinded, Baldr said he couldn't heal you—you hated him for that. You never forgave the first and never believed the second. So your hatred ate your honor and you set this whole wicked plot into motion."

Face red, Hodr shook his head. His fists were clenched. "I was angry with Baldr. And you. And mother and Thor and all the rest of you who got through that war without a scratch. So yes, I hated him —for all the reasons you said—and for a very long time, but I got past all that. I would never raise a hand to him or wish him harm. Not Baldr. Not my own brother."

Odin slapped Hodr and bellowed into his face. "What kind of womanish answer is that?"

Hodr's mouth fell open in shock. And then he was on his feet.

Hodr had always been stronger than most. The first punch came in fast and struck Odin in the cheek, sending him stumbling sideways. The follow-up stomp was clumsy but still caught his hip and skidded off. Mistilteinn clattered to one side.

Odin rolled away and came up on his feet.

"How did you find the witch, Hodr? Or did she find you?" His jaw throbbed; it felt like a horse had kicked him.

Hodr was standing, fists clenched and head cocked to one side, listening. He was pulling hard against the chains, so hard that the bolt holding the chains to the post broke with a loud *ping*. He came at him in a fast shuffle, hands out to grapple—smart. On the ground, Hodr didn't need his eyes.

Odin dodged away along the wall, putting several more feet between them but choosing not to trip Hodr. Neither did he grab the trailing chain.

Hodr's foot banged against the fallen Mistilteinn and sent it rolling. Like a hound after a rolling bone, he went after it. He scooped it up and spun. The way he squared off against Odin left no doubt in Odin's mind that the runes granted the sight Hodr had described.

And then Hodr gave a strangled cry, dropped the spear, and staggered backward. He braced himself against the longhouse wall, clutching his head.

Odin counted a dozen heartbeats before Hodr said, "I don't know any witches. I didn't come here to kill Baldr. All I wanted was to make peace and leave again. With or without your blessing."

After a long time in which nothing but the fire's crackle and

Hodr's labored breathing could be heard, Odin said, "I believe you, son."

He found that he meant it, too. It wasn't that his son had attacked him; he'd goaded him into that. But everything about what Hodr had said and done felt right. Hodr didn't care if anyone believed him. He'd learned the truth about who and what he was and had made peace with himself.

"You have my blessing, son," Odin said. "You and your woman, and all your children, will have what you came to ask about. If you want it."

Hodr sagged against the wall, laughing or sobbing or both. Not that he could cry anymore. "What good does that do me now, Father?"

"What do you mean?"

"I have to be killed—executed, don't I?"

Odin snorted. "I've lost one son, Hodr. I will not lose another."

27

LOKI

Day 4, late afternoon

"And so now I'm here," Loki said. "I know you hate me, Hel. I hate myself half the time. I've been working toward this moment for a very long time, and revenge means nothing unless I succeed."

Hel's gloved fingers flicked the words slowly at him. "So you tricked his brother into killing him? But why Baldr? Why not Ygg himself?"

He snorted. "Because I'm not a fool. I know my capabilities. Killing Ygg is beyond me—"

"Even if you surprise him?"

"There's no surprising him. Not like that, at least. Maybe with a knife from behind, but I still wouldn't chance it. So instead, I'll kill everything he's built. I'll burn it all down, shatter every stone. With the help of our people, the Aesir will be wiped out. When I'm done, Ygg will have nothing."

Because that's what Ygg had done to him. He'd taken everything.

Except Sigyn.

Sigyn had found him long after he'd lost everything, yet somehow she'd come to love him. Without her love and care, he never could have remade himself with a singular purpose, much like Mistilteinn, the spear he'd crafted.

"Do you know why I'll do that, Hel?"

"Revenge, obviously."

"That's part of it. Just as the haft is part of the spear." He wanted to say the next words aloud, but he couldn't risk it. So with his hands he said, "My goal is to free you and your brothers. Yes, I want revenge. I want him, and the others, to suffer as we have. But if you and your brothers aren't free, then I've failed.

"I'm no coward, Hel, despite what you think. I know it looks like I am—especially since I keep saying that I'm not—but I've deliberately cultivated that appearance. Who believes a coward will take action? The mouse scampers and hides. But predators stalk their prey unseen. Then they strike."

Hel frowned.

"Men turn and kill the stalking wolf when they see it. But the mouse? They laugh and turn away. I've suffered much to prove I am weak so that the strong discount me."

Hel's twisted lips became a sneer. "Where is the honor in that?"

"What does honor have to do with anything? You think Ygg acts with honor? After what he did to us?"

Hel leaned back in her chair, stubborn resolve—or misplaced pride—overwhelming her contempt for him. "The bargain's been struck. I have to go through with it."

"Don't mistake this for a game of tafl," he said, "or think that you have Ygg cornered. If he thinks he is, he'll upend the board and bury his spear in your chest. And if you happen to beat him? You'll spend all your remaining nights looking over your shoulder."

"You should know."

"No, I don't. Because I wasn't fool enough to oppose him. I rolled over and showed my belly like he expected."

She sneered again.

"Are you listening at all? I'm telling you—and you obviously don't want to hear it—that we want the same thing. I just went about it differently."

"What about Mother?" she said with her hands, the unmarred side of her face red with anger.

"You think I didn't tell her all this? She spat in my face, called me a coward, and refused to speak with me. Then she went down her own dark path."

Hel looked as though she was about to come out of her chair.

"Listen, Hel, please. Listen. We want the same thing. If you want to succeed, then we need to work together from now on. But don't fool yourself into thinking it'll be easy or safe."

Hel sat half in, half out of her chair, thinking hard. Her eyes had gone white.

Loki hardly dared breathe.

Finally she said, "So you don't think he'll free me or my brothers?"

How to explain this? "Since he killed Ymir, Ygg's believed that he is the mightiest of the Aesir. With the possible exception of Thor—I wouldn't want to be near if they ever went beyond hurling insults at each other. And then here you come, daughter, using powers he didn't know you had to pluck his son's spirit from its journey on the Gjoll. He didn't seem to know that was possible. And if that wasn't threat enough, you then used Baldr as a bargaining chip."

"I'm not following you."

"He'll keep his word. Then he'll kill you and probably your brothers too, just to be safe."

"But he gave his word."

"He and I were blood brothers, Hel."

She stood and paced. Her mother had always moved when she thought. "All I wanted was our freedom. I took the only chance I had."

"I know that, but if you'd talked to me before—"

She snorted.

"All right, that's fair. But still."

"I didn't know what you were planning—no idea you had any plans at all," she said. "When I saw Baldr board the Naglfar, I had to act. If we'd had this talk sooner, we could've done things differently."

True enough.

"You're right," he said. "And now that we have, let's figure out the best way to move forward."

She spread her hands. "My options are limited. You think he'll kill me regardless of what I do."

"Yes, but I have devices that will free all of you." Many winters ago he'd tasked the Svartalvar, who also hated Ygg, with building devices that would cut through the binding charms Ygg had sung over Hel, Jorm, and Fenrir.

"So free me now, and we'll instead use this time to free Jorm and Fenrir."

"I would, but I don't have the devices with me," he said, ignoring the frown that creased her brow and mouth. "They're safe in a cave beneath Franangr. Second, Goldtooth is paying close attention to you and I. He'll notice if you leave, and then there'll be an army between us and your brothers. And finally, this whole 'bring Baldr back to life' thing is an excellent distraction."

She smiled wanly but not, he hoped, without some affection. "So what, then? I go ahead with my original plan?"

The question Loki had asked himself the day before rushed back at him: Did it matter that Baldr would live again? With that murder, he'd wounded Ygg and kept him off balance and unable to fully focus on what else was happening. Events over the next few nights would contribute to that. Possibly the Sons had already attacked the city. No doubt Yelena and her fool coven would try for Ygg soon, as well.

He shook his head. That would be fun to watch.

"What?" Hel asked.

"The important thing is that Ygg stays off balance. So yes, I think keeping your word makes the most sense."

Chin in hand, arms folded across her chest, she stared into the hearth for a long time. As a child, she'd lain on her belly and done much the same. It made his heart ache.

"All right," she said aloud after a long while. Then with her hands, she continued. "He'll assume that despite the differences you and I have, you'll have impressed upon me how serious a situation

I'm in. So I'll play the role of the good girl. I'll keep my end of the bargain and trust that he will, too."

Loki nodded and with his hands said, "And even if he doesn't come here and free you, I will."

28

ODIN

Day 5, late morning

Hands clasped behind his back, Odin moved close to inspect the weapons and tools hanging on the walls of Smith Gundri's forge. The single-bit axes were well crafted, though the beards were a trifle too tapered for his tastes. The wooden hafts were also well made and fit snugly in the axes' eyes. Perhaps the woodcrafter too was a Son of Muspell? How widely had their disease spread? How deep did it run? If last night's quiet was any judge, perhaps the rot wasn't too bad.

"You do fine work, Smith Gundri," he said, facing the swarthy, sweating, burly man.

It hadn't taken long for the wardens to find Gundri, particularly with Ráta coordinating. Ráta had shifted shape and quietly watched the forge for a day. She reported nothing unusual.

Pack-Father, people gather.

As expected. *Sit outside the forge. Let the Einherjar keep the folk away.*

The forge was well-organized, all the tools set neatly in their racks and the smith's hammer placed atop the anvil. The skymetal he'd been shaping was set beside the forge. The pokers used to stoke the fire sat in their own rack beside the forge.

"Thank you, Alfather." Gundri wiped his upper lip and smoothed his beard but stayed silent. He couldn't quite keep his eyes from darting to where Ráta stood between anvil and forge.

Odin grabbed a stool that was tucked behind the forge's bulk. He sat in front of Gundri and spread his hands. "The Sons not only attacked the Great Hall and threatened the Almother, they also set those fires two nights ago. I'm puzzled as to what they thought to accomplish. Sure, they caused a great deal of damage and murdered one hundred and twenty-three of our people." He twisted his head. "Ráta, we captured those Sons who attacked the Almother. What have they told us?"

She shrugged. "They want to topple the jarls from power. That the jarls have ruled for too long. That the jarls gotten rich off the peoples' hard work."

"One hundred and twenty-three children, women and men," he repeated, "all dead. Murdered by the Sons. Can you guess how many jarls they hurt? Not one. And when I have food brought in from Ifington and the surrounding towns, well, the folk will thank the jarls while cursing the Sons. That makes sense, right?"

"Indeed it does, Sigfather," Ráta said.

"See, Smith Gundri, she agrees. And Ráta's not one to tell me only what I want to hear. I want honest opinions. Blind obedience does me no good. That's one of the few things I've learned in all my many winters."

Gundri's eyes flicked to Ráta. The hammer on the anvil. The open doors. Finally back to Odin.

"So you and I are sitting here, speaking as I would with any of my hersirs or baresarks. Man to man, in this case."

"What do you want from me, Alfather?" Gundri asked.

"Information."

Gundri said nothing. A brave man.

Odin turned toward Ráta. "Those other Sons we caught. What did they say about their willingness to talk?"

"That they'd take their secrets into the barrow, Sigfather."

"How well did that work out for them?"

"I'd have to say they were mistaken."

Ráta had a gift for understatement. Those who'd attacked the Great Hall had been questioned and eventually divulged the little they knew. They'd met a cloaked man at a stable near the eastern gate. They'd never seen his face or heard him speak. He'd given his instructions in the Jotunn hand language. The wardens had followed up on every detail they could, including the men themselves.

The best information had come from the apprentice who'd killed himself rather than be captured. Once the rest were all hanged tonight, Odin would sit beneath their bodies and speak with them.

Ordinarily, Ráta's reply would have loosened the smith's tongue.

"We caught one of the Sons who set those fires," Odin added.

An animal wariness crept into Gundri's eyes.

"He killed himself before anyone could question him, but I hauled his spirit back into his corpse and bade him speak. What was his name again, Ráta?"

"Madr, Sigfather."

Gundri paled. Sweat beaded on his upper lip.

"That's right. Do you know what Madr told me? That he was your apprentice. Is that true?"

After a long hesitation, Gundri nodded. A bead of sweat rolled down his forehead.

"See, we're getting somewhere," Odin said. "Your apprentice also told me that the Sons often met here. A good spot, really. Noisy. Many people moving about on the street—well, usually."

Gundri glanced at the wide entrance, where Freki lay. Freki licked her lips and panted, showing finger-sized fangs. Gundri visibly flinched.

"Madr also told me of a graybeard who typically came here."

Gundri stared at his hands, hairy-knuckled, scarred and singed from years in the forge. They bunched and released, the muscles in his forearms shifting. A brave man, indeed. Perhaps another little push.

"You know what kills warriors in battle, Gundri?"

The smith said nothing and kept his eyes averted.

"I asked you a question, smith."

"I imagine the enemy's weapons do." Gundri cleared his throat. "Alfather."

Odin laughed and clapped the smith on the shoulder. "I like you, Gundri. You've got guts. And while you're correct, it's really fear that kills warriors. Because of it, they can't think. They forget to guard their shieldmate, or they don't listen to the orders shouted at them."

He shouted now. "Who did Madr meet with at your forge?"

Gundri flinched, gathered himself, and after a moment, met his eye. It took no more than a heartbeat, but it was long enough for Odin to see the hatred in this man's heart. All that he'd done for the Aesir, and this was the thanks he got?

He picked up one of the pokers and thrust it deep into the hot forge. "Do you have a family, Gundri?" He ground the poker into the hot coals, feeling it crunch and watching for the iron to begin to glow.

Gundri spat on the frozen earth. "They're all dead. My sons died in their own shit when the plague hit. Grief killed my wife."

"I am truly sorry to hear that."

"You should be, you bastard. They're dead because your son, the famed healer, failed to save them."

Gundri was probably putting on a show for his neighbors— doubly so if he, and perhaps some of his neighbors, belonged to the Sons of Muspell. Odin held back a sigh. He could've had the smith taken from his forge and brought someplace quiet. But Gundri wasn't the only one putting on a show.

He heard the smith spit on the floor. "Do your worst, *Alfather*. Burn me with that thing. I won't talk."

Odin drew the poker from the fire. The tip glowed white hot. He could taste the ash in the air. "As I told your former apprentice, Gundri, alive or dead, I'll get the answers I need from you. It makes no difference to me." He pointed the poker at Gundri. "But it does to you."

Gundri stared at the glowing tip for a long time.

Another push?

"Let me be clear, Gundri. If you answer my questions, I'll leave you be. Or if you like, I'll send you to another town. I can't give you back what you lost, but I can give you a second chance."

Gundri spat again.

"Very well." He gestured at the smith. "Ráta, bend him backward over the anvil, please."

To his credit, Gundri tried to stand, but Ráta had him by the neck before he'd moved an inch. Odin brought the red-tipped poker toward the smith, the air rippling with its heat. Gundri's eyes widened. He thrashed in Ráta's grasp like a child throwing a fit. Odin's skin prickled as she pulled on her fylgja's strength. Once she did, the contest ended.

The smith tried to shrink away, tried to turn his head, but Ráta held him steady. Her expression was remote. Her eyes glittered with the white fury of her fylgja's power.

"I'll tell you what you want, I'll tell you, I'll—"

Odin set the bar against Gundri's right eye. The man's scream was deafening. His back arched, and he thrashed. The stench of burning flesh leaped into the air, chasing the hissing and burbling as Gundri's blood boiled away.

When he removed the glowing tip, Gundri's bowed back relaxed a fraction, but he still writhed in agony. His other eye was shut tight, tears streaming from beneath the lid. Snot ran into his beard; his mouth was a wide circle of agony.

Odin gave him a few moments, then set the bar against his left eye. Gundri shrieked even louder. He writhed so fiercely that Ráta almost lost her grip. The air buzzed with power as she drank more deeply from her fylgja's power.

More come, Freki said.

Odin pressed his lips together. As expected. Now to see if anyone had the courage to confront him.

When he'd finished, the stink of burned, ruined flesh hung in the air. Gundri was a limp, shuddering vestige of himself.

"Bring him to the door, Ráta."

The smith hung like a sleeping child in the baresark's arms. Odin racked the poker, walked to the wooden box full of spikes and spearheads, and removed six spikes. He took an axe down from the wall and followed Ráta out of the forge.

A crowd of people had formed where the road bent to leave this district. A half company of Einherjar stood between Odin and the gathered folk.

Odin swung one of the broad, heavy doors shut, threw the bolts at top and bottom, then shook it. It rumbled sturdily. "Hold him against the door, please."

Hands beneath the smith's armpits, Ráta pressed Gundri against the door as though he were a pelt they were about to dry.

They approach, Freki said.

Odin took the man's hand and raised it. He pressed the first spike against his wrist, reversed the axe, and hammered the spike between the bones of the forearm into the stout wood.

Hot blood spattered across his face.

Gundri woke, loosing a harsh scream and nearly wrenching his arm free before Ráta controlled him. The air hummed as she pulled harder on her fylgja's power.

Weakly, Gundri murmured, "Why . . ."

"Why did the Sons attack my wife?" Odin asked. He wiped his face with the back of his hand, withdrew another spike, and hammered it through the meat of the smith's upper arm.

Gundri screamed and writhed again.

"Why did the Sons you've aided burn my buildings and ships?" Odin asked.

". . . message . . ."

"Maybe that's what they told you, but I'm sure there's more to it." Odin stepped around Ráta and pressed a spike into the smith's other arm. Gundri flinched. "Where can I find them? Who leads them?"

". . . graybeard . . . comes here . . ."

Odin hammered the spike through Gundri's arm. The smith uttered a long, low groan of pain. Blood frothed between his lips. His bowels released, and that stink joined the others. The oak door was stained even darker.

Memories flooded Odin of his own breath rasping between his

teeth, of burbling blood as a cold spear slid between his ribs. Of ropes tightening around his neck and wrists as his weight came onto them.

Gundri's voice grew thready as he slid toward death. "Afi . . . his name . . . any . . . more . . ."

Afi.

Madr had used that name, too.

"Maybe. I'll find out soon enough."

Odin gestured for Ráta to step back and join his wolves and the line of Einherjar. When she let go, Gundri groaned as his weight sank fully onto the spikes. The door creaked, but its hinges held.

". . . monster . . ." Gundri coughed blood.

Geri's rumbling growl became louder.

Into both Geri's and Freki's minds, Odin said, *Easy now. One example is enough for today.*

He grabbed the smith's jaw in his hand, the beard wet with blood and slobber. "No, Gundri, there are no monsters here. I keep the monsters at bay."

29

FRIGG

Day 5, midday

Frigg tugged her hood forward against Sól's midday glare, pushed the gate open, and stepped from one of Ifington's busier roads onto the wide path that led to the way house run by Hodr's woman, Alara.

"Wait here," she told the two wardens that Ifington's gothi had tasked with guarding her. She'd refused the ten others and insisted these two dress as warriors rather than as wardens.

"Yes, Almother," said the burlier of the two men.

She walked down the short path toward the way house. The doors facing the street stood open, letting in fresh air. Silent shadows crisscrossed the interior whenever a rumbling, creaking shadow passed behind her on the road. Ice clung to the house's low-slung thatch roof, and barrels were set out to catch the dripping meltwater.

Perhaps her move had been shortsighted, but no one knew she'd come to Ifington. Pretending to be a rich karl seemed safer than moving through the city with a company of wardens around her, now that a witch had attacked her in her own hall. Besides, she needed Hodr's woman to open up, and frightening her or drawing more attention than necessary would make that more difficult.

By now, five nights after the murder, Alara had to know of Baldr's death. She must also have heard the name of Baldr's killer. Baldr's wife Nanna was still abed, weeping and keening. Would Hodr's woman be the same? Or would she be up and about, doing what still had to be done?

More importantly, could she tell Frigg where to find Lopt the smith?

The clink of cups and pots banged their way out through the open doors. The stewing fish and baking bread reminded her of meals she'd eaten as a child in her father's hall. Her stomach rumbled. She paused on the threshold, enjoying the wash of heat flowing out of the building. A few men sat hunched over tables on the far side. Directly across from Frigg, against the far wall, stood a waist-high table with barrels on a shelf. Cups and mug were lined up neatly on the table's right side. A stout woman stood at the big hearth opposite the kitchen, stirring a pot suspended above the fire.

"May I help you, mistress?" The woman's voice at her elbow range sweet-toned and polite.

She was committed now. Nanna was family; she had to deal with her grief. But Hodr's woman wasn't family yet; she might never be. Unless Frigg got the information she needed.

"That depends," she said, stepping into the way house. With the daylight at her back, she'd be a shadow in the doorway. She put her hood down.

The woman who'd spoken was tall and lean. Modest green dress with a high neck. Thin gold necklace. Very pale face with reddened eyes and dark circles beneath them. Her hair was light brown and neatly braided.

"Would you show me to the owner of this way house?" Frigg had already guessed that this was who she sought. Physically, this woman could be Nanna's cousin.

"I'm Alara. My brother and I both own this place, as I suspect you well know." Her eyes narrowed as her voice took on a sharper tone. "We're not selling this place, so please leave and tell your master to stop sending his people."

Frigg couldn't help but smile. Alara and Nanna might look similar, but where Nanna was meek, Alara was forceful in the way of those who'd worked for what they had.

"I can see why my son chose you," she said, to see how quickly Alara's mind worked.

Alara blinked. She drew back slightly. When realization dawned in her eyes, she gasped and stepped back.

The woman stirring the pot looked confused, as did the men at the tables who'd glanced over at the sound of Alara's raised voice.

"Be easy, child," Frigg said, taking Alara by the shoulder and smiling as kindly as she could.

Alara smoothed her dress and then clasped her hands together so hard that her knuckles whitened. "Almother, I can't believe you've—" Her raw hands flew to her mouth. "Oh no, what's happened to Hodr? Is he ... he's not ..."

"Can we speak privately somewhere, Alara?" she asked.

Alara's lips trembled and tears sprang to her eyes. She controlled herself.

"Of course, Almother." Alara pointed at the cook. Without a tremor in her voice, she said, "Thegn, please go wake my brother. Tell him he needs to watch the house till I return."

The thrall nodded and left.

"We can go to my house, Almother. It's out back. We won't be disturbed there."

"Lead on," she said, already fearing that Alara was family after all.

———

"I ASSUME you've heard what's happened?" Frigg asked, setting her warm cup of mead aside. Alara had insisted on preparing them both a small cup.

Alara looked more composed now. She put her cup down and wrapped her hands around the arms of her chair, braced to weather bad news. "The whole city knows, Almother. Not at first—the din was terrifying—but when the news reached us late the following day ... I'm so very sorry for your son's death."

"Thank you, child. Do you know who was responsible?"

Alara's head began to shake back and forth like a ship's jib about to burst its ties.

"Can you help me understand why he did it?"

Alara's shoulders crumpled, and her face fell like a glacier calving. She buried her face in young, long-fingered hands roughened by work and wept. The ragged, wet gasps filled the small longhouse.

Frigg rose and pulled Alara into a hug and rubbed her back in small circles. The young woman clung to her. Frigg suppressed a sigh as the familiar flame-visions kindled above Alara's head. In them, she watched . . .

. . . Alara move among the wounded. Her face was dirty, tear-streaked, and lined. She touched a brow here, smiled down into a bandaged face there. She stopped beside a man who'd lost his leg at the knee, tucked her loose hair behind her ears, and bent to check the dressing. Two helmeted warriors, bearded axes and shields in hand, burst through the side door. Fear and horror grew in Alara's eyes and she backed away, her empty hands coming up to . . .

So war would come here, too. But when? Had Alara looked older or just exhausted? And who were those warriors? Frigg peered deeper into the vision but couldn't answer her own questions. The warriors wore brown, non-descript leathers. Their faces were hidden. Their weapons were not unusual.

And Odin thought they could use these visions to change the future?

Alara gently disengaged and in a ragged voice said, "I'm sorry about that, Almother . . ."

Frigg took Alara by the shoulders. "I wept my way through the night after he was killed. Had my daughter not been with me, I might have gone mad."

Alara wiped her eyes and offered a sad, consoling smile. "I felt the same when a sickness took my parents. Were it not for my brother . . ."

"When was that?" Even with the aid of the valkyr Baldr had

trained and sent out into the towns and villages, many still died of sicknesses.

"About seven winters ago," Alara said.

"How old were you?"

"Twenty winters, I think. Maybe nineteen." Alara smiled and shrugged. "My brother had left the army and started working as a warden here in Ifington. I was here with my parents. They'd been running this way house for a couple years. They got sick—were sick for weeks before it really set in. Coughing, tired, fevers. And then I got sick, too. Wasn't much the valkyrs could do for them, but their potions and poultices helped me. When I got better, I started running this place along with my brother."

"It grieves me to hear it." After a respectful interval, she added, "They'd be proud—you've done well here."

Alara's eyes took on a sad, faraway look. "I like to think so. And thank you, Almother."

"May I ask when was it you met my son?"

"About eight winters ago. He'd been badly wounded. The Norns were kind, I guess, since his horse, Kona, happened to bring her master here. My parents helped him. I did, too, when they let me. It took a few weeks, but he recovered—and then he insisted on paying us back."

The Norns, kind? Odin would disagree. "That sounds like Hodr."

Alara smiled. "He started working in the stables, then in the yard. Took him a bit to figure out what was around him, but he did it. Kona helped him quite a lot."

"It must be hard to keep this place going," Frigg said. "There's plenty of work to do, I mean."

"Certainly enough to go around. It's quieter once the harvest's done and winter has the ships stuck in port or the roads get snowed over. My parents picked this spot well, though, that's for sure. We were the second way house in Ifington. We're right by the main road so we're easy to get to. Add in good food and a safe place to keep the carts, horses, and oxen, and well, it makes sense to weary travelers. We've been tested a few times by thieves and such, but we survived."

"It helped to have your brother with the wardens, I'm sure," Frigg said. She figured it was best to keep Alara talking rather than rush her, though she could feel her impatience rising.

"It did, for sure. An extra patrol out front each night, and Hleven made sure everyone knew he was a warden. Even so, we got tested. Not after Hodr started staying here, though."

"So he stayed on after he recovered?"

Alara nodded. "My parents told him he'd paid his debt, so they could offer him paid work. Only a few coppers a week, food, and a bed, but he took it gladly. And he's never tried to . . . well, you know . . . around me."

Frigg had dealt with some of that back in her youth when some of her father's strongest warriors had thought they could do what they wanted. Her father had made certain she could defend herself, though. Her experiences were probably nothing compared to what Alara had dealt with.

A wistful smile crept across Alara's face. "One time a merchant made the mistake of being loud about what he wanted from me. Happened he was standing right next to Hodr. Hodr told him to shut his fool mouth, but the man kept going. Hodr cocked his head to the side in that way he has . . ."

Frigg smiled lightly, hoping it would hide her upwelling sadness. The gesture Alara referred to must be linked to Hodr's blindness; he'd never done it growing up. She herself had only noticed it when she'd gone to interrogate him a few days ago. The thought that this young woman knew her son better than she did made her tears flow, even as something else welled up—relief, maybe, that Hodr's loneliness had ended.

For a little while, at least.

Alara's hands came down upon hers. "I've upset you, Almother."

She smiled through the moment. "You have, child, but in a wonderful way. Please keep telling me about my son."

Alara pursed her lips, hesitated, and then continued. "Well, he cocked his head to the side, and while that man—Fossen was his name—laughed at him and made all sorts of rude gestures toward me, Hodr shoved him.

"Fossen stumbled back and said something like 'Blind or not, you're a dead man.' Hodr smiled and said, 'I wanted to make sure you knew it was coming.' And then Hodr laid him out faster than anything I'd seen."

"Thor taught him how to fight," Frigg said. "Only Tyr and maybe Ullr were Hodr's equals."

Alara gaped at that, which was natural, she supposed. Most people had never seen Thor. They'd heard about his deeds in the Last War and the old tales from before then. Probably half of Ifington hadn't been alive during that war.

"After that, we didn't have many problems," Alara continued, "except a few weeks later, when he stopped Fossen and his friends from stealing the wares of some merchants who were staying at the house."

"A very fitting end to the story," Frigg said, nodding. "And I'm sorry to be blunt, but it's the beginning of another that's brought me here."

30

ODIN

Day 5, midday

Axe still in one hand, Odin faced the crowd. The smithy was slightly higher than the road, so he could see over the heads of the two dozen Einherjar arrayed before him, spears lowered at the crowd of more than a hundred folk. Sól's light glinted off their armor. Ráta stood ready to his right, arms by her side.

Behind them, Gundri the smith wheezed and coughed his way closer to the Naglfar.

"Should I have Hersir Saglund send more Einherjar, Sigfather?" Ráta asked in a low voice. "To disperse the crowd."

Noting her concern, Odin scanned the faces of the crowd.

Huginn, Muninn, give Saglund this message: Do not send more Einherjar into the southeast trade quarter.

"I've sent my ravens," he replied. "I told him not to send more men. One example is enough."

Some of the tension eased from Ráta's tight-lipped expression. She'd follow his orders. But he wouldn't put her in the position of having to do something she'd find foul, like killing these ordinary folk. Not unless he had to.

"I've sent for the wardens," shouted a husky voice from the crowd. "You can't do what you did."

"Can't I?" he shouted back.

The crowd rumbled, a beast at bay. More shouts came from around them.

". . . good man, didn't deserve that!"

"Alfather or not, what right do you have to . . ."

". . . can't torture 'im!" called a woman.

". . . known him all my life, never hurt anyone!"

Odin addressed Hersir Ungr, leader of the two dozen Einherjar. "I want one column on either side of the road. Do not draw your weapons without my order."

Hersir Ungr was blond and tanned and wore his beard in three intertwined braids. He'd seen maybe twenty-five winters. "Sigfather, if I may—"

"Coward! Come out from behind your warriors," called a man, his voice deep and hoarse.

"You heard me, Hersir."

Hersir Ungr saluted and shouted, "Part ranks!"

The Einherjar column split—they'd all heard the order to their hersir—and formed up on either side of the road, shields facing outward. Odin strode into the gap, stopped three paces beyond the last Einherjar, and spread his arms.

"Here I am." The crowd of folk edged backward. He pulled gently on his fylgja's power. Calling their bluff didn't mean being stupid; he had a knack for bringing out the best in people—and the worst. "Where is he who challenged me?"

Ráta stepped up beside him on his left. The air buzzed with her power.

Muttering, grousing, unintelligible shouts from the crowd. And then movement. A tall, dark-haired woman pushed free of the crowd. She put one hand on the pommel of her seax and squared her shoulders below hair as black as raven feathers. A fresh scar slid sideways beneath her left eye from nose to hairline.

"Do you lead this crowd?" he asked.

She glanced to her right and left, frowned, and replied in a husky voice, "No, Sigfather."

Odin's lip quirked. Interesting choice of title. "What about that man who challenged me? Does he lead?"

"I sent him home. Bit of a drunk," she added, as if hoping he'd let it go.

He said nothing.

She cleared her throat. "I came forward because I didn't like how this was going. I was there the other day when . . . when your wife was attacked. That wasn't right. Neither is this."

He said nothing.

"And I . . . I wanted to say I'm sorry—sorry for your loss, Sigfather. I knew your son. A little. He taught me."

"You're a valkyr, then?" The valkyr were the men and women who tried to heal wounded warriors both on the field during battle and afterward. Often, their choices and their care kept the wounded alive or eased the passing of the warriors' spirits.

She nodded. "I was. Nine winters with the army up north. The last two, I trained as a valkyr."

"You'd have made my son proud."

She colored slightly and looked down.

His vision went red as pain knifed through his missing eye. The raven-haired woman's face twitched, and as though she'd donned a mask, he saw . . .

. . . *her astride a black wolf. She held a spear in one upraised hand. Gray smoke wreathed her head and spilled down her shoulders. She looked right at him, her eyes the color of raw meat, and shook her spear. Then she and her wolf leaped into the air and ran through the sky toward a grasping forest of withered . . .*

And then the vision was gone, as quickly as it'd come. But the sense that he knew this young woman remained, that he trusted her—or had trusted her before with a very important task.

". . . because I've known Smith Gundri all my life. He's a good man. He doesn't deserve this."

"What's your name?" he asked.

She looked right at him—same as in his vision, except this woman seemed younger, less sure, and far less imposing. How had she become the one he'd seen? What had he seen? Even when the baresark drew fully upon the strength of their fylgja, they didn't look like this woman in his vision.

He held out his right arm. "I'm Odin."

The crowd rumbled. She shot a disgusted look over her shoulder then took his hand. "Obviously I know who you are, Sigfather. I'm Gondul."

She had a strong arm and a firm grip. And she looked him in the eye.

He released her arm. "Gladsheim needs women and men such as you, Gondul. May I ask why you left the army? I'm sure they need valkyr."

She shrugged. "Three winters ago, my father passed back into the Gap. My family needed help working their claim. It's gotten hard for them."

He shot a questioning look at Ráta.

"Likely skymetal, Sigfather," Ráta said. "In the time you've been gone, there have been several finds in the mountains to the east. The Almother allowed those who actively work the veins to own them and sell the ore. Can be lucrative."

"I see. Good to know." He smiled at Gondul. "I've been away."

She nodded. A ghost of a smile crept across her face as if to say *Everyone knows you've been gone. And now everyone knows you're back.*

Gundri groaned, coughed, and cried out wordlessly. Gondul's smile faded. She gestured toward the dying smith. "He was a good man. He didn't deserve that."

"He collaborated with my enemies. With our enemies."

"Maybe. But this?" She looked disgusted.

He spread his hands. "I've lived a very long—"

A hurled axe banged into his head.

The impact knocked him backward, staggering to keep his balance. The axe thudded to the ground.

Silence fell across the smithy yard, the road, and the crowd.

Odin caught his balance. Exuding menace, Ráta had moved forward. Gondul's expression was shocked.

Hersir Ungr shouted, "Einherjar, form wall!"

The warriors lining each side of the road surged into motion, lowering shields and spears. Those closest in the crowd yelled and turned to run. Those in the second and third rows, with nowhere to go, started a panic.

"No!" Odin shouted above the screaming, fleeing crowd. "Stand down, Einherjar!"

"But Sigfather, they attacked you!" Hersir Ungr shouted back, his voice outraged.

"Do I look hurt?" Had his fylgja's power not been coursing through him, that axe would have split his skull. It had been well thrown. Lucky, too, that the blade had struck rather than the wooden haft. "I caused this trouble. I'm not about to murder my people."

Not without a better reason, at least.

Hersir Ungr didn't look convinced.

"Einherjar, resume your positions," Odin shouted. "You'll answer to me if any of you wound the folk here. Do I make myself clear?"

"Yes, Sigfather!" The two dozen warriors stomped back to their guard positions.

Not that it mattered now; the crowd had only been a few hundred strong, and half were already gone.

"Ráta?" he called.

"Right after it happened, I saw three figures break out of the crowd and go running."

Huginn, Muninn. See if you can find anyone running who's further away than those who've fled. If so, try to see their faces and then follow them.

Yes, Wing-Father.

The two ravens clattered into the air from one of the nearby roofs. They were unlikely to find anyone, but it didn't hurt to look. These Sons of Muspell seemed intelligent enough to have planned a bolt-hole.

Gundri gasped wetly. His breath rattled out, and Odin felt the smith's spirit slip away. He'd have to interrogate the dead man soon.

But first, Gondul.

The young woman hadn't moved. She wore a resigned expression, as if she expected to be held accountable for the attack.

As he approached, she asked, "How are you unhurt, Sigfather?"

"Did you know that would happen?"

She smiled sadly. "No, Sigfather."

He crossed his arms and said nothing. Short of seidr, he'd never found a sure way to detect lies. She squared her shoulders, lifted her chin, and met his gaze. The resignation never left her face.

"I believe you," he said, well aware of how instinctively he trusted her. "You also understand that I provoked that attack?"

Confusion clouded her eyes. "I don't understand."

"War is coming. I've returned to find our people grown soft and lazy."

"Not everyone," she said.

"No, not you. Or those like you. But how do I find those who'll fight *before* war comes?"

She gestured at the Einherjar and then at herself.

"Yes, there are thousands who've served and will be called back to fight. But as a valkyr, you know what happens to those who fight."

"They're wounded. Many die," she said. "But how does torturing him, Gundri, benefit you? You've turned the folk against you."

"You said this smith was a good man."

She nodded. "I've known him to be. As have those here."

"And I'm sure he was. But none of us are only one thing or the other. Gundri harbored those who burned ships and, two nights ago, nearly thirty buildings. One hundred and twenty-three of our people are dead because of him. He may not have touched torch to tinder himself, but he aided those who did. I can't let that pass."

After a long moment, she said, "All right. But he's dead."

"That doesn't matter. He'll tell me whatever he knows, which hopefully will lead me to those who attacked us. And he now exemplifies what happens to those who betray our people, while you, Gondul, exemplify how I treat those who are loyal."

Roughly a hundred folk still stood in the street below them, watching. Listening.

"So you planned all this?" Gondul said, a note of outrage in her voice.

"Let's instead say that I hoped our people's temper would reveal itself," he said. And then, more loudly, "What I'd like now, Gondul, is for you to stay as witness to Smith Gundri's words and then, if you choose, tell what happened here."

"Why choose me?" She looked skittish, like someone who'd woken expecting her day to end in an entirely different way.

He couldn't help the grin that spread across his face. He'd heard those same words so very often over his hundreds of winters. His response was always the same. "You chose yourself by stepping forward and confronting me."

Indecision and fear warred with her curiosity and courage. Her lips firmed, and a hardness came into her eyes. "I'll stay."

"Well done, Gondul," he said, again offering her his arm.

She gripped it firmly.

"I expect to soon need women and men such as you. Consider what you've already learned today and what you're about to learn. Speak with Ráta, if you choose. She'll make herself available.

"And then, if you wish to enter my service, come find me in the Great Hall. I will set a place aside for you."

31

FRIGG

Day 5, midafternoon

Frigg listened to the soft *snick-snick* of Alara's knife as it sliced through the onions. That sound, and their aroma, were laden with memories of lean winters as a child, when onions were used in everything from flatbreads to soups. Alara was working in the kitchen on the opposite side of the hearth. Her long brown hair kept falling in front of her face—deliberately so, Frigg suspected.

"Keeping busy has helped keep my mind off things," Alara said, using the flat of the thin knife to scrape the onions into a pot. "You don't mind, Almother?"

"Not at all."

Alara tucked her hair into a loose bun and glanced at her. "May I ask you about that night?"

"It's why I'm here," Frigg said, "at least in part. I have questions for you, too."

"For me?"

"Indeed. You see, I don't believe that Hodr is guilty of what he did."

The chopping resumed, this time with carrots. "But you said—"

"Oh, he definitely threw the spear that killed Baldr," she said, surprised that the words came out so easily. "But I don't think he meant to do it."

Hope burned so brightly and suddenly in Alara's expression that it was hard to look upon. "He didn't go there to kill anyone, Almother. He went to see his father—the Alfather, I mean, begging your pardon —and ask permission for me to ea—"

Frigg raised a finger. "Not aloud. We don't speak of it." A rule Hodr had clearly broken.

Alara's cheeks colored. "Of course not. My apologies." She resumed slicing the carrots.

"He told me that's why he came, and that if his request was refused, he'd give it all up and return here."

Alara's knife broke with a *tink*. She set it aside and slowly turned. "He said that?"

"Not four nights ago. And I believed him. It's what convinced me he was innocent in intent, if not in deed." Had it only been four nights? She counted the time out on her fingers. By now, Loki should have spoken with his daughter, and Hermod should be with Hel. Baldr would soon be alive again. She'd need to stay in one place long enough for a message from Odin to reach her. She fought down a rush of excited joy when she realized that she hadn't heard what Alara had been saying.

"... wanted me to, you know," Alara said. "But I said I couldn't, not without my family."

She must be referring to the effect of the apples. "That's what it would mean. A wise realization. It shows why he favored you."

Alara blushed slightly and swept the cut carrots into a pot full of bones and other vegetables. She hung the pot on the iron arm suspended above the hearth, filled it with water, and swung it over the fire.

"That's dinner, then?" Frigg asked.

"For tomorrow," Alara said, crossing the small room to where Frigg sat.

"My mother used to cook us similar soups in the winter months. I may've been a chieftain's daughter, but we didn't eat that differently from anyone else. Worse, sometimes, since my father made a point of sharing his table with any in need."

"From what we hear, Almother, you've continued that tradition."

"Now, now, no need for flattery," she said, smiling to make sure Alara didn't take it wrong. "You've already won me over. I think you'll make an excellent wife for my son, and you'll have my blessing regardless what you decide."

"You say that like he won't be . . ."

Publicly killed and left to rot? That was the penalty for murder. She'd pronounced it only twice in all the time Odin had been gone. "With your help, he won't be."

"Whatever you need. Anything." Alara sat on the bench opposite Frigg.

"What can you tell me about the smith Lopt?"

Alara's hands flew to her mouth. "Was that the spear that—"

Frigg nodded.

"Hodr said that spear let him see like you or I do, but in fog. I didn't understand how it could be, but . . ."

Seidr was common enough to be known, but how it worked was a mystery to most—even to herself, and she was married to a man who practiced the art as naturally as he breathed.

"That's what he told me, too," Frigg said. "Do you remember how Hodr got the spear?"

"It'd be impossible to forget. He was coming back from the market when a horse broke loose and trampled him. Broke his skull clean open, caved in his chest—I'd never seen anything like it. But the worst of it mended before the valkyr arrived—"

"Why was that?" If the injuries truly had been that bad, it would have been impossible for him to heal on his own.

"The night before it happened, I think, he'd—" She mimed eating an apple, then resumed speaking in a whisper. "He'd kept it hidden, said it was probably the only thing that saved him."

That was interesting. She'd no idea that a year-old apple would keep enough of whatever it was . . . its magic . . . to restore wounds like that.

"How was the smith involved?" She felt guilty asking since Hodr had already told her, but she'd come here for proof of his innocence. So far, what he'd told her matched what Alara was saying.

"We found out later that it was the smith's horse that had broken free and trampled him. The smith didn't come that day to apologize, I don't remember why, but he came back a few nights later. They spoke for a while in the way house and then went outside. When Hodr came back, he had his new spear. The old one got broken in the accident. I don't know if I said that, or if that's even helpful."

"This is all helpful." Frigg said, leaning forward. "What happened next?"

"Hodr told me what the spear did and then he left—rode out with Lopt to Gladsheim."

"Did anything about that seem unusual to you?"

Alara pursed her lips and thought for a long moment. "I guess? It seemed a little quick. He'd talked about apologizing to his brother for a long time, but he'd never gone. When we heard that the Alfather had returned, he got more serious about it. Then it just sort of happened."

"So he went to apologize to Baldr and to ask about marriage and the future," Frigg said, holding up her hand as if she held an apple.

"Yes, Almother."

She sat back in her chair. Most of this she'd known already. It seemed that Lopt was a real person, rather than someone invented by a shape-changing witch. Time to see where that thread led.

She repeated her original question. "The first time you met the smith was roughly two weeks ago?"

Alara shook her head. "He'd been through maybe once a year for a while now. It's not like I really knew him or anything. He was, I don't know, someone who stayed a night or two and then left again. Dozens of folk do the same."

"So if his horse hadn't trampled Hodr, Lopt probably would've passed through again."

"That's what he'd always done before, as far as I know."

"Was the Lopt you met recently—this will sound strange, but was he the same man you'd known from the times he'd stayed here before?"

Alara gave her an odd look. "I'm not sure I . . ."

"Had Hodr ever told you about shape-shifters?"

Alara's eyes went wide. "Are you saying that—"

Frigg held up her hands. "I'm only asking if Lopt seemed the same. Someone might have pretended to be him."

"I really couldn't say, Almother. Like I said, I didn't know him well."

So much for this being easy. "Do you know where he's from?"

Alara pursed her lips and stared up at the beams. "A village near Ifington—near a bog, I think. I don't remember the name, though. One of the smiths in town probably does."

"I'll check with them. Is there anything else you can think to tell me?"

"About Lopt?"

"Him, or my son."

"Only that Hodr didn't go there to ki—do what he did. When he got that spear, he said he felt like a new man, even with that little bit of sight he said it gave him. I tried to tell him it didn't matter to me, but I didn't have the right words, I guess."

"I've been alive a very long time, and if I've learned anything, it's that most men need to be *doing* to feel whole," Frigg said with a wry smile. "But they never realize that almost always it's what they're *already* doing that's important, not what they could or feel they should do. At least, those are my thoughts on it."

"I suppose that's right, Almother."

She'd never listened to her own elders, either. Frigg put her hands on her knees and made to stand up.

"Almother?"

"Yes?"

"What will happen to him? To Hodr, I mean."

Custom required—demanded—that a murderer be publicly killed. And that was especially true if the murderer was a jarl's child. Examples had to be set. But Frigg was convinced, now more than ever, that Hodr was innocent of intent if not of deed. That was a very narrow ledge to walk, and even if she could prove Hodr's innocence, some folk might not believe it. They'd see the ruler's son escaping a crime. That would further undermine their trust and might eventually lead to more unrest.

Or she could kill her own son to set the example—and live another thousand winters regretting that choice.

"The benefit of being married to a restless man, Alara, is that he has more options at his disposal than most others."

"I don't understand."

Frigg stood and undid the ties holding her sheathed, falcon-headed knife to her belt. She presented it on her palms to Alara. "I saw you break your knife earlier. Take this and keep it with you."

Alara shook her head and stepped back. "I couldn't. It's too fine a —it was a kitchen knife, not a . . ."

Frigg took one of Alara's work-reddened, rough and scratchy hands into her own much softer palms. There'd been a time when she'd practiced with weapons every day, and her hands had shown it.

"It's only a knife, Alara." Vision-flames gathered above Alara's head. She continued, ignoring what was unfolding in the vision. She'd already seen it. "And you were—you are—my son's betrothed. Everything will work out. Accept it as a token of that promise and my love for you."

Tears poured from Alara's eyes. Her lips quivered, and she shook her head from side to side.

Frigg closed Alara's fingers around the knife and then touched her face. "You are worthy. Everyone forgets that Odin and I, and all the other jarls, lived as you do now for a very long time. Worse, perhaps. We didn't have it easy then; you don't have it easy now. But you're working hard, as he did—and me, too. Just because we live on a high hill doesn't mean our problems go away. We've set ourselves up as the wardens for all the Aesir. Believe me, I'd rather have your problems than my own. Hodr loved you for a reason. I see it clearly. One day, if you choose, you'll join him, and us, and find that the high hill is nothing to envy. Until then . . ."

The vision-flames flared, and she couldn't help but see . . .

. . . *Alara raise empty hands to show that she was unarmed. The warriors swaggered further into the hall, twirling their axes and laughing. They threaded through broken tables, shattered benches, and black stains. Something fierce flickered across her face. Her right hand darted down and flew back up clenching a foot of bright skymetal, a gold falcon's head on the pommel. And then everyone dropped to their knees, clutching their ears. Their faces contorted with pain. Alara recovered first. She pushed herself up and darted over to the prone warriors. The falcon-hilted knife flashed up and down, up and down, in a spray of . . .*

"Almother!"

Frigg felt hands take her own.

"Almother! Are you all right?"

She blinked. Alara was right in front of her.

"I'm fine, Alara. Just a . . ." She should tell the truth. ". . . a vision of what might be."

"Of me?"

"No, no, not like that."

But not that much truth. She forced a smile and patted Alara's hands. "Promise me you'll learn to use that knife."

32

LOKI

Day 5, late afternoon

From his perch in the shadowed rafters, Loki watched as Ygg's golden-haired daughter, Hermod, stepped into the hearth light escorted by Hel's corpse-servant. Hel rose to greet Hermod. The two women couldn't have been less alike. Hermod was broad-shouldered and well muscled in the way of most warrior women. Hel was comparatively slight and lean.

Hel smiled, the blackened, twisted flesh that comprised the lower half of her face splitting to reveal white teeth. "Welcome to my home, warrior. I hope you rested well last night. I understand the journey here can be taxing."

"I found it easy enough." Hermod's voice was loud and brash. She waved her hand at Hel's corpse-servant and did a poor job of hiding her revulsion. "An odd way you have of making a guest welcome."

"I grant no guest rights, daughter of Ygg," Hel said. "Your father told you that you were—you are—my hostage?"

"He did. Though I don't expect to be here long."

"As long as it takes for your father to release me."

"Which means you should be about your task, yes? The Alfather is impatient to restore my brother's life."

"I will. After I've eaten." Hel gestured toward the breakfast laid out on the table: dried meat and fish, flatbread. Some goat's milk. A stew warming in a cauldron over the hearth.

Loki was impressed. He hadn't thought it possible for Hermod's spine to stiffen any further, but she accomplished it and dismissed Hel's offer with an abrupt shake of her head.

Sit, girl, he urged. *My daughter means you no harm. Don't make this harder than it needs to be.*

Hermod remained standing. "Very kind, but I'd prefer to depart as quickly as possible."

Hel's smile looked forced to Loki. She was hardly more experienced at this battle of words than Hermod. "It's not a simple thing to unweave the net I cast over your brother's spirit. Nor will it be easy to ensure that your brother's spirit goes to your father when the Hvergelmir tugs so strongly upon it."

Hermod set her hand upon the pommel of her sword. "Then I hope for your sake that you can do what you promised."

Hel spoke after a long, brittle silence. "I don't care for your tone. And even less for your threats."

Hermod took one step forward. "Then be about it."

Had Ygg instructed his daughter to act like this? This should've been a simple transaction falling entirely within the bounds of custom: Provide a hostage to the foe. The foe does what is required. The hostage is released. The feud is ended. Simple and beneficial for all parties.

The wood in the hearth crackled and popped. One log shifted and fell. Hel's corpse-servant shuffled forward, but Hel waved him back. Then she sat down.

Hermod's face went dark with rage. Seems she'd inherited her father's anger issues. "What are you doing?"

"I'm about to eat, as I said," Hel replied evenly. "I'll need all my strength. Your anger is misplaced. I'm not the one who killed your brother. Your brother did that."

"Maybe—but you're benefiting from the deed and his death."

Hel broke off a piece of bread, set some fish upon it, and took a bite. She chewed slowly.

Hermod had more self-control than Loki had thought. She didn't fly into a rage or draw her blade. She gritted her teeth, clenched her fists, and closed her eyes for a brief moment.

Then she opened them, blew out a quiet breath, and surprised him. "Hár Hel, I have clearly offended you. I ask your pardon. Beg for it. We Aesir deeply mourn this double tragedy both because we don't understand it and because my brother Baldr was . . . unique. I loved him deeply. I loved Hodr, too, though I hardly knew him."

With an awkward, young smile, Hermod continued. "Regardless, all of Gladsheim mourns Baldr's loss. Over the last dozen years and more, he labored to bring a lasting peace between the Aesir and Jotunn. He was often in Jotunheim, healing their sick and dying and trying to figure out why so many Jotunn babies are dying.

"On my journey down here, I saw meltwater dripping from the trees and the stones, and to me it looked like they too mourned Baldr's death. I can't help but think, to hope, that everyone mourns him—my people and the Jotunn alike. I think that's one reason my father wants to bring him back, so that our people have a chance at peace."

Hel wore a grave expression. She rested one hand on the grip of the hand distaff hanging from her belt. Beside it rode a pouch and, on her other hip, a long seax in a black scabbard. When she spoke, her voice sounded distant. "Not long after I was stranded here, I named this knife Famine, for it's all that kept me from starving. I named my dish Hunger, for my belly rumbled every time I ate from it."

She gave a sad little laugh. "The entrance to this house I called Stumbling Block, since that's what happened not a month after my father and I finished building it. My bed became my sickbed. I lay in it for days. Weeks. Sick, finally, from this place's damp chill and my own labors helping my father. And then . . ."

Loki remembered how frantic he'd become when she'd fallen ill and then lapsed into a pale stillness. He'd flown back to Gladsheim, stolen medicinal powders and poultices from Baldr, and hurried back. She came back to him after nearly a fortnight of constant tending. She brought with her a new reason to hate the Aesir. She'd gotten sick because they'd exiled her; their medicines were all that had saved her.

Hel glanced up at the corner where he hid and shrugged. "Your father and brother tried to heal me, you know, after I was born. My father and mother—she's dead—brought me to him. They told me Baldr labored hard over me, and that what movement and feeling I have in my arm and face, and what sight I have in this white eye, may well be because of his efforts."

Yet another log on the fire of his hatred for the Aesir.

"I pulled Baldr's spirit out of the Naglfar because I wanted to be free, as I want my brothers to be. But I also did it to honor the help he gave me. To thank him again, as I thanked him when I was old enough to speak. He was kind to me. He kissed my cheek"—she touched the blue-black stain that marred half of her lovely face —"and said he was sorry he couldn't have done more for me. Three winters later, your father exiled me and my brothers from Gladsheim."

Hel's smile faded. "I loved your brother for trying to heal me and even more for his lack of pity. For his kindness. For not turning away when he looked at me because of this blight on my flesh that the Norns cursed me with."

Silence fell. Then it stretched.

Hel broke the silence, her voice flinty. "So I think I may keep him with me forever, maybe raise him like I did Ganglieri here," Hel said, indicating her corpse-servant. "But better."

Loki nearly fell from his perch.

Hermod's mouth worked like a dying fish's. "You can't. You made a deal."

Why had she changed the plan?

"Can't I? None can undo what I did except me. And why should I be free if everywhere I go, people like you treat me like you did?"

"But . . . I'm . . ."

They'd agreed that she would go through with her plan.

Hel raised a hand. "But I did make a deal. Which I'm changing. Just now you claimed something that I think should be put to the test."

Ygg would certainly kill her now.

"Wha—what did I say?"

"You claimed that all things weep for Baldr. Stone and metal, grass and trees. Jotunn. Hyperbole, perhaps, but let's see if it's true."

Hermod shook her head as if to say *No, no, I wasn't being literal*. He pitied her a little bit in that moment.

"Hear me, Goldtooth," Hel said loudly. "Tell your master that if he wants Baldr's spirit, then he must find the Jotunn woman named Thokk. If she weeps when told that Baldr is dead, then I will send Baldr's spirit winging back to him. If not, Baldr will remain here as an honored guest. Rest assured, Ygg, I will know if Thokk cries. What you do after that is on your own head."

Hermod's face was a thundercloud. Her hand had crept back to the hilt of her blade. "Who is this person?"

"A crone named Thokk. She lives in Utgard. I don't know where; that was not given to me." Hel gestured at the chair opposite her. "So, daughter of Odin, you are welcome to break your fast with me, or I will have a meal brought to you. This house is big enough for the two of us. Either way, you will remain here as my hostage until your father keeps his word."

The afterwalker, Ganglieri, lurched into motion. Hermod fell back a pace, outrage and disbelief etched on her face. She grasped her sword's hilt with one hand.

In that moment of tumult, Hel looked right at him and with her hands said, "I'll tell you where Thokk is. It's up to you now, Father."

Then Hel turned back to dealing with Hermod. Ganglieri had staggered toward the table and picked up a platter of food. Odin's daughter had let go her sword, evidently decided that an afterwalker with some fish and flatbreads wasn't a threat.

This was exactly why Loki preferred to keep his plans secret—he only had himself to blame when things went wrong.

33

ODIN

Day 5, night

Odin slammed his fist against the stone wall as Heimdall fell silent.

Until your father keeps his word.

Rán's piss, what was Hermod thinking to have started out like that? She'd known what was at stake. No, that wasn't entirely fair. It almost sounded as though Hel had been looking for a reason to take offense. By all the sweeps on the Naglfar, why would she change the deal? He would have kept his word.

Odin blew out a long breath and closed his eye, willing his sacrificed eye to open and grant him a sight he could use. A blood-red haze dropped across his mind's eye. He saw Hermod . . .

. . . standing opposite Hel, a hearth between them. The firelight made Hel's disfigurement even more awful. Surprise and anger, shock and embarrassment, and most of all, the realization of failure were cut in deep lines on Hermod's face. Hel's attention shifted. She looked directly at him, her eyes flared white . . .

He stumbled backward. Heimdall caught him by the arm.

"Odin?"

Carefully, he touched the patch over his eye. The socket beneath was warm, but his fingers came away dry rather than coated with the blood he'd expected. "I think I saw them, cousin. Hel and Hermod both standing inside Hel's home."

Heimdall raised an eyebrow. A long pale scar ran like a road beneath his eyes and over the bridge of his nose, making the tight press of his lips grimmer still. "That is what you'd wanted."

Indeed it was. "I'd hoped for more control."

"You've mastered more seidr than I knew existed," Heimdall said, releasing him and stepping back to lean against the north wall. "In time you'll master this sight, too."

"Is that all, then?" Odin asked. "That's all Hel said?"

Heimdall's eyes closed again as he listened. "All that's important. Hermod says, 'Sorry, Father. I failed both you and him.' "

"Did they say anything else to each other beyond what you've told me?"

Heimdall shook his head.

"Did you hear what Loki and Hel said to each other?" Loki would've used the Jotunn hand speech, but it didn't hurt to ask.

"Only the innocuous words they exchanged when he arrived and again when he left the following night," Heimdall said. "Do you suspect Loki of having done the opposite of what you asked him to do?"

Did he? That thought staggered around his mind like a drunkard on a heaving longship. It wasn't in Loki's best interests to betray him. And yet, Odin had uncovered that memory of Loki promising to rain destruction down upon Odin and all the Aesir. Was the memory true, or had it been planted in his mind by the thing that had attacked him from beneath Urdr's Well?

He had no idea.

He put his head in his hands and leaned against the stone wall. Heimdall gripped his shoulder. It was time to check on Baldr now, too. Four nights already, tonight marking the fifth. He should still have another four before Odin's weave failed and the rot took him.

"Who is this Thokk, Heimdall? What is she to Hel? Why make

such an absurd demand when the deal was made? I would have kept my word."

Heimdall gave his shoulder a final squeeze and gestured northward. "I'll start looking for her. I'm guessing she's a Jotunn woman, so . . ."

"Where is Thor?"

"On his way back to Thrudheim. I need to tell you what he found, Odin."

"And where is Frigg right now?"

"Ifington, but she'll be leaving for Jarnstadr shortly. It's a village northeast of Ifington."

He couldn't be the one to speak with Thokk; there wasn't enough time to travel there and back again. But Frigg could. In Ifington or now Jarnstadr, she was at least two nights closer to Jotunheim than he was.

"How long to find this Thokk?" he asked.

Heimdall wore a distracted look. He raised a hand. He inhaled deeply and held his breath, obviously listening.

"Heimdall?"

"I heard you," he snapped. "I've no idea how long it will take. Might as well ask me to search the beaches for a particular stone."

"I will help you, cousin," Odin replied carefully. "I'll leave for my High Seat—"

Heimdall gave him a forced, gold-toothed smile. "You know, it's not the seeing that troubles me." He tapped his ear. "It's this. Last night, a man named Rollo drowned in the Eastern Sea. I heard his death rattle as clearly as I heard his mates shouting his name. That was after Frigg spoke with Hodr's Alara last night. Did I mention that? Alara sounds like a sweet woman who brought peace to my nephew. She doesn't believe that Hodr intended to kill Baldr."

"Heimdall, I under—"

"And then as Sól rose this morning, Freyja sacrificed the priest who didn't capture Gulfinn's disir. In Utgard, the Jotunn shaman Vafthrudnir and the Skrymir discussed the best way to honor Baldr without offending you. As you and I speak, two drunken farmers are arguing over the boundaries of their fields. A cart's wheel has fallen off and its blocking traffic out of the western gate. A child's fallen sick in Ifington, coughing and vomiting. Thor's whistling, and Vidar's shouting orders. Hel tells her dead servant to make sure your daughter doesn't leave. And those birds in Vanaheim . . . They never stop squawking my name!"

His eyes sank closed. "But you know who I never hear unless he wants me to? Loki. Would that he'd buried his blade in my ears. I can close my eyes, Odin, but I cannot shut out the sounds."

Odin waited for his cousin to continue, but Heimdall had finished. "Are you done?"

Heimdall's pale face flushed with rage. "Am I—"

"Don't, cousin," Odin said. "You better than anyone know what's going on, what we face. And you stand there whining because a bunch of birds squawk your name?"

"You can't imagine what it's like." Heimdall's hand fell on the pommel of his sword, Hofud.

Odin took him by the shoulders. "No, I can't. But we need you. I need you. Find Thokk for me. I will help."

"It could take nights to find her," Heimdall said. "How will you get to her in time—"

"Leave that to me. Just find her. Once we have Baldr back, I'll bend all my strength to undoing Loki's mischief. All right?"

For a long moment, Heimdall looked as if he still wanted to fight. "All right."

Odin slapped his shoulder. "Good. Now, tell me what's happening with Thor and Vidar."

———

Máni was well above the eastern peaks before Heimdall had finished relating what Thor had discovered. Stars glinted overhead.

"So Thor found drag marks back and forth between the lake and the nearby cliff, which had been collapsed to hide whatever had been there," Odin said, "but he's uncertain it's the same lake that Vidar described."

Heimdall sipped the cold, fresh water the thrall had brought up the tower after restocking the firewood. "Correct. He said it was a Jotunn stone-home beneath the cliffs."

That made sense. Many long winters ago, the Jotunn had shaped entire villages into the stone beneath mountains. They abandoned most of them after the Last War, but perhaps some were still active. Perhaps this stone-home belonged to the supposed rogue tribe that had razed Háls. If that whole story hadn't been a lie.

"Sounds like an ideal place to plot against us."

"It does indeed."

"And Thor saw no other Jotunn activity on his trip up there?"

"Not that he said. If he'd seen something unusual . . ."

Thor would have destroyed any obvious threat. "We're reacting, Heimdall. Attacked from within, unexplained events outside. A plan's in motion, but it's hull down on the horizon. We're just glimpsing its sails."

"I agree, though I've seen no army—nor heard one." Heimdall gestured vaguely northward. "We know the Jotunn speak with their hands, but moving the number of warriors they'd need to attack either city . . . That'd make some noise. Someone would say something."

"Not to mention the fact that they shouldn't have enough warriors to be a threat. And if they did have enough—"

"—I should hear them," Heimdall finished. "So much for the peace Baldr sought, eh?"

Odin grunted and stared into the fire. What to do? Could he force another vision? His missing eye had shown him Hel and Hermod. Perhaps he could see more.

He threw a pair of logs onto the smoldering brazier at the center of Heimdall's tower and stoked the fire until the heat grew steady on his face and his hands warmed. He stared at the burning wood in the brazier, willing his missing eye to see.

Nothing. But, it worked before.

He closed his remaining eye.

Reds and yellows slithered across the blackness. Those dull colors faded to . . .

. . . *reddish-brown trails that crisscrossed around him. He lay flat on cold stone. He tried to sit up. Couldn't. Looking down, he saw his arms and legs and chest bound tight to gray stone with twisted ropes of guts. Those were his . . .*

"Odin, are you listening?" Heimdall said.

He blinked back to the night sky. He'd seen that bloody rope of guts before. Was it meaningful to have seen it twice? Frigg saw the same doom played out again and again, but that didn't mean his sight worked the same way.

"Odin!"

He blinked with irritation. "What? I'm listening."

Heimdall snorted. "Vidar's reported again."

"And?"

"The warband that had been chasing him since Háls broke off pursuit in the last day. He's going after it."

"That's odd, that they broke off." Did they think they couldn't defeat Vidar's warband? Or did they have another goal? "Can you see or hear the Jotunn warband?"

"I hear them moving, but I . . ." Heimdall squinted northward. "No, I can't see them. They're still in the forest."

Odin laid his hands flat on the stone wall. Bad enough to have a Jotunn warband marching through your lands. Worse to not know where it was. But fine, let them come.

"Vidar asks that you send reinforcements and spare horses so he can send his wounded back."

Huginn.

Yes, Wing-Father. The raven stirred from his perch on the tower wall.

Fly to Saglund. Tell him I need to speak with him in the morning.

Yes, Wing-Father.

"I'll speak with Saglund in the morning about sending a warband north," he said. "Can you tell the Einherjar where to meet Vidar?"

Heimdall pursed his lips and turned back northward. "I'll get them close enough that they should be able to find each other."

Beneath the moon's brightness, the Bifrost coursed like a river through the sky. The sight dragged a yawn from him. "Tomorrow I'll go to my High Seat and help you find Thokk. I'll look elsewhere, too. Maybe I'll glimpse what the Jotunn are really up to."

"Thank you, Odin."

He thumped the stone and turned to leave. "I must say, old friend, I don't relish this coming war."

Heimdall's gold teeth glittered in the yellow light of the brazier. "I thought you wanted to wipe the Jotunn out of existence. You should welcome this war."

"No, cousin. Only the wars I start."

34

ODIN

Day 6, before dawn

Odin stepped out of the larder into the snowy clearing behind the Great Hall. His breath frosted in dawn's chill. He tugged shut the door to the larder where Baldr's body lay. The charm he'd woven to protect his son's body from the rot had grown threadbare. At most, it would last another three nights.

Odin headed back toward the Great Hall, stepping in his own footprints as he went. Three nights wasn't much time. But it would be enough. He'd help Heimdall find Thokk, which meant eschewing his other duties and going to his High Seat.

A man cleared his throat.

He glanced up toward the sound. A stocky man in a heavy red cloak stepped out from the shelter of the pines.

"Sigfather. I hope I don't intrude," Hersir Saglund said, raising a hand in greeting. "You said we should speak first thing."

"I didn't mean it so literally," Odin said. "But I appreciate your dedication."

Saglund led the Einherjar. He'd done so ambitiously, more than doubling the number of Einherjar during the last twenty winters and increasing his influence and personal power to the point that Frigg had checked him. Odin would continue to prune the man's authority.

"I serve at your pleasure, Sigfather." Saglund crunched toward him, using the path Odin's feet had made through the fresh snow. He stopped about a sword's length away. "What did you want to discuss?"

"I'm sure Fimafeng has set some wine out in the hall," Odin said, gesturing toward the fir tree–lined path and his own track of footsteps in the snow that led back to the Great Hall. It was barely wide enough for them to walk side by side.

Saglund fell into step a half-pace behind Odin. Saglund's sheathed sword banged against his leg. He put his left hand on the pommel to steady it. "I have finally received reports from all the Einherjar garrisons, Sigfather, so I can tell you exactly how many there are and where."

Up ahead, the path narrowed as it turned left toward the rear of the Great Hall beneath a snow-laden branch that hung out too far into the path.

"Excellent," Odin said. "I'm glad you bring it up, because Heimdall heard from Vidar late last night."

Saglund stepped to one side and pressed the offending branch down and out of Odin's way. Lumps of snow plopped down. Odin nodded his thanks and stepped past. The distant rear door of the hall creaked, and yellow light flooded out over the snow, illuminating everything but the single set of footprints leading from the hall to where he stood.

A broad-shouldered man stepped through the open door, and a hunched figure moved into the yellow frame.

Odin heard Saglund's distant voice say, "Thank you, Fimafeng, but I'm warm enough. I'll wait for him at the tree line."

Saglund's distant voice.

A *single* set of footprints.

Behind him on his left came the sickening, crackling grind of bones breaking. No, not breaking—being reshaped. He drew on his fylgja's power and moved in toward Saglund, his left arm swinging out to block the low strike he knew was coming. Let the thick leather on his forearm take some damage rather than his lower back.

Saglund's thrusting arm slammed into his. Only his fylgja's strength enabled him to parry, even as white fire ripped into the flesh above his hip and dragged across his lower back.

Freki! Geri!

He brought Gungnir into his right hand and jabbed the spear at the false Saglund. False Saglund slipped to one side and grinned. A wet spike of bone jutted from where his hand should have been. He licked Odin's blood from the spike.

Stupid. You almost had me.

Odin dropped into the shape of a lean gray wolf. As he did, he sensed someone behind him.

A second attacker. Not stupid at all. A distraction.

The second witch's thrust with a knife passed through empty air instead of his now wolven back. The plot had almost worked. Almost.

"Sigfather?" came the real Saglund's cry, closer than before.

We come, Freki said.

"Run, sister," False Saglund hissed. "Help the others finish the work."

Odin charged forward and slammed sideways into False Saglund, knocking him back into the snow-laden boughs. The witch rebounded and slashed wildly with her bone-spiked arm, forcing him to back up.

He shifted back to himself. From the corner of his eye he saw the second witch shift into an owl and flee.

"He was right—you are hard to kill," False Saglund said, his eyes darting left and right. With a sickening crackle, his other hand became a matching bone spike.

"Yelena, I presume?" Odin brought Gungnir to hand again.

False Saglund's smile grew wider.

"Sigfather!" yelled the true Saglund.

"Were you behind my son's death?" Odin demanded.

We are near, Freki said. And indeed, he could feel them getting closer. He'd left them sleeping in his room. This would be the last time he went anywhere without them.

False Saglund surged forward, lashing out with both spiked hands at Odin's eyes. Odin slid back, avoiding the cuts. With a pop, False Saglund vanished. In his place, a black cat dropped into the churned snow and sprinted away beneath the low-hanging fir branches.

Odin swore and whirled to see Saglund standing on the path, sword out, breath pluming.

"Rouse the Einherjar!" Odin said. "We're under attack."

Saglund blinked, and his mouth opened and closed. "Yes, Sigfather."

Odin took a step toward the path. "Heimdall, hear me! Watch the tree line near where I stand. You may glimpse an owl flying away. If so, it's a witch. Track her."

The fir trees ran the entire length of the cliff behind him, from the road up to the highest tier, where Aegir's Temple was, to the other. The trees grew twenty yards deep at their widest. He doubted Heimdall would see the witches fleeing. They'd sneak away and regroup with their sisters. Their coven. What work were they about? Other than trying to kill him.

"And Heimdall, alert the wardens."

A few heartbeats later, the deep voice of the warden horn's rang out over Gladsheim.

Odin strode out of the fir trees into the clearing that ringed the Great Hall and the other buildings. Freki and Geri padded toward him, wary but no longer rushing. They could sense that the immediate danger had passed. From inside the hall came muted shouts and the dull thud of pounding feet. He headed toward the sounds.

Ráta rushed out. "Sigfather, we're under attack. Witches." Her eyes widened as she took in the scene. "But you've found out already. How many?"

"Two. One took Saglund's shape and got close enough to do this." He turned so she could see the slash. "They know our limitations. Be careful."

She nodded, hot fury in her eyes. "There are more in the city, riding the roofs. The wardens received reports of livestock slaughtered throughout the city and widespread spoilage of foodstuffs—rotted, as if they'd been left in the hot sun."

"A full coven?"

"I don't know. Hard to say from the reports."

"Are the Sons also involved?" The Sons of Muspell had already burned most of the city's storehouses three nights earlier. "What about the wells and the river?"

"No signs that they're being attacked. Since the Sons' attack, the Einherjar have been guarding the bridge and the wells."

Odin grunted. He reached back and touched his wound. It was deep enough to be irritating. He released Gungnir, removed his cloak, and pulled his satchel over his head to begin removing his cloak, overtunic, and shirt. His skin prickled in the morning air. "Anything from Heimdall regarding an approaching army?"

"No, Sigfather," Ráta said.

He cut his shirt apart, took half of it, and folded it into a compress. Then he took a winding cloth from his satchel and had Ráta tie it tight.

Thunder rumbled. He glanced up at the darkening clouds. "Heimdall said Thor was nearly back in Thrudheim."

Lightning stabbed down into Gladsheim's lowest tier. Thunder hammered the city.

He dressed quickly. "Find an Einherjar warband, Ráta, and stay with them. Show them how to fight these witches."

"Yes, Sigfather," she said.

"I'll send Freki or Geri for you when I draw the witches' attention and they converge on me. I'll need you watching my back."

Lightning flashed again. The thunder rolled, long and sullen. Smoke was beginning to rise into the sky above his city. Again.

He lifted his arms and with a powerful downstroke of golden wings, he soared up into the night sky. It was long past time to take the fight to his enemies.

35

ODIN

Day 6, dawn

Odin ripped Gungnir's blade from the chest of the dead witch. He held the spear crossways, ready to slash or club with the spiked butt. Freki had his back. He'd sent Geri to bring Ráta and some Einherjar.

He stood in a large paddock surrounded by the unnaturally rotted corpses of a hundred head of oxen. The ground was scorched and muddied. Lightning crackled through black clouds; flurries were falling. Though it was past dawn, Sól had yet to show her face.

So far, he'd fought three witches who'd tried to surprise him. One had sent fire roaring at him. Another had tried to bind his limbs with a song similar to his own. The third had taken a great-cat's shape and pounced at him. Freki had held the cat at bay while Odin had bent the fire back upon its sender and turned the binding song to his will by making it engulf the limbs of the great-cat. Then he'd gutted it. The two others had fled.

He whipped Gungnir around and severed the witch's head. Best to be safe.

The air stunk of burning hair, blood, and offal. The snow-covered, thatched roofs of the three buildings in front of him hunched like giants' shoulders. Three broad-winged birds spiraled down from the storm clouds, talons outstretched. Two landed together on one roof; the third landed on another. As they touched down, they shifted into women.

"Son of Burr," called the lone witch, her honeyed voice laden with hate. "That's the last of my sisters you'll violate."

Be ready, Freki.

He drank from the well of his fylgja's power. His body thrummed with her strength.

Freki rumbled eagerly.

"The day is young," he called back. "Is this Yelena who speaks? Or is she still hiding behind her sisters' skirts?"

The witch didn't answer.

"Or maybe I've killed her already," he said, and kicked the dead witch in front of him.

Huginn, Muninn, he said, *stay where you are. Watch.*

His ravens were perched beneath the eves of the nearby hall. He himself would feel the wounds suffered by his familiars. Freki and Geri were far tougher and deadlier than Huginn and Muninn.

We obey, Wing-Father.

Freki rumbled a warning. A trio of black-haired, silver-backed monstrosities with long, heavily muscled arms and shorter hind legs were moving into place between each of the buildings, maybe thirty yards away.

That made seven witches total—two on one roof, one on a second roof, three on the ground and one dead before him. A full coven.

From the corner of his eye, Odin saw the pair of witches on the first roof join hands and thrust their free hands up toward the sky. Sparks played about their shoulders. Their hair stood on end.

The three massive silverback-witches charged, knuckles driving into the ground and squelching into ox corpses. Freki snarled and leaped forward.

On the roof of the first building, lightning forked down from the clouds and blasted into the witches' arms. A ball of lightning crackled above their heads and between their upraised hands. The snow on the roof melted and the thatch began to smoke and burn.

Odin hurled Gungnir at the leftmost witch of that pair. He could have made the throw without his fylgja's strength; with it, Gungnir flew faster than an arrow, slammed into the witch's chest, and knocked her off the roof.

Her coven mate lost control of the lightning. It blew up in her face, knocking her lengthwise along the roof. She skidded to a halt and didn't stir.

The lone witch on the second roof who'd called out to him had vanished.

Odin turned to see Freki slam deliberately into the leftmost charging silverback, knocking it sideways into the path of the second silverback. They skidded to a halt. Freki cut back to block both of them. She'd need help momentarily, but the third silverback-witch was nearly upon Odin.

Odin braced for impact. The massive black-haired beast slammed into him, knocked him backward off his feet. It was like getting hit by a pair of horses. He flung his arms out behind him to absorb some of impact before his back hit the corpse of a dead ox. He rolled backward, heels over head, spitting putrescence as he rose to a crouch.

Geri, I need you.

I am near, Geri said.

The silverback that knocked him down skidded to a halt.

He could feel Freki's snarling fury, but he had no sense of how well she was doing against her two witches.

Where is Ráta?

The silverback-witch charged again.

Also close, Geri said.

Odin opened his hands. Gungnir swayed into them. Two-handed, he blocked the double-hammer blow of fists the third silverback was attempting to rain down on him. He drank still deeper from his fylgja's power, beginning to feel the familiar golden haze rising to distort his sight. Fist after fist slammed downward. Each time, he blocked with Gungnir. A lesser weapon would have splintered. He diverted the next two blows to one side and then the other, trying to unbalance the witch.

Freki yelped, and pain exploded in Odin's right arm and side. The witch closed her black, leathery hands around the spear and tugged. Weakened as he was by Freki's pain, the witch was able to rip Gungnir out of his hands.

She flung it away and followed up with a fast, unbelievably powerful pair of blows that cracked his ribs and sent him reeling. She charged again, massive hands lifted high to crush him.

Huginn and Muninn flew into her face, talons tearing at her eyes. The witch staggered backward, batting ineffectually at the ravens.

Odin brought Gungnir back to his hands and spun in a tight circle, slashing the witch's exposed belly. Steaming guts spilled free. The witch gave a great, hoarse cough that produced as much blood as sound. She fell heavily, one thick arm wrapped around the wound, trying to keep her stinking innards where they belonged. Even as she did, her form reverted to a woman's—small and lean, head shaved on the sides, dark hair pulled into a topknot. She vomited more blood in a wet, weak cough.

He cut her head off.

Well done my friends, Odin said to his ravens.

A throat-tearing chant resounded from atop the roof behind him. Lightning burned through the spiraling clouds. The witch who'd been alone on the roof again stood by herself, hands thrust up toward the sky.

Pain lanced through Odin's right arm. He glanced toward where he felt Freki, maybe ten yards away. Freki was standing but heavily favoring her right foreleg and side, head lowered, slavering, ears back. The two silverbacks she'd intercepted had backed her against one longhouse.

One of those witches glanced toward Odin. The witch's thick-lipped mouth parted to reveal large, yellowed fangs. Her huge head swung back to Freki and then her sister witch. Odin watched her deciding what to do—either charge him, leaving her sister to deal with the wounded wolf, or stay and help kill the wolf. Her muscles bunched, and she leaped at him.

Mistake.

I am here, Geri said.

The silverback had already closed half the distance.

Help Freki!

The air crackled around him; the small hairs on the back of his neck rose. He threw himself sideways right before lightning blasted a smoking crater into the ground where he'd stood.

Before he could roll to his feet, huge leathery fists slammed one after the other into his chest. More ribs cracked. He got Gungnir between himself and the silverback.

He had to stand.

He pulled hard on his fylgja's strength. The golden haze across his vision leaped higher as she answered, grinning, eager to wrest control from him. *Not this time, Slídr.*

And then Ráta was there, standing over him, golden knives flashing in each hand as she drove the silverback back with sweeping cuts and quick thrusts. The silverback bellowed and gnashed her yellow fangs as she retreated.

Odin came up on one knee.

Over her shoulder, Ráta shouted, "The Einherjar are on their way, Sigfather."

And then she threw herself at the silverback, knives again flashing in glimmering arcs. The silverback shuffled further away, roaring and spitting as she went.

"One of his whores takes her place beside him," shouted the witch from atop the roof.

Odin turned to face her, putting his back to Ráta. The silverback was still there, but for the moment seemed to have given up the attack. He felt Ráta moving back toward him.

Three witches were dead for certain. A fourth had maybe been killed when the lightning had blown up in her face. So, three, maybe four, left. Unless more than one coven had attacked.

"That's good! More flesh for the wyrm," the witch atop the roof shouted, her arm again shooting straight up toward the roiling black clouds. She was drawing more lightning, preparing to hurl another bolt.

Odin slammed Gungnir's spiked butt into the ground and reached into his satchel. He would bind these witches and beat answers out of them. His gaze passed over the empty roof where the two witches had been. He'd killed one from that empty roof and thought he'd done for the other.

But the roof was empty.

Then he realized that Ráta was wielding knives. She always used the axes he'd given her. And the air should have been buzzing with the sound of bees—the hum of Ráta drawing upon her fylgja's power.

Odin was turning to face the attack even as it came in. But he was too slow by far.

Ráta—no, false Ráta—buried one golden knife in the left side of his stomach, just above the long gouge given him by another witch not long ago. He grabbed the witch's hand in his left and kept her from ripping the knife out.

He was able to divert the other stabbing knife, mostly. Instead of plunging to the hilt into the right side of his stomach, it cut a long, deep furrow across his ribs. He caught the arm that held it.

She struggled, trying to free herself. He smashed her nose with his forehead. Hot, tangy blood ran into his mouth. He pulled her closer and rammed his head down again. Her shocked expression went slack, and she crumpled in his arms. She had Ráta's form but not her strength. This witch was only a woman right now. Odin squeezed his left hand and crushed her right forearm. She shrieked in agony.

A red-gold haze shrouded his sight and muffled his ears. His own blood pounded in his head even as it poured from his wounds. Through it all, he glimpsed the lone witch astride the roof. He heard her screamed chant. The air began crackling around him; his skin tingled.

He wrenched the witch's left arm, eliciting another hoarse shriek and then a gasping shudder as he stripped the golden knife from her limp hand. With that knife, he pointed at the witch standing on the roof.

Odin spoke a rune word.

The wind rose to a howling shriek and blew the witch from the roof. The tingling of imminent lightning vanished.

One golden knife in his right hand, the other still in his stomach, he turned back to the broken witch dangling from his left hand. The stab wound was agony itself. Blood sheeted from the sweeping gash across his ribs. He pulled still harder on his fylgja's strength, and the pain drifted away.

The witch hung in his grasp, panting. He could feel her trying to shape-shift, so he squeezed her hand. The broken bones grated on each other as he pulverized them. She howled again, twitching, weeping. He drove the golden knife up under her chin into her brain. She convulsed and went limp.

He dropped her. Now there were four dead witches. He turned toward Freki and Geri.

Geri had clamped his teeth on the silverback's rear left leg, while Freki had her by the throat. Geri released his grip. Freki shook the witch by the throat till her neck broke with a *crack*. The silverback dwindled to a small woman's form. Freki dropped her.

Five dead.

The silverback the false Ráta had been fighting stood unmoving about two spear lengths away. Horror and indecision warred on the battlefield of her intelligent, seamed face. It appeared that fear killed witches, too.

Odin pointed and spoke another rune word. The air sang like tempered steel, and the silverback reverted to a middle-aged woman, lean and lithe. Geri took the witch by the throat, Freki by the leg.

Six dead.

One left. Probably. Every coven he'd ever fought had been seven strong.

Driven mad by his rune word, the wind was blowing swirls of snow that obscured the longhouses and the ragged fence that now surrounded so much death. He stretched out his hand and calmed the wind with another rune word.

The last witch had climbed back onto the roof—or flown. It didn't matter. Even from this distance, she looked shocked.

"Yelena!" he shouted, though he was only guessing at her name. "I told you the day was young."

Thunder rumbled overhead. The lightning flashed. The witch had one hand up to the sky and the other pointed at—not him, but his wolves. Lightning began to stream downward toward her upraised hand.

Odin grimaced. She was a slow learner.

He snatched up Gungnir and hurled it at the witch. His wounds screamed at being wrenched, and he fell to his knees. Through a bloody haze, he saw the last witch become a vulture and leap upward. Gungnir clipped her left wing as she lifted off.

Odin leaned back and watched a few feathers drift downward. The vulture vanished into the gray sky while his red-gold haze faded to darkness.

36

FRIGG

Day 6, late afternoon

Hands on her hips, Frigg frowned down at the burial mound. It was about waist high, excluding the handbreadth of newly fallen snow that covered the hill west of Jarnstadr. The heavy white clouds above promised more snow soon.

"I'm sorry to ask this again, gothi," she said, "but you're certain the smith and his family are all buried here?"

Gothi Svar was a tall, slight man, middle-aged and balding, with a stained gray cloak over his thick brown woolen clothes, well made and well worn. "I helped lay their bodies in there myself, Almother. All eleven. Sad night that was. The whole family, lost."

"Any disturbances since then?"

"I'm not sure what you mean, Almother?"

She fixed her eye on him. He was nearly a head taller but so deferential that it hardly seemed that she was looking up at him.

His blue eyes widened, and his face flushed. "Absolutely not, Almother. This is a small town. We would've known—and dealt with it."

Rising as a draugr rarely happened, but when it did, it was

usually because the deceased had a score to settle. Dispatching them was never easy.

She gave him a tight smile and nodded. "I had to ask. I intended no disrespect to you, your village, or the dead."

He bowed his head. "It never occurred to me that you might, Almother. It's just that—well, it was a tragedy that rocked us. Not many of us here, and we're all into each other's business. Probably too much. And then to have the Almother herself visit and ask questions about our smith—former smith. It's another shock."

"You've handled it better than most," she said, putting some warmth into the words. "Come, show me the village. And if you would, introduce me to any who knew Lopt particularly well."

"AND THIS WAS THE OLD SMITHY." Svar gestured toward a large mound of earth with the vaguest outline of stone showing where the forge had stood. A sword's length deep trench ringed the entire site. "The fire was so freakish that we were all a little worried that, you know"— he wiggled his fingers toward the ruin—"magic was involved."

It was odd that a smith's house would burn down. Accidents could happen to anyone, and fire was always a worry. But for a house fire to spread to the forge? It sounded like something that involved magic. Or a witch named Yelena, perhaps.

"This is where Lopt forged the weapons he made for the Einherjar?" she asked.

The gothi nodded. "The army, too, I think. His eldest helped him. The others sons handled the ironwork for the village and the surrounding hamlets while they learned the finer arts of forging."

Eleven men, women, and children burned to death. A brutal way to cover your tracks.

"And you said it happened at the end of summer?"

"Yes, the night of the festival in the late hours before dawn," the gothi said.

"So Lopt and his family had been at the festival?"

"I think so. I remember Lopt's eldest limping around on crutches. That crazy horse of theirs had injured him. My memory's not what it was, but they must've all been there. The whole village goes, as do many from the nearest hamlets and homesteads. We hold it in yonder field."

He gestured eastward toward the wide, snow-covered field she'd flown over on her way into the village. She noticed now that the clouds above had fulfilled their promise. The snowfall was light but steady.

"It happened before dawn. Old Thom rang the bell that woke us; he never sleeps. When I arrived—not a long run, you just walked it— both the longhouse and forge were ablaze. Fire higher than the trees. I joined the line throwing water and dirt on the fire, but sweet Aegir, it was so hot we couldn't get close without catching fire ourselves. A few of the still-drunk ones tried, soaking their clothes and themselves and then running into the flames—Lopt's grandchildren were in there—but they couldn't do it. All we ended up doing was to keep the fire from spreading. You can see how close those other houses are."

To the left stood a longhouse next to the forge. On the other side, a few goats and sheep wandered in a large fenced area, their noses white from pushing through the snow. The fence ended at a weathered barn attached to a longhouse with a sod roof.

"How old were they?"

"The grandchildren?"

She nodded.

"The oldest was . . . Let's see, my own Bergl was six this winter, so Lopt's oldest had to be seven or eight winters, easy." He shuddered. "The youngest was only three."

Frigg concentrated, willing the vision-flames to appear above the gothi's head. To her surprise, they obeyed. In them, she saw that . . .

. . . fire had eaten everything right down to the ground. The gothi was nothing but one set of charred bones on a field of blackened, contorted limbs. Soot and ash swirled in the wind . . .

". . . so it didn't seem right to rebuild. Once the buildings had collapsed in on themselves, we kept piling dirt on the worst parts.

Then when we recovered the bodies—and that was awful—we covered over the whole horrible mess. Even so, it smoldered for days."

Tears coursed down Svar's face.

She touched his shoulder. "Your people are lucky to have you, gothi."

He sniffed and shrugged. "You're kind to say so, Almother. I wish we'd been able to save them—and I wish I knew how it happened."

She had a good idea, but she'd spare him that.

"May I ask why you've come asking questions about Lopt, Almother?"

No good would come of being honest. "Some of his weapons fell into the wrong hands. I came to ask him about it."

"I see," the gothi said, a hundred more questions swimming like fish in his eyes. "Would you join us in the hall tonight, Almother? We'd honor you and, if I may, the passing of your son."

She glanced up at the gray sky and the now heavier snowfall. It weighed on her heart, but she squared her shoulders and smiled at the gothi. "It would give me great pleasure to spend some time with the brave folk of Jarnstadr."

———

LATE THAT NIGHT, Frigg lay awake in the gothi's bed listening to the howling wind. He and his wife had insisted she take it. It would've insulted them had she refused. And besides, she couldn't fly during a blizzard.

The smith Lopt had lived and worked in Jarnstadr all his life, supplying weapons to the army and then, in later years, to the Einherjar. He'd regularly traveled through Ifington and then down to Gladsheim making his deliveries. Both of his sons had become smiths. One would take over his father's forge; the other would open a forge in Ifington.

Lopt and his sons were known in Ifington, where there was a large army garrison and they carted in shipments of weapons for the

Einherjar and the army. They often rode down to Gladsheim to make deliveries for the Einherjar, but never up to the Breach, which made sense. Around Jarnstadr, they handled local ironwork.

But they'd all died in a freak fire, along with their wives and children. The bodies were burned past recognition, but the number was right, and the villagers had no reason to doubt anything about the fire or who died in it.

By Alara's account, Hodr hadn't met Lopt until this winter—perhaps a month ago, maybe a little more. At that time, the real Lopt had been dead since summer's end, roughly two months before that. Whoever Hodr had met—whoever had given him the spear, taken him to Gladsheim, and stood by his side while he hurled that spear at Baldr—was not the real Lopt. So who was the fake Lopt?

The obvious candidate was Yelena. Frigg knew other shape-shifters, but only two with the ability to take any shape they chose: Odin and Loki. Obviously, Odin wouldn't kill his own son.

Which left Loki.

A sickening thought occurred to her. What if Yelena didn't even exist? What if Loki *was* Yelena? Loki could be anyone he chose. He also had no trouble taking a woman's shape.

Loki was Yelena. Loki was Lopt.

Frigg sat bolt upright, flinging the blankets aside.

Heimdall had never been able to find Loki, even when he was sober—and sweet Aegir's blood, it was Loki who'd dulled Heimdall's senses. With Heimdall crippled, Loki had more freedom than he'd ever had. And she'd asked Loki to plead with his daughter for the release of Baldr's spirit?

She meant to laugh out loud, but stopped herself. She'd wake the gothi and his wife.

Instead, she strode the few paces to the outside wall and listened. If anything the blowing wind sounded stronger. She swore. She still couldn't leave. She paced back toward the bed.

This was all Loki's doing. He'd tricked Hodr into killing his brother. But what about the Jotunn attack? Was that coincidental, or part of a larger—

Wait.

When Yelena had tried to kill Frigg, she'd used seidr. Loki couldn't, could he? So Loki couldn't be Yelena. But could he have been Lopt? Quite possibly.

She wanted to scream. This was too complex. Loki could have done all of it, from start to horrid finish. Yelena could have done the same. Was there anything that argued against them being the same person?

Frigg thumped down onto the bed. *Think, Frigg. Think!*

The witch had mentioned a mistress. Could that be, or have been, Angrboda? That would make Yelena at least a hundred winters old. Not that it had to have been Angrboda; she only thought that because in her gut, she felt Loki was involved. Could the witch's mistress be Hel? It could easily be some unknown Jotunn hag. Or maybe there wasn't any mistress at all, and Yelena had been lying.

Still, there was something about that night Yelena had attacked her that bothered her. Yelena had killed Gulfinn, fought Ráta, and escaped. That was the night before Baldr was killed. Hodr said he and Lopt had arrived in Gladsheim the day before Midwinter. He was certain they'd been together the entire time, which maybe didn't mean much when magic was involved, but it suggested—

And then it hit her.

Lopt and Yelena couldn't be the same person, not only because that fight had happened while Hodr and Lopt had been elsewhere, but Yelena had been that pregnant woman, the sister of that murdered girl. She'd bewitched Harald. And Yelena had said she'd been in Gladsheim weaving many plots. Klakki, Yelena's pretend husband, had revealed one of those plots, revealing he'd been magicked into helping her cut the mistletoe.

She breathed a sigh of relief. She was getting somewhere. Yelena wasn't Lopt.

So who was?

Odin said he'd killed a lesser shape-changer on the road back from the Gjoll's shores. But what about Loki? She kept circling back to him.

It felt right. Odin had uncovered that memory of Loki swearing revenge. Angrboda had died cursing Odin's name and had also, presumably, laid a trap on her old house that had snared Mimir and nearly caught Odin. Her shade had cursed Odin and prevented him from getting back to Gladsheim in time to possibly prevent Hodr from killing Baldr. All those things might've helped Loki, if Loki were Lopt.

But why kill Baldr? Why not just kill Odin?

As quickly as the thought arose, she snorted. Kill Odin? In the last hundred winters, only the spirit out of Urdr's Well had come close. Loki didn't command a fraction of the power Odin did. So he must've decided to go after Odin's children instead, the ones he had a hope of hurting. It was fitting; Odin had hurt Loki's children, so Loki would hurt Odin's. And in hurting them, he also hurt Odin.

Revenge. That felt right.

But not everything made sense. Take Hel's gambit, for one. Loki had been genuinely surprised by that; she'd stake her life on it. And then there was the apparent lack of a Jotunn army. It had felt as if Gladsheim was being softened up for an attack: the Sons of Muspell's burning the ships a couple of weeks earlier, the rioters that had attacked her. Line up enough coincidences, and you got a spear pointed right at your heart.

It looked more and more like Odin had been right. She and Baldr had been foolish to trust the Jotunn. And worse, they'd missed a sickness in their own city.

She had to get back to Gladsheim, and quickly—which raised another concern. She hadn't heard anything yet about Odin's success bringing Baldr back to life. That worried her. But maybe his ravens were on their way even now with the good news.

And yet she couldn't go anywhere tonight, not with the blizzard raging. For now, she could only let Odin know what she'd discovered and figured out. She'd leave in the morning no matter what.

"Heimdall, hear me. Heimdall! Tell Odin what I'm about to tell you. Loki was behind Baldr's murder—or at the very least, involved somehow. He has to be. Let me explain . . ."

37

LOKI

Day 7, late morning

The merchant staggered the final dozen steps toward the warm yellows and reds reflecting off the cave wall. He'd stopped bleeding about a mile back, so it might be a little harder for the snow bear to track him here. He laughed at the thought—weakly, ending with a coughing fit that brought blood to his lips. If it hadn't been for the winter ox pulling his wagon, he'd be dead—or in the bear's belly, as his ox no doubt was by now.

"Someone there?" The voice quavering out of the cave undoubtedly belonged to an old woman.

"Hoe—" He ended with a wracking cough that brought him to his knees.

A shadow darkened the cave entrance. "Who are ye?"

He saw a frail hand gripping a seax and raised his own hands. "I'm Hoenir. I was attacked. I need help, if you'll give it."

The old woman stood there, chewing her gums and thinking. Her eyes flicked from him to the woods below to the brightening sky and back again. "What's your name, boy?"

"Hoenir, mother."

She spat. "And who attacked ye?"

"I'm a merchant. I was headed up to Skirnirsberg—"

"That was yer first mistake. Good people there, but rough travel this time of year."

"I've a cousin," he added, a fact he'd intended to mention later in his story.

"Who's that now?"

"Buskin Godlison," he said, coughing. More blood flecked his lips.

She grunted as if he'd confirmed something for her. "I know him. You're in bad shape, boy."

The merchant waited for more, but she stared at him with blue, watery eyes.

He coughed, spat blood, and cleared his throat. "Anyway, a snow squall hit, and I hunkered down with a small fire. Just me and my winter ox. I was about to sleep when I heard this horrible rumbling growl."

"Been a lean winter for snow bear," the old woman said. "You'd be little more'n a snack."

"My ox had been skittish, but I didn't think—"

She cackled.

He shrugged. "More fool me, eh? Normally my son goes with me, but he and his wife lost their baby."

"We're dying out, I tell ya." Her expression softened slightly. "Fewer births every winter, and nary a live one."

He suppressed a violent shiver. "Indeed. Makes it hard to go on..."

"What's that now?"

"Not having children around. Makes it hard to go on. No one to carry on the line."

"The Norns are cruel."

An awkward moment passed while she ran a hard eye over him. "Get on up and follow me in. I've little enough, but I'll give what aid I can."

"Thank you, mother," the merchant said.

She sheathed the knife and, with the aid of the wall, made her slow way inside.

A new low, duping an old woman, Loki thought. Even so, the ruse was for a good purpose. He had to learn what this woman thought of Baldr and his death. Hel had sworn she would know if the old woman cried, and she would free Baldr's spirit in that event. Exactly how she might accomplish that, he had no idea.

When he'd pressed her about why she'd changed the deal, she'd shrugged and said with a lopsided grin, "You wanted him distracted, right?" Then, more soberly, she'd added, "I thought about what you said. That'd he'd kill me, or try to, regardless of what I did. I'd rather spit in his eye than roll over for him."

Once Goldtooth found Thokk—and he would, eventually—someone would show up to speak with her. Probably Ygg. And if Thokk wasn't naturally inclined to grieve at Baldr's passing, then Ygg would motivate her. Not that torturing an old woman would fulfill Hel's terms.

He stood, wincing, and spat more blood. He began shifting his cracked ribs back together. No point continuing to feel the pain of an injury he'd inflicted on himself.

The question before him now, though, was whether he could allow Baldr to be brought back to life. He really didn't see how it mattered either way. Sure, having Baldr come back would be annoying, but he'd accomplished his goals. Not only had he made Ygg suffer the kind of pain Ygg had forced Loki to live with all these winters, but he'd successfully distracted him from what the Jotunn were doing.

And Loki could always kill Baldr again.

The Skrymir had said they needed a month for their final preparations. By killing Baldr, Loki had bought them about a week. If Baldr stayed dead, they'd get maybe another week while the Aesir prepared for and held the funeral. If Baldr were restored to life, however, the resulting celebration would probably last twice as long.

Either way, the whole storehouse issue would complicate matters. He'd gotten the Sons of Muspell to burn some storehouses in Gladsheim. Assuming they went through with it; it was also possible that they'd been stopped. If they'd succeeded, then more supplies for a funeral or celebration would have to be brought in from the surrounding towns and villages. Not only would that take time, but it'd weaken those places.

And all of it would require Ygg's personal attention.

The old woman's sharp voice rang from out of the cave. "Well, boy? Coming?"

Loki grinned to himself and shuffled toward the entrance. "Yes, mother."

The old woman shuffled into her—well, it was a cave, but homey though, with rugs and skins covering the smooth floor. Hundreds of winters ago, some Jotunn shaman had had the ability to make stone flow like water. They'd used that seidr to shape stone-homes like these, as well as bigger dwellings like the place he'd met with the Skrymir and Vafthrudnir a few weeks earlier. This home was roughly square, with a crude bed and a table holding a knife, assorted roots and vegetables, and maybe some meat. The ceiling was uncut stone.

The old woman dropped something into the pot suspended on an iron arm, stirred it, then swung it back over the fire in the hearth. "I had a little rabbit left, and some roots and vegetables. Was saving it, but now's as good a time as any."

"Thank you mother, you're too kind."

She sniffed, glared at him, and pointed at a spot by the hearth. "Sit down, boy. If you collapse, you'll lay there till you wake."

He bobbed his head and limped over to the spot she'd indicated.

"Hold on, let me give you a hide." She wrestled a bear hide off her bed and dragged it over to him.

"Are you sure, mother? I'll be okay without."

She glared at him again. "Never let it be said that old Th—"

He coughed loud, long, and hard, willing blood and phlegm to come up into his hand. When he finally finished, he stood swaying in place and shaking.

"Shoulda left you outside for the wolves, boy," she said, shaking her head. But she didn't say it unkindly. "Less trouble that way."

She set the bear hide behind him, hitched it a few times so it was closer to the hearth, then offered him a surprisingly strong hand as he collapsed onto it. Never let it be said that old Loki couldn't fake an injury.

"Thank you, mother," he said maybe a little more breathlessly than necessary. "I'll repay your kindness a thousand times over."

She sniffed, shuffled over to her rocking chair, and collapsed into it. Her tired sigh wasn't at all faked. Loki felt a little more shame creep into his heart.

38

ODIN

Day 7, late morning

Something wet and warm and itchy was striking Odin's forehead. Another drop hit. Then a third. Then the burning started, sizzling fat dripped onto his skin.

Aegir's balls, it burned.

He writhed, trying to sit up, to escape the burning pain. He couldn't. His arms had some play, but he could feel a tightness around his wrists and waist, knees, and ankles. He lay on what felt like cold stone, smooth and broad.

Something cool and wet and soft wiped across his forehead. It took the pain away.

His sight was blurry, and he blinked. On the fang of stone above his head, a droplet glistened like venom on a serpent's tooth. He watched it fatten, then drop free. Pale hands appeared with a stone bowl that caught the venom.

A familiar woman's voice said, "No more pain, not for a little while, my love."

His sight began to clear. Scattered witchlamps threw a weave of light and shadow upon the looming stalactites, but the bowl blocked his view of the woman. All he could see was her slim, pale hands and slight figure.

Again he tried to sit up but couldn't. He looked down at the red-brown ropes of his bindings and . . .

Odin woke, warm and comfortable, in a bright room. Through his bleary vision, the light cast by each witchlamp seemed to stretch tall like burning swords. He tried sitting up, expecting resistance. None. Nor pain. He touched his forehead. Smooth skin.

He probed his right side, where he'd shared the damage done to Freki. No pain there, but his stomach was bandaged. Beneath the bandages, he felt the tender edges of stitched wounds and wet poultices where he'd been stabbed, but there was no pain as he stretched and twisted.

He swung his feet out and put them on the cold planks.

Freki lifted her head, pink tongue lolling out, and bared finger-long teeth in a smile.

You are healed, Freki?

Yes, Pack-Father. The silverbacks cracked my bones, but your mates brought relief.

He petted her head. To Freki, all women were her pack-father's mates. No point correcting her.

And Geri. Where are you?

Tracking, came Geri's voice, distant. *Nothing.*

Found nothing, came Huginn's thoughts in his mind. He, too, was distant.

Heimdall likely searched, as well.

How long have I slept?

Freki's ears twitched, and she looked toward the room's entrance as a slim hand pushed the hanging rug to one side. A thrall entered holding a platter of food and a flagon of wine. Her golden skin was rich honey against the simple white dress. Her head was bald, and the long tattooed lines from nape to brow line still looked red.

Freki rose, head lowered as she sniffed. Fear danced in the woman's eyes, and she backed away.

Scared, Freki said, flopping back down. *Probably not the witch.*

"Come in and set it down," Odin said, gesturing toward the table built into the wall. His clothes were stacked on it; his boots were beneath it. "How long have I slept?"

The thrall flushed and placed the platter with downcast eyes. "Not that long, Alfather. It's been one night since the wi—they attacked us. It's midday right now."

He'd slept through all yesterday, last night, and some of today. Not good. Baldr had two nights left.

Has Heimdall found Thokk yet?

Hurried footsteps came toward them from down the hall. Freki sniffed the air and yawned.

"Thank you. Leave."

"Yes, Alfather."

Ráta pushed past the departing thrall. Fresh blood was smeared across her forehead and one cheek. She'd seen much of war—and bore the scars. Dark hair, braided, head shaved on the sides, tattoos around her neck, and a horizontal scar beneath her left eye along the cheekbone. She was lean, almost as tall as he was, and in armor and shoulder guards made of bear hide, imposing.

"So the last witch escaped, I take it?" Unless more than one coven had been involved.

"Yes, Sigfather, I . . . I apologize for not arriving sooner. If I had—"

He held up a hand. "I knew what I was getting into. You brought me here?"

"Yes, Sigfather. Eir and Idunn helped restore you."

He moved to his clothes. "Tell me, what's the damage to Gladsheim?"

"It's significant." Her voice betrayed no emotion. "But there's worse news. Ifington's also been attacked. The city's northern third was destroyed. Hundreds dead, at least."

A pit opened in his stomach. Only a bright spark of fury kept him from falling in. For a moment, the scream that had sustained him while he hung from Yggdrasil almost burst forth. Not yet. Not now. But soon.

———

ODIN STOOD by the hearth in the main area of his longhouse. Hersir Saglund and Chief Warden Orgrandr were with him, along with Ráta. She'd brought both men along.

"So how bad off is Gladsheim?"

The two men exchanged glances.

Orgrandr cleared his throat. "Hundreds of livestock throughout the city are dead of a blight. More food supplies destroyed, too, grain and salted meats and smoked fish. All rotted."

He put his hands behind his back and gripped one wrist tightly as he told of a populace terrified by the Sons, the witches, and the death and destruction that had been visited upon them in the past week, since the equally traumatic murder of the beloved Jarl Baldr.

"I wouldn't say the people are rioting, Alfather," he said. "Not yet, anyway. But food has grown scarce and, well, they're afraid that war is coming."

Odin kept his tone neutral. "War *is* coming. We're being softened up."

Both the other men sobered. He'd confirmed their worst fears. Best to keep them focused on problems they could address. "How long do you estimate the remaining food stores, including those privately held on the upper tier, will last?"

"If we ration to, say, two meals per day, I'd give us a couple of weeks," Orgrandr said. "There are over thirty thousand mouths to feed, Alfather."

"And once the all the wagons return with supplies from the surrounding villages and towns?"

The chief warden blew out a breath and stared into the hearth. "Another three, maybe four weeks? Harvests were good this past summer, but..."

Not nearly enough food to get through to summer, nor enough to sustain the city if the Jotunn attacked. And if the Sons of Muspell burned more buildings? Or another coven attacked? If the Jotunn attacked, they would need to bring everyone in the nearby villages into Gladsheim, only compounding the food shortage.

"If I may, Alfather," Orgrandr said, "I think we should ease the folk into severe rationing: two meals per day for a week and then down to one meal per day with two on the last day of the week."

"The people won't like that," Saglund said.

"No, they won't," Orgrandr said, "but it's either starve quickly or starve slowly."

Odin spoke. "I'll have Freyr and Freyja send supplies, but it will be at least a month before those will arrive."

"That will certainly help, Alfather, and give the people hope," Orgrandr said. "No matter what, it will be a lean, hungry year."

All too true. "Also, have our remaining supplies and livestock moved to the second tier. We can't afford any more losses."

Saglund cleared his throat. "The Einherjar will assist in that, Sigfather."

"Good, thank you, Hersir," Odin said. "How many Einherjar warbands are in the city?"

"Seven, Sigfather."

"Send three of them out to protect the incoming wagons," Odin said. "And another north to reinforce Vidar. Heimdall will tell you where."

"Sigfather, if we're attacked—"

"Then those warbands can converge and harry whatever army the Jotunn throw at our walls. In the meantime, they'll help keep our food safe, which will help ease the peoples' minds. Those who aren't here cannot eat what food remains. The Einherjar can hunt and forage on their own."

"Yes, Sigfather, I'll see to it," Saglund said. "I think the more experienced warriors might take to that task more readily than the younger ones."

"I leave their disposition to you, Hersir," Odin said. Blood sheeted down across his vision and . . .

. . . *Saglund stood before a burning hall, his sword raised and his shield held in a loose guard position. His face was dirty and streaked with sweat. No helm. Gray hair matted and dirty. A building burned behind him, and he was shouting and gesturing with his sword as though he was giving orders. The sword's blade flashed as if it, too, was on fire. Warriors trooped past him . . .*

Odin blinked as the vision cleared. His eye socket ached, and he wondered why there was never any sound in his visions. Twice it seemed as if Saglund had shouted the word "Muspell," but he couldn't be sure.

He met the chief warden's gaze. "Have the wardens organize hunting, fishing, and foraging parties. That should keep everyone focused on solving problems rather than creating new ones."

"Yes, Alfather."

He turned to Ráta. "Heimdall's still seen no trace of a Jotunn army?"

She shook her head. "Not since the witches attacked. The only significant force I'm aware of is the warband that Vidar's pursuing."

Odin stared out through the open door. Here beside the hearth, it was warm and comfortable, but a few steps would carry him through the door into the chill, sunny afternoon. What if the doorway Vidar had found was mixed up in all this?

What if he'd been a bigger, blinder fool than he thought?

He dug into his satchel and withdrew a charged spindle. "Ráta, please take this to Vidar. Tell him to return to me. You will take command of his warband and the Einherjar the hersir sends."

"Of course, Sigfather, but—"

"There are many pieces to this puzzle before us. This doorway Vidar found has to be one of them—and I've been ignoring it. Too many other things on my mind."

She accepted the spindle from him. Confusion had clouded her eyes.

"I'll explain," he said, including both Orgrandr and Saglund. "The door beneath Háls led to Utgard just as the door in this longhouse leads outside. Vidar said that with one step, he was in Utgard."

"You don't believe him?" Ráta asked.

He shook his head. "I do. But what happened in that step? How did he cross the hundreds of miles separating him from Utgard?

Vidar can help me answer those questions and see what's happening here in a different light."

"I don't understand, Sigfather."

Nor did Saglund and Orgrandr, by their expressions. "What do we always say about snow bears that are stalking you?"

She grinned. "There's always more than one. And you never see the one that gets you."

"Exactly. What if there are more of these doorways? The Jotunn knew there was one. It's not too far a leap to think they'd look for more. I would. What if the Jotunn found them and figured out where they lead?"

She began to nod. "If they happened to be in the right places, well, they could send a thousand warriors through and destroy us."

Orgrandr paled. Saglund was fidgeting, as well he might. He was responsible for Gladsheim's defense.

"Maybe that's why Heimdall hasn't found an army marching. They don't need to march."

Ráta blew out a long, slow breath. "I'll bring Jarl Vidar back at once, Sigfather."

"I know you will." He clapped a hand on her shoulder.

She dropped into her snow lynx form and shot out through the open door like an arrow.

He regarded Orgrandr and Saglund. "Any questions regarding your orders?"

They shook their heads and rose.

"Let me know if you need anything. If it's within my power to help, I will. I'll meet you both back here this evening."

In the meantime, he had to check on Baldr's body to make sure witches hadn't ravaged it. And then he needed to see a sharp-eyed friend about finding an old Jotunn woman.

39

LOKI

Day 7, midday

Loki sipped the thin broth and found it not terrible. When he'd ladled out their portions, he'd pretended to take more than he had. He felt bad enough already about his ruse; he wouldn't take food from her, too.

"I've been here"—the old woman smacked her gums as she sipped—"seven winters now."

"By yourself?"

"Aye, my husband fled back to the Gap nigh on three winters past. He's the one who made this old stone-home livable."

"So this *is* one of those?"

"Oh, aye." She twisted and pointed with her cane at the back wall where her bed was. "He said there's a door there; can hardly see the lines. Won't open, though. No idea how deep it goes. So he put our bed in front of it and said, 'Best way to find out if anything's coming through.'"

She cackled and slapped the arm of her chair.

Loki couldn't help but laugh, too.

"So tell me, you said you have a son?"

"I do, mother. Four sons and a girl."

Her eyes went wide and she made a soundless whistle. "Now how'd you manage that?"

"My family were farmers. Back when we had fields, I mean."

She leaned forward, squinting at him. "How old are you?"

He swore to himself. *Careful.*

"Older than I look," he said.

She sniffed. "Who cares about looks? It's how you feel that matters. Can barely make it outside to piss anymore." She lapsed into silence, rocking back and forth. He thought he'd dodged the question, but she said, "But five children, eh? Same woman out of those cursed pits?"

"I knew the minute I looked at her," he said, which was true, since he meant Angrboda. "So I bought her free."

"You *are* older than you look." She gave him another shrewd glance.

"My father had some influence." He switched to the hand speech. "And I promised three of my boys to the sleep."

"Ah, that must've been hard," she said aloud. And in the hand speech: "But at least they live."

"Others have borne worse. But what about you, mother?"

"Me?" She rocked and sucked her gums. "It's a too long, too sad story."

"Some say it helps to—"

"Some people are fools," she spat. She rocked in silence a while longer. "The Aesir took all but one of my children from me. Three died in that pointless war. The fourth, my daughter, survived and found a man and had a child before"—she switched to the hand language—"the shaman came to haul her away to those cursed pits."

Loki replied in the hand language. "She visits you here?"

The old woman shook her head. "She's gone back to the Gap, too. Wasting sickness took her. She had two boys and a girl."

Which meant that one boy went to the sleep, the other was probably dead, and the girl . . . He wouldn't ask about her.

"I'd give my remaining winters—along with these miserable past few without my man—to Rán if she'd let me see my granddaughter," she said.

Loki said nothing.

In the hand language, she said, "They said it's war. We all must sacrifice. And maybe that's true. But what's the point, really, when we fight Aesir who can murder us by the hundreds? Have you seen what Thor can do?"

Obviously he had, but this merchant he'd become hadn't. "No, mother."

"Too right. You're sitting here, after all. I heard that he's been at it again. Broke a mountain a few weeks back. A mountain!"

"I heard that, too." Which he hadn't, but it wasn't surprising. He'd seen Thor do much worse.

"You're a father," she said. "You know what it's like to lose your children."

He blinked, swallowed, cleared his throat. "I do."

"Don't hide the tears, son. That's your blood calling to your kin. Nothing breaks that bond, not pain or suffering or even that long trip back to the Gap. Or rebirth, when Aegir and Rán grant it."

"You believe that."

She swatted at the air as if she'd have hit him were he closer. "I said it, didn't I? Now fetch me my cup and that blanket from the bed. I'm tired."

He struggled up, not making too big a show of it, and did as he bid. Then he resumed his spot on the hide by the hearth. "Don't you hate them, though?"

"Who, now?"

He switched to the hand language. "The Aesir. It was them who took everyone from you."

She shrugged. "Sure I did. There was a time when I would've put a knife in old Ygg's eye if I'd had the chance." She snorted and shook her head.

"What?" he asked.

"I guess a part of me still wants to kill him. Or die trying." She shifted her ancient, knobby shoulders beneath the wool blanket. "But all that hate and those thoughts, those were a young woman's fantasies. No point thinking like that anymore. Doesn't do any good. Doesn't bring anyone back. And all of it twisted the time I was with my husband. I chose to see the evil and feel the hate and anger, rather than focus on the love and hope. Precious little of either. Sounds stupid saying it, I know."

"I don't think so. Sounds wise to me," Loki said. "But if you had the chance, would you have? Put a knife in Ygg's eye, I mean."

She turned a sharp eye on him. "Now why would you ask that?"

He shrugged and gave a quick smile. "I've lost family to the Aesir, and I . . . I'm not like you, mother. I *hate* them."

She pointed at her cup, steam rising from it. "Fetch me that, please."

As he handed it to her, she wrapped her old bony hands around his and met his eyes with her own rheumy gaze. "Let it go, son. It only hurts you and those you still have."

Her hands were cold and dry, but a warmth passed from her into him. He blinked away the sudden tears and backed away. He couldn't let his hate go, could he?

After she'd taken a few sips and set the cup on the floor, her fingers went back into motion. "I saw his son, once. Ygg's."

"Which one?"

She grinned. "The nice one."

His heart sunk like Jorm into the sea.

"What did they call him? Baldr the . . .?"

He shrugged and gave a weak smile. "I've heard so many."

"It was more'n a dozen winters ago. I was hobbling my way through Jotunheim on my husband's arm. They'd brought out all the sick and even some of the pregnant ones. My husband and I tried not to look, afraid we'd see—or think we did—our granddaughter."

"What, right out on the street?" he asked.

"Haven't been in Jotunheim in a while have you, son?"

"No, I . . . I try to avoid it."

"Why do you think I'm up here? Anyway, one of the pregnant ones was in labor. Not sure what they were thinking bringing her out, but they did. That Baldr, though, he dropped to his knees in front of her and went to work like any midwife would. We didn't want to watch—knew the baby was stillborn. They all are, these days. They say Baldr's touch heals anything, but he can't bring back the dead. Who can, eh?"

Who indeed.

"Specially not babies who never had more'n a toehold on life," she continued. "But we stayed, right to the bloody end, along with dozens, maybe hundreds of others. He held that dead baby in his hands, and he wept—I swear to Aegir, he did. Old Ygg's son cradled a dead Jotunn baby in his arms and wept. I looked at my husband and he was crying, too. Looking back, I think that was when I gave up the hate. After I don't know, thirty winters? Just gave it up. Couldn't believe it. Couldn't believe any of it."

Her hands fell silent and she rocked back and forth, staring into the dwindling hearth fire, lost in the memory. And she was crying now.

He hadn't planned the conversation to go this way. Not in a thousand winters could he have planned this. Maybe the Norns had cast a lucky rune his way. Regardless, he could now outright ask the question he needed to ask.

With a somber tone, he said, "You know he's dead now, right?"

"Who now?"

With his hands he said, "Baldr."

"What?" She sounded shocked. Shocked and . . . upset? She had to be upset, particularly given the story she'd told. But he had to be sure.

"He died on Midwinter."

She snorted and wiped her cheeks. "Don't be a fool. They don't die. None of 'em do."

"His brother—the blind one—killed him with a spear."

"That's crap."

"It's true. I heard it straight from a crier's mouth." And it was true. He'd stopped in the nearest village south of Thokk's cave for a warm meal and a quick, safe nap.

"Where?" Suspicion radiated from her.

"Back in Gerdja, before I left for Skirnirsberg."

"Which crier?

"Helgi Holtsson."

She swore. "So it's true then."

The dying hearth fire popped as the logs settled. In that wan light, fresh tears flowed down Thokk's weathered cheeks. "He seemed like a good'un," she whispered.

He had his answer. When Ygg showed up and asked this poor old woman if she'd weep for his dead son, she'd say, "I already have." Worse, he didn't know what to think now or what to do. Hel would release Baldr's spirit, and Ygg would bring him back. And then Ygg would free Hel.

By killing her.

"I think I'll get some rest," the old woman said, her voice heavy. "Throw a log on that fire for me, please."

"Yes, mother," he said.

"Call me Thokk, son," she said. "Call me Thokk."

Loki froze in the act of placing the log on the fire. Of course she'd had to repeat it. He glanced at the entrance to the cave, only a spear's length from where he knelt. They were nowhere near deep enough. Goldtooth had to have heard her name.

So much for the Norns being kind. Now he didn't have much time at all.

40

ODIN

Day 7, early afternoon

Heimdall greeted Odin with a broad, eager smile, and uttered four words that lightened his heart.

"Odin, I found her."

"Well done, cousin!" He pulled Heimdall into an embrace. Not only had Baldr's body been spared by the witches, but his weave still held strong and likely would for another two nights.

Muninn, Huginn, I need you, he said.

"She said her own name aloud recently. She was speaking with a man, I think."

"You can describe where Thokk lives?" Odin dug in his satchel and withdrew a handful of dried meat and one of his last two witchthread spindles.

"Yes, but—"

His ravens landed on the stone wall. Odin spread the dried meat out on the cold stone.

Eat. You'll need the strength.

"I also have a message from Frigg to relay."

"That can wait," Odin said. "Where is Thokk?"

"A cave on the northwest flank of the barrier mountains that girdle southern Utgard. About a half-day's flight from the Breach. Thor passed within a few miles of it on his way back."

"And Frigg is where?"

"Ifington. But Odin, I need to relay her message. It's important. I would've done so sooner, but Eir said you shouldn't be disturbed."

Sped by his seidr, Huginn and Muninn could fly to Ifington by nightfall. Even if Frigg left tonight, she wouldn't reach Thokk's cave until—

An icy dread gripped him. Frigg would arrive the very day that his spell unraveled. They were right up against it now. No room for mistakes.

"Odin!" Heimdall's hand was on his arm now. "Frigg thinks Lopt was Loki."

He may as well have drawn Hofud and struck him. The words rang inside Odin's mind. His missing eye throbbed. Loki's threat swam up into his mind: *I will free my children. And when I do, we will destroy everything you've built. We will set such a fire to your works that the heavens themselves will burn.*

". . . talked through the timing of everything. It fits. Yelena couldn't have been Lopt because she—Yelena—was busy here while Hodr and Lopt were traveling from Ifington."

"I just killed six witches who could all shift as well as I can," Odin said. "Any one of them could have been Lopt."

"True, but—"

"You want Loki to be the culprit because of what he did to you."

Heimdall lifted an eyebrow and cocked his head. "It makes sense that he's behind all of what's before us—or some of it, at least. I heard you relate that memory of Loki threatening you."

Odin withheld a sigh. He really needed to start using the Jotunn hand speech. "Did Frigg offer any other evidence against Loki?"

"She spoke to me from Jarnstadr, the village that was home to Lopt."

"She found the smith, then?"

"In a manner of speaking."

"Heimdall . . ."

"Lopt and his wife, and their family—sons, their wives, their children—were all dead. Burned to death in their house," Heimdall said.

"So?" Odin crossed his arms over his chest. Frigg had suspected Loki's involvement from the moment he'd uncovered that missing memory. He had, too, if he was honest.

"They died at Midsummer, over six moons ago. Which means Lopt was almost certainly an imposter—and probably a shape-shifter."

"That's possible. Or it was an old man playing a part."

Heimdall laughed. "Seriously?"

"Fine. Say it was a shape-shifter. What proof do either of you have that Loki was Lopt?"

Heimdall snorted. "Why is it so hard to believe that Loki has betrayed you?"

Odin frowned. Fair point. He gestured toward Huginn and Muninn. "How about we send my ravens on their way so they can guide Frigg. Afterward, we can discuss this theory of hers."

After a long moment, Heimdall crossed to where glossy black birds perched on the stone wall. He told Muninn how to reach Thokk's cave. Then he told Huginn what Hel now required.

As Heimdall spoke, Odin unwound the final strand of witchthread from his second-to-last spindle and began to sing, weaving the thread around his ravens and tying it off. He made Huginn's weave stronger. Their feathers took on a golden shimmer under the bright sun.

You know what to do, Muninn?

Yes, Wing-Father, Muninn replied. *Find Frigg in Ifington. Guide her to Thokk's cave.*

Excellent. Huginn?

Tell your mate what Hel did, Huginn said. *And then return.*

Very good. I've sped your flight. You will reach Frigg before nightfall.

Wings clattering, Muninn and Huginn launched themselves into the air. Odin watched the trail of golden light marking their flight until they passed below the wooded northern horizon.

Why was it so hard to believe that Loki had betrayed him? Truth was, it made sense. Loki was absolutely capable of it. And he'd been genuinely furious when Odin had admitted six nights ago that he shouldn't have trusted the Norns. That admission alone would have justified striking back at him.

But Loki hadn't lashed out. And six nights wasn't enough time to hatch any serious plan.

"Did it seem to you that Loki faked his shock at learning that Hel had taken Baldr's spirit hostage?"

"No, it did not." Heimdall stood on the opposite side of the tower, one hand resting on Hofud's pommel.

"We didn't think so, either." That suggested that Hel had been truthful when she'd dealt with himself and Frigg. "So what did Hel gain by breaking her deal with me?"

"Nothing." Heimdall thought for a moment. "She's all but guaranteed that you'll move against her at some point, particularly if this meeting with Thokk goes poorly."

Heimdall knew him well. As did Loki. "She only changed our deal after Loki spoke with her."

"You think Loki suggested it?"

"Hel was smart, capable, and powerful when I went up against her in the spirit realm," Odin said. "Why would someone smart do something dumb?"

"We can't all be like you."

Odin gave a thin smile.

Heimdall's eyes narrowed. "You're suggesting that Hel's not truly acting against her own interests."

"Is she still bound? And what about her brothers?"

Heimdall's ice-blue eyes narrowed as he looked into the far distance. "I can see the chain binding Fenrir. Jorm still sleeps. And Hel, she's—"

Heimdall cried out and staggered backward. Odin leaped forward and steadied him.

"I'm fine," he said, blinking his eyes rapidly. "Bitch blinded me for a moment."

Not a good sign. He would have to act against Hel. "Does it make sense that Loki convinced his daughter to break her deal?"

"Only if he has a better plan. He's like you, Odin. He does nothing without thinking it through first."

Loki might have bought her cooperation with the same coin he himself had paid with: freedom. That Fenrir, Jorm, and Hel weren't yet free didn't mean they wouldn't soon be. Maybe that explained the long delay between Loki's threat and his actions now. He had gained the means, somehow, to overcome Odin's magic and break Fenrir's unbreakable chain.

And what did this meeting with Thokk amount to? More time. Was it enough? If Loki was acting now, that meant he thought he'd succeed. Even so, he'd only gained about four nights—two since Hel changed the deal, and another two till Frigg talked to Thokk.

Odin thumped the stone wall with one fist. "Is everything else—Háls's razing, the attacks here and in Ifington—somehow tied into Baldr's murder?"

"Possibly," Heimdall said.

"You heard what I said to Ráta earlier?"

"About Vidar's doorways?" Heimdall nodded curtly. "It might explain why I don't see armies gathering. But we're explaining something we don't understand by pointing at something else we don't understand."

"Which is why I need Vidar back here." Odin stared out at firs so laden with snow that their boughs hardly moved in the building wind. Rather than figuring out why Háls had been razed—and how the doors worked—Odin had stayed in Gladsheim fighting literal fires. Loki, the Jotunn, the witches, and the Sons all benefited from these distractions. Maybe it was as simple as Loki's knowing these attacks would happen.

How had he gone from refusing to believe Loki was plotting against him to believing it possible?

He closed his eye and breathed out. Blotches of red and white mingled in the blackness. He forced his missing eye to open. He looked . . .

. . . up from beneath the water at the barnacle-crusted bottom of a longship . . .

. . . down at a burning forest . . .

. . . at rot spreading across Baldr's face . . .

. . . at a body bound tight against cold stone . . .

He opened his eye and saw little more than he had before: snow-laden trees, blue sky, wispy clouds.

"You asked why I found it so hard to believe Loki had betrayed me?" He knew he had, though he still hoped he hadn't.

Heimdall said nothing.

"Because he and I are too much alike."

41

FRIGG

Day 7, afternoon into evening

Frigg landed amid the ruin of a street she'd walked two nights before. The smithy and its side yard were smoking rubble now. As was the house beside it, the leatherworker's shop down the street, the small yard where goats had bleated, and the patch of snow on which had stood a makeshift man sculpted by a child's imagination. All of it gone.

Ifington hadn't been attacked. It had been burned.

Yesterday she'd been in Jarnstadr contemplating the scorched bones of another building and a barrow mounded for the victims of those flames.

This morning she'd flown south toward Gladsheim only to turn east when she spied heavy black clouds hanging above Ifington.

This evening she walked down a street devastated by fire, avoiding the twisted, burned limbs that had once held up homes, shops, docks, ships, markets, warehouses. A third of the city—everything north of the River Ifing was a scorched ruin.

Along with so many of her people.

She realized, finally, what she was looking at. Not fallen, fire-blackened timbers, twisted by heat. She could have borne that. But not this. Who could bear this? The burned-out husks of people, limbs blackened and withered, contorted by the agony of flame, had clearly been placed in neat, respectful lines alongside the streets.

She closed her eyes against the horror. Baldr's scorched face gibbered in her mind's eye. She turned away, one hand over her mouth, tears falling freely.

Her gaze fell on a swaddled baby that lay as if asleep, except that her tiny chest neither rose nor fell. The babe's mother still cradled her child, though her body was charred to within a whisker of bare bones. She'd shielded her, hoping that someone would come and save her daughter. No help had come.

And where had she been? Asleep in Jarnstadr. What right did she have to seek Baldr's rebirth when all these lives had been lost?

"Mother, are you all right?"

Frigg blinked away her tears, hauled in a shuddering breath, and turned around.

A young man approached with a sad expression on his dirty, beardless face. He held a spear in one hand. A warden's brooch bound a warden's cloak that looked too big for his frame.

In the vision-flames that burned above his head . . . *he stood arms akimbo before a tree from which a sword hilt protruded.*

"You might be," she replied. She hadn't seen war and death associated with this boy. Why?

"Mother?" His sadness faltered as confusion creased his face. He was tall, broad-shouldered, and lean with youth. His blond hair stuck out in all directions. His eyes were gray, like Odin's.

"What's your name?" she asked.

"Sigmundr," he said, his smile returning. "Volsungsson."

Frigg put her arm out in greeting. "I am Frigg Logrsdottir."

He blinked twice, and his eyes went wide. But he took her arm. His forearm felt like stout ship's rope. "It is an honor to meet you, Almother. If I may—"

"What am I doing here?" she finished for him.

He nodded once.

"Are you from this part of Ifington, Sigmundr Volsungsson?"

He shook his head. "I'm from a village to the west. My father brought us here when my youngest brother saw the smoke."

"That was well done. Why are you alone?"

"We split up to look for survivors, Almother. I haven't"—his face fell, and his eyes clouded over—"found any. Only . . ." He gestured toward the bodies that lay in neat rows.

Frigg reached up and took him by the shoulders. "Few things are harder than what you're doing right now. Thank you for doing it."

He gave a small nod and turned away to cough. When he looked at her again, wearing an embarrassed smile, the dirt on his face was smudged and streaked.

"Do you have any idea who did this?" she asked.

The vision-flames flickered above his head. Sigmundr's youthful frame had filled out with a warrior's physical presence. The sides of his head had been shaved and tattooed. His hair was long and tidied with silver rings, and he wore a single-braided beard that reached his chest. In the vision, he . . .

. . . *spoke to an older man in gray, tattered clothes with a worn blue cloak and a wide-brimmed hat . . .*

It couldn't be.

. . . *The older man indicated the sword with one hand. With the other, he removed his hat. A simple leather patch covered one eye . . .*

Frigg heard herself gasp.

. . . *The other eye, gray, pierced her like a spear. And Odin said to her . . .*

Distantly, she heard young Sigmundr say, "Almother!"

. . . *"He will be one of the first. Train him. Guide him . . .*

Gray smoke raced with white clouds across a blue field.

. . . *we'll need thousands like him . . ."*

Her back was cold.

Frigg felt herself lifted and the double-thump of a heart against her ribs as she was jostled up and down. She heard heavy breathing and then, nothing.

FRIGG WOKE IN A WARM ROOM. Exposed beams were high overhead. A blanket covered her, though she still wore the dirty dress she'd left Ifington in.

She sat up. A bowl of clear water sat to her right beside a plump towel. She drank some of the cold water, then bathed her face and arms in what remained.

The last thing she remembered before—

She couldn't think about that yet.

But how could she not? Somehow, Odin had not only looked at her through one of her visions, but he'd spoken to her. She grabbed the back of the bed and steadied herself. How was that possible?

And what had he meant? She should guide and train the young boy she'd met, or the grown Sigmundr in her vision? Both? And That they would need thousands like him—what did that mean? These visions didn't make their choices easier; they made them more difficult. Ignorance would have been better.

A knock came from behind her. The wife of Ifington's gothi stood in the door, the hanging pushed to one side. "I thought I heard something. I'm happy to see you up so soon. Can I get you anything, Almother?"

Frigg turned around, smoothing her dress. "Just information, Hugalla. How long have I been here? What happened?"

Hugalla stepped into the room. Her usual radiant kindness lay buried beneath exhaustion and grime. She gestured toward someone Frigg couldn't see, then tied the door hanging back. "Not long, Almother. A young man brought you here—carried you. Said he spoke with you in Northwall—well, what's left of it, I suppose. And then you collapsed."

"I was flying back from Jarnstadr," Frigg said. "I saw the pall above the city and came to see what was happening—or had happened."

Footsteps thumped against the planks. Gothi Mus stepped in. Black half-moons hung beneath his eyes. From bald pate to brown boots he, too, was covered in the remnants of soot and ash that had been brushed from his clothes.

The gothi and his wife exchanged a quick look. Mus shook his head slightly. Hugalla's shoulders slumped and she turned away.

"What's going on?" Frigg asked.

Gothi Mus raised his arm and indicated the door. "Best to show you, Almother."

―――――

With a grinding groan, Aegir's Hof collapsed in on itself. Out of its corpse, black smoke billowed up from red, hungry flames. Over a hundred people stood in a loose ring around the temple. Some held blankets, some had shovels. Others had buckets.

"We've been fighting that fire since dawn," Gothi Mus said. "Thought we had it beat, but then a column collapsed. Flames shot up, and what was left of the roof caught."

"Saving his hof would have buoyed everyone's spirits." The tone of Hugalla's voice made it clear that they'd have to rally around something else now.

Maybe she could help with that.

With Sól nearly wended nearly down to the western horizon, Frigg guessed that she'd only been asleep for at most a handbreadth of Sól's journey. Despite the wind, which was strong enough to clear most of the smoke from the burning temple, the day wasn't much colder than it had been.

"Where is the young man who carried me here?" Frigg asked. "I'd like to thank him."

"He went back into Northwall," Mus said. "Said he needed to finish. Should I have him brought?"

She shook her head. "Everyone's too busy for that. We need to speak about how badly Ifington's been wounded."

"Come with me." Gothi Mus nodded toward a pair of tables, where a handful of men and women soberly conferred. He gestured to a tall, dark-skinned woman on the opposite side of the table. "This is Hersir Umbuth. She leads the army warbands garrisoned here."

Frigg extended her arm.

Umbuth gripped it. "An honor, Almother. I wish it were under better circumstance."

In the vision-flames above her head, Umbuth fought alongside her fellow warriors. Her face was bloody, her dark eyes fierce and her full lips pressed tight. Much like she was now.

"Likewise," Frigg said. She regarded Umbuth and Mus. "So who attacked us? In Gladsheim, the Sons of Muspell attempted something similar but were stopped them before too much damage was done."

With a gauntleted finger, Umbuth began indicating areas on the map of Ifington spread before them on the table. "According to reports—and those are still coming in—witches appeared before the Northwall guards, touched them, and then flew away. Those they touched died. Other witches, or maybe the same ones, appeared atop warehouses, halls, houses, and shops. They called fire from their hands in long gouts and then flew off. We also have some reports from wardens of torch-carrying people touching off other blazes. If that's true, they might be the Sons you mentioned."

Witches in league with the Sons of Muspell. Frigg felt numb.

"Did I hear correctly, Almother, that you flew over part of the city?" Gothi Mus asked.

Ifington sat astride the River Ifing which split into three fingers as it approached the shore of the Great Eastern Sea. The Old Bridge spanned the southernmost finger; Newbridge spanned the northernmost finger. Everything north of Newbridge and that finger of the river was bounded by Northwall.

Frigg cleared her throat. "Yes, almost everything between the northern shore of the Ifing and Northwall is gone—burned down to their foundations. Same for Northwall."

Northwall had been the outermost wall, a wooden palisade atop mounded earth and stone, with many platforms for defenders.

Frigg traced her finger along the sweep of the Inner Wall, which was built on the southern shore of the Ifing. It ringed the original, largest section of Ifington. "And large sections of the Inner Wall are in sad shape, both from fire and neglect."

Umbuth said. "We're mustering the supplies and craftsmen to shore it up, particularly the span that faces north."

"Almother, I've seen to it that the Hersir has the authority to gather what she needs," Gothi Mus said. He gestured toward the burning temple. "It's taking longer than desirable."

Frigg nodded. "Heimdall's heard all we said, which means Odin has, too. They'll send aid."

"Whatever they send will be much appreciated." Umbuth hesitated and pursed her lips. "You seem to expect another attack, Almother."

Frigg felt like a hot ingot awaiting the next hammer blow. She said nothing.

"I received word from the Breach a little while ago," Umbuth said. "They reported no sign of a Jotunn army."

Frigg put her hands behind her back and channeled all of her anger and frustration into gripping one wrist with her other hand. Could it be that they were *only* being attacked by the Sons of Muspell —along with a coven of witches? Did it make sense that a *rogue* Jotunn tribe had destroyed Háls?

Before she left Gladsheim, she'd believed they were being softened up for an attack, yet no Jotunn army had been sighted. "Jarl Heimdall hasn't seen an army, either," Frigg said. "Not when I left a week ago."

"Plenty of time for a message." Gothi Mus's frown made it clear that he'd had no word from Gladsheim.

Dusk was falling. Torches, bonfires, and witchlamps were being brought into the market surrounding Ifington's Great Hall. Wardens and other able-bodied men and women stood watch. The wounded were being brought into the buildings on the southern side that had survived the fire.

A shout went up nearby. "Up there, southward! Witches!"

And then, "Archers! Find archers!"

Two streaks of golden light came toward them faster than flaming arrows shot from Ullr's bow. As they drew closer, Frigg discerned two winged shapes—Huginn and Muninn.

"Stop! Those are Odin's ravens. They bear a message for me."

The ravens' wings flared and they landed on the table. The gothi and his wife each took a reflexive step back. Umbuth drew herself up a little straighter.

One of the ravens fixed an eye on Frigg and croaked, "Wing-father sends word."

———

FRIGG ABSORBED THE NEWS NUMBLY: The deal with Hel now broken. Gladsheim attacked and burned. Hundreds dead. Food stores destroyed, livestock slain by witches. All but one of the coven dead at Odin's hand—which meant there must be at least two covens active in Asgard.

Hersir Umbuth and Gothi Mus took the news as well as could be expected. They left her alone after the raven had spoken. The next message was for her ears only.

Make Thokk weep, or Hel will not free Baldr. Fly northwest to the mountains, then west to a cave on the southern ridge. Muninn will guide you.

Baldr's chance at renewed life hung by a thread two nights long.

Muninn and Huginn cocked their heads as if asking if she had anything further to say. When she didn't respond, they clattered upward and roosted.

What right had she to a reborn son when thousands in Ifington and Gladsheim had said goodbye forever to their daughters and sons, wives and husbands? And now she had to fly into Utgard to plead with an old Jotunn woman who'd no doubt lost family to Aesir spears.

Frigg stared up at the darkening sky for long enough to watch the first stars emerge. After enduring their indifferent stares, she turned her back on them and addressed herself to the south. "Heimdall, tell Odin I'll leave at first light."

42

LOKI

Day 8, before dawn

Loki, called a familiar voice.

Loki opened his eyes. He was on his back, tall green grasses around him. Red, yellow, and orange leaves swirled beneath a blue sky. Birds darted; tree limbs creaked.

Loki, the same voice called a second time.

The sky's blue became icy, and his back went cold. Snow gusted across his vision. The forest sounds faded.

He sat up and looked around. Instead of a grassy plain near a forest, he was on a white wasteland of snow and ice and rock. A shape wavered in the air before him, fuzzy and indistinct, snow blowing through it.

Loki, answer me, called the voice a third time.

"Vafthrudnir?" he asked.

Like a released bowstring, the figure snapped into focus.

Loki stood on a big raft. He wore a shirt and breeches that rippled in the breeze. The sea rolled beneath him and bubbling fragments of ice drifted past. A very young-looking Vafthrudnir sat cross-legged before him, eyes closed, a witchstove before him. Steam drifted up from the cup atop the stove.

Thank you, Loki. You're difficult to find.

"What's happening?" Loki asked, looking around. A whale's tail slapped the water and sank beneath. White birds wheeled above. The last thing he remembered was falling asleep to old Thokk's snores, so he must be dreaming. Either Vafthrudnir had slipped into those dreams, or he was dreaming of Vafthrudnir—disturbing in and of itself.

Yes, Loki, you're dreaming. And yes, I'm actually speaking with you. It's difficult, and this isn't my first attempt. Far from it. But we needed to talk.

Vafthrudnir's mouth didn't move as he spoke.

Would you feel more comfortable if it did?

Loki cloaked himself and drew the hood up. "How are you able to enter my dreams?"

That's not important. All that matters is that I deliver a message: We've advanced our plans. We attack in four nights. Is there a—

"Four nights? You're changing the plan again? When last we spoke, you said I'd have to wait a full month between killing Baldr and your attack—a month I didn't want and argued against, if you'll recall."

I do, Loki. Gladsheim and Ifington were attacked by witches and the Sons of Muspell. We don't know why. Because of those attacks, the store-houses from which we were stealing supplies have been destroyed—along with many other buildings.

Hmm. Well, that was unfortunate, and partly his doing. Okay, mostly his doing. Best to not admit that, though. "Why were you stealing supplies? And how? It'd take weeks to—"

The doorways. Remember the ones the Skrymir showed you? And we needed those supplies for our wakened armies.

"Ah, of course. But to need supplies . . ."

Yes, Loki. Vafthrudnir was sounding exasperated. *Our situation really is that dire.*

Loki calculated rapidly. "So including tonight, I have four nights?"

We could delay slightly if you absolutely need it.

He laughed. "So now you seek to accommodate me?"

The raft Loki stood upon sank into a trough as the old shaman sighed.

"You'll attack on the fourth night from now? I have your word on it?"

Yes.

"I'll be ready. And I have another distraction planned. For that night. Take full advantage of it."

Oh, we will. Vafthrudnir's eyes opened on such a look of vicious anticipation that—

—Loki sat up and gasped. The cave was warm, the fire low, and the old woman no longer snoring.

He wrapped the blanket around his shoulders and slipped outside, sticking to the shadows, until he stood beneath a snow-laden fir. Aurvandil's Toe glittered blue in the clear, predawn sky.

He had a choice to make.

Somewhere, his sons Vali and Narfi marched, or slept, with Beli Stormseye and Helveg. They were the spear that would strike deep into Gladsheim's heart. In four night's time.

He looked back at the cave and then up at the sky. Did it matter if Baldr lived again? Would Ygg be more or less distracted if Baldr were alive or dead? Would a living Baldr pose a greater threat to Helveg, his two sons, and the Jotunn armies? Would a Ygg with a dead son be less inclined to mercy than a Ygg with a living son?

He snorted. It didn't matter either way. Ygg wouldn't stop until his enemies were dead. And Thokk would weep when whoever Ygg sent came calling. He knew it.

Yes, he had a choice to make—and not one he'd ever dreamed of having to make. He stared down at his hands, made red by the dawn.

He knew what he must do.

43

ODIN

Day 8, morning

Odin folded his golden wings and landed on the wide shelf he'd shaped out of Yggdrasil's bark. Clear water trickled down the bark, pooled in a hollow he'd shaped, and fell away. Familiar stars dotted a black sky to his right. To his left was the tree. Before him, hard against the great tree's trunk, was his High Seat. He knelt, removed his cloak and satchel, and splashed cold water on his face, combing it through his hair and wetting the back of his neck.

After speaking with Heimdall last night, he'd stood in the Great Hall and dealt with his people's anger—over the attacks, the destruction, the forced rationing, and all the chaos in their once peaceful city. Naturally, they blamed him. But he'd endured worse. This very place bore witness to that. This was where he'd hung for nine nights, a noose around his neck and a spear through his side, riding the threshold between life and death.

Thresholds. Doorways. There was a connection there that he wasn't seeing. Not yet.

"Hello, Hangi," said a voice from behind him.

Odin threw himself into a roll, came up, and spun around. He brought Gungnir into his hands.

Staring into his face were the big black eyes of a squirrel roughly the same size as Sleipnir.

"Is that the spear you shoved through your side?" the squirrel asked, unperturbed by the three-foot length of bright skymetal pointed at his face.

"Ratatoskr." He sighed and dismissed Gungnir. "You shouldn't sneak up on folk like that."

The squirrel cocked his head to one side. "Sneak? I've been told I sound like a landslide running up and down my tree."

"Well, my friend, you're quieter than you think. Or I was more distracted. Either way, it's been a long time since I've seen you. How does the morning find you?"

"Morning, is it?" Ratatoskr glanced up at the star-filled sky. The long red fur on his ears wafted gently back and forth. He sniffed.

"Indeed it is, at least where I'm from." Here, the sky never changed. "Would you care for some wine?"

"What is wine?"

He smiled. "I've offered you some before. Let me pour it."

He found a knot in the bark that was deep enough, pulled the wineskin around, and filled the hollow. Ratatoskr padded over and sniffed, his long whiskers twitching up and down like fishing lines. He drank a little, then sat up, his paws rubbing furiously at his nose.

"I remember now. I'll stick with water. But thank you, Hangi."

"Next time, maybe, eh? The taste grows on you."

"Where?"

"Where what?" Odin asked, as calmly as he could. Ratatoskr was a challenging conversationalist at the best of times. And truth was, he didn't know what the squirrel was or why it lived on Yggdrasil. He'd met him thrice before, each encounter stranger than the last.

"Where does it grow on you? That sounds unpleasant."

Despite himself, he laughed. "No, no. I meant that over time, you come to like the taste."

The squirrel wiped his nose with both paws. "I doubt that."

Odin took a mouthful of wine, then tossed the skin onto the ground. "I don't mean to be rude, Ratatoskr, but—"

"I have a message for you, Hangi."

"A what now?"

"A message," Ratatoskr said. "I'm always rushing. Up and down; down and up. From the birds to the wyrm and back again. But this time, the wyrm told me to find you, Hangi. You're right where he said you'd be!"

"The wyrm?" Odin's mind raced, twin ravens of thought and memory. A wyrm—the wyrm—was below? What was above? He'd tried looking up a long time ago, but the brightness there had blinded him as completely as the darkness below had swallowed him.

The squirrel's huge head bobbed up and down. He leaned forward, his apple-breath warm and oddly pleasant. "The wyrm said, 'Tell Hangi that his spirit will be safe from me should he come visiting. Tell him he can ask me the questions to which he wants answers.' "

"That's it?"

"Yes."

Answers.

"All right. Bye now, Hangi!"

"Wait!" Odin shouted, reaching out.

The tension in Ratatoskr's bunched haunches relaxed slightly. He flicked his tail in a way that conveyed impatience. "I have another message to deliver."

"I won't keep you long, I promise, it's . . . I don't know who—or what—this wyrm is."

Ratatoskr's shield-sized eyes grew wider. He came in close on his belly, so that his head was closer to level with Odin's. "You don't know the wyrm, Hangi?"

He had a pretty good guess, but best to make sure. He shook his head.

With one red-furred paw, Ratatoskr gestured downward. "It lives down there, below the women, among the roots. I'd thought you'd seen him when you stabbed and hung yourself."

The women must refer to the Norns. "No, I couldn't pierce that darkness. And when I looked up, the light blinded me."

"It is bright. But I'm used to it." Ratatoskr's chest puffed up. "So you've never seen Hawk and Eagle, either?"

Odin shook his head again.

"They seem nicer than the wyrm," Ratatoskr said, "but I still don't get too close. Dain told me not to."

Who was Dain? He rubbed his face. Priorities. "Can you tell me about the wyrm?"

"Yes," the squirrel said.

He waited.

Finally he asked, "Will you?"

Ratatoskr's whiskers twitched back and forth. He glanced up the mountainous height of Yggdrasil.

"How about I bring you some food? As thanks for sharing what you know with me."

"What kind of food?"

"What do you like?" Odin asked.

"Apples. But there are plenty near where I sleep."

Was it too much of a leap to assume that Ratatoskr ate the same apples that he'd found—the ones that kept the eater young and strong?

"I like apples, too," he said, "but I also enjoy nuts. In fact, all the squirrels I know eat them. They love them so much that they gather them up in great numbers and hide them away."

Ratatoskr flicked his tail. "Are they better than the wine?"

"I think you'll like them," he said, smiling. "How about this: I'll bring you some. If you don't like them, I'll bring you something different. Sound fair?"

Ratatoskr's shield-sized clawed paws combed his whiskers and then his ears and then over again. His tail flicked three times. "All right. Hawk and Eagle can wait a little. The wyrm says mean things to them, anyway. And they're mean right back."

Well that was interesting, confusing—and again, not relevant. Hopefully. "That is very kind of you, Ratatoskr."

The long whiskers twitched.

"What else can you tell me about the wyrm?"

"Which one?"

"There's more than one?"

Ratatoskr's head bobbed up and down. "Oh, yes. There are many hatchlings. They're always gnawing on the great tree's roots. And then there's the bigger wyrms. I've only seen a few of them. When they speak to me, their teeth glisten and drip like wet leaves."

"How many of the bigger wyrms?" he asked, hoping that Ratatoskr could count.

"I've seen this many." Ratatoskr held up one of his front paws. It had four nails, each as long as a sword. "And then there's the biggest of all. I've only ever heard it moving and speaking."

"How do you know it's the biggest?"

"Its voice hurts my ears." His paws darted up to cover his red-tufted ears. "I hear it sliding through the darkness. It tries to trick me into coming closer, like Hawk and Eagle do."

So in the darkness beneath Yggdrasil there lived one wyrm bigger than all its brood, perhaps four large wyrms (assuming Ratatoskr could count), and "many" hatchlings. And in the brightness above, there were at least two birds.

"One last question, my friend," he said. "May I hear the message from the wyrm to the birds? It seems as though they must hate each other, since they're always exchanging insults. If I have to choose sides, I'd like to make a good decision."

The huge tail flicked a few times, and Ratatoskr cocked his head to one side then the other. "The wyrm said you'd ask."

Did he now?

"He said I could tell you. The message was: 'Soon I'll be free, and I'll loop my coils around you. My broodlings and I will sink our fangs into your flesh and devour it.'"

"You're right, that's quite a mean thing to say," Odin said. "And how do the birds respond?"

"With taunts of their own: 'You never will, blind wyrm. Trapped wyrm, you never will. Not even when the heavens burn.' Sometimes they say worse."

Loki had said something like that—'when the heavens burn.' *Coincidence or significant? Both?*

"Thank you for that, Ratatoskr, you've been a great help. I'll bring you berries as well—they're sweet, like apples. I think you'll like them."

"You're welcome, Hangi," Ratatoskr said, bobbing his cart-sized head up and down. He bunched up, ready to leap away. "Don't trust the wyrm."

And then he was gone, scrabbling up the tree, grit and crumbling hunks of bark falling down behind him. Odin watched until he couldn't tell the red-brown squirrel from Yggdrasil's trunk.

He'd come here to sit upon his High Seat and watch as Frigg spoke with Thokk. While here, he could also learn about the threats facing both his family and the Aesir. But all he'd done so far was find out how little he knew. Ratatoskr had helped him make one connection, though. The spirit from the well that had attacked him was probably the wyrm in the darkness. It had taunted him then. Hurt him. But now he knew what he was dealing with—or had a better idea, at least.

Should he accept the wyrm's invitation? Absolutely. But trust it? Never.

He needed answers. That meant risk.

He could handle the wyrm.

44

LOKI

Day 7, morning

"Good morning, mother," Loki said to the old woman. "How did the night treat you?"

Loki wasn't sure which creaked louder, the rude bed frame or Thokk's ancient joints. He rose and offered her a hand.

"Thank you, my boy," she said, showing what few teeth remained to her. "I've always slept a bit better with a man in the house. Not that this is much of a house. Or much of a bed. Or . . ."

"Very funny," he said.

She knocked the bedpost with her cane and sniffed the air. "What's that I smell cooking?"

"I was up early and feeling better, thanks to your care, so I killed us some hares," Loki said. Which he had done, but in a snow cat's shape. Easier to hunt as a hunter.

Thokk's delighted laugh was nearly as creaky as her joints. "Now how did you catch one of them? They're quick. And wise to my little traps."

"Just have to be a little quicker," he said, still holding her arm as she shuffled toward the hearth.

"Maybe I'll step outside for a pee," she said. "Get it over with now before I have to haul myself out of that thing pretending to be a chair."

"All right, mother," he said. "I'll get the bread frying, too. I had some in my bag."

She smacked her lips and looked into the pot, stirring it. "Meat, soup, and are those mushrooms in there? A lucky morning for old Thokk."

Loki dropped the pot lid a hair too late; the cave rang with the clang. "Sorry, hotter than I thought."

Besides, he wanted to be found now.

"Careful with that, boy," Thokk said, glaring at him. "I've only got the one pot."

"Not for long, mother." He used a rag to pick up the hot lid.

"Eh, what's that now?" She stopped her slow shuffle toward the door and looked back over her shoulder.

"Just that I need to repay your kindness," he said, smiling. "I'll make sure this is the last day you spend with this dented old pot."

"Don't need more'n one," she said with a sniff. She swung a thin cloak around thinner shoulders and shuffled out into the cold.

"NOW THAT WAS SOME FINE SOUP," Thokk said, sitting back after her third helping. She slapped her chair's arm. "Might fatten me up yet, eh?"

"If the Norns so desire." He took her bowl and spoon. Both were pitted and scarred with many winters' use.

"As cruel as they are kind, I think. When I was younger, I thought they had a purpose in mind. Now I'm not so sure."

"You think so? What about Aegir and Rán? They're not unkind. Just . . . remote, maybe?"

Thokk frowned. "Maybe. But those two definitely aren't kind. I don't think they care one way or the other. Sacrifice a bull to bring life to the fields, and maybe it works, maybe it doesn't. Why kill the bull, then? And what sense, what kindness, is there to our people dying out? None that I can see."

"None I see, either," he said.

She waved a gnarled hand at him. "No, I tell you, all you can rely is yourself."

"What of family and friends?" Loki rinsed the bowls and spoons with some melted snow. "Without your kindness, I'd be dead now."

"And I'd lack a full belly," she said with a near toothless grin. "No, I tell you, friends and family are like trees. Some roots run deep and can take all the tugging in the world. Others run shallow. A solid pull and they come free. And where does that leave you?"

"Ass over head?"

Thokk clapped her hands together and rocked back and forth, wheezing and cackling. It hadn't been that funny. She trailed off into a hacking cough. "That's exactly where, boy," she said between coughs. "And you never know which till you start pulling."

"All too true, mother," he said, stacking the dried bowls atop the table. "Are you all right?"

"I'm fine," she said, fanning the air with an age-ruined hand. "I still think you're looking pretty spry for a man half-eaten by a bear a night ago."

He shrugged. "I slept well and had a good dream. Besides, it's already well past midday. Never doubt the restorative power of sleep."

She grunted. "Well, you're welcome to spend another night if you like."

"I'd like that, mother," he said. "Besides, if I venture out now, the wolf will have me."

"Or the bears." She put a hand to her head. "You know, my boy, I think I ate too much. I'm not feeling all that well."

Loki took her arm and helped her up from her rocker. "Let me help you to your bed."

Her arm felt like two sticks wrapped in sailcloth. She shuffled a couple of steps, winced, and shuffled a couple more. He helped her lay on her side and pulled the wool blanket up to her chin.

She shivered. Pain shot across her face, and she twisted to look for reassurance.

"Why are you crying?" she asked.

He wiped his tears. "You were very kind to me."

She spasmed again. Blood flecked her lips. He fetched the bear skin and laid it over her, then took her thin, feverishly hot hand in his.

"I really don't feel well," she said, her eyes screwed shut. Her voice was slurred a little, and the way she lay made her look even older than she was.

He brushed her thin white hair back from her face. "I'm so sorry, mother."

"For the food? Don't be. Tasted so goo—"

She hissed in a breath, and her eyes rolled back in her head. And then she convulsed, her hand gripping his impossibly hard and for what seemed far too long.

"For the pain. I didn't have enough to make it quick."

Her breath rattled out. She went limp.

He kissed her brow. Seemed he was a coward when it came to murdering old women.

45

ODIN

Day 8, midday

Odin pressed his head against the sharp bark of his High Seat. With the pain came both release and a tether. The latter let him find his body again; the former let his spirit fly free . . .

. . . *down Yggdrasil's immensity toward Ithavoll and what lay below.*

Clear water trickled down the rough bark, pooling, overflowing, and then continuing down. He recalled the enchantments he'd cut into Mimir's severed head, the songs he'd sung and how he'd placed his uncle's head so that the water would always flow over it and—

There was a spot of decay on the tree.

Then another, and then many more as he plummeted alongside Yggdrasil's trunk. Where the clear-flowing water touched the rot, the bark turned murky and stank. He wondered what this meant, if anything. Everything rotted in time.

He pushed away all thought of black decay spreading across Baldr's face.

Ithavoll's white mists and green grass loomed before him. He dove through them, burrowing through the rich black soil that lay beneath. It smelled fresh, a newly turned field ready for seed.

He burrowed deeper still, following Yggdrasil's taproot down into the soil.

The soil pressed upon him.

There was no light. No sound. No movement, save his own.

Darkness above, darkness below.

Was he still moving?

It grew hard to breathe.

He thrashed in his seat.

He hauled in a deep breath. He was in both places at once. His spirit unmoving, perhaps, in the lightless soil, aware of his struggling body and yet unwilling to return.

He needed to know.

Pain rippled back and forth along the tether. He willed himself to go deeper into the soil, deeper into the darkness. The lightlessness persisted until, eventually, green dots winked into life. Were they real or just the spots seen by the hanged man choking out his last breath?

He must know.

The weight on his chest grew. His ribs creaked. He couldn't breathe.

More spots. Hundreds.

He thrashed.

Still more spots—thousands of green-glowing lights. He was in among them.

You'll die, his body said. *Not yet*, his spirit replied.

The spots were wriggling.

He went closer and then recoiled.

They were wyrms, and they were chewing on Yggdrasil's roots, swarming over her roots like flies on a corpse.

He broke through the soil into—

A gasp ripped at his throat.

His spirit screamed its triumph.

His lungs filled; his thrashing eased.

———

HE STARED down into a familiar place—the Ginnungagap. Red, roiling fire blasted into the Gap from below; flowing ice plummeted from above. Where the two torrents met, the Roaring Cauldron churned, stretching out eleven mighty arms across the Gap.

And still the Gap was unfilled.

"Welcome to my home, little father," said a familiar voice. "I knew you'd make it."

He spun in place, resisting the Roaring Cauldron's outward shove.

"Look up," the voice said.

He did. He saw Yggdrasil's taproot, thick as a mountain, and three other roots that reached down past the vast black canopy of soil, as if drinking from the Roaring Cauldron itself. An immensity slithered through the soil above. Two glacial eyes opened in the darkness, black slits in the center of each with yellow-green pupils. A double row of iceberg teeth yawned open.

"Do you like the view, little father?" the voice asked. The impossibly immense, toothy jaws didn't move. "You may find it hard to believe, but I long for more."

The thing was between him and his body.

Fear—and it was gut-wrenching, bladder-loosening fear—reverberated up and down that slender sliver of a tether. Could the beast see the tether?

"We have something in common, then," Odin said. He felt the wyrm's pleasure. It knew he was afraid. He couldn't believe that he *was* afraid.

"More than one thing," the wyrm replied.

Fear killed warriors and witches alike.

"Ratatoskr delivered your message," Odin said, "if you are the great wyrm."

The two huge eyes grew bigger still as the immensity propelled itself forward. The teeth vanished as the jaws closed.

Fear could kill him.

He saw the snake-like snout first, a forked tongue flickering in and out. Dead-white scales, the yellow of old bones at the edges, covered a sinuous neck that stretched toward him. The yellow-green pupils never shifted focus as they approached.

He was a speck floating before a monster.

"You tell me," the great wyrm said.

Through the tether, he felt his gut tighten. His body was sweating. "Ratatoskr said you promised answers. And safe passage."

"Did I?" The glacial eyes blinked.

Was that a sly glint in the monster's eyes? Odin thought back to the message Ratatoskr had delivered: *He can ask me the questions to which he wants answers.* Panic wormed its way through Odin's mind. He should've considered that promise more carefully.

But he still would have risked this conversation.

"Ask your questions, son of Burr."

Odin began drifting toward the right. Best ask his questions while he could. "Were you the spirit in the well that I fought? It also called me 'little father' and 'son of Burr.'"

"Do no others address you similarly?"

"So that's a yes."

"What if it is?"

"Then I'd have an answer."

The wyrm's eyes seemed contemplative. Odin accelerated his rightward drift, arcing upward.

"Yes," the wyrm said. "I am the spirit you fought."

"Thank you, great wyrm," Odin said. "I suspected as much."

"I am benevolent."

No more than he himself was.

Was the canopy above a little closer now? It had to be. Best to ask another question; perhaps he'd get another answer.

"I have a memory—a forgotten one, newly remembered," he said. "Loki threatened me, my family, and everything I've built. Did you plant that memory in my mind?"

The wyrm blinked. "And how would that advance my ends, little father?"

Fair question. Odin racked his memory for what it had said when they'd fought. It had kept asking him to come down to visit. "That's not an answer."

The wyrm said nothing.

"When last we met, you warned me that my doom was set no matter what I did. That you'd read it in Yggdrasil's bark."

"I also said that you could join me here, that that was unwritten." The wyrm's immensity doubled in size, its iceberg teeth bared in open threat.

Odin flung himself backward, realizing that the beast had slithered forward. "You seem to bear me some ill will."

"Not especially."

That sounded truthful, but the wyrm was toying with him. Why? He'd once surmised that the spirit in the well wanted to possess him. Was that the beast's goal now?

"Then why have you lured me here?" he asked.

The wyrm gazed upward. "Has the sun grown dark?"

"I don't understand."

"What of the winters? I yearn for the three long years when the winter never ends. Have they begun?"

Odin said nothing. Was the wyrm asking about future events? He accelerated his upward progress.

As if the wyrm could hear his thoughts, it said, "Ah well. You see, son of Burr, I don't know everything that happens in your world." Then it seemed to smile. "We share a prison, you and I. Each of us in our own way seeks escape."

"You could break through." Odin waved his hand toward the canopy of soil and roots above. "You're big enough."

"You'd think that, wouldn't you?" Now the wyrm seemed to shake its cliff-sized head. "But no, the same force that you rail against, little father, constrains me. Can you believe it?"

Odin had flown high above the wyrm now, but the beast was so huge it hadn't yet had to change where it was looking. "I can indeed."

"I wonder if this is the time the Weaver foresaw," the great wyrm said. "I know what you're doing, son of Burr. You will only succeed if this is not the time."

"You promised safe passage," he said, knowing that promise had been as intentionally vague as the other. Ratatoskr had said there were at least four other big wyrms.

The glacier-sized eyes watched him go. "I did."

Odin felt the attacks coming, one from below, two from either side. He shot upward, a salmon leaping impossible waterfalls. You never saw the one that—

He dodged sideways, down and then back up again. Jaws clamped shut on the space he'd just occupied. Fire flared in his arm.

Stupid, stupid, stupid.

"Which part was stupid, little father? Coming here or listening to a squirrel . . ." A rhythmic rumble coursed over him, and Odin realized the great wyrm was laughing. "Just think, that squirrel's more wits than you."

He glanced down. Four wyrms coursed toward him. They were white like the great wyrm, but smaller—merely as long as winding rivers, their eyes a feral green. He doubled his pace and dove into the black soil, burrowing upward past the wriggling green-glowing wyrms. He crushed one in his hand as he passed, to see if he could. A wet, slimy stink coated his numbing hand.

"Now, now, don't be petty," the great wyrm said. "This isn't the time after all, little father. I didn't think it was, but one can hope."

Gasping, Odin clawed his way upward.

"Regardless, you've danced with some of my brood. They'll be looking for you."

He broke through into Ithavoll, the wet mist cold on his face.

The wyrm's voice continued, fainter now. "Perhaps they'll bring you back down to me. Or you'll brave another journey by yourself. Regardless, little father, you are welcome any time.

"I, Nithogg, invite you."

———

SCREAMING, Odin opened his eye.

His hands trembled. His right arm was numb from the hand up.

His left side burned. His legs were weak. He hauled in air like a starving fisherman his nets.

What was that thing?

Nithogg.

Are you all right, Wing-Father? Huginn asked. *I am worried. The Watcher is, too.*

The back of his head was wet with blood. His hair was matted with sweat. Odin looked out across the unmoving, twisted bark sea of Yggdrasil's branches.

For now, yes, Huginn.

For Heimdall, he said, "Yes, I'm all right."

Huginn said, *The Watcher says Frigg will reach Thokk's cave by dawn tomorrow.*

"Thank you, Heimdall," he said aloud. "Has night fallen over Gladsheim?"

Huginn spoke again. *The Watcher says yes, he will have Huginn tell you when Frigg arrives.*

Odin swore to himself. Sometimes, time beside the tree felt slower than back in Gladsheim. This was Baldr's last night as a corpse, and here he was, a living wreckage from having confronted . . . what, exactly?

Nithogg.

He shuddered again, hating himself for that reaction.

"Again, my thanks, Heimdall." When this was over, he'd speak with Heimdall about Nithogg and its brood. But for now, he had to recover his strength.

Grunting, he forced his stiff limbs into motion. He pushed himself up from the High Seat and on trembling legs, his left side burning still, he staggered to the comparative safety of the platform. His left leg gave way and he fell nearly face first into the knot from which Ratatoskr had lapped the wine. One indignity avoided, despite two others—he stank of his own piss and shit. He'd fouled himself like a boy on a battlefield. Never, never had he confronted something like that. Ymir had paled in comparison.

He pushed himself up and stumbled to where he'd left his gear.

He snatched up his wineskin and, gulping, drained it. He dragged a shaking hand across his mouth.

It called him "little father." It had called him the same when he'd fought the waters of Urdr's Well. It had also said it'd been born when Odin slew Ymir, something else he didn't understand. How in Aegir's name could he not have known this wyrm existed? That answer, at least, was obvious.

His pride and arrogance.

A strutting cock thought its yard and few hens comprised the entire world. So, too, had he thought his puny realm, and those adjacent, were his to control, that he could stretch forth his hand and exert his will upon them. And so he had, for a long time. He'd stood on the threshold of pain between life and death. He'd won power and knowledge and wisdom because of it, not once, but many times. And he'd believed himself the equal of it all.

His missing eye throbbed. Here he sat, again reminded of his blindness. His ignorance. His stupidity. It had only taken the murder of his son to shake him from his stupor. Empty despair crept over him, a blanket drawn up over a child woken by a nightmare.

But he was awake now. He knew how little he knew.

Faced with one nightmare—Ymir—a lifetime ago, he'd become one himself. He'd found the power he needed, and he'd taken it. Nithogg was no different.

Odin hadn't become Ymir's equal till he'd remade himself. He wasn't Nithogg's equal either.

Not yet.

46

FRIGG

Day 9, early afternoon

Tired and hungry, Frigg landed in the deep, drifted snow before the cave's entrance. Her spread wings reverted to her cloak and her own arms. The wind shrieked over the ridge, tugging her long hair free of its loose braid. She dug in her pouch for another strip of cloth, then reached up with gloved hands and tamed her hair.

Muninn had settled onto a high branch of a fir that overlooked the cave's entrance. The raven had delivered Odin's message and guided Frigg to Thokk's cave. Frigg turned away. It was up to her now. All she had to do was make an old woman cry.

She wiped melting ice from the sun-warmed rock wall in front of her. It wept from the warmth of Sól's smile. Perhaps a similarly warm approach would thaw the old woman's heart. No way to know except to walk in there and start talking.

Frigg clenched and released her hands. This was what she'd wanted, wasn't it? To be out in the world doing something important rather than stuck in a hall issuing judgments about other peoples' mistakes without making her own. To step away from days spent judging others when she herself had done so little.

The neat row of dead women and children laid out in Ifington's destroyed streets welled up in her memory. Everyone lost children. And here she stood, unique among mothers, since she had a chance to get her child back.

Frigg fought back fresh tears and drew her seax.

The rough entrance to the crone's cave gaped with a yellow warmth that contrasted with the stone grays and ice whites of the mountainside. Frigg knocked the hilt of her knife against the stone of the cave mouth. No reply. She stepped out of the wind to stand beside the manmade wall that helped keep the warmth in and the cold out. The rich scent of a simmering spiced stew drifted around the corner.

Her voice chased the echo of her knife's knock. "May I enter? It's Frigg. I've come to speak with Thokk."

"Who now?" The reply sounded wintrier than cracks opening on a frozen lake.

Frigg stomped the snow from her boots, knocked the snow and ice from her cloak, and threw it back over her shoulders. She sheathed her knife and followed the stew's inviting aroma, pushing past the rough woolen blanket strung across the inner entrance with her hands open and her arms spread.

A fire danced in a deep recess to one side, past a small table. It must have drafted to the outside, for the air inside was mostly free of smoke. She drew a deep, relieved breath.

"Now that I see ye, I still don't know who ye are." The speaker looked more like a dark lump in a rude chair than an old woman, as Frigg's eyes adjusted to the dark, smoky dwelling. "Second visitor in as many nights. Old Thokk was never this popular."

So this was Thokk. The chair creaked as the old woman shifted, beckoning her forward with a claw-like hand.

"Closer now, child, I don't bite," Thokk said with a wheezing cackle. "Not hard, anyway."

Gradually, the features of the cave became clear. Hides covered the floor, but Frigg could still feel the chill radiating from the stone beneath. A haze of smoke clung to the high ceiling. A crude bed was off to her left, maybe two spears' lengths away.

Every part of the hearth and cave showed signs of Jotunn stone shaping. The chambers in the mountain behind Jotunheim were like this, except far more expansive with room for thousands of families. She'd roamed them as a child. Like Thokk, she was a Jotunn. If she had to, she could use that.

As Frigg drew closer, Thokk's features became clear. Her face was a shriveled fruit; her fingers, gnarled roots; her limbs, bare winter branches.

"May I sit, mother?" Frigg asked.

"Depends. What have you brought me?"

"I don't—"

"I gift you with warmth from my hearth, shelter from the wind and snow, and"—with her wooden cane, she tapped the iron pot hanging in the hearth—"food from my meager stores. What do you offer me?"

She'd brought no more than a wineskin and some flatbread. She set both before her. "Little enough, mother, for I've traveled light and swift to reach you. Grant me some of your time, and I promise to bring whatever you want."

"And what's a promise from you worth, eh?" One of the old woman's eyes was watery and half clouded, but the other fixed her like a thrown spear. "In all my winters, I've only ever heard of one Frigg. It's said she left her people to marry that old goat, Ygg."

"I am that Frigg," she said, no more ashamed of who she'd become than who she'd been.

Thokk leaned in, her chair creaking. "And still so young? Quite the magic he tempted you with. Did you bring any of that with you?"

The old woman's withered face split in a toothless grin, and she wheezed with laughter till a cough took her. She hacked into a fist and then smacked her lips together with a wet sound that sent a shudder down Frigg's spine.

"I have none to share," Frigg began, "but as I—"

Thokk waved a hand, then tapped the cauldron again. "This smells ready to me. Take it off the fire and pour me a bowl—and one for yourself, if you wish."

Frigg set a steaming soapstone bowl and wooden spoon into Thokk's hands. Then she took a small bowl for herself and sat down cross-legged before Thokk. She sipped the stew. It tasted gamey and earthy, with small strips of meat—hare, maybe—mixed with roots, herbs and mushrooms. Better fare than she'd expected.

Thokk drank from a wooden cup. "So, Frigg, why have you come so far and so fast to Thokk's cave?"

This was it. Her moment. Could Heimdall hear her? Probably, since he'd heard Thokk speak her own name. Was Odin watching? Not through stone, unless he'd sent his spirit.

Was Hel?

Frigg's stomach gurgled. She carefully set down her bowl. "You've lived a long time, mother. Is it safe to guess that you've lost friends and family along the way?"

Thokk's face split like cracked leather, and her keen eye twinkled. "Oh, aye, great lady. I'm the last of my family. You and yours saw to that."

"I'm sorry for—"

Thokk slurped her soup with a sound like a knife being honed.

Frigg cleared her throat. "There's been too much death and suffering among our people, thousands upon thousands over the winters. I've come because Odin—"

"Ygg." It was a stab with her voice.

"That's what the Jotunn call him, yes. And with good reason. For a long time, that was my own name for him. But perhaps we can move past that. So much harm has been done on both sides."

"And yet the Aesir are free to roam, farm, trade, or whatever, while the Jotunn are penned like cattle—worse than cattle—and left to fend for themselves."

Already she was off on the wrong path. Frigg raised her hands. "I'm not here to argue the sad history of our tribes. I'm here to plead for our future."

Thokk smacked her lips. "So why talk to me? I've had nothing to do with the course set by the Skrymir—except that I've watched my sons slaughtered in one pointless battle after another. My poor old husband gave his life saving my daughter from rape and worse at the hands of the Einherjar."

"I'm here because of my son, Baldr."

"I heard he's dead."

Frigg blinked, and her stomach heaved.

Thokk fixed her with an iron eye and leaned forward. "Not easy, is it? Never does get better. Just more familiar."

"I suppose it wouldn't." Frigg stared down at the hides she sat on. Her stomach churned. What could she possibly say to a woman—a mother—who'd lost everyone and everything? Why would this woman show any mercy at all?

"Well, great lady, say what you've come to say. I've little enough time left. I'd rather not spend it looking at the top of your head."

She met the crone's eyes. "I'm here because you can save my son."

"And how am I supposed to do that?"

"Weep for him."

Thokk slurped in another spoonful and set the bowl aside with a clink. "Give me some of that wine."

Frigg handed her the wineskin. The old woman tilted it back and drank. She rasped with enjoyment and smacked her lips.

"Been a long time since wine passed these old gums." She hung the skin from the arm of her chair and rocked thoughtfully. "Weep for him, you say? That makes no sense to me."

"To me either, I suppose," Frigg said. "But that's the condition that was set."

"By who?"

"Hel."

"And who's that?"

"Loki's daughter."

Thokk slapped her hands together. "That wicked old liar, eh? He's still around?"

"He certainly is. As are his children." She steeled herself against a shiver. Hel could be there now, watching as they spoke.

"And how did his daughter come to have such power over your son?"

"I don't know. Odin says she has some power over the dead, power that's different from what he himself has. She—Hel, I mean—netted Baldr's spirit on this side of the final plunge into the Ginnungagap. Odin's magic keeps Baldr's body whole, but not for much longer."

"So how does my weeping for Baldr affect anything?"

"My guess"—she spread her hands—"is that Hel somehow knows of all you've suffered. And maybe she thinks if you can shed enough of your hatred for the Aesir to weep for Baldr, then maybe that's a good enough reason to let him live again."

Thokk sat back and rocked for another few moments. "I've heard of your son. He brought food and healing arts to Jotunheim. Not enough to reverse whatever curse killed my daughter and her unborn child, but enough to give us a little more hope."

Frigg nodded encouragingly.

"I suppose some Jotunn killed him?"

"I don't know who killed him," Frigg replied. "His brother threw the spear that took his life, but I believe someone else guided his arm."

Thokk quirked her lips at that. "Shrewd distinction."

Frigg drew herself up a little. She ignored the muted rumble in her belly.

"Who's his brother now? Thor?"

Frigg shook her head. "That's his half-brother. The one who threw the spear is my son Hodr."

Thokk folded her crooked hands in her lap and said nothing. Was that sympathy glimmering in her black eyes, or Frigg's own hope reflected back at her?

"Well, that's a sad thing," Thokk finally said.

"Indeed it is."

"So you're in a bad spot? Son killing son. About to lose both probably, eh?" She took another pull on the wineskin. "It's not that I don't feel for you, great lady. But weep? Seems like the ravens have finally come home to roost."

Frigg inhaled sharply, then stopped herself from lashing out. This old mother didn't deserve a harsh response. But did she? She bowed her head.

Yes, she did.

47

FRIGG

Day 9, midafternoon

Frigg rubbed her eyes. She deserved this old woman's contempt. Three nights ago, she hadn't known Thokk existed. Two nights ago, she'd learned Thokk was the key to bringing Baldr back to life. Yet how many others like Thokk lived among the Jotunn and the Aesir?

What would convince this woman to weep for an enemy's fallen son?

Thokk picked up her bowl and scraped her spoon across the bottom.

"My son was trying to end the war between Jotunn and Aesir," Frigg said.

Thokk slurped in another mouthful.

"All the tragedy you've experienced traces back to a conflict that only a few now living remember—a few who took part in that conflict," Frigg continued. "Those few hate those who sprung from Ymir's loins. And yes, I speak of Odin, his brothers—if they yet live—and his cousins. But Baldr is Odin's son, and mine, the product of a literal union of our tribes. He spent many winters—too many—fighting the Jotunn alongside his kinsmen. But when Baldr saw his brother blinded, all that changed."

The spoon renewed its grating against the bowl. How was there even soup left?

"He saw how pointless the fighting was. He gave up sword and spear. He dedicated himself to the art of healing. Every winter since the Last War, he went to Jotunheim and helped everyone he could. In the last dozen winters, Baldr has worked tirelessly to bring our tribes back together—or failing that, to at least end the bloodshed."

Thokk sniffed. "Maybe Ygg set one brother against the other because he wants the fighting to continue. Because he wants every Jotunn baby dead."

That was absurd. And a strange thing for Thokk to say. "No. Baldr convinced his father to give peace a chance. He convinced Odin to wait, to let him continue mending this split in our tribe. We're all of one stock. We share Ymir and Audhumbla, revering them as the father and mother of Jotunn and Aesir, just as both our peoples revere Aegir and Rán—for different reasons, and with rituals grown different over time. But our roots spread from the same tree."

Frigg made an expansive gesture. "As a girl I played in stone-homes like this. We have common ground, you and I, as our people do. Yet all we've done for many hundreds of winters is fight. We can end this age of spear and sword and axe. Right here."

"There'll never be an end to all the killing." Thokk punctuated each word with a rap of wooden spoon against wooden bowl. "The Aesir wanted good Jotunn land, so they took it. Then they forced us into this rough land that's grown less fertile with each passing winter. Just as the Jotunn women have."

"I know. Baldr knew. He had a plan to end all that, to reverse it. Baldr had a plan for the Jotunn to leave Utgard for Asgard—"

Thokk laughed. "Asgard and Utgard, is it now? Those names say it all. You think the Aesir will accept the Jotunn into their towns and villages?"

"I do, mother—"

"Don't call me that. I'm no mother to you—or to anyone anymore."

Frigg held up her hands. "I apologize. I intended only respect. We

Aesir have done wrong, I know. The Jotunn have, too. Baldr meant to heal the rift between our people. He knew it'd take time and trust and a willingness to change on both sides. Part of that means a willingness to set aside old hatreds."

Thokk pushed herself as much upright in her chair as her bent spine would allow. "So you rebuke me, *Almother*? Odd tack for one who wants something from me."

"If I didn't, you'd accuse me of groveling."

"Maybe."

"May I add, Thokk, that I think you were perhaps much more in your youth than you'd have me believe."

Thokk's black eyes glittered as they shifted from the fire back to her. "And why do you say that?"

"You argue well. Better than most I've had dealings with."

"My husband was a chief." She waved one age-ruined hand. "I paid attention."

For a long time, the only sound in the small cave was Thokk's labored breathing and the crackling fire.

"You've grown so quiet, great lady, and after such a plea, too." Thokk wiped a crooked finger beneath a dry eye and held it up. "You came here to make me weep for your son. I've yet to do so."

"I'm not sure you will. I'm not sure that anything I say will move you."

"Sit there long enough, and maybe it'll come to you." Thokk's black eyes were twin snake pits.

"My son doesn't have much time left. Otherwise, I'd sit here forever."

"Eh? What's that mean?"

"I told you he didn't have long. I meant that literally. My husband wove a charm that has kept the rot from Baldr's body. He said the magic would only last nine nights."

"And?"

"Last night was the ninth."

"So Baldr is gone now?"

Frigg hated herself for it, but she gave a small, helpless shrug. "I don't know. I think maybe he has a little time. I hope he does. As I hope you'll—"

"Weep?"

Frigg nodded. She felt small and tiny and naked and raw. And she hurt, as if she'd caught her thumb under a rasp—not the pain afterward, but the realization of how much pain was coming when the rasp ground across her skin.

She hated the agony of hope inside her chest.

Thokk's glare transfixed her. "Maybe you'll weep for me and all those who've suffered thanks to the boot Ygg's planted on their necks. For all the promises he's broken and all the lives he's destroyed. I'd be with my family now but for him."

Spittle flew from Thokk's mouth. Despite herself, Frigg recoiled from the old women's rage.

"Maybe if you and your wicked husband had spent more time thinking about the repercussions of all your lies and wars and petty hatreds, more Jotunn—and Aesir—would be alive to enjoy the prosperity that you believe your dead son might have brought to the land." Thokk smacked her hand against her chair and jabbed a crooked finger at Frigg. "Why should you have your boy restored to you when thousands of others will never, ever get their children back?"

Frigg said nothing.

What could she say? Thokk was right. Nothing about any of this was fair. It was only because Odin was exceptional that Baldr's restoration was even possible.

But Baldr, too, was exceptional. Thokk had hinted as much without intending it. Baldr had once been a killer of Jotunn just as his fathers and brothers had been. But he'd changed. He'd chosen the path of healing to set the break between Aesir and Jotunn and help it mend straight.

In his own way, that was maybe what Odin wanted to do with their visions.

Thokk swiped both hands beneath dry eyes and thrust her crooked fingers at Frigg. "I have no more tears to give. This old body is worn out. Tired. All I have to look forward to is death and maybe seeing my loved ones again before we all fall back into the Gap and are lost in its currents." She made a shooing gesture with both hands and with spittle-flecked lips shouted, "Now get out of my home! The only tears you'll ever get from me is the dew that gathers on my dead eyes."

Numb in the face of such ferocity, Frigg stood. Her feet tangled in the stool and she stumbled backward, caught herself on the rough stone wall, and fled the cave.

The cold air hit her like a fist in the stomach. She fell to her knees, chest heaving.

She had failed.

48

LOKI

Day 9, midafternoon

Loki heard Frigg's scream as if he were beside Angrboda again, trying to comfort her even as she pulled away.

Angrboda had blamed him. Never mind that he'd been the only one facing reality. If you heard a bear, you didn't wait till it saw you; you changed course. You didn't beg the avalanche to turn aside; you got out of its way.

If you wanted to kill a bear, you prepared a trap. If you wanted to turn the avalanche aside, you labored for years to build a channel.

And that's what he'd done.

Frigg's scream trailed away into ragged weeping.

Loki exhaled.

Angrboda had keened for weeks. She'd torn at her clothes and her hair. She'd destroyed her hands and nails, clawing circles in the earth. And then, screaming, she'd poured power into those circles until he thought the rocks would shatter from the sound. He'd assumed she was flinging charms at Ygg. But for all her prowess as a witch, those spells had never reached him—or if they had, Ygg had given no sign.

Yet she had berated him for not fighting Odin.

Week after week, month after month, Angrboda had cut and re-cut circles in the dirt. In a broken voice, she rasped rune words and sang charms he didn't want to understand. He kept her alive, setting out broths and meats and breads. He built fires to warm her at night. He prowled the Iron Wood and kept the predators away. For all that, she rarely saw him, even when she looked into his eyes. The Angrboda he knew and loved had given herself over to hatred and the need for revenge so completely that she'd lost herself.

Or so he'd thought.

He'd approached her one evening as Sól was setting while Máni was rising. The sky seemed split equally between light and dark. Silence shrouded the glade around their home—no insects, no wind, no babbling from the nearby river.

That barrow silence took even Angrboda. She kneeled in the center of one of her circles, head cocked as though she were listening to someone, clasping filthy hands between her breasts and rocking back and forth, back and forth.

Then a hideously thankful smile split her face. She'd stood and walked into what became her house alone. Angrboda had made her choice.

Two weeks later, she was dead.

His beloved brother Odin—Ygg—had set those events into motion. It wasn't Loki's fault.

It wasn't.

But wasn't it? Maybe a little?

But what else could he have done?

When he'd told Angrboda that he'd changed Ygg's mind so that Hel, Fenrir, and Jorm were exiled rather than executed, she'd mocked him. Then she'd withdrawn into her grief and crazed witchery. And when she was gone, he spent the next two hundred winters planning for this very moment.

Frigg's weeping was the sound of his success.

He tried to savor it, like fresh wine in his mouth. He'd worked for it. He'd sacrificed for it. So why did his gut churn? Why did his old woman's face burn with shame?

Because all he'd done was break a grieving woman's heart.

Lies, the hearth whispered. *You have succeeded.*

He hadn't. Success meant Ygg's ruination.

And all he's built—that includes his family.

Frigg hadn't wronged him. She had in fact made efforts to include him—which he'd rebuffed.

After the fact. Out of pity and her own shame for what they did to you and yours. They knew it was wrong, but they did it anyway.

Which Ygg had admitted six nights ago—but it was only wrong because the Norns' prophecy had wounded Ygg. If someone else suffered, well, that was all right.

And here you sit, having suffered much.

He'd taken the brotherhood oath seriously. It had elevated him from the son of a minor jarl's daughter, who'd been married off to a Jotunn, to the blood brother of the chief Aesir himself. Men had killed for less.

Yes, and then you were used, humiliated, and mocked.

He'd mated with a stallion so the Aesir could have their wall. He'd been captured and tortured, forced to aid in the theft of Idunn and her apples. Even after he saved Idunn, all he'd gotten was blame. He'd won a bet—barely—and so the Aesir received fabulous items and potent weapons crafted by the Dark Alvar. What had he gotten? His lips sewn shut.

Your revenge is justified.

All of it had led to where he sat now. So why did he feel this—

It's called doubt. Worry.

Nonsense.

No? What happens when they figure it all out?

Ygg would kill everyone Loki loved. And then make an example of him.

Exactly.

The Skrymir had said he'd make sure Sigyn got away safely. Vali and Narfi were with Helveg—the spear tip that would be thrust into the Aesir's side.

First you trust Ygg, and now you trust Skrymir?

What choice was there?

Weep.

If he wept, Baldr would live again and his children would remain prisoners—until he could retrieve the devices he'd had crafted and free them.

Two nights ago, Vafthrudnir had said the Jotunn would attack in four nights. He had two nights left. Would Ygg be more or less distracted with Baldr alive or dead?

That doesn't matter now.

Ygg would kill Hel for changing their deal. He might even kill Fenrir and Jorm to remove their potential for future threat.

A dead Baldr would give you more time to free them, wouldn't it?

Possibly. If Baldr remained dead, Ygg would have to remain in Gladsheim until the funeral. It'd take at least one night to prepare that. If they waited longer, the Jotunn would attack.

And under cover of that, he could free his children.

"Thokk!" came Frigg's shout. "I ask you to reconsider."

If you wept, Baldr would live again. What if he interceded with his father on Hel's behalf?

Loki snorted.

Had Hel not acted, Baldr's spirit would have rejoined the Ginnungagap long before Ygg returned. You yourself could argue that.

He could. And maybe it would work. But that was a big maybe. If Ygg decided to kill Hel, neither Baldr nor Frigg nor anyone besides Thor, perhaps, would try to stop him. Loki could fight, but Ygg would sweep him aside.

If you don't force tears from those ancient eyes, Ygg will definitely kill Hel. But if you do weep, Ygg might keep his word and free Hel—and only possibly kill her.

But then he'd have his son back.

So what? Baldr will argue against killing the woman who saved him.

"Thokk!" Frigg sounded angry. Determined. Perhaps she intended violence against the woman whose refusal to shed tears kept her son from renewed life.

Why had Hel put him in this position? She'd looked right at him when she'd set the new condition, as if she were putting the decision into his hands. Life or death for an enemy's son.

You murdered Thokk because she would have wept.

Didn't that mean he'd chosen death for Baldr?

All those winters past, he'd been afraid that Ygg would kill his children. Fear had set his feet on this path. He couldn't change that any more than he could un-kill those he'd slain to get where he was now.

Are you a coward?

What would a coward do?

He'd weep. He'd show a small mercy, hoping he could wriggle free of a hard decision. Cowards kept quiet.

He'd been quiet because he was stalking his prey.

Loki dug gnarled fingers into the pouch at his side and produced one of the black pebbles the Svartalvar had made for him.

He had a choice to make.

49

FRIGG

Day 9, late afternoon

Rage and grief and horror and guilt burst from Frigg's throat as if from a broken dam. On her hands and knees in the snow, she screamed on and on until her throat grew ragged and her voice hoarse. Gradually, the keening died in her raw throat and she panted, eyes closed.

She was the pot after a stew had been poured out, full one moment, empty the next. No, not empty—spent. A horse after a sprint. Done in.

Finished.

She looked up at the blue sky. Clouds encroached from the west. She tasted snow on the breeze. They'd know she had failed just by looking at her. She laughed at herself. By *looking* at her? She'd probably deafened Heimdall.

She said it anyway. "I've failed, Heimdall. Tell Odin." Then, more quietly, "Tell everyone."

But she'd proved Hodr hadn't intended to kill Baldr. She'd saved one son. She sat back on her haunches. Sure, she had. Just as the Norns' prophecy had saved Baldr at the expense of Hodr's eyes.

Muninn fixed her with a black eye.

"Is that you looking at me, Odin?" she asked.

Muninn cocked her head. She fluffed her wings and croaked, "No."

"You couldn't have done any better," she said as if Odin were present.

Muninn blinked again, her eyes corpse-white and then beady black again.

"What should I do?" Frigg asked the raven. "What would you do?"

Even as she asked, she knew the answer. Odin would make the old woman weep tears of blood if need be. But could she? Should she? Even if she did, what good would those tears be?

She drew her knife—not the falcon-hilted seax Odin had given her, but the new one she'd bought from a smith in Ifington. The blade's spine was blackened and bore distinctive, artistic hammer marks. Sunlight burned along the skymetal blade, accentuating the wavy line that ran from tip to oval-shaped guard. A gold braid was engraved into the guard; the heavy pommel echoed the guard's design. The smith had engraved the F rune into it; he said he did it on all his weapons, to bind them to their owners. His own master mark was subtly marked on the flat, unsharpened part of the blade above the guard.

Muninn croaked and made an upward gesture with her head. Encouragement?

"There was no getting past the hate in that woman," she said, tasting snow on the breeze even as Thokk's words echoed in her mind.

Why should she have her boy restored when thousands of others would never, ever get such a chance? She hadn't spoken her instinctive answer to that question: Baldr was exceptional. But weren't all children exceptional?

Why should Baldr live again?

He's my son and I love him wasn't good enough. All parents—well, most—loved their children. Any parent who'd lost a child wanted them back. But that wasn't possible. Even for Odin, it was barely possible to bring Baldr back.

Why should Baldr live again?

Muninn's talons scraped along the rock. "Wasting time."

Frigg glared at the bird. "I'm not wasting time. There's still a chance I can convince her."

Muninn blinked.

"Leave me be," she said.

Baldr should live again because he was exceptional. Why should she shy from that? He was. Exceptional people could change everything.

Baldr could bridge the gulf between Aesir and Jotunn. Odin couldn't; he and Ymir were the reason for the gulf. She couldn't, because she'd sided with the Aesir. But the Aesir loved Baldr because he'd brought healing to all who needed it. She'd seen them, the Jotunn, reaching out to touch him as he walked among them in the streets. She'd heard them calling out their thanks to him for trying, for caring, for weeping as he pulled dead babies from their mothers' wombs. Hel herself had recognized that Baldr was exceptional.

So why had Hel changed the deal? Odin would have kept his word. Hel had known about Thokk—how didn't matter. If she'd also known how intransigent Thokk was, then why had she acted against her own best interests? Hel had said that if she hadn't acted, Baldr's spirit would have gone back into the Gap before Odin could have saved it. Hel wanted to be free. Hel wanted her brothers to be free.

So why had she changed the deal?

"Muninn, do you remember the message you delivered to me?"

The bird cocked her head at her.

"Muninn, repeat Odin's message."

The raven coughed as if she were clearing her throat. *Make Thokk weep, or Hel will not free Baldr. Fly northwest to the mountains. Then west to a cave on the southern ridge. Muninn will guide you.*

And that was it.

The naked blade in her lap flared in the wan sunlight, and in it she . . .

. . . *saw Baldr, corpse-white, walking through surf. He was whole.*

Unburned. He moved like a man asleep. He was one of dozens, hundreds, thousands plodding through the surf toward a gray-pebbled shore.

Her vision skipped away to . . .

. . . a Gladsheim that had burned. Black smoke hung above the first tier. A line of bow-wielding warriors watched from atop the second tier's defensive wall. Bundles of arrows were stacked every few feet. Spears leaned against the battlements.

A horn sounded from below.

A thick, iron-tipped bolt blasted into the wall next to her, killing the man who stood there. Sword-sized splinters flew outward, slashing and stunning those warriors close to the impact.

Her sight lifted. She saw beyond the wall into what had been the first tier. Beneath old, frayed war banners denoting their tribes—Hill and Lake, Mountain and Plain, Forest and River—stood a thousand Jotunn warriors.

Frigg came back to herself, gasping. The knife lay in the snow and she was on her knees, hands braced against the stone where Muninn had perched. The raven had fled to a snow-laden branch that bobbed up and down with the added weight.

She'd finally glimpsed a war with the Jotunn, her city destroyed, her people slaughtered. Could it be happening right now? Her stomach lurched. Her visions had never worked like that before. They were future events.

She hoped.

Were the two separate visions connected? In the first, Baldr was dead. In the second, a Jotunn army, far larger than should conceivably be possible, had razed a third of Gladsheim and was set to finish the job. Would that war happen because Baldr wasn't around to prevent it? Or would it happen because Baldr lived again? She refused to believe the latter. If he were alive, at least they'd have a chance of preventing that war. It was selfish to believe that, but that didn't necessarily make it untrue.

Odin had wanted to combine their visions so they could make more informed decisions. What happened in the future depended on the choices that came before. It was all choices.

She had to choose.

Frigg looked down at her knife lying in the snow. Melted snow glistened like tears along the blade. Her own distorted reflection stared back at her.

She couldn't lose him. Nor could the Aesir or Jotunn. Baldr was too important.

She snatched up the knife and stalked back toward the cave. "Thokk! I ask you to reconsider."

Muninn croaked. It sounded like approval.

50

FRIGG

Day 9, late afternoon

Frigg paused a few paces inside the cave until her eyes adjusted. "Thokk! I've had a vision of a coming war. May I tell it to you?"

She waited, heart in her throat. No reply. No sound at all. Just the hearth's faint, outflowing heat, the musky smell of the ancient, and the wind's whisper. She stepped to where the tunnel curved inward.

"Thokk!"

No response. She went forward, knife gripped tightly, her palm beginning to sweat.

The humble cave opened before her. The rude bed shoved into the corner showed itself. The table, crowded with dried herbs, was still there, as was the neat stack of firewood.

Thokk sat in her chair, staring into the fire. She was rolling something between her fingers.

"Thokk." Frigg drew closer.

The old woman closed her hand around a small black stone and nodded at Frigg's blade. "Come to do some carving, dearie?"

Frigg felt a flush rising in her cheeks. The knife's grip was almost slick in her hand. She sheathed the blade. "No."

Thokk cackled. "Would this Hel really accept tears cut from me?"

"I've had a vision. War between Jotunn and Aesir. May I tell you what I saw?"

"Sounds like you already are."

Frigg spread her arms, palms open. "I saw a Jotunn army inside Gladsheim's lower tier. They'd burned it and driven the folk up into the second tier."

Thokk pursed her lips. "You want me to cry because my people are finally giving as good as they got?"

"That's not what I meant."

"Would you be here telling me this if that was an Aesir army standing in the remnants of Jotunheim?"

"Absolutely."

Thokk sniffed and looked into the fire.

"I'm telling you this because if Baldr's alive, he could prevent all that death, Aesir and Jotunn alike. What do you imagine will happen when Thor arrives?"

"I don't have to imagine it," Thokk said.

"You see?" Her heart raced; her mouth was dry and her stomach churned. "If Baldr were alive again, he could stop that war. I know he could." She hated how desperate she sounded. But she was.

"You don't know that. No one can. You just want your son alive again."

"Of course I want that," Frigg said. "But I can hope for more— want more—for both our peoples."

"So I'm the selfish one? The one who should ignore all the wounds you and your husband and his armies have inflicted? All the death? All the families separated?" Thokk jabbed a twisted finger at her. "Maybe there were a thousand Baldrs among the Jotunn. Maybe even one of my own children. We'll never know, though, since ten times—a hundred times—have been slaughtered by the Aesir in one senseless war after another. Did you ever think of that?"

The past truly was a heavy stone, handed down father to son, mother to daughter. Frigg clasped her hands together. "Odin didn't start the hatred. Ymir did. He slaughtered Audhumbla and murdered

Odin's parents because he felt like it. He would have kept on killing, too, if Odin hadn't stopped him."

Thokk sneered. "So we've been told by the only people to have survived that bloodbath. Were you there? I wasn't. Yet here we are, enemies. Because of old stories."

Just because children had always picked up that heavy stone didn't mean they always had to. They could set it down, a rock in the flowing river. Enough rocks deposited would dam the past, or channel it. And Baldr had done that. She'd watched him carve a new way forward, one that led to a future peace that he would build stone by stone, timber by timber. She'd watched him convince others that a future was possible. But it wouldn't come without effort and sacrifice. Or forgiveness.

"So let's you and I tell a new story," Frigg said.

Thokk's old eyes bored into her, one raspy breath after another wheezing into and out of those ancient lungs. She couldn't even sit up straight because her spine was so curled.

"It's not that easy, great lady," Thokk said, rolling the pebble between her gnarled fingers.

"Things worth doing rarely are." The low-burning hearth threw a fitful light across the old woman's time-ravaged face.

The firelight.

Frigg froze in place. Thokk's raspy breath wheezed in and out. The pebble rolled around and around.

Frigg's eyes flicked back to the light on Thokk's face. Yes, there was light—but no vision-flames burning above her head. Over the past few weeks, virtually everyone had manifested vision-flames above their heads. On the rare occasions she didn't see them, Frigg had been able to summon them.

She concentrated. Almost reluctantly, the vision-flames came to life above Thokk's head. In them, she saw . . .

. . . *a black-checkered sail flapping overhead . . .*

. . . *a wolf's corpse on her left, a young man's corpse on her right. Ropey red and brown sinews wrapped tight around a man's thighs and knees and stomach . . .*

. . . thick, black-haired arms ending in black-skinned, leathery palms grasping a spear . . .

Frigg gasped.

Thokk raised an eyebrow.

"You?" Frigg drew her knife.

"Me? I don't know what you mean, great lady."

"It *has* been you, Yelena. All along."

Thokk looked confused for a moment. She flicked the black pebble into the fire, then winked and spoke in an all-too-familiar, all-too-silky voice. "Took you long enough."

Frigg lunged.

Black smoke exploded out of the hearth and filled the cave. Frigg's lunge carried her into the now-empty chair. She couldn't see anything. Her eyes burned, and she coughed.

A cold, hard hand grabbed her by the hair, and a leg swept hers out from under her. Only the hand in her hair stopped her face from smashing into the floor. Before she could move, a knee in her back pinned her flat against the stone. The hand in her hair tightened its grip as a sharp-nailed hand snaked across her throat.

That familiar, hated voice whispered in her ear. "I could kill you now, Almother. I probably should. But I want you to live the future I bring."

The taloned fingers cut shallow furrows across Frigg's throat from one ear to the other, then shoved her hard, face first into the stone floor. The weight and bony knee that had driven into her back vanished.

Flat on her belly, mindless from shock, Frigg coughed and retched, spitting bile onto the stone floor. Eyes screwed shut, tears streaming from smoke and terror and grief, she pushed herself up and crawled till she banged into the wall. She crawled along it, coughing and gagging on the smoke, till she felt a draft and followed the wafting air out into blinding sunlight and cold snow.

Muninn croaked.

Frigg collapsed in the snow, hauling in deep lungfuls of clean air and spitting out black phlegm till she dared to open her teary eyes.

She wiped snow from her numb right cheek, did what she could to dry her eyes, and staggered upright. Half-blind, she tottered over to the tree where Muninn perched.

Thokk had spoken with Yelena's voice.

Thokk hadn't been Thokk. She'd been Yelena.

For Yelena to be here as Thokk meant . . . what?

She swabbed at her eyes again. This was all planned. Yelena had definitely been in Gladsheim before Baldr's murder. That had been nearly eleven nights ago—more than enough time for a witch to fly here.

Had Hel been in on the plot? She was the reason Frigg was here in Thokk's cave, but the original deal hadn't included Thokk. That original bargain had made sense; Hel wanted freedom for herself and her brothers. But then she'd changed the deal. Which meant what? Hel had been brought in on an existing plot, probably because her capturing Baldr's spirit had disrupted that plot. Something must had happened between the deal they'd struck with Hel and Hel's changing the terms. Something . . .

Loki's visit. They'd begged him to intercede with his daughter.

Frigg's laugh was as bitter and as short and as full of self-loathing as it was possible to be. Loki had gone to Hel and convinced her to renege on the deal she'd made. Then they'd concocted this pointlessness involving Thokk. Baldr had never had any real chance. And since Thokk had been Yelena, Loki and Yelena were working together. They had to be.

Delay and distract. Keep your opponent off balance.

Her stomach dropped.

It all clicked together: the Sons of Muspell attacking and burning, the witches doing the same, the Jotunn destroying Háls. Loki had thrown in with the Jotunn. Maybe they'd promised to free his children in exchange for betraying his blood brother—a blood brother who'd already betrayed him by exiling his children. Odin's memory of Loki's threat had been real. Loki had tricked all of them as completely and as fully as it was possible to be tricked.

She'd been a blind fool idiot. She should take this knife and jab it through her stupid heart.

"Heimdall!"

Muninn jumped sideways, startled by her scream.

"Tell Odin that Yelena was Thokk. This was all a trick. Loki's behind most of it—maybe all of it. He's thrown in with the Jotunn."

Frigg glared up at the setting sun, now darkening behind red clouds like the black spots of rot that Odin's magic had swept from Baldr's face. Baldr was gone. That was beyond any doubt now. She had to accept it.

For months now, visions of his death had plagued her. She'd refused to speak of them, believing, as her old shaman had told her, that the future was fixed. Odin had argued otherwise and all but begged her to tell him what she saw. He believed it possible to determine their own future, claiming he needed to know as much as possible to make that happen. She understood that now; she'd glimpsed that truth before. She'd already shared some of her visions with him.

But now? Now, she would share them all. Together, they'd choose their own doom rather than stumbling blindly forward.

Her visions had shown Baldr's body rising amid a flaming ship to speak with her. Frigg racked her memory. What had he said? She couldn't remember. All she could recall was the flesh scorching from his bones and the clacking of his white teeth. Now she would send Baldr's body on fire's wings to join his spirit. She couldn't bear to think of his body rotting away in the dark; if he spoke from those flames, then so be it.

She had a funeral to plan.

51

ODIN

Day 9, late afternoon

From his High Seat, Odin looked down upon a snow-covered ridge broken by a cave opening. Muninn sat upon a boulder outside that cave. The big raven cocked an eye toward the sky, ruffled her throat feathers, and bobbed her head. It looked very much like a greeting.

Hello to you, Muninn, he said. If only they could speak with each other across this distance.

Through Huginn, Heimdall had told him that Frigg had failed to convince Thokk. So here he was on his High Seat, his sight winging via Muninn to Thokk's cave where smoke billowed free.

Not a good sign.

Frigg crawled from the cave and collapsed in the snow. Long heartbeats passed as she struggled to recover. Finally, she pushed herself up and stared into the sky, her face filthy and tear-streaked and more beautiful today than it had been when they'd married. She was speaking—shouting—but he couldn't hear her. He couldn't take her in his arms and provide what comfort he could. He couldn't advise her. He could only watch.

A hound scratched at the door of his mind. He ignored it.

Frigg was speaking to Muninn. He stared hard at her lips, but he couldn't tell what she was saying.

The scratching outside his mind became a man's fist, banging.

Frigg's mouth firmed, her lips a tight white line. She stood, became a falcon, and flew southward. Black-winged Muninn followed.

Odin's eye snapped open. Pain thrummed through his body as if he were a fraying harp string. Trembling, he swung away from the High Seat and collapsed onto all fours on the ledge beside the seat. "Heimdall, what happened?"

Huginn replied. *The Watcher says, "Frigg said that Thokk admitted to being Yelena and that Yelena and Loki must have been working together. Frigg also said that this betrayal confirms Loki has thrown in with the Jotunn. She wants me to find him and his family."*

"So Baldr is truly dead," he said to no one but himself. The first to die since the Vanir war ended over two hundred winters ago. Frigg was probably correct that Loki had thrown in with his enemies.

He slammed his fist against Yggdrasil's rough bark. A bloody haze fell across his sight. He saw . . .

. . . a long sword burning with reflected fire held aloft in one gauntleted hand . . . slimy guts sliding through his hands . . . drawing blood from his own knuckles as they scraped across cold, jagged rock . . .

He opened his eye and found himself at the brink of the platform. More hints of things to come. He needed answers, not hints. His eye was open, but it wasn't seeing enough. Would it ever? Answers. He needed to know what was coming.

He stepped back resolutely. Who best to ask but those same three bitches who'd set his family on this course?

Wait. "Heimdall, you said that Frigg believed Thokk was Yelena?"

Through Huginn, Heimdall said, *Yes.*

That couldn't be. Yelena had led the coven that attacked Gladsheim. Or perhaps he was assuming that; she'd never answered to that name. All seven witches he'd fought had been strong; the last one had channeled lightning by herself. Ifington had been attacked on the same night as Gladsheim by, reportedly, a coven of witches working with another group of the Sons. That took a high level of planning and coordination. The strongest witch always led the coven. They would have sent their strongest, led most likely by Yelena. And who would've lasted longest in a fight against him? Probably Yelena.

So it made sense that the witch he'd wounded as she fled had been Yelena. If that were so, it was highly unlikely that Yelena had also been Thokk. It would take a full day to fly to Ifington; Heimdall said Thokk's cave was another two beyond that. He'd fought Yelena three nights ago. Healthy, it might've been possible for her to make that journey, but wounded? Never. Even with healing magic, she'd have to have spent some time recovering.

But it didn't matter. He knew who Thokk could have been. Who she had to have been.

Who she was.

Loki.

He stared out at the inky sky. Twinkling stars stared back.

Loki would know about Thokk because Hel had changed the deal after he'd visited her. Loki was even better at shape-shifting than Odin himself. And Loki hated Odin more than anyone alive. Even though Nithogg hadn't directly answered his question, it had confirmed that Odin's memory of Loki's promised vengeance was real. The wyrm didn't care about Odin or his sons or anything else. Nithogg wanted freedom—exactly what Loki wanted for his children as well.

Hel had sought freedom, too, but her plan must have conflicted with Loki's, so she'd changed her own deal and sent them chasing after a woman Loki impersonated. Maybe there'd never even been a real Thokk. Maybe everything that had happened after he'd so stupidly asked Loki to intercede with Hel had been part of one grand scheme. Perhaps all of it was—the attack on Háls, the Sons of Muspell, the covens, whatever was happening up north with Vidar. Even Baldr's murder. Perhaps Loki had planned all of it.

Perhaps.

Loki was certainly capable of long-ranging deceit and clever, secret plans. Regardless, Odin had been tricked and snared in an expertly set trap. Neither pride nor power had brought him low; it had been his own ignorance.

But no longer.

Odin stood. He looked downward.

"Heimdall, I go to speak with the Norns."

52

ODIN

Day 9, evening

Odin launched himself forward into the middle Norn, knocking her back against Yggdrasil. Her sisters lost their grip on her hands. She collapsed to her knees, gasping for air and clutching her ribs. The rightmost Norn, the youngest, staggered backward, arms wheeling as she tried to catch her balance.

He grabbed the oldest Norn by her robe and slammed her against the tree next to her sister. She shrieked and clawed for his face, but her arms were too short to reach. Her nails scrabbled along his shoulder and arm. He banged her against the tree a second time, then a third. She went limp. For the briefest moment, the memory of doing this to Frigg broached the surface of his mind; she'd been made of sterner stuff.

The other two Norns charged him. He backhanded the youngest in the face and sent her sprawling. The other had a sharp chisel clutched in her fist. The iron tip punched through his overtunic and broke against his chest. The golden haze at the edges of his vision crept higher. He hit her in the face, and she dropped at his feet.

His wolves advanced, heads lowered, snarling.

The young Norn he'd backhanded rose on wobbly legs. Her robe did the least to conceal her full breasts, narrow waist, and wide hips. Blood dribbled from her nose, and her right eye was swelling shut. She froze in place, good eye wide and staring as Freki took a single step toward her.

The Norn he'd punched lay still at his feet. He rolled her over with one booted foot. Geri positioned himself over her.

He still pressed the oldest Norn against the tree, limp in his hand. He lowered her to the ground and leaned her back against the tree. She had graying brown braids, deep crow's feet around her eyes, and the seamed skin of an old woman. Her head lolled forward on her chest, but breath still wheezed from her lungs.

He grabbed the other unconscious Norn at his feet and leaned her against the tree beside her older sister.

Watch these, he told Geri, pointing at the two unconscious Norns slumped against the tree.

He walked toward the young Norn. She scrabbled backward still further, and Freki's jaws opened to clamp down on her ankle.

Wait, Freki.

She lurched to her feet and stumbled toward the nearby house, panting and sobbing. Why did these women think walls and a door would stop him? He opened his hand, and Gungnir flickered into it. He took a quick, skipping step and hurled the spear at her. The cross guard grazed her shoulder and knocked her down.

Now, go!

Screaming, the Norn scrambled to her feet. Then Freki slammed into her and knocked her down again.

Drag her back, he said to Freki.

He returned to where the oldest Norn lay slumped and unconscious against the tree. He slapped her awake. She awoke with a start, panic flaring in her eyes until she recognized where she was. Resignation bloomed in her eyes.

Freki deposited the youngest Norn beside the middle-aged Norn.

"I don't mean any of you lasting harm," he said to all of them.

"Do what you will," the middle-aged Norn said. "We've told you what we could."

"Which implies there's more you can say." He knelt on one knee in front of the oldest Norn and gestured around them with one hand. "So I want you to answer my questions—fully and with no tricks of language."

The old Norn spat in his face. It hit his cheek and dribbled down. He wiped it off and cleaned his gloved hand in the damp grass. "I take it that's a no?"

She made to spit again, but he grabbed her by the neck and squeezed. Pain blossomed beside the fear in her eyes.

"Leave her alone!" screamed the youngest Norn. She was up on her knees, ignoring the gigantic wolf on her left. She was terrified—he could smell it—but she had guts, unlike the middle-aged Norn, whose expression had gone slack while she stared at the grass.

"Be nice," he said, leveling a finger at the old Norn. He released her neck and hooked his thumbs in his belt.

"We don't exist to answer your questions," the old one said.

"Yet you've done so in the past. You'll do the same now." He waited, looking from one to the other, not expecting assent but still hoping. "Fine. I'll start." He held up a finger. "Where and when will the Jotunn attack?"

The Norns said nothing.

He held up a second finger. "Where can I find Loki?"

The Norns said nothing.

He held up a third finger. "Where can I find the coven that's been attacking my cities?"

The Norns said nothing.

"Let me see if I can work this out. If you record past, present, and future as if they were all memories, then you already know you don't answer me. And you know what I'll do because of that." He drew his seax from its sheath at the small of his back and pointed at each Norn with the long blade. "I reject that explanation."

He lowered the knife to his side. "I believe that you three, Frigg, and myself only glimpse what *could* happen, not what *does* happen. If I know enough of the coulds, then I can pick what happens. You three can help me do that."

The oldest Norn shook her head. "That's not possible, Valfather."

"You said you serve neither life nor death," he said. "That implies you serve a different power."

"Does it?" asked the middle-aged Norn.

"You serve yourself." The youngest Norn spat blood into the grass.

"Of course. That's what everyone does. But I've also chosen to serve my people. I've worked to make their lives better."

"At the expense of all who oppose you."

"That's sometimes how the world works, child. And yet those with whom I've made peace became my people. The Vanir and Alvar knew that along, as did those Jotunn who've joined the Aesir. If you three help me, I can end the coming war before it starts. I can begin building the peace my now-dead son wanted so badly."

The Norns looked at one another. All three closed their eyes and cocked their heads as if they were straining to hear a whisper. Was there a power beyond Aegir and Rán that spoke to these three Norns? Were they telling him the truth?

One by one, they took deep breaths and slowly exhaled.

He would not accept that all of this had already happened. He controlled his own wyrd.

Their lips firmed.

Maybe there was a power beyond life and death that spoke to these Norns. Maybe he could speak with it, as he'd spoken with Nithogg. And like Nithogg, maybe it had power beyond his own—for the moment. But he was Odin. He'd killed Ymir. He could defeat these other powers.

And he made his own choices.

The Norns opened their eyes and stared at him from above determined, set mouths. The stench of their dread was thick in his nostrils.

They had made their choice.

Odin grabbed the old Norn by the throat and hauled her upward. She shrieked and batted at his gloved hand. He slammed her against Yggdrasil. She tried to knee him in the crotch, but he turned his thigh into it. She started wheezing as her weight came onto his hand. Her wrinkled, brown-spotted hands ripped at his fist and forearm.

Her face reddened as she thrashed her entire body trying to wiggle free.

He pulled very slightly on his fylgja's strength to maintain his grip and looked right into her weeping black eyes. "Elders should set an example for the younger folk, don't you think? Here's your chance. Answer me, and I'll leave you three alone. If you don't, I'll make an example of you—and then offer the same choice to your sisters."

She managed a sneer and hauled in a ragged breath. "Get on with it."

"Question first, now," he said, scolding her with the knife. "How can I get the power you serve to speak directly to me?"

She spat in his face.

He laughed. "You'd think I'd have seen that coming."

The spittle had hit his eye patch. Another irony. He removed it and flung it aside. He reversed his knife and punched the old Norn in the guts. She made a wet, vomiting noise. He eased his grip, and the old woman hauled in a deep breath.

Odin pointed his knife at the other two. "Pay attention. I expect you know it gets worse from here. Unless you change it."

The middle-aged Norn gave no sign that she'd witnessed anything.

"Stop!" shrieked the youngest Norn. "She'll never answer you. She can't. Let her go! Please! You don't have to do this."

"But if this is a memory, child, then I've already done this."

She was about to say something else when the middle-aged Norn glanced askance at her and said, without heat, "Be quiet. You know what happens."

If this *was* all part of what they'd seen—remembered—then they were fools to go through with it.

The old one made a gurgling sound, and the scrabbling of her hands grew more frantic. Her face had nearly purpled.

To the young one, he said, "You can change what happens. Answer my questions."

The young one clasped her hands between her breasts and rocked back and forth. Her pretty, unlined face was blotchy and awash with tears. Her black eyes grew unfocused as if she were staring at something far away.

Heartbeats passed. He eased his grip on the old Norn.

The young Norn blinked back to herself. She exchanged a resolute glance with the middle-aged Norn and took her hand in hers.

No one spoke.

Their resolve wasn't even a fraction of his.

Odin caught the youngest Norn's gaze and slammed his knife so hard into the old Norn's stomach that the blade bit into Yggdrasil's bark. The old Norn screamed and vomited blood, which he sidestepped, and clawed at the knife hilt protruding from her stomach.

"No!" screamed the youngest Norn, coming to her feet and charging.

Freki moved to stop her, but Odin stopped the wolf with a thought. She wasn't coming for him; she was headed to the old Norn.

"Urdr, no, no," she said, sobbing. "I'm so very sorry."

Urdr, eh? Was she named for the well behind them, or was it the other way around?

The middle-aged Norn sat in the matted grass, tears streaming down her face. But she hadn't otherwise moved. The youngest Norn began tugging on the blood-slick hilt of his knife. She couldn't free it.

The old Norn, Urdr, still coughing, took the young one by the shoulders. Her fingers left red marks on the girl's cheeks and stains in her hair. She smiled. "Verdandi, please. Stop. Remember. Be strong."

Urdr coughed and went limp. Verdandi shrieked as she embraced the old dead woman.

Urdr's spirit dart free from her corpse like a salmon headed upstream. With a word and a gesture, Odin wrapped her spirit around Gungnir's blade. It settled there and waited, like that caught salmon might for the cooking fire.

Perhaps sensing what he'd done, Verdandi spun and threw herself toward Gungnir with outstretched, grasping hands. She clawed at the blade, slicing her fingers on the sharp edges as she presumably attempted to free Urdr's spirit. Odin grabbed a fistful of her robes, took a single step forward, and ripped his spear free from her hands even as he banged her against the tree. The girl sobbed, went limp, and slid to the matted grass.

He stood over her, looking down at the sobbing mass at his feet. "By now, you should understand the difference between a thing foreseen and a thing experienced. Let's start again."

53

ODIN

Day 9, night

Odin flicked a long trail of Skuld's blood from his knife, wiped it on her robe, and walked toward the youngest and last Norn. "It's you and me now, Verdandi."

The middle-aged Norn, Skuld, had also refused to answer his questions, despite the increasing persuasiveness of his blade. Her spirit had joined Urdr's around Gungnir's blade. Verdandi, a yellow lump in the green grass, had crawled back toward the stone table as Skuld gasped her last. Freki and Geri had stopped her from going any farther.

Odin nudged her with his boot. She flinched away. "Shall I repeat my questions, Verdandi? I should think you'd know them by now."

"We've already given you the only answers we can." She drew herself up but kept her eyes downcast. "Everything you do has already happened."

"Prove it. Tell me where I can find my enemies."

Verdandi said nothing.

From the stone table, he snatched up a bit of the bark on which the Norns had cut and painted their runes. Hundreds of lines were cut from one side of the bark to the other. Some lines came down from the top edge; others came in from the bottom. They'd painted many of the lines red; he traced them with a finger. Some dead-ended. Others looped back upon themselves. Some were thicker; some were thinner. All intersected other lines.

He turned the bark so that the top edge became the right side. He couldn't tell which way the bark should be oriented. He turned it again. A silver-painted rune caught the light. He didn't recognize it. He stared at the rune till it wriggled like a caught fish trying to free itself.

Verdandi stabbed a steel chisel into the meat of his thigh. It snapped against his skin. The surprise of it knocked all thoughts of the unfamiliar rune out of his mind. Verdandi was already sprinting away, angled more toward Urdr's Well than the longhouse.

Stop her.

Freki and Geri leaped into motion. Geri barreled into Verdandi, sending her into a sprawling tumble. Freki blocked her way forward.

Bring her back.

Geri locked his jaws around Verdandi's ankle and dragged her back through the grass. Verdandi kicked the wolf with her other foot, but Geri bit down till she screamed in pain.

"Tell me about this bark. What do these lines and runes signify?"

Geri released her ankle. Blood stained the hem of her robe. She sobbed into the grass.

"I came here for answers, Norn. All I've gotten are new questions and deeper mysteries." He kneeled on one knee, knotted his hand in her hair, and jerked her head backward. He shoved the bark toward her blotchy, tear-streaked face. "Tell me about this bark."

"It's yours, Valfather. One of many."

Shocked, he stared at the painted lines and the silver runes inscribed on each corner. "Tell me what it means."

"That one tells of what brought you into this moment. Others in that stack continue the lines into that which is becoming and from there into what will be."

"Find them," he said. "Show me."

"No."

That single word struck him like a hammer. His fury boiled over.

He stood, his hand still clutching Verdandi's hair. He banged her against the table, shoved the bark in front of her face. "Tell me what it means!"

She screamed and clawed at his hand in her hair. She kicked and thrashed.

He drew his knife and pressed it against her cheek. He stopped himself. He needed her still. For a little while, at least.

He shoved her into the grass, where she lay weeping.

Watch her. She'll probably run again.

Freki and Geri converged on the prostrate Norn.

He went through the stacks of bark on the table till he found two more with runes that matched the one he'd held. He compared all three. The patterns of lines and paint were different on each. He could tell them apart, but couldn't tell how they should fit together.

He turned back to Verdandi, a downed doe in lush grass. "Show me how to read this."

She kept sobbing.

This was absurd—he'd be laughing if he weren't so angry. Her two sisters (if sisters they were) had died because they wouldn't answer his questions. She was clearly willing to accept the same.

But he had other options.

He reached for Gungnir, and the long spear swayed across the glade into his right hand. With left thumb and forefinger, he drew down the spirits of Urdr and Skuld, twisting them together into crudely spun witchthread.

With the spirits of the dead Norns to power it, he began singing an ancient song that had not been heard since Gunnloth had barred his path. The song had made her yield to him. He'd taken her, what she guarded, and then flown away with his prize.

This song would *make* Verdandi yield. She would surrender that which she guarded.

He flicked his wrist and cast the rough-spun witchthread toward Verdandi. She didn't try to avoid it. The song slipped between her lips, softened the hard creases around her eyes, and deepened her breathing. When she looked up at him, an inviting smile on her red lips, her eyes were a riot of colors.

His song brought her up onto her knees, moaning. She edged her legs apart. He sang till desire made her eyes heavy-lidded, till need brought a red flush to her face. She tore at her robe, exposing firm, young breasts. She hitched up the hem and ran her hands into the deep well between her thighs.

Her sisters hadn't answered him, but Verdandi would.

He ended the song and tied off the witchthread so that its loop ran through her into him and back again. He felt his own face grow warm; he himself stirred. Desire thrummed between them like lightning between the storm and the ground.

He ignored it. He needed answers.

"What power do you serve?"

"That which reached into the Ginnungagap, set the rivers flowing and the tree to growing." She smiled and arched her back, offering herself to him.

He shook his head, clearing the fog of his own heady magic. He didn't want her; he wanted her answers. "How can I speak with the power you serve?"

"You cannot." She lay back in the long green grass.

"Show me how to read the cut lines and runes upon the bark."

"You cannot read them. Only the priestesses may do that."

His rage was a cold spike driven through his heart. "Where can I find the coven that's been attacking my cities?"

"They have fled into the Iron Wood. Seek them there."

"Where is Loki?"

"In two nights, he will present himself to you in your hall," she said, digging both hands into the lush grass.

"Where and when will the Jotunn attack?"

Verdandi smiled.

Blood dripped across his vision. He blinked, and . . .

. . . *a mist rolled across the plains. A yellowed ship sailed toward the broken wall, its mast reaching high into the sky, black sail taut before the wind. He stood atop that wall. Hermod gripped his arm. A slice beneath her right eye had covered her cheek and neck in blood. She was mud-spattered, but her eyes shone clear and strong with defiance. "We'll hold, Father. We —" A howl unlike any other cut across the sky, and he knew now that Rindr had meant . . .*

. . . clutched his head. A battle was coming.

"That's only the beginning, Valfather," Verdandi said, her voice throaty and warm.

"When will it happen?"

"You'll need warriors, Valfather." Her eyes were a rainbow scatter from his magic. "I'm supposed to give you one."

She meant that he sire a child upon her?

His song's magic thrummed through them, dulling his anger and clouding his thoughts. But it stoked his lust. He shook his head. He needed to think, to ask better questions while his magic still muddled Verdandi's mind.

She smiled again. Blood dripped down across his vision and he stood . . .

. . . atop the outer walls, the armies opposing him covered the plain from horizon to horizon, a hundred leagues in every direction. This was it. Finally. No matter what he'd done it all led here. Through gaps in the racing storm clouds he spied the swallowed sun. Below him, beyond the spiked ditch, thousands upon thousands of stick-like limbs shook spears and banged axes. But they were otherwise silent, rotting eyes and empty sockets alike staring . . .

. . . turned and looked down upon his own army of Einherjar and Aesir lining the walls. Still more marched from Valhol, the full promise of Glad-sheim's past and present power. A valkyr dashed through the sky on wolf-back toward him, her familiar face wreathed in fire and smoke. They'd brought so many of his children to him for so very long, and it still wouldn't be enough. If he'd only known the . . .

. . . sword of fire struck down from the heavens. Nine heartbeats later, the snow-laden ground bucked and everyone staggered, trying to keep their balance. A hot, howling wind full of grit and rot swept across the city. The howl persisted after the wind had settled. He remembered what throat brought it forth . . .

. . . himself, but gray-bearded and bleak-eyed. Himself to himself, he exhorted, 'Prepare better than I did' . . .

. . . and blinked back to where he now leaned against the broken table. He retched. The bile burned his throat, and he spat into the grass.

"He told you to prepare better, didn't he?" Verdandi asked, tugging at his belt. His magic still clouded her eyes.

He shoved past her, staggering through the tall green grass toward the well and its cool water. The mists swirled around his legs. Yggdrasil rose tall and straight while wyrms gnawed its roots, hissing *You are welcome any time, little father.*

"You'll need brave warriors who won't break when they see what fills the plains of Vigrid," Verdandi said, taking him by the shoulders and turning him toward her. She smiled, full red lips parting.

He'd seen himself in a time yet to come, an Odin who'd survived winters he'd not yet lived. But how many? That future Odin had felt despair and fear, the likes of which he himself hadn't suffered since Ymir had slaughtered and dismembered his parents before his eyes.

Realization struck: The future Odin faced the Jotunn. Innumerable Jotunn.

"Oh it's much worse than that, Valfather," Verdandi said. "Much, much worse."

But he barely heard her. The heavens had burned; the seas had roiled. The future Odin had exhorted him to prepare better, despaired of not having enough children to—

"So do more, Valfather. Bring more." Verdandi lay a warm hand on his cheek. "Sire a thousand heroes, then a thousand more. Just think how many peoples you've seen strewn across this realm."

Like seeds in the wind.

"Exactly."

His magic was a dazzling swirl of color in her eyes. She'd refused to tell him of the power she served. Instead, she'd shown him a future in which all he built was destroyed.

As Loki had promised.

Odin grabbed her by the arms. "I need to know more."

Her eyes cleared for a moment as she fought the magic pounding through her body and his. Her mouth worked as if she was about to spit in his face. He willed it otherwise, and his magic made her part her moistened red lips.

He'd lost Baldr because of her and her sisters. Now he'd learned of a future him who needed more children, sons and daughters who would fight.

He ripped off the rest of her robe, exposing her slender body, tawny skin, and wide hips. Her heavy breasts swayed gently. He shoved her back down into the grass.

She resisted.

He used his magic to change her scream into a moan, to smooth her attempts to shove him away into an embrace. His song pounded through both their veins.

He unbuckled his belt.

When he was on top of her, he saw such fear and horror and dread in her eyes that he blinked, and . . .

. . . *a charred hand reached over the wall. A head rose between the wooden stakes, the bare skull visible through the scorched flesh. Its other skeletal hand clutched a rusted axe with a blackened haft. A naked, rotting baby rode a grandmother's shoulders. Fluids slicked her bony shoulders and rolled down between her withered breasts. Maggots wriggled from one to the other and back again. An afterwalker's mottled skull lurched up into the space before him. He threw himself backward even as its bony hand clawed scratches into his face. He met its milky eyes right before Hermod's blade sheared its head in half. The rank, sickly sweet putrescence rolled over him like a wave. For the first time in a thousand winters his stomach churned. More dead clawed their way up the wall, while below, the ground swarmed with dead warriors, as if they were flies and his city the rotting corpse . . .*

He had to stop that future. He would stop it. Baldr was lost, but he would bring new children into the realms.

Starting now.

PLEASE LET ME KNOW WHAT YOU THINK!

I hope you enjoyed the story.

I can't overstate how important your reviews are to making sure other people get a chance to read my story. I'd love to hear your thoughts — positive, negative or anything in between.

And if you see any errors, please let me know and I will fix them immediately!

Please leave a review on Amazon!
Kinsmen Die
Dark Grows the Sun

Contact me directly
mattbishopwrites@gmail.com
fb.me/mattbishopwrites
m.me/mattbishopwrites

ACKNOWLEDGMENTS

Jen: Without your love and support, this book would not have been written.

Emmett and Maeve: Thanks for understanding, without quite getting it, what "Daddy's writing" meant—and continues to mean.

Mom & Dad: I'm truly grateful for everything you've done for me.

ALSO BY MATT BISHOP

AND THE HEAVENS BURN SERIES

See my blog for details and updates

https://mattbishopwrites.com